HEAVY PLANET
AND OTHER SCIENCE FICTION STORIES

MILTON A. ROTHMAN

HEAVY PLANET

AND OTHER SCIENCE FICTION STORIES

MILTON A. ROTHMAN

PREFACE BY FREDERIK POHL

EDITED BY DARRELL SCHWEITZER
AND LEE WEINSTEIN

SPONSORED BY
THE PHILADELPHIA SCIENCE FICTION SOCIETY

WILDSIDE PRESS

CONTENTS

MILT ROTHMAN

THE DAY I met Milt Rothman for the first time was one of great historical significance. That being so, you might imagine that I would remember what particular day it was. I don't, though. All I know for sure is that it was a Sunday, some time in the year 1936, probably in the summer, maybe in the fall. What made it special was what happened, for the first time, on that day:

That morning half a dozen kid science-fiction fans from New York City (including me) had taken the train to Philadelphia to get together with a similar number of Philly fans (including Milt).

In those days science-fiction fandom was poorly organized and sparsely populated, and nothing quite like what we kids were doing had ever been done before. In fact, that sort of thing didn't even have a name yet, and over the course of the afternoon we New Yorkers and Philadelphians spent together we began to wonder what to call ourselves.

As it happened, 1936 was a presidential year. The political parties had just finished naming their candidates in what they called their conventions . . . and someone suggested what we were up to was a kind of convention, too, wasn't it?

The rest is history. We did call ourselves the first science-fiction convention ever, and we set such a good example that they've been happening ever since.

The aspect of our little get-together that was most unlike those big political conventions was that we all got along pretty well. In fact most of us New Yorkers became pretty good friends with our Philadelphia opposite numbers, and some of those friendships turned out to be for life. Milt was such a friend for me, for more than sixty years.

In 1936 Milt Rothman was a sixteen-year-old high-school student with no very clear idea of what he wanted to do with his life. He liked music, and in fact was already pretty good at playing the piano, but it didn't seem very probable that music was something you could support yourself at. Milt liked science, too, or as much of it as he had been exposed to—both in school and in the pages of *Amazing Stories, Wonder Stories* and *Astounding Stories*—but this was 1936, remember. There were no such places as California's Silicon Valley or Boston's Route 128 as yet, so there weren't all that many jobs for scientists in the private sector, and perhaps even fewer in government.

The other thing that Milt Rothman liked was science fiction.

That didn't promise any very highly paid lifetime career, either. (I once calculated that the average income for a science-fiction writer in the 1930s was not much more than $6.00 a week.) However, writing science fiction had a special advantage over those other careers. It didn't require any great investment of either money or time to start with; you didn't have to go to college for four or more years before you could write for one of those science-fiction magazines that we all so avidly read. All you had to do was write a story that one of the three practicing science-fiction editors was willing to buy.

True, the potential financial rewards were not enormous. The most you might hope to get for a short story was fifty dollars or so, perhaps no more than half that, and perhaps not very promptly, either. (When Jack Williamson's first story was bought the editor hadn't sent him a check, or even a letter to say that it was accepted; When Jack happened to be looking over a nearby newsstand he was astonished to see that there the story was, already in print.) But we were teenagers, remember. We lived at home. Our parents provided us with food, clothing and shelter, and if we did happen to get one of those checks it would be pure gravy. 1936, moreover, was a year that was still stuck firmly within that drab and scary era of American history called the Great Depression, and those prospective checks, however tiny, looked good.

I would be telling an untruth if I said that Milt Rothman, or any of us, began trying to write science fiction primarily for the money. That wasn't the reason at all. We all did it for the pure love of it, and because none of us could imagine any greater glory in life than to have some work of ours published in one of those magazines. But, whatever the reason, nearly all of us did do it.

That includes me. In my own case, I had one small advantage over the rest of us hopeful beginners. It was simply that I lived in New York City. That was the city where every one of those science-fiction magazines had their offices. Would-be writers in most of the country had to rely on the mails to submit their work to the people who might buy it. Not me, though. At the expenditure of only a nickel in subway fare each way, which I could easily save out of my lunch money, and a few hours of time, of which I had a lot to spare, I could deliver my manuscripts in person.

I'm not suggesting that that really helped me to sell my own stories. It didn't. The editors had no compunctions about pinning a rejection slip on each one of them as they handed them back to me. Some of them, however, were reasonably friendly about it.

That gave me an inspiration. I had heard of a kind of creature called a "literary agent," and it occurred to me that, as long as I was seeing these editors anyway, I might as well try to sell other people's work to them. So I hung out my shingle and a few writers entrusted their future to me. Most of my clients were beginners as green as myself, but they learned; and so did I; and by and by the very rare occasions when I got any acceptance of any of my own work began to be supplemented by the slightly less rare (but still not at all frequent) occasions when someone accepted something from one of my clients. Among these was Milt Rothman.

In Milt's case I did a little more for him than for most of my clients. Before I offered his manuscripts to any editor I did some revising and rewriting on them, for which he agreed to pay me an extra 10% beyond the then regular 10% agent's commission (it's usually higher now) on anything I sold of that sort.

I'm not now sure whose idea it was, but by gosh it worked. The first story I touched up for Milt was "Heavy Planet" and it sold at once to John Campbell's *Astounding,* the top market in the field. So did "Shawn's Sword," the second one to get the treatment. And there was much rejoicing in Milt's house and my own, because the future looked bright.

There was one little problem. That problem was born in the mind of John W. Campbell, who was probably the greatest editor science fiction has ever had, but not without his occasional evidences of feet of clay.

The difficulty, Campbell explained to me earnestly, was Milt's name. *Astounding's* readers weren't used to seeing names like "Rothman" attached to the stories they loved. (He didn't explain what he meant by "names like 'Rothman, '" but then he didn't have to.) Campbell's readers, he maintained, liked bylines that sounded, well, like regular American fellows. Scotch-Irish names were best, he told me—like, well, for instance like "Campbell." (And as a matter of fact when H. L. Gold began to write for Campbell's magazines, not much after that time, the byline Campbell imposed on him at first was actually "Clyde Crane Campbell.")

So I reported all this to Milt, who grumbled, but was too thrilled at the prospect of being in *Astounding* at all to mount any very strong resistance. He agreed to letting himself be known as "Lee Gregor." It wasn't a very Scotch-Irish name, but at least it didn't sound particularly Jewish. Campbell frowned but accepted it.

(Was John Campbell an anti-Semite? You can get an argument on either side of that question from most of the people who knew him. He certainly had a lot of Jewish friends and bought a great deal from Jewish writers; and after a while he stopped asking them to hide under non-Jewish pen names. Perhaps he really was right about how the readers felt. . . . But in the late 30s that was where he stood——along with a large fraction of the rest of the American population, I should point out. I've always thought that it was very lucky for Isaac Asimov that he had sold a couple of stories to *Amazing* before Campbell bought one, so that his own name had already been exposed to the readers. Otherwise, I suspect, every one of those 400-odd books that Isaac ultimately produced might have been published under some such name as "Kevin MacIsaacs.")

How far Milt and I might have gone with our cooperative venture I don't know, but fortune intervened. Very good fortune, as far as I was concerned, because what happened was that, mostly through dumb luck and happening to be in the right place at the right time, I fell into a job as an honest-to-God real professional editor of not one but two real (if low-budgeted and not very successful) science-fiction magazines, *Astonishing Stories* and *Super Science Stories*.

That meant I couldn't be an agent any more. Like most of my clients, Milt accepted that development philosophically, and went on to keep right on selling stories on his own.

Writing science fiction didn't turn out to be a career for Milt Rothman, though. Maybe it could have been, but those two other interests, music and science, got in the way. His hopes of a career in music got a big boost when he was actually invited to audition for a prestigious music school, but nothing came of it. What did come along was World War II, and shortly after Pearl Harbor Milt was a private in the U.S. Army.

There were advantages that might accrue to being in the service in those days, and one of them came from the fact that someone among the higher brass began to worry about where they were going to find their next crop of commissioned officers as what looked like a long war ground along. They wanted a reliable supply of college graduates who could become second lieutenants and ensigns when needed. To provide for that future need they instituted a program under which a corps of bright and lucky, soldiers were assigned the duty of going to school instead of manning a foxhole. Milt was one of the bright and lucky ones, winding up with a B.A. in electrical engineering from Oregon State University in 1944.

By 1952, long out of the Army, he had added an M.A. and a Ph.D. in nuclear physics, and a real career was on the way. His first hope was to get where the nuclear action was, at Oak Ridge, where the first atomic bombs had been developed. That didn't work out, because a few long-ago Marxist flirtations had ruled out a security clearance. However, there were other places glad to provide an opening for a new-minted nuclear physicist, including the Plasma Physics Laboratory at Princeton, and that's the sort of work Milt did in his daytime job until his retirement in 1985.

I'm not sure how much Milt Rothman might have achieved as a science-fiction writer. He never got the chance to show us. His other career got in the way. All the years he was working on the frustrating job of trying to make nuclear fusion produce the kind of dividend that might some day light people's homes, he didn't really have the time to write sf.

That didn't mean he didn't do any writing at all. There exists an organization known as the Committee for the Scientific Investigation of Claims of the Paranormal—CSICOP for short—which spends most of its time debunking the endless cases of psychic powers and alien abduction and all the other crackpottery that befouls our age. CSICOP publishes a magazine, now known as *The Skeptical Inquirer,* and for years Dr. Milton A. Rothman was the magazine's house scientist, writing a regular column that attempted to shed the light of scientific reality on those murky areas of human credulity. It's not easy to say how successful his efforts were. His arguments were persuasive, informed and put with literary style. There isn't any doubt that the magazine's readers cherished his writing, but I can't say whether he ever convinced any of the believers that they had misplaced their faith. I wouldn't bet that he had because, unfortunately, the believers weren't reading *The Skeptical Inquirer* in the first place.

Then Milt's health began to get in the way of even a part-time writing career, so that he gave up the column for CSICOP. He could not even make it to the Millennial Worldcon, over Labor Day weekend in Philadelphia, although he was a fixture at Philadelphia's World Science Fiction Conventions, having chaired two of them. A month later, on the 6th of October, 2001, he died.

But he left something behind for the rest of us. His stories remain, and they are gathered in this volume. Enjoy them. He was a good writer . . . and a good man, and a good friend.

—Frederik Pohl

HEAVY PLANET

ENNIS WAS COMPLETING his patrol of Sector EM, Division 426 of the Eastern Ocean. The weather had been unusually fine, the liquid-thick air roaring along in a continuous blast that propelled his craft with a rush as if it were flying, and lifting short, choppy waves that rose and fell with a startling suddenness. A short savage squall whirled about, pounding down on the ocean like a million hammers, flinging the little boat ahead madly.

Ennis tore at the controls, granite-hard muscles standing out in bas-relief over his short, immensely thick body, skin gleaming scale-like in the slashing spray. The heat from the sun that hung like a huge red lantern on the horizon was a tangible intensity, making an inferno of the gale.

The little craft, that Ennis maneuvered by sheer brawn, took a leap into the air and seemed to float for many seconds before burying its keel again in the sea. It often floated for long distances, the air was so dense. The boundary between air and water was sometimes scarcely defined at all—one merged into the other imperceptibly. The pressure did strange things.

Like a dust mote sparkling in a beam, a tiny speck of light above caught Ennis' eye. A glider, he thought, but he was puzzled. Why so far out here on the ocean? They were nasty things to handle in the violent wind.

The dust mote caught the light again. It was lower, tumbling down with a precipitancy that meant trouble. An upward blast caught it, checked its fall. Then it floated down gently for a space until struck by another howling wind that seemed to distort its very outlines.

Ennis turned the prow of his boat to meet the path of the falling vessel. Curious, he thought; where were its wings? Were they retracted, or broken off? It ballooned closer, and it wasn't a glider. Far larger than any glider ever made, it was of a ridiculous shape that would not stand up for an instant. And with the sharp splash the body made as it struck the water—a splash that fell in almost the same instant it rose—a thought seemed to leap up in his mind. A thought that was more important than anything else on that planet; or was to him, at least. For if it was what he thought it was—and it had to be that—it was what Shadden had been desperately seeking for many years. What a stroke of inconceivable luck, falling from the sky before his very eyes!

The silvery shape rode the ragged waters lightly. Ennis' craft came up with a rush; he skillfully checked its speed and the two came together with a slight jar. The metal of the strange vessel dented as if it were made of rubber. Ennis stared. He put out an arm and felt the curved surface of the strange ship. His finger prodded right through the metal. What manner of people were they who made vessels of such weak materials?

He moored his little boat to the side of the larger one and climbed to an opening. The wall sagged under him. He knew he must be careful; it was frightfully weak. It would not hold together very long; he must work fast if it were to be saved. The atmospheric pressure would have flattened it out long ago, had it not been for the jagged rent above which had allowed the pressure to be equalized.

He reached the opening and lowered himself carefully into the interior of the vessel. The rent was too small; he enlarged it by taking the two edges in his hands and pulling them apart. As he went down he looked askance at the insignificant plates and beams that were like tissue paper on his world. Inside was wreckage. Nothing was left in its original shape. Crushed, mutilated machinery, shattered vacuum tubes, sagging members, all ruined by the gravity and the pressure.

There was a pulpy mess on the floor that he did not examine closely. It was like red jelly, thin and stalky, pulped under a gravity a hundred times stronger and an atmosphere ten thousand times heavier than that it had been made for.

He was in a room with many knobs and dials on the walls, apparently a control room. A table in the center with a chart on it, the chart of a solar system. It had nine planets; his had but five.

Then he knew he was right. If they came from another system, what he wanted must be there. It could be nothing else.

He found a staircase, descended. Large machinery bulked there. There was no light, but he did not notice that. He could see well enough by infrared, and the amount of energy necessary to sustain his compact gianthood kept him constantly radiating.

Then he went through a door that was of a comfortable massiveness, even for his planet—and there it was. He recognized it at once. It was big, squat, strong. The metal was soft, but it was thick enough even to stand solidly under the enormous pull of this world. He had never seen anything quite like it. It was full of coils, magnets, and devices of shapes unknown to him. But Shadden would know. Shadden, and who knows how many other scientists before him, had tried to make something which would do what this could do, but they had all failed. And without the things this machine could perform, the race of men on Heavyplanet was doomed to stay down on the surface of the planet, chained there immovably by the crushing gravity.

It was atomic energy. That he had known as soon as he knew that the body was not a glider. For nothing else but atomic energy and the fierce winds was capable of lifting a body from the surface of Heavyplanet. Chemicals were impotent. There is no such thing as an explosion where the atmosphere pressed inward with more force than an explosion could press outward. Only atomic, of all the theoretically possible sources of energy, could supply the work necessary to lift a vessel away from the planet. Every other source of energy was simply too weak.

Yes, Shadden; all the scientists must see this. And quietly, because the forces of sea and storm would quickly tear the ship to shreds, and, even more vital, because the scientists of Bantin and Marak might obtain the secret if there was delay. And that would mean ruin—the loss of its age-old supremacy—for his nation. Bantin and Marak were war nations; did they obtain the secret they would use it against all the other worlds that abounded in the Universe.

The Universe was big. That was why Ennis was so sure there was atomic energy on this ship. For, even though it might have originated on a planet that was so tiny that chemical energy—although that was hard to visualize—would be sufficient to lift it out of the pull of gravity, to travel the distance that stretched between the stars only one thing would suffice.

He went back through the ship, trying to see what had happened.

There were pulps lying behind long tubes that pointed out through clever ports in the outer wall. He recognized them as weapons, worth looking into.

There must have been a battle. He visualized the scene. The forces that came from atomic energy must have warped even space in the vicinity. The ship pierced, the occupants killed, the controls wrecked, the vessel darting off at titanic speed, blindly into nothing. Finally it had come near enough to Heavyplanet to be enmeshed in its huge web of gravity.

Weeaao-o-ow! It was the wailing roar of his alarm siren, which brought him spinning around and dashing for his boat. Beyond, among the waves that leaped and fell so suddenly, he saw a long, low craft making way toward the derelict spaceship. He glimpsed a flash of color on the rounded, gray superstructure, and knew it for a battleship of Marak. Luck was going strong both ways; first good, now bad. He could easily have eluded the battleship in his own small craft, but he couldn't leave the derelict. Once lost to the enemy he could never regain it, and it was too valuable to lose.

The wind howled and buffeted about his head, and he strained his muscles to keep from being blasted away as he crouched there, half on his own boat and half on the derelict. The sun had set and the evening winds were beginning to blow. The hulk scudded before them, its prow denting from the resistance of the water it pushed aside.

He thought furiously fast. With a quick motion he flipped the switch of the radiophone and called Shadden. He waited with fierce impatience until the voice of Shadden was in his car. At last he heard it, then: "Shadden! This is Ennis. Get your glider, Shadden, fly to a45j on my route! Quickly! It's come, Shadden! But I have no time. Come!"

He flipped the switch off, and pounded the valve out of the bottom of his craft, clutching at the side of the derelict. With a rush the ocean came up and flooded his little boat and in an instant it was gone, on its way down to the bottom. That would save him from being detected for a short time.

Back into the darkness of the spaceship. He didn't think he had been noticed climbing through the opening. Where could he hide? Should he hide? He couldn't defeat the entire battleship single-handed, without weapons. There were no weapons that could be carried anyway. A beam of concentrated actinic light that ate away the eyes and the nervous system had to be powered by the entire output of a battleship's generators. Weapons for striking and cutting had never been developed on a world where flesh was tougher than metal. Ennis was skilled in personal combat, but how could he overcome all that would enter the derelict?

Down again, into the dark chamber where the huge atomic generator towered over his head. This time he looked for something he had missed before. He crawled around it, peering into its recesses. And then, some feet above, he saw the opening, and pulled himself up to it, carefully, not to destroy the precious thing with his mass. The opening was shielded with a heavy, darkly transparent substance through which seeped a dim glow from within. He was satisfied then. Somehow, matter was still being disintegrated in there, and energy could be drawn off if he knew how.

There were leads—wires of all sizes, and busbars, and thick, heavy tubes that bent under their own weight. Some must lead in and some must lead out; it was not good to tamper with them. He chose another track. Upstairs again, and to the places where he had seen the weapons.

They were all mounted on heavy, rigid swivels. He carefully detached the tubes from the bases. The first time he tried it he was not quite careful enough, and part of the projector itself was ripped away, but next time he knew what he was doing and it came away nicely. It was a large thing, nearly as thick as his arm and twice as long. Heavy leads trailed from its lower end and a lever projected from behind. He hoped it was in working condition. He dared not try it; all he could do was to trace the leads back and make sure they were intact.

He ran out of time. There came a thud from the side, and then smaller thuds, as the boarding party incautiously leaped over. Once there was a heavy sound, as someone went all the way through the side of the ship.

"Idiots!" Ennis muttered, and moved forward with his weapon toward the stairway. Noises came from overhead, and then a loud crash buckled the plates of the ceiling. Ennis leaped out of the way, but the entire section came down, with two men on it. The floor sagged, but held for the moment. Ennis, caught beneath the down-coming mass, beat his way free. He came up with a girder in his hand, which he bent over the head of one of the Maraks. The man shook himself and struck out for Ennis, who took the blow rolling and countered with a buffet that left a black splotch on a skin that was like armor plate and sent the man through the opposite wall. The other was upon Ennis, who whirled with the quickness of one who maneuvers habitually under a pressure of ten thousand atmospheres, and shook the Marak from him, leaving him unconscious with a twist in a sensitive spot.

The first opponent returned, and the two grappled, searching for nerve centers to beat upon. Ennis twisted frantically, conscious of the real danger that the frail vessel might break to pieces beneath his feet. The railing of a staircase gave behind the two, and they hurtled down it, crashing through the steps to the floor below. Their weight and momentum carried them through. Ennis released his grip on the Marak, stopped his fall by grasping one of the girders that was part of the ship's framework. The other continued his devastating way down, demolishing the inner shell, and then the outer shell gave way with a grinding crash that ominously became a bumbling rush of liquid.

Ennis looked down into the space where the Marak had fallen, hissed with a sudden intake of breath, then dove down himself. He met rising water, gushing in through a rent in the keel. He braced himself against a girder which sagged under his hand and moved onward against the rushing water. It geysered through the hole in a heavy stream that pushed him back and started to fill the bottom level of the ship. Against that terrific pressure he strained forward slowly, beating against the resisting waves, and then, with a mighty flounder, was at the opening. Its edges had been folded back upon themselves by the inrushing water, and they gaped inward like a jagged maw. He grasped them in a huge hand and exerted force. They strained for a moment and began to straighten. Irresistibly he pushed and stretched them into their former position, and then took the broken ends in his hands and squeezed. The metal grew soft under his grip and began to flow. The edges of the plate welded under that mighty pressure. He moved down the crack and soon it was watertight. He flexed his hands as he rose. They ached; even his strength was beginning to be taxed.

Noises from above; pounding feet. Men were coming down to investigate the commotion. He stood for a moment in thought, then turned to a blank wall, battered his way through it, and shoved the plates and girders back into position. Down to the other end of the craft, and up a staircase there. The corridor above was deserted, and he stole along it, hunting for the place he had left the weapon he had prepared. There was a commotion ahead as the Maraks found the unconscious man.

Two men came pounding up the passageway, giving him barely enough time to slip into a doorway to the side. The room he found himself in was a sleeping chamber. There were two red pulps there, and nothing that could help him, so he stayed in there only long enough to make sure that he would not be seen emerging into the hail. He crept down it again, with as little noise as possible. The racket ahead helped him; it sounded as though they were tearing the ship apart. Again he cursed their idiocy. Couldn't they see how valuable this was?

They were in the control room, ripping apart the machinery with the curiosity of children, wondering at the strange weakness of the paperlike metal, not realizing that, on the world where it was fabricated, it was sufficiently strong for any strain the builders could put upon it.

The strange weapon Ennis had prepared was on the floor of the passage, and just outside the control room. He looked anxiously at the trailing cables. Had they been stepped on and broken? Was the instrument in working condition? He had to get it and be away; no time to experiment to see if it would work.

A noise from behind, and Ennis again slunk into a doorway as a large Marak with a colored belt around his waist strode jarringly through the corridor into the control room. Sharp orders were barked, and the men ceased their havoc with the machinery of the room. All but a few left and scattered through the ship. Ennis' face twisted into a scowl. This made things more difficult. He couldn't overcome them all single-handed, and he couldn't use the weapon inside the ship if it was what he thought it was from the size of the cables.

A Marak was standing immediately outside the room in which Ennis lurked. No exit that way. He looked around the room; there were no other doors. A porthole in the outer wall was a tiny disk of transparency, he looked at it, felt it with his hands, and suddenly pushed his hands right through it. As quietly as he could, he worked at the edges of the circle until the hole was large enough for him to squeeze through. The jagged edges did not bother him. They felt soft, like a ragged pat of butter.

The Marak vessel was moored to the other side of the spaceship. On this side the wind howled blankly, and the sawtooth waves stretched on and on to a horizon that was many miles distant. He cautiously made his way around the glistening rotundity of the derelict, past the prow, straining silently against the vicious backward sweep of the water that tore at every inch of his body. The darker hump of the battleship loomed up as he rounded the curve, and he swam across the tiny space to grasp a row of projections that curved up over the surface of the craft. He climbed up them, muscles that were hard as carborundum straining to hold against all the forces of gravity and wind that fought him down. Near the top of the curve was a rounded, streamlined projection. He felt around its base and found a lever there, which he moved. The metal hump slid back, revealing a rugged swivel mounting with a stubby cylindrical projector atop it.

He swung the mounting around and let loose a short, sudden blast of white fire along the naked deck of the battleship. Deep voices yelled within and men sprang out, to fall back with abrupt screams clogged in their throats as Ennis caught them in the intolerable blast from the projector. Men, shielded by five thousand miles of atmosphere from actinic light, used to receiving only red and infrared, were painfully vulnerable to this frightful concentration of ultraviolet.

Noise and shouts burst from the derelict spaceship alongside, sweeping away eerily in the thundering wind that seemed to pound down upon them with new vigor in that moment. Heads appeared from the openings in the craft.

Ennis suddenly stood up to his full height, bracing himself against the wind, so dense it made him buoyant. With a deep bellow he bridged the space to the derelict. Then, as a squad of Maraks made their difficult, slippery way across the flank of the battleship toward him, and as the band that had boarded the spaceship crowded out on its battered deck to see what the noise was about, he dropped down into a crouch behind his ultraviolet projector, and whirled it around, pulling the firing lever.

That was what he wanted. Make a lot of noise and disturbance, get them all on deck, and then blow them to pieces. The ravening blast spat from the nozzle of the weapon, and the men on the battleship dropped flat on the deck. He found he could not depress the projector enough to reach them. He spun it to point at the spaceship. The incandescence reached out, and then seemed to waver and die. The current was shut off at the switchboard.

Ennis rose from behind the projector, and then hurtled from the flank of the battleship as he was struck by two Maraks leaping on him from behind the hump of the vessel. The three struck the water and sank, Ennis struggling violently. He was on the last lap, and he gave all his strength to the spurt. The water swirled around them in little choppy waves that fell more quickly than the eye could follow. Heavier blows than those from an Earthly trip hammer were scoring Ennis' face and head. He was in a bad position to strike back, and suddenly he became limp and sank below the surface. The pressure of the water around him was enormous, and it increased very rapidly as he went lower and lower. He saw the shadowy bulk of the spaceship above him. His lungs were fighting for air, but he shook off his pretended stupor and swam doggedly through the water beneath the derelict. He went on and on. It seemed as though the distance were endless, following the metal curve. It was so big from beneath, and trying to swim the width without air made it bigger.

Clear, finally, his lungs drew in the saving breaths. No time to rest, though. He must make use of his advantage while it was his; it wouldn't last long. He swam along the side of the ship looking for an opening. There was none within reach from the water, so he made one, digging his stubby fingers into the metal, climbing up until it was safe to tear a rent in the thick outer and inner walls of the ship.

He found himself in one of the machine rooms of the second level. He went out into the corridor and up the stairway which was half-wrecked, and found himself in the main passage near the control room. He darted down it, into the room. There was nobody there, although the noises from above indicated that the Maraks were again descending. There was his weapon on the floor, where he had left it. He was glad that they had not gotten around to pulling that instrument apart. There would be one thing saved for intelligent examination.

The clatter from the descending crowd turned into a clamor of anger as they discovered him in the passageway. They stopped there for a moment, puzzled. He had been in the ocean, and had somehow magically reappeared within the derelict. It gave him time to pick up the weapon.

Ennis debated rapidly and decided to risk the unknown. How powerful the weapon was he did not know, but with atomic energy it would be powerful. He disliked using it inside the spaceship; he wanted to have enough left to float on the water until Shadden arrived; but they were beginning to advance on him, and he had to start something.

He pulled a lever. The cylinder in his arms jerked back with great force; a bolt of fierce, blinding energy tore out of it and passed with the quickness of light down the length of the corridor.

When he could see again there was no corridor. Everything that had been in the way of the projector was gone, simply disappeared.

Unmindful of the heat from the object in his hands, he turned and directed it at the battleship that was plainly outlined through the space that had been once the walls of the derelict. Before the men on the deck could move, he pulled the lever again.

And the winds were silenced for a moment. The natural elements were still in fear at the incredible forces that came from the destruction of atoms. Then with an agonized scream the hurricane struck again, tore through the spot where there had been a battleship.

Far off in the sky Ennis detected motion. It was Shadden, speeding in a glider.

Now would come the work that was important. Shadden would take the big machine apart and see how it ran. That was what history would remember.

SHAWN'S SWORD

"Nothung. Nothung—I name so this sword, Nothung, Nothung—Notable steel—"

THE SULLEN red glow of the fire flickered over the man's face as he beat violently on the anvil in time with his lusty singing. He was big, in height and in girth, and his face was ruddy with a mighty joy. Sparks pounded from the anvil; the incandescent strip of metal lying there gradually assumed form. It was a sword, straight, double-edged, and of diamond-hard metal.

Big shadows crawled blackly over the walls of the darkened chamber. Machines stationed around the room assumed grotesque form in the flickering light. It was curious that with the wealth of metal-working machinery present, the man should choose to forge the sword—archaic weapon—by brawn of shoulder and arm.

He roared on, making the surrounding shadows quiver with the song of the ancient hero, Siegfried. More fervent it grew, combating the ear-shattering clamor of the hammer.

"What the devil's all the noise about?" A rough voice broke into his mood. "I could hear you at the other end of the asteroid." The intruder, squat, bulky, unshaven, advanced into the room.

"What d'ya have there!" He reached out for the strip of metal in the singer's hand.

"N—no—" Arthur Shawn shrank back. His big, rotund figure seemed to collapse on itself, and the light seeped out of his eyes. "It's nothing." His face seemed childlike in its fear as he battled with a devastating slowness of speech.

"A sword!" the other shouted. "King Arthur's making a sword!" He roared in laughter. "Here y'are, King Arthur, some more books for you. They just came in the mail torp. Maybe ya can make yourself a white horse out of them."

He dropped a heavy package on the floor and staggered laughingly out of the room. Far down the hall—at the top of his voice—hilariously he roared: "King Arthur's making a sword! A sword!" It echoed faintly in the room, where the fire on the crude furnace wavered dimly.

Arthur Shawn's eyes reflected hurt. Slowly he turned and, shoulders stooped as though he feared his own six-and-a-half foot height, he shuffled out of the room.

The corridor was small for his huge bulk. But now, away from the inspiration of the forge and song, his size seemed more round and soft than muscular and strong. His face, relapsed into its normal rotundity, was expressionless and empty. Only his eyes—the lines around them showed pain, as of a child rebuked for doing something it thought was good.

His room was a cubicle that seemed to shrink as he entered. A bed at one corner, a desk opposite, and around the walls shelves of books.

Shawn's eyes lit vaguely as he stood there scanning the books. With eager expression he placed the package on the desk and cut it open.

"Ah!" he breathed in delight as the titles spread before him. Curious titles they were for an asteroid miner. Likewise were the hundreds of books that lined the walls. Children's books of adventure, mostly very old—about medieval knights, King Arthur, Robin Hood, Don Quixote. Recordings and the scores of romantic operas: "Die Walküre," "Siegfried." Their spirit breathed life into Shawn's frame.

He was lonely here on the asteroid. It was hard for him to talk to people—some misconnection in his brain made it necessary to fight over each word. Withdrawing into himself, he kept to his room and his books, only venturing forth for his daily work of mining cosmolite crystals.

Like most stutterers, when he sang, he had no trouble with his voice. At first he had tried singing, but the men's ridicule stopped him. He never told them he had once tried to he an opera singer. That would have made things intolerable.

He never had become a singer. His figure was ridiculous, in the first place, and, too, he wasn't very bright. He never seemed to be able to cope with situations the way other people did. His mind worked so slowly, and his halting speech accentuated it.

Escape—his life was a continuous escape from reality. Off to the asteroids to be far from civilization; persecuted by the men there for his lack of wit and his strange ideas; then escaping into children's books to wallow in the romantic and mighty deeds of the valorous men of old.

Those were men! Galloping on their white steeds, battling, swinging their mighty swords—there was always a sword. *Excalibur— Nothung—*

Why wasn't he like them? Gradually he became so, in the closed world of his mind. In his own fancies he did all those wonderful things. In his mind he rode as an armored knight, steel-clad on a wonderful horse, until that alone was real to him and everything else was trivial, passively to he borne for the sake of his dream-fantasies. They *were* only fantasies, but—why have them so? Why not make them real?

*   *   *

A sword—he must have a sword against the ridicule of men. A sword to make himself invincible.

He was clever at making things. Sometimes he wondered if part of his brains—he had so little brains—were not in his hands. For they, big and clumsy though they seemed, had a very curious skill at doing delicate work.

He would make a sword, a very special sword. The men would marvel at its beauty and prowess.

Shawn thrilled as he sat there reading the new books. Such wonders they told. If he could only live thus. Perhaps he could make enough money, strike a rich pocket of crystals.

He stood up, face set in as close an approximation of determination as its soft lines would allow. His shoulders drew back. He'd show them.

The clang of the bell announced the next work shift. Abruptly his shoulders slumped. He was back in his own skin, his dream broken. Through the door he slunk, and down the corridor. Shouts of laughter greeted him in the big room that led to the air locks.

"Where's your sword, King Arthur? When you rescue a maiden in distress, O King, don't forget to get me her visiphone number!" They crowded about him derisively.

The incoming shift surged on, shedding spacesuits.

"Listen to this!" The loud-mouthed one who had caught Shawn at the forge told them the hilarious news. "King Arthur's making a sword! When he's finished he's going out to fight dragons on a white horse—with a special spacesuit for the horse!"

The chamber resounded with laughter.

Shawn seemed to shrivel. "G-go away," he mumbled inaudibly, and pushed through the mob to where his spacesuit hung. His eyes were moistly bright.

Outside was silence. Shawn felt better there, with the clean, searing rays of the distant sun etching the jagged landscape in vivid outline.

He allowed his driver units to waft him away to his digging site. The lack of gravity exhilarated, and a momentary extra touch of oxygen cleared the trouble from his mind. It was pleasant, floating out there alone. From the small height he could see nearly a tenth of the total area of the asteroid. The view was fantastically beautiful.

Shawn spied the cairn that marked his site of operation, and settled down beside it. into the well-worked cavity. The electric chisel in his hand vibrated gently, until a shower of reflected light revealed the presence of a cosmolite crystal.

As he worked there silently in the vacuum, Shawn wished that he had enough brains to understand what cosmolite crystals were

used for. All he knew was that they were essential in atomic generators, power broadcasters, and beam radiophones. They had curious
properties of focusing electromagnetic vibrations, whatever they were.

They were found only on those asteroids which had been part of
the center of the original planet; very brittle, their mining was a
tricky job.

It was very difficult for Shawn to think and work at the same
time, so presently he gave up the one and merely worked.

Inevitably, the signal came through for the end of the shift. He
stayed out some minutes longer than usual this time. He did not want
to encounter the crowd in the air-lock room. There were a few there
still, when he arrived, but he pushed stolidly through to his own
chamber, where he could be alone and could escape into his phantom
life.

Exhausted, he ate and then slept for some hours. Day and night
mattered little to these men, where the sun rode on the hands of a
chronometer.

The handle of his sword was a beauty. He worked on it the next
day for several hours. It was carved of a ruddy alloy that seemed to
glow with an inner fire and etched with intricate designs. There was a
book, a thick, heavy volume, that he pored over constantly while as-
sembling the haft. A sword maker of old would have wondered at some
of the things he did.

Another work period, while he silently endured the jests of the
men.

Then the final working of the blade. Behind locked doors, he lived
in the character of a hero, while the blade was pounded and polished
to a mirror-finish and a razor-sharp edge. The polishing was tedious,
for the metal, after undergoing his treatment, was incredibly tough.
Shawn disdained the use of machines. This sword must be done entirely by hand, and it took more than one work period before—

"How's the sword getting along, King Arthur?" The usual cry
greeted Shawn as he entered the air-lock room to watch the coming of
the small police ship that patrolled the lanes among the asteroids.

"It's finished." He spoke with a mixture of pride and shyness. The
clang of the landing craft vibrated through the buildings, and metallic
rattles sounded as the air-lock connection was made.

"W-wait." He turned and ran back to his room followed by laughter that didn't seem to matter so much, now.

When he returned, the air lock had been opened, and the five pa-
trolmen were emerging, filling the room with their clamorous greeting.

"Look! King Arthur has a sword" His name was known throughout the asteroid belt.

"Let's see it. Is he strong enough to use it?" This as Shawn, with the expression of a child exhibiting a toy, held it up.

"Here . . . let me see it."

"No!" Shawn drew it back. Their hands should not defile his metal. It was a wonderful sword. Like *Excalibur,* which had made King Arthur invincible, or *Nothung,* with which Siegfried had defied Wotan, king of the gods.

A current flowing from it seemed tangible, giving him strength to defy them.

"I won't break it," the man growled, advancing. "Let me have it."

"No!" Shawn's voice rose operatically, and with a spasmodic motion he rapped the man's unkempt skull smartly with the flat of the blade.

The room howled at the miner's discomfiture.

"It's a magic sword," one of the police explained gleefully. "He can't be beaten with it!"

"If you want to kill dragons," another patrolman continued, "why don't you go to Ganymede? The dragons there are even uglier than Carlos!"

Shawn's face shone. Was it really courage the weapon gave him? Was that strange recklessness, that feeling of unconquerable might, courage? He had never felt like this before.

So hard to express himself in speech.

Words struggled to escape, but his throat clogged, throttling the sentences. Sweat leaped out on his face as he struggled to say the thought that had come to him.

Sing it!—his mind whispered. Singing frees your tongue! What if it is melodramatic! Drama is the life you seek!

From his throat broke forth great volume of tone. Uncertain quality, perhaps, but the spirit behind it—The incongruous spectacle of this living inferiority complex uttering such vibrant song struck the men motionless. Across the floor to the air lock he swung fiercely. No one moved to stop him.

"I go, then, to Ganymede; dragons will I slay! For with the sword, *Nothung,* giving strength to my arm, I defy the world to inflict on me harm!"

The last note, loud, high, sustained, broke off suddenly with the slam of the air lock. Simultaneously the men awoke from their astonishment and in a turbulent wave crossed the room to pound vainly on the metal.

The other half of the connection was released, the valve shut, and with a bound Shawn was at the controls. The exultant spirit still drove him, and with but a glance at the simple controls he flipped on the antigravity driving the ship straight up.

He had never piloted a ship before in his life. Far from the asteroid, out in the emptiness of space, fears began to creep back into his brain. But a hand on the sword hilt reassured.

Was he not invincible? Was not his destiny to do things heroically, as men did in books and opera? Ah, if life could be as it was there! His eyes gleamed as he. whirled about, listening to the swish of an imaginary crimson-lined cape, and the click of sword against sword.

Ganymede—the man had said there were dragons to be killed. There he would go. He exalted with the thought of the great deeds he would do there. Since the mathematics of course-plotting were too complex for any ordinary human mind anyway, the machines took care of that, and the trip, guided by the humming, clicking course plotter, was spent in dreams as thin and unsubstantial as the space outside the hull.

Ganymede spun below after a week. The orbit the plotter put the craft in gave him a distinct, kaleidoscopic view of many-colored vegetation. A small town, domed for higher-pressure air, came into view. Shawn ignored it. Where was the land of the dragons? There, perhaps, where such foliage as Earth never knew reared up for hundreds of feet.

How to land? The automatic machinery, so simple when it came to traveling through space itself, gave no clue. His hands, clever and swift with most operations, were clumsy with the few levers and switches he now had to manipulate.

The ship lurched downward. Too fast. The forward motion then decreased too rapidly. He cut off the anti-gravity. The ship dropped like a plummet. Frantically he shot on full antigravity: upward surged the vessel, the sudden motion sending him into the control panel. His arm depressed the forward power lever, while the nose of the ship fell abruptly.

Panic-stricken, his mind ceased operation and fear moved his suddenly paralyzed fingers. Antigravity worked against motive power, and staggeringly the ship careened downward. Then an abrupt deceleration, a flash of tangled branches and spiny leaves, and a jarring stop while mud spattered in sheets and gobs from the swamp.

After some minutes Shawn lifted himself from his uncomfortable position draped over the control board. His nerves quivered, and his hands shook. He felt cold, and an uncontrollable shiver passed over him. To be back in his little room, with his wonderful books—Then his hand touched his sword, and he recalled why he was here.

Everything was ready. He had prepared a pack with necessaries, and the respirator to boost the tenuous atmosphere. No need to wait longer. Shouldering one and adjusting the other, he was through the air lock in another moment.

The ground was soft and muggy, sucking him in almost to the top of his boots. With difficulty he advanced, regretting momentarily his decision to leave the antigravity lifter behind. But no—a hero must endure hardships without the softening accouterments of civilization.

The marsh continued for a short distance, and then the ground rose. It became dryer, and the character of the vegetation changed from bushy, sharp-spined plants to long, ropy, brilliant-hued growths. Shawn advanced cautiously, watching for signs of alien motion.

Something small on the ground seemed to change its shape, or was that a trick of vision? A bright streak of color shot out from underfoot and disappeared in the brush. Shawn thrilled with alarm and recoiled a yard.

Breath came quickly. Pulse beat fast. Stooping slightly, eyes darting from side to side, he continued slowly. The foliage thinned out; a bare stretch of land was ahead.

Then from one side—Shawn was paralyzed as by a bolt of lightning—a shrill, sirenlike shriek wavered and wailed. A series of heavy crashes sounded, and then Shawn saw it—vaguely, through the branches. Big, reptilelike, with eyes of yellow and hide composed of millions of tiny scales that scintillated and sparkled in the sunlight. Like a coat of jewels it was, glimmering with all the colors of the rainbow in incredible mixture.

Shawn was running suddenly, without volition.

Why are you running, Shawn? There's your dragon following you! You mustn't run, Shawn; you're a hero. Put your hand on that sword. You are invincible with that sword. Why are you running away? Stop, turn, face the monster and kill him! There he is—right on top of you.

Shawn looked back—a confused mass of colors—right behind—closer—above!

A sudden flash of incandescence—a wave of heat. Then Shawn's foot caught on a root and the ground flew tip to meet him.

A man was standing over him. At first he seemed to be far away and in a poor light, but presently he was close and more visible. The stranger was a little past middle age, but was healthy and robust, alert. He was dressed in the rugged clothes of a planetary pioneer.

His hand held a still-warm neutron blaster. On his face was a puzzled expression.

"Where did you come from?" he asked, helping Shawn to his feet. "And why are you carrying that? A sword is no sort of weapon for this place."

Shawn spoke slowly, absolute misery lined his face. "I . . . I made the sword. I was mining the Belt, and I came here to kill a dragon. The sword makes me invincible"—he choked a little—"but I keep forgetting."

"Oh, I see"—dubiously. The stranger closely scanned Shawn's countenance, and his pursed lips showed the revolving of inner thoughts. "My name is Briggs, John Briggs," he proffered his hand, which Shawn took loosely. "I own this land and raise Rainbow Dragons. People pay a lot for their skins."

The two circled the prone monster that lay among smashed bushes, noticing with satisfaction the gaping, smoking wreck of what had been the head.

"I'll come back later," Briggs moved on, following the rising ground, "and get its skin. This one, unfortunately, was not to have been killed for a while. We try to conserve them; they don't breed very fast." He motioned vaguely ahead. "My house is up there. We should be having dinner soon."

He stopped abruptly, and his face darkened with the suddenness of a Venusian thunderstorm.

"Poachers!" he grated explosively. Pushing through a clump of hushes that obscured the vision to the right, Briggs came upon a mountainous heap of bare flesh that lay there in a swamp of gore. The spectacle of the skinless, bloody carcasses was nauseating, and already an army of little things was at work.

"One, two, three of my beasts killed." He studied the tracks. "They didn't go to the house. But there'll be more of my animals slaughtered."

"Poachers?" Shawn queried blankly.

"Yes. Gangs of them roam about, killing our animals and underselling our price. They don't have to stand the cost of raising them." Bitterly, "I think the police are fixed. They never seem to get here soon enough. I don't even bother to call them now." His hand tightened on his neutron blaster.

"We'll go up to the house and see if everything's all right. Then we'll find those rats and make them pay." Briggs' eyes belied his gray hair.

"Can you fight?" he asked suddenly.

"Yes!" Shawn brightened. "My sword—"

"No." Briggs was very impatient. "That's no good. Can you use a blaster?" He talked ferociously to himself, striding up the hill. "We'll finish them this time. We'll wipe them out so clean nobody'll ever dare come here again!"

Reaching the house, a low, sturdy metal structure, he punched at a button to the right of the entrance. A snap answered from within, and the door opened. The two crowded into the airlock, closed the portal, and after the pressure had been raised by a hissing inflow of air, opened the inner panel.

"Hello, sweet," Briggs greeted the woman who stood expectantly within. "We have company. This fella's ship was wrecked down in the swamp. By the way," to Shawn, "I don't think I got your name."

Shawn's gaze jerked back from the path it had been following around the comfortably furnished room, lined with hooks, pictures, and other evidences of culture incongruous to this frontier planet.

"Oh? Oh . . . Shawn, Arthur Shawn."

"This is my wife, Shawn. You make yourself at home while I get things ready. I'll only be a minute."

Mrs. Briggs followed her husband out of the room at the invitation of a beckoning glance.

"Who is he?" she asked when they were out of earshot.

"You know as much as I do about him. I found him being chased by a Rainbow down in the bush. He looks a bit . . . a bit weak, here." He motioned significantly. "But harmless."

"It's a pity."

"Yes, yes"—abstractedly. "But we have real trouble on our hands. The poachers got three more out of the herd. If I can get Shawn to help, we'll wipe them out. No waiting for the patrol this time. I'll let him have the small blaster and I'll take the big semiportable. Then with the bombs I made—"

"Take care, John!"

"Don't worry—but what's that?" Noise came from the other room.

Mrs. Briggs started—then relief. "It's the phonograph. Why—he's playing 'Die Walküre'!"

Briggs nodded. "He would. You noticed his sword? He has an idea that he's one of the old heroes. Siegmund killing dragons, you know."

He had unlocked a heavily armored closet, and now he pulled out of it the big blaster and several small cylinders, some of explosives and some of gas.

'Oh, Lord! He sings too!"

Together with the recording rose Shawn's voice, slightly off pitch. *"Whose hearth this may be, here I must rest me."* Answered by the gruff tones of the basses, followed sweetly by the violins.

The raucous door buzzer broke in, sharply. Briggs laid down his armload and snapped on the vision plate.

"So! A patrolman. You wouldn't think one could possibly come around when you needed him." He worked the door control.

Through this Shawn stood ecstatically following the music.

The policeman was in haste. "I'm looking for—" His eyes, sweeping the room, came to rest on Shawn's oblivious figure. "There you are!" Angrily, "You're under arrest!"

"What's up?" Briggs queried, none too pleasantly.

"This man's under arrest for stealing a patrol ship!"

Briggs exploded with laughter. "Stealing a patrol ship! Why didn't you get police protection!"

The policeman flushed. "Stay out of this. He's the guy we want. That sword, and that stupid face—"

"Stupid?" Shawn suddenly noticed what was going on, and his eyes dilated in fear as he saw the patrolman.

"Yes, you. You're coming with me, stupe."

"No. I won't let you take me."

"So, resisting arrest, too?"

"Watch out!" Warningly. Shawn had his sword unsheathed, and brandished it clumsily.

"Stop that! You'll hurt somebody!"

The policeman was alarmed as Shawn waved the sword wildly. He drew a gun.

"Don't . . . don't!" Shawn thrilled with insane fear as the gun appeared in the man's hand. A mad, thoughtless sort of courage activated his arm—not his mind. The flat of the sword glanced off the patrolman's head, stunning him, while the edge, slicing a flap in his scalp, stained his hair red.

"Don't come near me!" Frantic, Shawn snatched up his respirator and retreated to the air lock, while the wounded man sank to the floor with Briggs springing to his aid.

The door opened and shut. Hiss of air, outer door open, and Shawn stumbled, ran—mind blankly afraid. Had he killed the policeman? The question was driven into him by the pounding of his heart. He must escape! All his life the one thing. Escape. Escape from reality, escape now from the law.

Branches tore at him and creepers tried to twine about him as he ran blindly down the hill. A ravine was suddenly across his path. A stone rolled under his foot, and he fell, gently under the mild gravity, to the bottom of the precipitous slope.

Bruised, he dared not wait. On he must go, far from here, where he could find complete solitude. People were dizzying to him, nauseating. Even the nice old man and his wife. He had learned, after a long time, what that expression on people's faces meant. Even *they* thought he was crazy. And he wasn't—really. He ran on.

The ravine deepened as he scurried along it. The swamp, where the wrecked spaceship lay, was behind and to the left. He had left the house and gone down the hill at an angle other than that of his approach. The distant, tiny, but intensely brilliant sun was near setting. Jupiter raised a gibbous face over the opposite horizon.

An abrupt turn of the canyon plunged Shawn into deep shadow. The gloom that settled about rapidly approached the intensity of that within his mind. The overhanging shoulder of the cliff obscured vision from above. The space below deepened until it became cavelike. Wildly tumbled and massed rocks gave some protection.

Why not rest here? It would be hard to find him, hidden far back under the cliff.

Grateful for the opportunity, he sank down on a flat rock. The words of that old opera came to him, the one he had just been singing a while ago. *"Whose hearth this may be—"* Here was no hearth, and no storm raged without, but the situation was similar: a hero fleeing from vengeance, finding haven from danger. A glow of pleasure at the thought began to warm him. After all, he had defended himself with his sword. Perhaps he really was a hero, but always in trouble, like Siegmund: *"Peaceful may I not call me; Joyful would I had been. But Woeful—"*

Clamor outside startled him. Rough voices calling, shrill in the thin air.

"Here—set the packs here. We'll camp for the night. Hey! Douse the light. Do you want to be seen?"

Shawn quaked. From his position he could dimly see several figures, momentarily outlined by the flash of light. A scintillating iridescence sparkled from one of the packs, and Shawn knew they were the poachers. It was the stolen skins; it could be nothing else.

Farther back into the dark he shrank If he were seen—his mind refused to follow the thought further. A fear-hounded, quivering mass of flesh with a sword stuck in the belt was what remained of the hero.

"Under the ledge!" the authoritative voice bawled. "As far back as you can go. We won't be seen."

To compress Shawn's bulk into as little space as he attempted was impossible.

"Fine place. Like a cave. We'll have. to remember this—Hey! Who's there?"

The darkness was cut by a knife of light.

"Come out of there—quick!" The heavy gun in the poacher's hand looked like a cannon to Shawn. In darkness, behind the searchlight, with respirator around his head, the man appeared monstrous and grotesque.

"My finger's nervous—come quick."

Shawn tried to speak. Gurgles came from his paralyzed throat. From behind a rock he crawled, trembling.

"So! What the blazes are you doing here? Having a picnic?"

"I . . . I'm Arthur Shawn." The reply was ludicrously stammered.

"Pleastameetcha," the poacher rasped sarcastically. "Fellas, meet Mr. Shawn." His voice was broad and unpleasant. "Mr. Shawn was going hunting when we interrupted him—with a sword. What were ya hunting, Mr. Shawn—Rainbow Dragons?"

Shawn's face lit in innocent surprise. "Why, yes. How did you know?"

"Ha-w-w-w!" The bellowing laugh burst from the poacher, echoing weirdly along the canyon walls. "Just hunting dragons with a sword! Maybe it's a magic sword! Lemme see it."

"No." Shawn drew back. Always like this. Always laughter and ridicule at the sight of the sword. When it was the most wonderful sword in the universe. He had made it so. It was magical—almost.

"Pipe down!" one of the gang complained. "Do you want to be heard on the other end of the moon?"

"What's that noise down there?"—from above, unexpectedly.

The poachers whirled, diving for weapons and cover.

"The poachers! They're under the cliff!" Shawn knew the voice as he slunk back. Briggs and the policeman; they'd tracked him here.

Scrambling sounds came from down the ravine. Briggs must be mad, to attack like this. Shawn must warn him. Briggs was a good man—even if he did think Shawn was crazy. Briggs didn't laugh at Shawn's ideas like others did. Shawn must help him.

He tried to shout. "Bri-i—" the noise was tiny and swallowed in his throat. His treacherous voice! Then, he had the idea. To sing! The way he could say what he wanted without the hellish clutchings in his throat.

"Briggs! John Briggs!" He opened his mouth and the notes came freely. "They're here, too many of them, go back."

"Shut up!" A surprised and savage face turned to him, distorted with fury. From the gun held by the owner of the face spat a sizzling beam of incandescence that made the air reek with choking brown fumes. Behind the man, at the same time, another ray lashed the rock to furious heat, while splinters of stone exploded from it. The poachers' blast went wild.

Beams leaped back and forth, lighting the ravine with a flickering and flashing brilliance. Briggs and the patrolman were shooting aimlessly. A hit was impossible in the intermittent illumination from the succession of bolts. But the poachers could do no better: two tiny targets, somewhere down the ravine, lost in darkness, with the light shifting and confusing.

Shawn jerked and twitched with fear. The rock to his right flared and cracked suddenly, beginning to melt. A bomb of terrific power shattered deafeningly, but thrown short.

Activity among the poachers. Something being removed from a case. A squat, thick barrel on a heavy tripod: a semiportable blaster. Shawn knew its work. The five-inch beam would scream down the canyon. Frightful energies powered it. Briggs would last in it for the veriest instant required for his body to he torn molecule from molecule, atom from atom.

And Briggs was a nice man. No one else had ever talked to Shawn as Briggs had. No one else had refrained from laughing at the sword in Shawn's belt.

And he remembered. The sword leaped out of the scabbard.

Was he mad? Defeat a gang of weaponed poachers with a sword.

But this sword was a very special one. Even the heroes of old had never seen a sword like this.

For an incredible instant the walls of the ravine were outlined with light that dazzled and seared with sheer intensity. Noise thundered back and forth, deafening even in that thin air. Wind shrieked; chips of rock flew madly as shrapnel.

Shawn felt himself thrown very violently against the rocks: and then, startlingly, everything was very silent, and he was flat on his back with Briggs flashing a light in his eyes.

Briggs' face reflected unmatched astonishment. In his hand he held Shawn's sword, unconsciously turning it over and over.

"Shawn, did I really see what I saw?" he said. "I mean . . . did this sword really . . . how?" Words failed, and he groped helplessly.

Shawn rose to snatch the precious sword from Briggs' hands, but the universe spun and he fell back.

"If you really did that," the patrolman gazed wonderingly for the tenth time at a seared and blackened area strewn with twisted metal—of poachers no sign— "I might forget you stole a patrol ship. But how—"

Shawn grinned pridefully. His voice came slowly, but with more firmness than it had had in a long time. "It was in a book. I saw in a book how to make a thing that—well I don't know exactly what it did, but the book showed how to make it. So I put it in the sword with a cosmolite crystal to make it work It would only work once. It was a very special sword."

"It certainly was." Briggs glanced with awe at the sword, and at the place where the forces from it had struck.

"Tell me—" Shawn was eager to know something that had bothered him. "Do you think I could stay here with you and kill dragons? I want to kill dragons."

It was not hard for Briggs to take pity on this big, hulking man whose brains were in his hands.

"Sure," he said. "Rainbow Dragons."

ASTEROID

THE SUN WAS setting on Ansen, and the reflecting light made a jewel of the planetoid. The jagged mineral crystals scattered the slanting beams in a shower of iridescence.

Sinsi floated, swaying slightly at the summit of a slender peak, watching the last sparkles die out of the mountain tips across the tiny valley. His body, an impalpable swirl of tenuously bound atoms, glowed a placid hue, a color that was three places past violet in the spectrum.

Of a sudden there came a change, an agitated vibration of the tinge in his extremities. He leaped a little and whirled about, then saw the two who approached.

Aio was smaller than Sinsi, and of paler shade. Emonit was older than the two, and his violet was nearly in the visible range. The trio pulsed in greeting with an undercurrent of something that was deeper. Aio flew to Sinsi, and the two coalesced vibrations, while Emonit hovered near and added a satisfying bass note.

Sinsi male; Aio female. What was Emonit, with that curious third-member relationship? Emonit, the elder, who, once upon a time, had been the active member in a triplet.

"Sinsi," Emonit pulsed, after the pair had completed greeting. His hue was somber and his tone serious. "I feel something wrong in space. There is a vibration that does not belong there, and it comes closer."

"You were always more sensitive than I," Sinsi said. "I have felt nothing."

"It is faint." Emonit suddenly gave a nervous jerk and flew lightly around the mountain tip. "But it will not be faint for long."

The asteroid was black and white like a too-contrasty photograph. George Hames kept looking at it through the port. "I never thought that Mitchell was batty. You don't accumulate as much money as he has if you're not all there. But what he sees in a hunk of rock like that to make him spend a million dollars for habitizing is more than I can understand. Why come all the way out here when you can get what you want right on Earth? 'Build your summer estate in the heart of the Himalayas,'" he quoted—roughly—from an advertisement. "'Midst dizzying heights and awesome depths you can commune with nature in her most glorious state. The sweeping lines ...'"

"Mitchell said I'd know it when I saw it." Arno Murray stood at the port also. He kept looking at the asteroid, but where Hames hadn't expected to see anything, and hadn't seen anything, Murray was looking for something, but he couldn't find it.

"Know what?" Hames finally turned away from the port and walked over to the machine that paneled the wall, where he studied for the hundredth time the plotted course that was automatically carrying the ship to an orbit around the asteroid.

"I don't know." Murray kept looking out at the asteroid. "Mitchell said I was to landscape the place. He said I'd know what there was about it as soon as I saw it, and then I'd know what to do. He didn't say any more."

"A screwball! A million dollars worth!"

"Ah-hhhh!" It was an abrupt indrawn sigh, like of pain. The sudden explosion of light that sparkled from the asteroid reflected from Murray's eyes brilliantly. The sun was on the crystals, and they shimmered and flowed like they were incandescent.

Murray didn't move for fifteen minutes after that. Hames left him alone. To Hames the glory was a lot of light reflected from shiny rocks. But Hames was an engineer who did the landscaping that Murray designed. Murray was an artist, and Murray saw things that Hames couldn't. Murray stood motionless and silent for fifteen minutes while in his mind was building a picture of what that land of scintillating crystals could be with the engineering and manipulating of Hames' crew and machines.

Fear was a sibilant whispering in the ether. The people of Ansen milled about in agitated eddies, shrieking their fright of the cylinder of metal that had come blasting out of space to circle their little world.

In the chant-like speech of their kind. they shrilled panic and stirred space with frenzy.

"The monster comes!" they called, and the fear went around the planet in a hysterical wave.

"The monster comes and kills our people! It is hot, almost like the sun itself. It propels itself against the ether, and when space warps to slacken its speed, our people are caught in the vortex and hurled to annihilation in the furnace! Emonit, tell us what to do!"

Emonit was there. From the tall peak he had shimmered down, trailed by Sinsi and Aio. His color was disturbed, and his vibrations tense with thought. He swept up to the center of the fear-stricken mob, and flashed sharply.

"Quiet!" His emanation sped outward. "This puzzle will be solved. The monster is impossible by all we know, but it is there, so it must be. It is hot, of a temperature that cannot support life. But there are life vibrations there. Many of them. Vibrations and vibrations all uncontrolled and intermingled so that I cannot separate one from the other. All I know is that there are life vibrations, and where they are—then they can he destroyed."

"How?" All asked as one.

Emonit's shade grew tinged with a hue that was rarely there. He sank back a little.

"It is fearful. . . ." he began.

And chaos was awhirl in space. The hot and dense cylinder of metal shrieked through the ether above; the braking grasp of forces that tangled in the fabric of the universe caught the followers of Emonit, and tugged them into the dissolution of heat. Shrieks of pain shrilled out, and then the mass was gone into the distance below the horizon, and there was silence, save for the whisper of space itself.

One by one they straggled back—those who had managed to flee before the grip had become too strong. Emonit was still there, and those left flurried their colors in relief, for he was their wisest, and the only one who could know what to tell them. Sinsi and Aio timorously floated back along the ether breeze, entwined with each other.

Emonit, quivering with horror, was silent for a long time. Those about him, waiting for him to say something . . .

And then horror was gone. Sometimes horror is not enough. Sometimes there can be worse than horror. Emonit's color grew deeper. It deepened until it was almost below ultraviolet. Almost until those who were in the monstrous metal cylinder might have seen it.

For from the other side of the planetoid messages had come to him. Messages of such urgency that in their shrieking crescendo they had reached him through the insulating rock and around the shifting currents of space—before breaking off.

"It has landed! It has landed, and from its base has come streaming forces and currents of power that are of a magnitude vast enough to break the rock atom from atom and electron from proton and combine it again into vapors that blast outward and overwhelm us with their fury and incandescence!"

Murray looked at the thermopyle and said: "It's cold down there."

"Darn right it's cold." Hames disdained to lift his face from the computing machine he was ticking away at. "What did you expect? We're practically incandescent compared to what they call hot down there. Now go away and let me get some work done. Did you ever think what kind of arithmetic I have to go through so dopes like you could walk around on asteroids without getting their toes frostbitten? Figuring mass and specific heat, and rates of absorption and radiation, and air insulation—and figuring what disintegration proportions to go into air and how much into heat and how much condensed into lining for the central chamber. . . . Wouldn't it be fun without a shipload of machines to do the work on? Go away to your paint-box, now, and let me work."

If Murray could stand and look through portholes all day long, Hames could spend his time with his nose in the calculators. They were accomplishing the same thing, but each in his own way—one dreamt and made beautiful pictures in his mind. The other dreamt with figures and equations and turned the beautiful pictures into solidity.

It needed both.

The control board burped, and winked coquettishly at Hames with a solitary pink light. A half dozen meters jiggled as the drive dug its toes into the fabric of space and set the ship to decelerating. Hames kicked and rolled halfway across the room in his swivel chair so he could give his attention to the orbit-setting. The ship spun around the planetoid in a narrowing circle.

In night for a half hour, the darkness was stark. The rapidly rising sun, though far away, was refracted and reflected into a glorious sight by the crystals, and Murray could not take his eyes away from it. Then a day of bare rocks, jagged peaks, and two tiny valleys. Briefly. And night again.

The ship spun and spun, and its speed became less, with its kinetic energy absorbed by space. The landing jarred a little, and Hames cussed the instruments. Then he was leaping downstairs and cussing the crew into their spacesuits.

He didn't waste a second. He had the converters roaring before the machines were set up for the other work.

The beam bit fiercely into the rock below, exploding it into a mixture of heat and expanding air. The remainder went into a dense, glassy slag that lined the tube which was beginning to extend into the center of the planetoid. The artificial atmosphere was running away, but later a gravity machine would be working down there, holding it in.

The ground heated incandescent and then bubbled vigorously for a yard around. And heat started to seep through and through the interior of the planetoid.

"To cancel a vibration—the cancelling wave must be destroyed also." There. Emonit had told what the sacrifice must be. He had said what had to be done, and now he stood there in silence, and all the others stood in silence around him. There was no more torturing of space with hysteria. No more wailing and shrieking with agonized fear. Emotion was beyond that.

The deadly, annihilating heat was seeping through the asteroid. The ship, at the center of the inferno, was on the other side of the world. Half the people of Ansen were destroyed. Soon the heat would reach this side, and there would be no more people of Ansen. No more. All would be gone. And the subtle color harmonies that sparkled from the sun-lit crystals would no longer be seen—by anybody. For the optic instruments of the invaders were too gross to catch the delicacy of the flavor in the light that came from the crystals.

Horror had gone beyond horror, and the heat was approaching.

"Who shall try first?" The whisper seeped vaguely through the group, coming from no one in particular, from everybody in general.

Silence again, while each seemed to shrink into himself. Then a convulsive movement in the corner of the crowd. A swirl of frightened light darted up and off to the horizon.

"Brave one." Emonit's faint thought followed him. "Remember what I said. Choose a life vibration. Attune your own to it. Absorb energy from space. Blanket the other vibration. Destroy it. You must be strong. Strong without measure. For the strange ones have power that we know not."

The converter was running at pitch, boring out the guts of the asteroid. The soil machines were pulverizing the hard rock and turning it to fertility that would grow lush plants of a design to match the hard, brilliant crystals.

Murray was at his drawing board, dragging pictures out of his head, and putting them down onto the white.

Hames patrolled the control room, surveying the multitude of recorders that had been constantly at work—many eyes and ears and fingers to detect what was happening, visibly and invisibly, in space, and partly out of space—and leaving them on the tape so that Hames could see them when he wanted to.

The room was about as silent as it usually was. The generator made a far-off drone that was so quiet it was almost a hush. The little clickings of the instruments as they puttered away at their endless tasks. The pop of a relay every once in a while. Little tiny mechanical noises that all put together made silence. Then there came another noise that was not mechanical, and it intruded. It came from Hames, and it was a whistle. It started high, and it came down in a glissando that ended when he reached the bottom of his range. When that happened he kept his mouth puckered, and his band came halfway up to his chin, and then stayed there.

"Hey, Murray!" he called, softly.

No answer.

"Murray, come here." Louder.

'What do you want?" Murray's frame intruded itself in slow sections through the door. His voice was peevish.

"Look at the counter tape." Hames didn't notice the frown that was on Murray's face. "At hour eleven we hit a flock of gamma rays. They kept averaging five times normal. Sometimes more. And at sixteen thirty the counter went wild, like somebody stuck a can of radium down its gizzard."

"So what?"

Murray wasn't usually dense like that and Hames shot him a curious glance.

"Don't you see? Eleven was when we started digging in with the brakes. Sixteen thirty was when we started up with the converter. We've stirred up something."

"What do you do for a headache?" Murray's contributions to the conversation were becoming unusually brilliant.

"Gawd!" Hames felt the height of frustration. "I make discoveries, and he bothers me with headaches. There's a medicine chest. Take whatever you want."

"I never had a headache before."

"Twice—and both failed." Emonit had felt the death of the pair, and a cloak of gloom spread itself over the few remaining of Ansen. They gathered more closely to Emonit, and their chanting mass-voice whispered. "Too strong. Too strong." Over and over. And there was nothing hut despair, for the asteroid was being disemboweled to give heat, and the heat was leaking through the miles of rocks to find them wherever they might hide, and leave nothing where they had been.

"I'll go." Sinsi suddenly rose. "If it requires more power, I am the strongest. I can do it."

"No!" Aio fluttered to him, her color livid.

"No!" Emonit towered over them all. "None of us is strong enough. Not even you, Sinsi. You must not be sacrificed. Not you."

Sinsi quivered. "Why not I, as well as others?"

Emonit faltered. "Let that not matter. We know that one cannot go alone. Many might."

"Many might—yes! Many, each in tune with the other, totalling enough power to clamp the life vibrations of the monster. Who will come with me?"

"You?" Aio danced in protest.

"Why not me?" Sinsi was defiant. "Do you think I could stand here and let others die to save me? It is not a mere danger of dying, but it is death itself.".

Emonit wearily put in his voice. "Can you forget the heroics of youth? Can you think of the future? Rather that I should lead the attempt than you. For I shall not last long anyway, and you must survive to be the leader of our people. Born to that."

"Born to nothing!" Sinsi glowed furious. "Leaders mean nothing.

While you waste time preventing each from sacrificing himself, all will be destroyed when the heat comes. I'll go myself, and any who want to come can follow."

A shrieking and howling of ether made a crescendo around the group. A swirl of tenuous shapes arose.

"Sinsi. You stay." The tone was sharp and decisive. "Emonit is right." Sinsi fell back from where he had risen. "You must stay and we must go. Let us hope that we win."

And the horizon rose high behind them.

"Will." Emonit's thought flew fiercely out to them. "Your will and the forces of your life to destroy the monsters. Make your vibration a mighty power that will be withstood by nothing."

Sinsi stood there, agitatedly. Aio hovered about him, but he would not be calmed. "I should have gone," he kept saying. "To stay here while they blast away their lives. To do nothing while they save us . . . Oh, yes. Aio. I know that we three belong together, and that we must not be separated, but can that overpower the knowledge that we stay in safety, while others meet terror for the sake of us? To take sacrifices from others is harder—so much harder—than to make sacrifices oneself."

Aio flew to him, and they were as one, comfortingly.

"If the time comes," Aio was fierce and soft, "we shall go together."

"It's not only irrational, but it's insane. It's not only illogical, but it's batty. It's nuts. It's screwy."

Hames talked like he meant it. He paced the little room, glaring at the meters that goggled cooly into his face at the end of each lap, and raising a fuss like the insides of a rocket motor.

Murray stood at a porthole, looking through it. He'd been standing there for an hour now, while Hames had been gently going mad tearing through all the books on atomic physics in the ship's library. Now Hames was deadlocked, and Murray still stood looking through the porthole at the landscape outside. It got on Hames' nerves.

"Haven't you seen enough of that bunch of colored glass out there?" he yapped, irritably. "You haven't done anything since we've landed but stand and look through the porthole."

Hames was a hunch of nerves. Murray was lax, and he hardly moved his face to answer.

"I've got a headache," he said. "I never had a headache before, and it bothers me."

"Well, why in cosmos don't you take something for it?"

"I dunno." It was with a loose little sigh. "The crystals are so beautiful. The colors—I'd almost swear there are some I'd never seen before." He closed his mouth, and looked out through the port, while his hand went up to his hurting head.

Hames gave up and went back to his books. The engineer couldn't see things that Murray saw, and it irritated him. They thought too differently.

He mashed his book shut, and started pacing again. While the drone of the converter made an accompaniment to the click of his shoes.

The converter, blasting atoms apart and boring away down into the center of the little world. . . .

"We come close to the planetoid and dig in with the brakes, and the Geiger counter jumps to five times the average." Hames roared it out as he pounded the floor. Maybe if he made a lot of noise about it the answer would come from somewhere. "We start digging with the converter, and counter acts like somebody dropped a ton of radium on it. Maybe the force fields touched off some radioactive substance around here. Maybe the stuff is right underneath, and the converter beam is multiplying its rate of disintegration. But it ain't, because the stuff coming through is all gamma rays, and no alphas or betas. And there's no direction. It comes from all around. Enough gammas to singe our hair if we weren't shielded. From all around. Look at the counter jump!"

Hames made a prayer to the little gods that inhabited that section of the universe in thanks for his not being outside the shield, where the counter units were.

"I never had a headache before," Murray whispered, vaguely. "I don't like it."

"You and your headaches and your blasted colored crystals." Hames turned fiercely upon Murray. "You don't know what a headache is like until you've tried to untangle a problem like this."

It roused Murray. "Scientific observations and deductions—" Caustic! "Why don't you make something out of my getting a headache as soon as the digging started and the rays began to come in?"

It was a weary little group that gathered around Emonit and Sinsi and Aio. The bottom was gone from their universe, and there was no longer any future for their world-line. "They failed. They failed." Reiterated over and over again, the words were dug into their consciousness, and there was no answer to their fate.

"Power." Sinsi was bitter. "What good is the most power we can get against a wall that cannot be broken through?"

"Perhaps power is not all." Aio hesitated in saying her thoughts. "Maybe the three of us...."

"The three of us?" Sinsi puzzled. "Why three any better than a score or a hundred?"

"*We* three." Emonit saw, quickly. "The bond that is between us. The subtler vibrations that only play among us, because we are a special three. Not unique. This grouping of three is the basis of life, but each is special to itself. And being special."

"And futile, unless we do something." Sinsi, impatient lest courage seep away entirely. "Come, and stop wasting talk."

Space whispered to itself. It was like the whistle of a wind that has traveled far distances of desert and sea, and now breathes with a sibilant voice through tree branches, so softly telling a portent of something that is to come.

The three felt the whisper gently caress them as they sped around the circle toward the cylinder that lay there like a blood-sucking insect. This was finality.

Murray's eyes were bloodshot.

"Good Lord," thought Hames. "This is going too far. An artist might visualize differently than I do, but Murray looks like he actually sees things that are different. Maybe even different from what *he's* supposed to see. Maybe he's cracking."

Murray saw Hames looking at him. "Whatever you're thinking, it's not so."

"I'm not thinking anything," Hames lied. "But your eyes look strained. Maybe you've been using them too much."

"I don't see a damn thing." How did Murray seem to keep knowing what Hames was thinking? "But I feel funny." He shivered.

A great flare of gammas hit the counter, and the tape reeled merrily off the spool. Hames bent over to watch closely, and abruptly a gasp hissed from his mouth.

"They've stopped! The gammas have stopped, and the counter's back to normal cosmics. The converter is still running. Why should they stop, and after the big flareup?"

He was bent over, eyes fixed on the counter tape, and not seeing anything, for he was thinking, and when you think you don't see. Hames was thinking. His mind was pacing at red speed, and he didn't see Murray.

Murray's face looked like it was going to cry. It twisted, and its eyes were bright, and suddenly words exploded from it. *"Oh—you engineers just can't feel—what you're doing."*

And Murray ran out of the room, slamming the door behind him. Hames sat and stared at the space where Murray had disappeared, as if his eyes could see through the metal. The footsteps clicked down the corridor, and then there came a rasp and a whirr.

*　　*　　*

43

"Murray-y-y-y-y!" Hames bellowed.

The door was behind his leap, and the corridor seemed to drag unendingly beneath his running feet, but the inner airlock valve was irrevocably sealed, and the hiss of the opening outer came through to the inside.

Murray was a shapeless mass that staggered, hopped, floated, and fell lightly to the bottom of the cold vacuum.

"Good Lord. Why did he do it? Why did he do it?" The question channeled into Hames' brain and burned like fire there.

Hames stood looking through the porthole. He tried to see what Murray had seen there, but all he could see was what looked like a lot of jagged colored glass sticking up in a crazy pattern that had no meaning. Artists saw things differently. That's why they were artists, and not button pushers. They thought differently. Hames stood looking through the porthole, and he wondered what Murray had meant when he had burst out: *"You engineers just can't feel . . ."*

Hames hadn't felt anything. What had Murray felt? What had his mind, more delicately organized than Hames, felt to drive him mad and send him with twisted face through the airlock?

The unending whisper of space hissed gently about the asteroid. The little people who had shimmered in the delight of bathing in the ether breezes were not there to feel the whisper, nor to see the strange colors of the crystals. They had been as a wall of soft mud holding back the tide of the sea. They had been like children hammering at a massive bronze door to break it down.

And now they were gone, and space was empty of their strange life. They had fought bravely, and with that might of spirit and that curious love they had. Now they were gone, and their utmost power had been like the touch of the breeze against the side of a battleship.

But *had* they accomplished anything? What had Murray meant when he said, *"You engineers just can't feel?"*

Hames looked out of the porthole at the blotch that had been Murray, and began to frame the words of his new thesis:

"Report on the form of gamma-particle radioactivity found on the asteroid Ansen."

FLIGHT TO GALILEO

I

Emergency Call

"THERE IS A large block of sentiment in favor of sending out a force to quiet the disturbances among the asteroids, to return the lost colonies to the control of Earth, where they belong," said the radio.

"Rubbish!" snapped Bern Ryder, silencing the unseen speaker by flicking in another station. "They'd get their noses bitten off. The asteroids are tough."

"It was a mistake to let them go in the first place." Richard Flemming's voice drifted out from behind the complex switchboard. The upper part of his body was buried in the machinery while he worked with pliers and welding tools.

"Ridiculous!" Ryder seemed to give each sentence a push with the first outspat word. "They couldn't do anything else."

"Consider the condition that existed at the time of the colonization of the asteroids." The voice from the radio came in as if it had been rehearsed. "There was a group of tiny worlds, each with its little settlement of the most intelligent and hardy men in the system, each with its own artificial gravity and atmosphere. At the beginning, a ship would set out from Earth or Mars perhaps once a month; each colony was lucky if it was visited once in six months. These men were too intelligent and too individualistic to allow a distant government to keep control over them; they simply allowed the bonds to slide loose, and set up whatever system happened to be most convenient to them at the time.

"No one could do anything about it. A ship coming up there once a half year—in that time so much could happen on the asteroids that control from the Earth was impossible. And even if someone wanted to do something about it, there were no battleships with which to apply force. The spaceships then were too delicately organized to allow the extra weight of weapons and armor.

"And now that war craft are available, the colonies have grown from the status of colonies. They are independent states, each with its own economic system and form of government. And what they do is no business of . . ." Click, the radio was off.

"The asteroids! We hear nothing except the asteroids." That came from Flemming, behind the big oil switch, a little below the rack of oscillator tubes. "Squabbling little upstart states. Capitalistic Sandrona at sword-points with Communistic Leninovdra presumably for reasons of principle. Regimentation of souls, and all that sort of thing. When it's really because Leninovdra has beryllium that Sandrona wants. Christiana on the warpath against pagan, feudalistic DeVoybus—but really because DeVoybus has uranium. And Adriana wants the fantastic crystals of Christiana for the jewelry they're nutty about. The whole bunch working at cross purposes, because they all want, want, want, and the others won't give. They should be united. We should do it."

"Just like that." Ryder snapped his fingers. "When each one of those settlements has arms and protection that a spaceship couldn't possibly beat down. A ship just can't carry enough power or armor. And you know they won't listen to conciliation. They are each too intensely nationalistic. It will take a long time, or something very big, to make them get together."

"Let's forget it, then, and get on with the final testing." Flemming squirmed out of the switchboard, stood up straight. He towered a full two heads above Ryder. Not that Flemming was particularly tall. Ryder was small and compact, with hands that were delicately muscled like a musician's; black, curly hair that persisted in hanging over his right eye.

Flemming flicked over a tiny tumbler switch that was answered by the thud of a relay somewhere behind the panel. Three pilot lights went on. Ryder ran his hands over the metal form that stood in the center of the room.

Gently, caressingly. His hands knew every centimeter of the surface, for they had made the machine. The skillful hands had fashioned the delicacy of the finger joints, the complexity of the electro-neural system, the multitude of motors and mechanisms that gave the machine motion. The ingenious eyes that surpassed human optics. The mouth that spoke when impulses carried through a wire from somewhere. The ears that heard sound and sent impulses through a wire to go somewhere.

Somewhere. That was the main thing. It wasn't a brain. It wasn't a mind. But there was going to he a mind in it later.

"You don't have a mind yet, old thing, but you will have soon," Ryder spoke to the mechanical body. For it was a robot, you know— tall, of shiny black metal. "A mind will be pushed into you. Not a brain; not the mushy piece of protoplasm that's the storage battery for the mess of forces known as the human mind. But the forces themselves will go into the artificial battery; then you'll be the person— whoever it is."

"Stop talking to yourself, little one." Flemming hardly wasted a glance on Ryder. "Let's get some work done."

"Okay." Ryder said it so that it was hardly audible. If Flemming had looked at Ryder when he had spoken, he might have seen the dark little man wince when his size had been so lightly and thoughtlessly mentioned.

Ryder moved back from the robot to the testing instruments, and the manner in which his eyes pointed towards Flemming was not right for one who was a friendly fellow-worker in research.

The big oil switch gave a sudden thump; a bank of meters surged in unison. The laboratory was silent, except for the faint clicking of the recording instruments and the sharp signals that Flemming whispered at each move. The circuits to be tested were of a complexity difficult to imagine. The two spent a long time in that room of gleaming metal and glass and flowing energy. Their work could not be merely a matter of conceiving and making a machine, and then trying it to see if it would work. A human mind was the stake in the gamble, and it was test, test, test, before they were satisfied.

Wa-a-a-. The buzzer was shrill. Flemming looked up irritatedly; Ryder gave a curt exclamation. Ryder was all sharpness and bluster again, and he didn't look like the little man who had flinched and shrank at a word from Flemming a moment ago.

They'd cut out the regular door signal; they didn't want to be disturbed, but a spot of light burned a steady red now. It was an emergency.

Flemming walked over and pulled the door open. A battery of feet clattering down the hall suddenly crescendoed. "What's up?" Flemming and Ryder found themselves in the crowd making for the escalators. How they'd gotten mixed in the mob was rather confusing. There they'd been, perfectly innocent bystanders, until tubby Rubinstein and heroically statured Nicotera had surged by, and they'd been lost in the wake. Rubinstein and Nicotera looked less like physicists than almost anyone you could mention, but they were a pair you couldn't beat.

No, you would have to look pretty far to find a pair that knew more about their field of work than they did, and you'd have to look still farther to find an assortment of brains equal to that bunch in the Research Building. In fact, you would have to go clear out to the asteroids—to the Science Colony on Galileo.

II

"Can You Help Us?"

"What's up? What's up?" Nobody knew, and everybody asked everyone else, until the crowd of erudite intelligences streamed into the assembly hall as wondering as a bunch of freshmen on their first day in school.

The Chief of the association—he was called Chief, but all he seemed to do was to call meetings to order and read announcements that came every once in a while—the Chief was rather breathless, and the miniature crowd that weighted the platform was white of face.

"Gentlemen, please be seated. All right, then, stand if you will." He waved the paper in his hand as if he weren't quite sure whether it was a Japanese fan or a handkerchief with which to bid someone farewell. He mopped his brow, which was a libel on the perfectly functioning air-conditioning. He suddenly emitted a gasp and sat down, himself.

Reuning, the big, pompous biologist, moved impatiently. His eyes were red. He'd been at the microscope for five hours, and the sudden grate of the emergency buzzer had caused him to ruin a slide, in addition to giving his nerves a bad jolt.

An elevator load of men flowed into the room. Some irritated by the interruption, some vaguely amused. They all wanted to know what it was about. What was going on, and when they could get back to work.

They never could take that emergency signal seriously since the last time it had been used. That was the time a little pine snake had sneaked out of one of the biology labs, into Johnson's chemistry lab. Out of all the labs in the building the critter had to pick that one—and Johnson mortally afraid of snakes of any size and color. When the mob found where the signal was coming from and sped to the rescue, they found Johnson atop a table, besieged by the reptile amid the wreckage of broken glass and overturned bottles. Johnson still has a murderous dislike for certain organic chemicals, flasks of which he brilliantly chose to overturn at that moment.

Johnson didn't think it was very funny, but thereafter, when the signal went off and fond memories were evoked, the atmosphere did not contain as much tense expectancy as would have been proper.

"Millard, you read them. I'm too jittery." Smitty, the Chief, handed a bundle of paper to Millard, the famous engineering research man. They'd elected Smitty Chief because he could say "The meeting will please come to order," more beautifully than any of the others. They hadn't really expected him to do anything, so when something had to be done they found themselves in a hole. Afterwards, the group who had supported Ross for Chief, said I told you so, that they shouldn't make jokes out of such serious things as elections. But try to tell a bunch of scientists not to make jokes out of anything that is outside science.

*   *   *

Millard cleared his throat. He was an engineer; the pure scientists purported to despise him, but he was able to make things. That was more than some of the others could do.

"Three radio messages have come from the Asteroids. Two are general news broadcasts. The third is directed to us, and is the reason for this special meeting. No messages have come since. None can come, and none can leave, for the ether is blocked with interference." Millard paused and looked steadily at the faces before him. He was a good orator even when not speaking; in a few moments the group began to catch on that the emergency buzzers hadn't joked this time.

"The first," Millard read, "from Cardwell City on Ceres, about half a million miles from Brenn. Quote: 'A spaceship of unusual size was seen to take off from Brenn. From its direction, and from rumors that have been traveling about the asteroids, it is believed that the ship is heading for the science colony at Galileo. Its purpose is officially unknown.' Unquote. The second," Millard ran on with hardly a pause, "From Kleerol, about a million miles from Brenn, more in the direction of Galileo. Quote: 'A large spaceship left Brenn at hour zero with constant acceleration of one gravity in the direction of Galileo. Rumors indicate that the ship is up to no good—for Galileo.' Unquote. And now the message from Galileo itself."

Nobody seemed to have moved, but where there had been a bunch of annoyed, amused, growling, laughing men lounging about the four corners of the room, was now a compact group of grim scientists clustered silently at the foot of the platform.

"This came on our own private, tight beam, scrambled phone hook-up, just before the interference broke it up. Quote: 'Report just received of take-off from Brenn. Brenn is after our ore deposits. Also unconfirmed rumors that Brenn is after consolidation of asteroids under Brenn. We believe that plans for the electron-proton projector discussed last month with Ruhinstein and Nicotera have been copied by agent from Brenn, and since only we two asteroids know the weapon, Brenn is out to see that only one asteroid remains with the weapon. We are building an opposing field generator, but have no time to manufacture special tubes; the ones on hand will give way after five hours. Can you help us?' Unquote."

Can you help us? The Terrestrial Institute of Science and the Galileo Science Colony. Mock rivals, squabbling at every turn—on the surface. But no knowledge one learned was a secret from the other. And when one needed help it knew who to ask.

Can you help us? A cluster of great domed buildings surrounded by a fairyland of parks: the science colony. Not a fortress of war. The power they had gushed through instruments of science, not fighting machines.

The best brains in the system were working out there on that little world at tasks that were unfamiliar to them: defense. Even the best brains can be conquered by lesser brains when the lesser brains are out to get what they want. Perhaps with—this is the joke—forces that the best brains have invented.

Millard spoke flatly and decisively. Our own government washes its hands clean. It will not spend any ships of its own to help a group with which it has nothing to do. Anyway, the asteroids are too far away to get help there in time. Moreover, Brenn is conducting a trade treaty with our own government. Which means that anything we do will have to be done by ourselves on our own hook.

"I propose that we immediately organize ourselves into a committee to declare war upon Brenn and combat them with all the scientific means at our disposal. Does anyone object to my acting as chairman of the committee?" No one did. Millard was hitting on all cylinders, and he could get the facts straight better than any other.

"Rubinstein, what weapon is this that the message mentions?"

"We didn't think of it as a weapon," Rubinstein lamely began. Scientists rarely think of that. "It's got plenty of power. Ten times more than a neutron or ion blast. You disintegrate piles of matter to get piles of energy to separate electrons from protons of matter. You shoot them off in parallel beams, and you keep them from coalescing by means of a force field. That's the rub to the situation. When the thing hits something the electrons and protons come together, and where you would have neutrons formed you get cosmic rays. And all the energy of all the matter disintegrated comes out at once. Wow!" The last was either descriptive, or a result of saying the entire speech with one breath.

"And the defense?" Millard had to think of everything.

"Oppose the field of force that holds the two beams apart, let them come together before they reach the target. Takes loads of power. No wonder their tubes won't hold up. Ten times more powerful than any neutron or ion blast. Oh, lots more powerful."

No wonder a lone ship could hope to defeat an asteroid.

"Aren't Brenn, Ceres, and Kleerol rather close together? Half a million miles isn't much." That came from Richard Flemming, and the group stared.

Bern Ryder began to look interested. When Flemming started asking questions that apparently had nothing to do with what was going on, it meant that Flemming was starting to dribble bubbles from his think-tank.

"They're part of a group. Ceres, Brenn, Kleerol, Astor, and two others I can't remember. But what does that have to do with anything?" Millard demanded.

"How far is Galileo from Brenn?" Flemming persisted, this began to be getting more to the point.

"Twenty million miles, about," Millard answered.

Flemming had the inevitable slide rule out of his coat pocket and was working away, mumbling to himself. "At one gravity, or 32 feet per second per second, that means, approximately thirty-two hours for the trip. The enemy has been en route one hour, which leaves thirty one. Gentlemen, do any of you know how we can reach Galileo, which at this season is approximately two hundred million miles away, in thirty-one hours?"

They had all suspected that, but Flemming needn't have rubbed it in.

"If we don't get to Galileo in time we'll get to Brenn later on." The promise came from the middle of the room and remained unidentified. It meant one thing: that each person in the group was slowly and gradually getting mad. Those men didn't do things suddenly. It took them time. But when they did get mad the results wouldn't be nice at all. Those men knew a thing or two, even though they were merely scientists; and they had a few toys lying about the labs that no one had thought of putting to practical use. Killing people isn't practical, but—Constantine, Galileo's chief astronomer had been a roommate of Fisher, chemist at the Institute. Hummel, the lanky chemist up on the asteroid, had been pals with Flemming way back when. They'd all gone to school together, and the sounds of Ray for Dear Old Tech could still quicken a pulse and moisten an eye.

So when Brenn marched in on Galileo she also declared war on the Terrestrial Institute of Science.

III

Robot

AT THE MOMENT, however, the thirty-one hours and two hundred million miles seemed an insurmountable obstacle.

Flemming continued his cross-examination. "What ship available will take the highest acceleration, and what acceleration?"

Millard began to be irritated by Flemming's air of mystery. "Our own *Bluebird's* as good as any. She'll do over fifteen gravities. Past that, delicate parts begin to be overstrained. And I suppose, my dear superman, that you are going to fly to Galileo under fifteen gravities and do a one man rescue. As a messy pulp you wouldn't get much rescuing done."

Flemming continued to mumble over his slipstick. "Fifteen gravities will do very nicely. Two hundred million miles in twenty-six hours, very approximately. Giving a five hour difference, and adding another four or five hours for their defense to hold up, means that we've got to get under way in less than nine hours, that we've got to work fast. Ryder, get out own stuff ready. Rubinstein and Nicotera make your weapon. Millard, prepare the *Bluebird*; I'll race the enemy to Galileo and get there in time to lick them with their own weapon."

"Wait a second Flemming," Millard objected violently. "I'm only chairman of this outfit, but I would like to know what's going on. If you know what you're doing, that is. Perhaps you don't."

"It's like two and two, Millard. We have to get help to Galileo. We have a ship that will do it, and we have a weapon to use; but a man can't do it without being crushed to a pulp. Ryder and I have a robot. A metal body that will contain a mind and that will take the fifteen gravity acceleration without a murmur. What could be simpler?"

Millard rapped for order. "All right, then. Since no other plan of action is forthcoming, we will proceed immediately. All of you who have anything to do know it. The rest will keep out of the way." Millard stepped off the platform and strode away.

Flemming and Ryder left the crowded room. Flemming walked swiftly down the hall with a purposeful look on his face, taking no notice of Ryder, who dogged his heels. Three times Ryder started to say something, but nothing came out. Suddenly he blurted: "I was to be the first one to enter the robot. You promised me. You can't break your promise just like that."

Flemming didn't look around. "You're awfully anxious to take on a lot of danger. What do you know about space navigation? You'd never come back. I've got little enough chance myself."

"You've got plenty of excuses," Ryder persisted. "But you only want to be a hero and pull it off single handed."

"My God, shrimp!" Flemming stopped short and turned upon Ryder, who seemed to shrivel at the words. "The way you can act like a baby is nauseating."

And that ended that. What could Ryder say? How could he tell Flemming that the reason he wanted to use the robot was because he had always been so little, and everything about his nature was warped because he had always been so little, and now he wanted to be big. That's why he had loved making the robot so much: it was so big and strong. And when the time came that it would be finished and ready for his habitation, then *he* would be big, and he wouldn't be stopped by anything.

Ryder absently stared at the brain case that lay complete on one of the tables as they entered the lab. It was bare and unadorned; the contact wires stuck out like tentacles. The two arms were neatly ranged beside it, with the torso still a skeleton of metal.

Flemming was shedding his clothes. There was a body to be taken care of when the mind was in the robot. That little detail had cost them almost as much trouble as the robot itself. The biology staff at the Institute had finally taken charge, and built them a suspended animation freezing chamber.

So Flemming got frozen. That was pretty routine, and Ryder had nothing to do but watch dials and push buttons, while the other nine-tenths of his mind was elsewhere. About the time the mind transportation had to be carried out, Ryder was decided on what he, himself, was going to do. Then he was ready to give all his attention to the big job.

It was unspectacular. The things that went on were hidden among shielded wires and tubes; all that you could see was the flickering of the meter needles. When it was all over, what had been Flemming was without a mind, and the metal thing *should* have had Flemming's mind. Ryder was wiping the perspiration from his face with a shaky hand. Mark, now, Flemming—that is, the body that had had Flemming's mind wasn't dead. There was no sharp line of demarcation; the involuntary motions went on as per usual, and metabolism went on as much, or as little, as the suspended animation process normally allowed.

But the robot had Flemming's mind.

The robot moved its right hand across its goggling eyes.

"My God," Flemming's voice came out of the face. "I feel awful."

"How?" Ryder didn't let his face show the excitement he felt.

"I don't feel. That's the trouble. Lord, it's awful."

The robot moved forward; a hum from within rose sharply as the gyroscope kept balance. It—Flemming, we'll have to call it now—staggered and went partly down to the floor. Ryder was quick and grasped the machine's arms. Flemming gripped Ryder's shoulder, who gasped, and twisted away.

"Be careful!" he bit out. "Those claws of yours are strong."

"You should know. You made them."

"Yeah. I made them." Ryder turned away and picked up his coat which he had thrown across the back of a chair. He'd mask his disappointment, but the last laugh would be his.

Flemming finally learned how to use that was himself. He made a sight walking down the hall, big and strong and black, with a kind of polished grace that came from the perfect functioning of the intricate joints Ryder had designed and made.

This that was Flemming created a greater disturbance in the Terrestrial Institute of Science than had the news of the attack on Galileo. Things worked that way. It was a shock and a horror to hear of the things that were happening far away, but good grief, look at this tall metal thing walking through the building calling itself Dick Flemming, the physicist. The big room at the top, where the Institute ships and planes were kept, rapidly filled with scientists and assistants—everyone down to the boy who ran the bottle washing machine.

Mechanics swarmed over the *Bluebird,* the swank little boat that was the pride and joy of the Institute. Its fifty foot length of blue was filled with all the power and gadgets that the personnel of the Institute could devise. There was only one thing it had lacked before; something to fight. This was being supplied now, in the shape of a bulk of machinery that was being installed in the cavity of one of the forward rocket exhausts.

Rubinstein and Nicotera were directing the installation, arguing with each other, as usual. They argued not only with their voices, but with vivid motions of the arms and their entire bodies. Then Flemming and Ryder marched in, pied pipers at the head of a flock of gaping ones.

"You worked fast," Flemming remarked.

"We had the things built already," Rubinstein explained. "All you have to do is to fix it onto something solid enough so that the back blast won't push the projector clear back to the next galaxy."

"Strong, eh?"

"Plenty strong. And works like a dream."

"More like a nightmare, I'd say," Ryder, the cynical, broke in. "That the only one you made?"

"No. This one is the biggest of three. Sends out a pair of three inch beams. The force field itself uses over a million kilowatts."

"Oh, oh, hit a snag somewhere." This from Flemming, as a mechanic gesticulated wildly from a porthole. Something had broken, had to be welded together again. The ion generator wouldn't fit into the narrow part of the rocket exhaust. So the exhaust had to be pulled apart and the machinery jammed into there somehow, then the whole business welded together again. It was the worst makeshift job ever seen; by the time it was complete, seven hours were done.

He gravely shook hands with Ryder, with Rubinstein, with Nicotera, and with Millard, and with the mechanics; he would have shaken hands with everyone in the crowd, but Ryder prodded him into the ship.

"Go on, you tin can, and let the neutrons fly. The battle will have been on for three hours by the time you get there, so you'd better not waste any time if you don't want to miss the fun."

IV

Margin of Safety

THE PORTS SHUT and locked themselves.

The antigravity droned, and the ship slowly rose through the back-flung ceiling of the room. Air props shoved out and spun, keeping the hulk on the straight and narrow, because it wouldn't do to use the big rockets so close to the Institute. There would be little left of the building and immediate vicinity if he forgot that.

Bern Ryder suddenly put his head back and laughed. It was the first good laugh he had had in a long time, and he took pains to extract a great deal of pleasure out of it.

"What's so funny?" Millard wanted to know.

Ryder cut off like somebody had pulled a switch. "Flemming thinks he's going to a rescue," he snickered. "but he'll never get there in time."

Millard looked, startled. "What makes you say that? What do you know is going to happen?"

"Oh, nothing is going to happen to Flemming—that I know of, anyway. Don't worry, I haven't sabotaged him. No dirty secrets in my closet. It's just that I'm going to get there ahead of him; when he arrives, there will be nothing left but congratulations. Won't I enjoy that, though?"

Millard raised his eyebrows. "So, more tricks up sleeves. Everybody has tricks up their sleeves. The genius running rampant in this Institute overwhelms me. I suppose you are going to go Flemming one better, and make the trip at fifty gravities instead of fifteen."

"Precisely. At fifty gravities I'll get there in fourteen hours, and that gives me twelve hours advantage over Flemming, which is none too much for what I am going to do. Let's get to work."

"Not so fast, there. Not so fast. Flemming is fixed up pretty well. What makes you think he can't do the job by himself, without you putting us to a lot of work just to get a lot of glory for yourself?"

"Maybe he can do it himself, and maybe he can't. He's got an ordinary ship. Fifteen gravities is a lot of pull, and if some weak little thing breaks down, that might be the end. It's not an armored warship. The enemy has the big weapon too, and Flemming doesn't have a shield. Flemming might be able to do the job, hut he doesn't have a strong enough punch to be sure."

"I give up." Millard threw up his hands. "Give the orders and your wishes will be law. The resources of the Institute are at your command."

"Thanks, bud," Ryder drawled, sarcastically, and was off to the nearest mechanic, who made a completion of his state of near-collapse when he heard what Ryder wanted.

"You can't kill my men that way," the head mechanic protested. "They've been working eight hours straight already, and now you want them to work ten hours more. Its against all principles. It's unethical. Tbe Union won't stand for it. What the hell do you want us to do?"

It was a crazy thing that Ryder wanted to make. He didn't have any plans or calculations, or anything to go by, except the idea that was in his head. He had half a robot. Less than half. He found some tons of scrap iron. Somebody went flying to the shipyard and came back with a load of rocket motors. Just motors. Plain, bare, unadorned motors. The biggest they could find.

Somebody else discovered a generator and an anti-gravity machine, and fuel tanks. Nicotera and Rubinstein stalked and waddled down to their laboratory, and came back on a truck loaded with one of their remaining double blast machines. The one that worked most of the time.

They threw all the junk together with a big flare of the welding machines, and when the smoke cleared away, an egg had been laid. It looked like an egg. At the center the very innermost center, was the brain from the robot.

Then came course after course of tough, laminated metal that made an impenetrable shield for the vital delicacy of the "brain." The two biggest motors had been laid end to end, and welded immovably together with heavy beams. Smaller motors had been stuck judiciously over the body at the proper angles for steering. Fuel tanks had been inserted where they would fit; the all-important generator had been been tied down with beams and plates welded to a solid mass. Eyes from the robot protruded heavily protected. Fingers from the metal hands connected to the brain and operated the controls. And sheath after sheath of thick metal smoothed the surface.

The thirty foot egg was far from being a fragile little thing. It was heavy—nearly a solid mass of metal, and the antigravity had been turned on before it had been half completed, to keep the floor from collapsing. A floor that supported half a dozen ordinary boats.

It was a monstrous thing, and its surface was dull in the glare of the lights. It was not pretty but there was something about it—perhaps the bareness of the metal and the crudity of the finish that made it look strong and slightly irresistible. It looked like you could just throw it right through any armor, like a projectile.

Ryder moved with a smouldering spark of vitality that had kept him going for eighteen hours. He knew that if he stopped he wouldn't he able to start again. Millard had long been curled up in the most remote corner of the room; Ryder kicked him to wake him.

"Up! We're on the last lap, and you have to run the mind pump. Just punch a button or two, and that's all. You'll learn."

"I think my mentality is equal to the task," Millard countered.

Ryder suddenly stopped before the monster. "We haven't named it. What'll we call it?"

"A thing like that doesn't deserve a name."

"Oh, but it must have one. What does it most resemble? An egg. Then its name is the *Egg*. Short and sweet."

And so down to the laboratory.

"Oh, Lord," Ryder wailed. "We can't move the stuff, and we can't bring the robot down here, because we can't move the robot without moving the entire *Egg,* and we can't—"

"String a cable," Millard broke in, but already Ryder was rooting through the cabinets looking for one long enough. It took several of them, and an hour. But they finally got a sufficiently shielded connection between the machinery in the laboratory, and the mechanical brain in the *Egg*. Work commenced.

Steve Dorsey made as if he were going to tear up the papers, but Mike Kunsak put out a fist that was as big as a melon and took them away from him.

"Now, now," Mike—his full name was Michael Vladistovitch Kunsak, Ph.D.—said. "You can't go throwing your work away like that."

"There's not much else to do," Dorsey slumped in his chair. "I spend my years planning and building all this, making thousands of drawings and blueprints, and now that I'm just about ready to put a complete shell around Galileo, everything goes bust."

"It hasn't yet," Kunsak said, his face in the papers. "This is some stuff you have here. You didn't tell us."

"Surprise, surprise," Dorsey muttered, tonelessly.

"You're taking this entirely too hard," Kunsak rose. "We'll have to put you to work."

"Ha. I've been working for the last fifteen hours. What do you think an engineer's for?"

"Then go to sleep. I've got my own work to do."

Kunsak went in to confer with MacPherson, temporary Chief of operations. "How goes the field generator?"

"Smoothly. Fifteen hours now, and fifteen more to go. We'll make it, and to spare. Then to set it up on the trips, and let it go at the first squeak from the magnetic detectors."

"I wish we had some offensive weapons," Kunsak said.

"I do, too. But every way we figure, we can't work it. Our own new double blast won't go through our screen. If we could hit the attacking ship first try, that will be fine. But we'd probably miss."

"You know what we can do, don't you?" That came from a young fellow with the beginnings of a mustache, dressed in a soiled leather jacket. Reeves had been quite an airman in his school days, and he was finding difficulty in settling down to his job as a chemist. "We can hook the double blast machine onto the nose of our fastest boat, and I can go out and wipe up the Brenn ship."

"Listen, Reeves. You've asked me that a dozen times, and I still say no. You would make a fine picture going out there in your little tincan, waiting until the attackers came. They would float in with lights and most power out, everything shielded so that we couldn't detect them. You might smack into them. You might not, but they would detect you first; and they would make hash out of you."

Thunder came from the machine that worked madly to cover the domes with thick layers of the latest product of the metallurgists. It was an incredibly tough metal after being cooled within certain fields of force, and certain other fields of force gave its molecules a tendency to cease motion, so that the metal stayed cool, though being bombarded with a practically solid blast of high speed particles. It took power and power and yet it wouldn't last for an instant under the new double blast. That had to be fended by the screen of force, which would still allow the straight neutron and ion beams to come through as if there weren't any screen there. It was just because of the way the thing worked. But the screen wouldn't stay up more than five hours, and then what would they do?

At the bowels of the asteroid were the power generators and the gravity field machines. Men labored there, for power was needed for many things—and the scientist knew things about the gravity machines they hadn't told yet.

V

Mad Race

SPACE IS CURVES and motions and velocities and accelerations. Navigation of space is something not to be done with impunity unless you have power to waste measured in the tons. There is no such thing as traveling in a straight line to a destination. The most efficient route is a highly complex series of curves. The more power you can spend the flatter your curve can be.

The ship from Brenn made a compromise, navigating a pretty fair sweep, but well on line for Galileo, twenty million miles away. It started at an hour—call it zero. It kept a steady acceleration of one gravity: thirty two feet per second per second. Every second its velocity increased by thirty two feet per second. Every minute its velocity curve soared upward, and its navigation curve flattened out.

At the end of nine hours well over three million miles had been covered; the mighty warship was speeding at a rate of two hundred miles per second.

That was when Flemming started.

Flemming, the tall, black robot, whose body of metal was strapped into the controlling chair of a ship otherwise empty of life. Life? Was Flemming living? Was there life in the ship at all? But Flemming was there, too busy to ponder philosophy. He was easing through the atmosphere, and spinning around the earth for precious minutes to attain the proper angle to set acceleration. And an *acceleration!* Not a piddling single gravity, but a force that a ship with organic life in it had never attempted. Life was not in this ship, only Flemming. And Flemming was pushed down into his chair with a weight fifteen times the weight he was accustomed to handling. Even the robot was in trouble.

The ship did not increase its velocity by thirty-two feet per second per second, as the warship from Brenn was doing. Every second saw it boring along four hundred and eighty feet per second faster than it had gone the previous second. It added up. In only one hour it was going 330 miles per second, very nearly the highest velocity the ship from Brenn was to make in its entire trip.

But Flemming had farther to go. Two hundred million miles of vastness, empty and black, lay ahead. Grimly he pounded through it, rehearsing in his mind the action that would come upon his arrival, keenly ferreting out each possibility of events he might meet, and planning ways to meet them. And all the time his body chained down by the irresistible force that the comet-tail of the rocket blast pressed on him.

On and on, among the whirling motion and curves of the solar system, the two vessels sped to their meeting place on the heads of the shrieking swords of radiance that were the rockets.

At hour sixteen the ship of Brenn reached the halfway mark. Ten million miles it had gone, while Flemming's slender little vessel was already looking back upon twenty-nine million. Ten million miles, and reaching out over 350 new miles each second.

Whirling gyroscopes hummed; the battleship slowly turned to present its tail to the fore. Then again the blasts lashed out, and again the force of one gravity applied itself to the ship, but in the opposite direction. Its speed decreased.

Hour twenty-one; the race was nearing it finality. The ship from Brenn had accomplished three quarters of its trip, Flemming would be halfway in another hour. Something, then, happened, which was the one possibility that Flemming, in his planning, had not given the slightest thought.

Ryder entered his ship.

Ryder, now, was not the body that had been called by that combination of syllables. He was not a robot, like Flemming was. He was a complex network of vibrations and forces in space conducted along a cable from the protoplasmic battery which had contained it, to a new metal battery that was to be its habitat. In the exact center of the *Egg* the little mechanism rested, hidden by layer after layer of metal, surrounded by generators and motors that consumed power of a magnitude very nearly to warp the immediate space.

Ryder opened his eyes. That is—the metal spheroid down below emitted an impulse that flowed through wires to a mechanism that opened the shields covering the optic instruments sunk into the armor of the *Egg*.

Ryder felt—well, he could not feel; there was an absence of sensation that went beyond the ordinary meaning of the phrase. He could not even feel ill at the lack of sensation; there were no bodily organs to cooperate with a production of the sensation of feeling ill. So—he did not feel.

He saw, and he heard, when there was air; he had orientation by virtue of the tiny gyroscope within the shell.

His hands, hidden somewhere among the machinery, wriggled their fingers, and touched the buttons that were the controls. A motor spun; the pair of eyes slowly protruded themselves from their recesses.

This was joy for Ryder. Looking down from the twenty foot height, he at last felt big. He at last felt as though he had the power to do something, instead of bluffing and being caustic as a defense against being little. The grey metal looked so strong.

The fingers moved, pressed buttons. The eyes retracted and became domed with protective transparent sheathing. The antigravity hummed; the *Egg* rose, slowly, then with increasing velocity. The roof of the chamber spread wide, and then was below; the people gathered in there became tiny, then were gone in the distance that pulled the city together in a ragged splotch interrupting the earth's curve.

The heavy gyrowheels roared; slowly the *Egg* responded, turning its nose away from the sun that was going down in the—west. Then the rockets—quickly building up from a thin sliver of incandescence to a fervent flame that stretched part way across a continent— blasted.

Flemming was halfway to his destination Brenn three-quarters gone, but Ryder was going under fifty gravities of acceleration. He was all metal, and the ship was as nearly solid as any ship had ever been made before. It held.

For seven hours he bored on through the blackness, pushed by that spear of light. And for seven more hours he continued on, with the spear of light grinding him to a stop.

Damn Reeves!" Mac Pherson exclaimed. "Who let him out the air-lock?"

Reeves was gone, and with him one of the experimental double-blast projectors. He had disappeared from sight for several hours; MacPherson had thought he was sitting in a corner moping. But all the time he had been installing the projector in his little ship; now he and the ship were gone.

Up in the sky was the tiny streak that marked his distant rocket trail; it snapped out as he began his silent vigil, hanging up there in an orbit, watching for something to come.

"He wins," MacPherson sighed. "We'll send him the signal as soon as we know something. Jones!" he called. "Are the torpedoes ready?"

"Two of them. No time for more. They're devilish things to make. Lord, I'm sleepy."

"Okay, shoot them out and sign off. You'll know when things begin to bust. Get some sleep in the meantime."

The torpedoes, hastily built things, were sent up into their orbits, where they would spin until the glare of the enemy's rocket would set off the photo-cells; relays would guide the torpedoes relentlessly to the source of that glare. The double-blast would flame out ahead. If, of course, there was anything left of the torpedo by that time.

A body moving head-on in an unswerving line, is a lovely target.

VI

For the Freedom of Science

"PILOT!" spoke the commander of the battle ship from Brenn. "Report on position and velocity."

"Position now one thousand miles from Galileo, at velocity of one mile per second. We have been on a straight line from Galileo for the past fifty thousand miles."

Fine work. From that distance and position the rocket exhaust would not be a comet tail, but a tiny star not to be told with casual glance from the other thousands of stars.

"Good," the commander said. "Cut rockets and drift until fifty miles from Galileo. Then decelerate at rate sufficient to bring us to rest within that distance." To the power room: "Cut all power as per plan." To the gun stations: "Commence firing immediately at fifty mile range with the double-blast projector. Neutron and ion blasts handle defense."

The lights winked out; the ship became a dark wraith floating indetectable, except to the magnetic and gravity instruments, which were in pretty bad shape among the complex fields of the asteroids.

A mile a second. In fifteen minutes the detectors blared out their warning down on Galileo. The big double blast screamed out of its projector towards the estimated point of disturbance, but the spotting was vague, with an error of plus and minus one degree; at a hundred mile range the beam might be off one and three quarter miles on either side. According to the laws of chance they *could* have hit the ship with the two foot beam. But of course they didn't.

Nearly a minute fled by, and suddenly all of the detectors on Galileo went wild; the electron-tube relays reacted with the speed of light, throwing the power screen through the already warmed-up tubes at almost the same instant that the enemy's double blast reached the asteroid.

Almost the same instant. That beam was a pencil of fire impaling upon its tip a fragment that might have been from the very center of the sun. It darted down to the surface of the asteroid, lingered there for a time too small for human senses to realize, then quailed back as the screen set up its repulsive power. In that instant Galileo shook, and the rock that had been touched disappeared in a blaze of power.

The defensive shield fought the beam, and where the electrons and protons came together was that little center of radiation that was like the sun.

The battleship's rockets were on full. The two torpedoes that had been drifting above, went into action. Their propulsion blazed; the double beams fingered ahead. These were little beams. They had not the hundred mile range of the battleship's. But their power was intense.

From two different directions they sped. Their mechanical controls knew one lesson. Aim for the ship and hit it. From opposite sides of the battleship spat ion blasts, caressing the simple targets of the torpedoes for an easy moment. And then the glare and the debris scattered.

A comet zoomed from the other side of the asteroid. Reeves, in his little boat, groaned against his chair straps. He'd been far away; it took time to get where he wanted at a speed low enough to be of any use.

His weapon was fixed. He had to aim the ship; to do that he had to get the ship pointing directly at the *Conqueror*. The ion blasts were spitting around him; the mechanical sighters were getting on to his orbit. He cut out of the gyrations, tried to shift his path, but at a thousand miles an hour the blood spurted out of his nose; before he had time to lose consciousness from the pressure the blaze of his rockets coalesced with the incandescence of the ion blasts, and space was filled with little droplets of molten metal . . .

The battleship went into an orbit about Galileo, spraying the big double-blast over the asteroid. But the blast never quite hit, because the screen made the two beams come together in that fierce fireball. The ion blasts poured downward, but the soil merely melted and ran, while the protected domes absorbed them without a murmur.

An immense neutron beam speared out of the base of one of the domes. The skin of the battleship began to glow. Five powerful blasts concentrated their fury upon the projector down there, and suddenly it snapped off.

Galileo was without offense.

"Prepare for landing," the commander ordered. Rockets thundered, and the ship spiraled inward.

Then it was that the generators at the center of Galileo, heretofore comparatively silent, began to hum and groan.

"Acceleration failing!" the pilot called, a frown marking his face.

The commander glanced over the meters and gasped. "Report!" he shouted as he flipped a connection to a room at the bowels of the ship.

The man with the detectors and analyzers was on his toes with the information—and excited.

"The gravity field opposing us is of a type predicted recently by the Science Colony, probably just created by them. Its effect is identical to that of the field about an atomic nucleus. The ion blasts have sufficient momentum to penetrate, but we do not."

The commander irately snapped the connection. A most lovely force screen that was, repelling all that came from without, but not affecting that which was on the surface of the asteroid.

Siege commenced. The question that hung in the balance was whether the ship could hold the beam longer than the asteroid could hold the shield.

When Bern Ryder—the *Egg*—that scarred little metal ovoid came streaking upon the scene, the status quo still held.

During that long voyage he had practiced target shooting. He thought he knew a way to hit a thing without heading straight for it and making a beautiful target himself. It made the enemy almost as hard to hit as himself, but the enemy was bigger, so maybe he had a chance.

If he'd had perhaps ten years to practice the maneuver he might have done it successfully. It was mad.

Ryder's rockets pounded him to a momentary stop, then he leaped again towards the enemy. But in that instant of rest, and in the moments required to gain speed, even at the fiercest acceleration at his command, the forces came beating upon him with devastation. He sheered off from their grip, but his forward motor was gone, and with it the blast projector. His *Egg* was lopsided.

It took tiny moments of time, where the fleeting thoughts raced, and Ryder, the wreck, went sixteen hundred feet per second, thirty two hundred feet per second, forty eight hundred feet per second, up and up every second; the metal fingers of Ryder made the slight turn in the flight of the *Egg* that sent it shrieking for the *Conqueror*. Ions and neutrons pounded him. The nose of the *Egg* ran incandescent from its concentrated force of many projectors, but all the mass was still there, and the space between the two ships narrowed swiftly.

Ryder's eyes went out when the projectile that was him made the plunge—through the armor of the *Conqueror* in a sweep of devastation that left garbage of the immediate vicinity; he could not tell what he had done. But the beam that came up from below left nothing remaining of the battleship to be seen.

Ryder, incredibly retaining the thread of connection to the metal brain that hid below sheaths of armor at the center of the broken *Egg* could not tell how or to where he moved, nor could he tell that Flemming was just then flaming in upon the wings of his rockets.

But he had faith; he knew that Flemming would find him. And in that utter darkness he lived for a time that was unmeasurable to him, thinking of what he would say to Flemming when the light would strike his human eyes, and when he would have a voice to speak:

"Maybe I was a little man, Flemming, but with the hands that created the robot I made myself big. Don't ever call me little any more."

POWER PLANT

JOE STONE WAS working on top of one of the generators when Willard called him. From where he stood he could look across the tremendous backs of the machines, all the way over to the other end of the cavern, and he was beginning to be able to trace the patterns of the maze of tubes and pipes. The mistiness of the air had cleared up; they had gotten the steam leaks under control, and the system, from the boilers that took off the heat wasted in the mercury turbines, to the condensers that tapped the cold underground river, was tight as a drum.

He saw Willard down there, at the side of the room, motioning for him to come down into the laboratory.

Joe waved back and replaced the hatch that covered the port through which he had been examining the exciter-field oscillators. He screwed it down and began to descend the ladder which clung to the side of the generator. Willard must be ready for more work, he thought. It took more time to set up the apparatus than to do the experiments and it was a shame Willard didn't get more help. It was a very pretty machine be was going to have when he was through. It wasn't for nothing that the high Command allowed him the time, and half an assistant, and an insulated laboratory.

It was not a very pretty machine that was spread out over the tables and along half of a wall. Frankly, Joe thought, it looked a mess. But it was hardly the finished product. It was just about the middle of a big piece of research. Willard was soldering wires at the far end of the room, and his hands, so restless when not occupied, moved very swiftly and surely among the delicate instruments. Taber was at the workbench, filing down a piece of metal.

"I'll soon be ready," Willard said. "You handle the potentiometer and 1 will take the readings from this end. Run through it the same as last time."

Funny, Joe thought, as he worked. They spent so much time trying to learn how to get atomic energy. Now they have had it for a while and we spend all this time trying to learn how to stop it. No doubt, though, there would be an advantage in being able to stop an atomic generator at a distance. At a good distance. We could win the war just like that. Simple enough.

But this job right here isn't so simple. You don't go about it the obvious way. You might think that you should neutralize the exciter field to stop the disintegration, and, true, you might possibly do things to a generator by messing around with the exciter field, but it was something difficult to handle. No, what you wanted to do was to eliminate the softener field, the space strain that put the atoms into a condition to be destroyed easily by the exciter field. The energy went off mostly as heat, some as high frequency rays, in these old machines here, and you had to run mercury and steam turbines with them, but with the new machines you could pick the energy right off.

So the work went. It was monotonous, and the only sounds were the scratching of Willard's pencil, the occasional hum of a machine, the dry sound of a word of instruction.

And then there was the heart-tearing, frightening sound of the alarm siren, the noise of shouting voices muffled by the insulating walls, the change in the rhythms of the generators, the flaring of the red light on the laboratory instrument panel.

Joe stood still; his stomach felt tight and there was a constriction around his chest. The roar of the generators outside rose imperceptibly in pitch and created a tension that stopped his breath.

"Switch off the oscillator," Willard said, as he moved over to the wall panel on which the red light shone. Willard studied the meters and the line on the recording radiometer. His hands were quite still, and there was only an in and out motion of the muscle in his cheek as he ground his jaws together.

Taber stood by the workbench, waiting for something else to happen, just like they all were. The sound of the shouting voices began to die out.

Willard said nothing, but he walked over to a computing machine; calmly it seemed, but very quickly. He began punching, and was soon finished.

"It is a very rough estimate," he said. "I have thought all along they might do this, but I suppose I was too interested in what 1 was doing to follow the other line, for it is the opposite of what I was trying to do." He spoke more and more rapidly, as though he were trying to excuse himself for something. "We were trying to extinguish the softener field. They—the enemy—have done the opposite. They have sent down on us from somewhere above, perhaps from a ship, perhaps from the moon (I don't know how much power they have) an exciter field that increases the disintegration in the power plant to a rate that increases with a curve that will cause the power plant to explode in ten minutes, plus or minus one minute. The secondary radiations from the generators are penetrating the generator insulation with a strength that makes impossible more than momentary life outside of the laboratory insulation." He stopped.

The three of them then thought, and there was an intensity and coldness of logic about those thoughts that drove very quickly to a conclusion that was inevitable and inescapable.

Taber thought: in ten minutes the power plant will blow up, and that will be the end of this entire sickening business. The colonists will win the war, and all the right they have for that.

Willard thought: in ten minutes the power plant will blow up, and my damper will be destroyed, and with it will be destroyed the hopes of bringing the war to a quick and victorious end.

Joe Stone thought: In ten minutes the power plant is going to blow to hell, and all of us with it, unless a person goes out of the laboratory to switch off the softener field, which would make the exciter field useless, no matter how strong. But that person would die.

What was he doing here, he continued the thought savagely. Why was it he that was down here in the clammy underground factory instead of on top where a person could live and fight and die as he had been taught a person should? Three weeks ago he had had thoughts like that. Three weeks ago he had stood at the entrance to the passageway halfway up the side of the hill. It had been raining, and across the valley the parallel Appalachian ridge could barely be seen through the thick air. The road up which he had been driven wound closely around the side of the hill and disappeared around the bend a hundred yards away. The trucks had gone on, leaving Joe and twenty others standing in the rain before entering the tunnel.

He allowed his face to get wet, and the water trickled down his cheeks feeling very cool and fresh. It would be warm always once he was inside, and he did not know when he would be allowed to come out again. So for a few moments he stood there and once again tried to puzzle things over.

Am I lucky or not, he thought. Am I luckier than my friends who were taken into the army and shipped off to Venus six months ago to fight the war? Was it good that I was better than they at physics and mathematics and therefore sent to tech school to study atomic engineering so that I would be able to run the power plants that supplied the munitions factories? Is it right that because I was better than they, that they should have the excitement and adventure of the army, while I must go below into the hot factory to slave over the dirty power plant?

To him, naturally, the army was excitement and adventure. That was what he had been taught. That was what they had all been taught.

So this mixed him up, and he stood there and once again the questions buzzed round and round his head, without end and without solution. What had been the use of his working so hard, if this was the net result?

What was the use? What was the value? What was the purpose?

They had never been answered, although Mary had been able to help him without exactly giving answers. She had been able to buoy him up with some reserve of feminine certainty, and had convinced him that he was doing the right thing, and she had kept him from thinking too much. Now she was not here; he would not see her for a long time, and the confusion was returned to his mind.

Well, the door was open, and the little group trooped into the tunnel. The lieutenant at the desk within checked over their papers and gave each a destination tag. They walked a little way into the mountain and climbed aboard a monorail car.

The track led downward in a series of curves. At each of the several stops the car made, one or two of the recruits climbed out. Joe was left, finally, and he rode on into the depths below the mountain. The tunnel slipped by; its walls were unfinished rock shining with hanging water. The black of anthracite coal occasionally lined the tunnel; Joe recalled that there had been coal mines here.

With a shock of booming sound and glaring light the power plant suddenly spread out before the car. The cavern was huge, and the opposite walls were dim from the mist in the air. The boilers and turbines filled the floor with their massiveness, and the whitely insulated pipes spun a complex web through the chamber. The roaring generators stung his ears, and it was a sound that he was to hear constantly. It beat down on his head, it made the air heavy, it oppressed him and made his heart pump fiercely.

That was the first sight Joe had had of the big place, and as he stood now in the swift silence of the laboratory he still had time to recall the dismay with which he had viewed the clumsy, monstrous mercury and steam boilers with their spinning turbines.

"Gawd," he had said to Martin, the corporal who had met him and was leading him to the quarters through the jungle of machinery. "This place is an antique."

"Sort of," Martin smiled. "It was left over from the last war. But we still manage to squeeze a billion or so horsepower out of it. We have been having some trouble with the steam turbine system. The place is steamed up like a Turkish Bath." He pointed to the drops of water clinging to the metal plates and pipes.

"It feels like one." Joe dragged out a handkerchief and wiped his face with it. "Bathing suits seem to he in season."

Martin's face suddenly turned wistful. "I haven't been swimming for a year and a half. I was district champion—four hundred meters free style. I can't wait to get back into the water. Think the war will be over soon?"

"To hear my crowd talk before they embarked for Venus, the war was going to be over very shortly after they landed. I sort of wish I was with them. It won't be much fun down here."

"Oh, we manage. It gets tiresome after a time. For we are short-handed, and to get leave is like busting an atom with a nutcracker, even a chromium-plated one."

Then they had entered the living quarters, which were air conditioned, and vastly more comfortable than the plant itself. There had been the going around to all the people and shaking hands and hearing their names and forgetting them, and hearing the clatter of table tennis balls and the jangle of year-before-last's songs on the phonograph, and smelling the dinner cooking.

Say, this isn't so bad, he thought. A person could have a decent time down here. The work is hard, the people swell, the books in the bookcase—but what happens when you have read all the books twice and know all the records by heart?

He came to know Taber at the first dinner. Taber, with the massive head and the twisted, useless leg. Taber was a character. All of them down there imitated him—his cynicism and his vulgar humor—for they thought it was clever, but they didn't know what it was all about. It was what Taber showed him at that first dinner for which he would always remember him.

The dinner plates had rattled back to the dishwashing machine, and the beercans were on the table as Taber showed Joe how to fold beercans in his hands. "You see, you hold the seam away from you, place the tips of your fingers on the seam, and the heels of your hands on tine can as the fulcrum of a lever, and you push with your arms instead of trying to squeeze just with the muscles of your hands. No, you don't have the trick yet. When you can't squeeze any more cans flat, then you know you have had enough beer."

That was Taber. It was so humorless above. The wars after wars, the strictness of the government, the constant militarism, had kept things grey, and while there was plenty of fun it was of a frantic, hilarious sort, not this sober kind of humor that you felt pretty deep but did not laugh at much.

So now where was the humor? What did Taber's humor say when the word *none* was measured in ten minutes? And what did Willard's science have to say concerning the sudden breaking off of the world line ten minutes ahead of you?

Willard hadn't belonged down here in the first place. Lord knows I was satisfied to teach atomic physics at the university, but they needed someone to run the power plaint, so they made me a captain and here I am. I had an idea, and they thought it was nice, so they gave me a laboratory insulated from the secondary radiations that might leak through the generator screens. So I worked on this, and did not think too much about the rightness of war. Taber was the one who did that. Enough for three people. How he pounced on Joe the first day Joe was here and commenced the same old argument.

"What news is there from the top?" he asked Joe after dinner. "You're the first new man in a month. Tell us everything."

And the others crowded around, literally hungry for gossip from above.

"What could I tell you that you don't know? You have radios and newspapers."

"Ah, son. Censored down to the advertisements. Don't you know? Minor skirmishes inflated to decisive battles it we win, desultory firing mentioned along the border if we lose a three-month campaign. But haven't you heard anything real? What about the end? What are the plans?"

"The end? Why, we beat Venus and win, that's all. What more could there be?"

"Ah, what's the use? You've just come out of school, with all the pap they taught you still in your head. They never mention whether a real victory is possible or not; what kind of peace could he made to ensure against another war just like this in another fifty years."

Joe was bewildered. "If we beat them, how can there be another war?"

"And they said the same at the end of every war, from the beginning of time."

"At it again, Taber?" That was Willard, entering the room with his boomng voice and hands that moved constantly as if with an excess of nervous energy.

"While there's life there's an argument," Taber misquoted, cheerfully. "There's no fun arguing with you anymore. I've gone through the field completely, and you are as stubborn as an ox and still persist in the foolish belief that Earth ought to defeat the Venerean colonists."

He paused for a moment to become amused at the shocked expression that finally came over Joe's face.

"Oh-ho. The schoolboy is shocked. Just like I'd said a four-letter Anglo-Saxon word in the presence of his best girl. What a mass of conditionings and inhibitions they make of the youngsters nowadays. I know," he looked at Joe, "exactly what you believe about the war. That bookcase over there is full of the books which have become the brains of the schoolboys of today. You believe that the colonists on Venus are engaged in a rebellion with the intention of finally conquering Earth. You believe that the colonists, because of the primitive conditions on Venus, and because the toughest had to survive, have degenerated into semicivilized people with the advantages of a few machines. You believe that their barbarism, if not checked, will overrun the solar system with its vicious ways. And therefore Earth must completely and totally conquer Venus.

"The only trouble with that is—I was on Venus for ten years, and I know exactly how things are. The colonists are tough, yes. No more barbaric than any pioneers. And they were lucky enough—oh, what a marvelous accident—to have a pair of really honest men to lead them through the beginning."

"Pratt and Zanderfeldt," Joe gasped. "Those . . ."

"Mind what you say about them," Taber snapped. "What do you know about them except what the people who write the books care to tell you? It is no wonder that the Venereans became sick and tired of being tied up to Earth, robbed and exploited up and down the line."

"Suppose we break it up." Willard then said. "Stone hasn't even seen where he is going to sleep, and you shouldn't subject him to all this on the first day. There's plenty of time later. All the time in the world."

But now there was only ten minutes. Ten cold minutes that throbbed at the three of them in rhythm with the crescendo of the generators outside. Ten minutes that depended upon the pull of a switch and the burning away of a life.

Taber thought: Damned if I'll do it and cause the colonists to lose.

Willard thought: I can't go. My machine is not yet finished, and I must remain to complete the work so that we will be able to end the war.

Joe Stone thought: I don't want to go. It's cutting me off too short.

If one of us does not go then we're all done for.

Willard put out a tentative feeler. "If someone went out and switched off the softener field the power plant would be saved."

"One of us, that would have to be," Taber said. "There is nobody living out there."

"That puts the problem in its most concise form," Willard stated.

"Like a problem in sophomore philosophy," Taber grinned. "I'll tell you right now. I won't go. You have known me for a long time. You know that I never believed in this war in the first place, and I was lucky to have a bad leg so that they didn't want me for the army and I didn't have to act the objector and get clapped in jail or shot. You know I have always thought the colonists were in the right, and that the war was an aggression upon them. You don't expect me to act heroic and give myself up in order to cause their defeat."

"You fool," Willard shouted. "What a low thing it is for your to sit there speaking your false ideas when such a tremendous issue is at balance. So many lives will be lost."

"A marvelous balance it is, where one person with the proper realistic ideas may swing the course of the entire war to the proper ending. Why don't you do it?"

"Because I haven't finished my work. If this machine is successful we can stop the war very quickly with the saving of many lives, for all the machines are dependent upon atomic energy, and they could not change rapidly enough. If I am killed now before the machine is completed, the war may not be finished for a long time, and thousands of lives will be lost in the meantime, and neither we nor the colonists will win in the long run."

"Your ways of thinking are very clearly shown by the manner in which you said 'we can stop the war,' instead of, 'the war can be stopped.' I can't help in a thing like that."

Nobody said anything for a while, and the drone of the generators increased in pitch so that the tension was unbearable. All the while Joe had been standing there, his gaze snapping from one face to the other as they talked, and the expression on his own face had changed from shock to amazement, to scorn and to rage.

"We have only *four* minutes now, plus or minus one minute, Mister Willard." he said, and his voice was terribly tight. "And the two of you have been conversing most philosophically in the most beautiful, logical language, and have stated your points very clearly and decisively, and so now there is nothing to do but wait for the remaining three and a half minutes, plus or minus one minute, to swing by, and then we shall all be finished, and we shall never worry about how the war ended, and we shall never have any more arguments.

"But how about me? I am being cheated. I have given a lot, a hell of a lot, so that I could be here instead of in a uniform with the common soldiers. I have worked very hard at studying, for I had to learn very fast, and I worked and ate and slept and worked and ate and slept again, and got little enjoyment out of it, and I was paid nothing for it, except by the thought that when it was over I would be in a better position than the common soldiers. For the past two years I have not lived as a person should live, and I cannot say that before that I lived very well either. But I expected something for all of that later. I expected that finally, sometime, I would be able to relax and enjoy what there was to enjoy. Now if things are going to be cut off short all of *my* work will have been wasted. You speak of your work being wasted, Mister Willard, but my work was just as important to *me,* and right now, *me* is what counts the most, for up to now there has been no *me,* but only a lot of work.

"So if I get chopped off it will all have been wasted, and I do not like waste." And he was very angry right then, for his face was white and his slender body trembled.

Taber gazed keenly at Joe and said, sympathetically, "Yes, you have a great right to be angry. But yours is a matter of emotion, and when it is all over you will no longer be angry. Mine is a matter of logical necessity, and concerns a subject which is of great importance. The freedom of Venus depends upon their success in this action."

"Damn your logic!" Joe Stone cried. "Your whole stinking, cold-blooded, traitorous mass of falsities. Don't you think that if Venus had the damper also it would stop the war on both sides at once and they would have something to say about the peace that was made?"

He violently wrenched open the thick door that led to the power plant, and fell back with his arm over his face as a crackling sheet of air-ionizing radiation flooded in from the tortured generators.

"No! You can't go out!" Taber sprang forward to stop him.

"Don't touch me!" Joe twisted out of Taber's grip.

The twist and the fault of Taber's trailing foot threw Taber to the floor, and he was in the path of the radiations. Taber's skin began to darken immediately under the terrific beating, and his face contorted from the burning.

"All right. I'm cooked." And he could still grin at the joke. "I'll pull the switch. I'll save your silly lives and your silly world. If what you just said about Venus possessing the damper can be true, then make sure it becomes true."

He disappeared through the door.

LAST NIGHT OUT

THE UNFRIENDLY STREET stretched ahead of them, pouring bitter waves of hostility through their nervous systems. They had ridden the bus from the spaceport into town, and now they stood on the pavement soaking up the profusion of sensations which permeated the atmosphere of the brawly town.

Joe, his iridescent fur registering a pale blue of distaste and his antennae quivering in a controlled agitation, kept a warm tentacle curled firmly in the hand of Jed Grey. Since his native name was a soundless, telepathic abstraction, the records of the Solarian Fleet labeled him Canopus 647-B-43G. To Ensign Jed Grey, his Terran teammate, he was Joe.

The blue of Grey's Space Fleet uniform matched, for the moment, the evanescent hue of Joe's pelt, as, in a curious manner, the pattern created by Joe's thoughts matched that of Grey.

The sky had created a raucous sunset, challenging the lurid glitter of the neon signs which lined the main street of Selby, Texas. The light reflected garishly from the multicolored and multishaped uniforms which swarmed about the thoroughfare.

Terrans, scaly-headed Arcturians, spined Sirians, the dark and stocky inhabitants of a strange planet which circled a star whose name to Terran astronomers was only a number in the star catalogue—all of these walked in small groups along the length of the street, seeking a spot where they could relax for the evening and forget where they had been or where they were going.

Jed Grey asked Joe, "Where are the rest of your boys?"

Joe allowed his perceptual sense to range through the town, his sensitive antennae erect and rigid. Through the murky welter of conflicting thought patterns he sought the familiar, gentle sensation created by the furred Canopans.

"It's hard to find them," he transmitted to Grey. "I know they must be in town somewhere. They came on the bus before ours. But there are too many Terrans about and it is bad. . . ."

Jed Grey knew precisely how bad it was. Habitually en rapport with his Canopan partner, he sensed in every nerve the hostile atmosphere of the street, tearing at the hard shell of defense which he bad learned to erect.

The Arcturians, habitually suspicious of strange planetary types, were sufficiently unpleasant in their thought patterns. However, it was from the native earthmen, whose blue uniforms vastly outnumbered all others, that the bulk of the torment arose.

Grey could sense it even though he avoided observing their faces. He could feel the alcoholic thoughts of the mechanic across the street: "An Earthman holding hands with a snake! Damned snake man!"

It was now months since Grey had learned what that meant. The pain with which he had learned that was by now gone. He did not think that Joe's tentacles looked like snakes, and he cared nothing for the opinions of the others. Yet it was difficult to keep out of his mind the intruding thoughts of the Fleetmen who glared at him with disgust on their faces.

"I have found the others," Joe thought to Grey. "They are in a small bar at the other end of town called the Purple Claw. It seems to be an interesting place."

There was no need for Joe to ask, "Shall we go there?" For there was no place else to go. This was a repetition of the problem which always occurred when the pair arrived at a new base or a new town. Where could they spend an evening?

It never occurred to Grey that he might go off by himself.

Making their way through the crowded street was no longer the ordeal which it had been when Jed Grey and Joe had first been assigned to work together. By this time it no longer turned Grey sick when a highly-painted female hysterically turned around and whined: "It's reading my mind! The damn snake's reading my mind!"

"I see that the Arcturians hang out at the Zig Zag," Joe observed. The Zig Zag's brilliant mercury-vapor sign made Grey's complexion a virulent blue as they passed beneath it.

"And extra police floating around," Grey noticed. "This is a bad town. Many transients here—on their way in or out. Coming to town for a big time—either the last one or the first one in months."

The Purple Claw was housed in a ramshackle building of ancient vintage, and sported as publicity a modest violet lobster which glowed erratically above the door.

Within, the air reeked of tobacco smoke, beer, telka. It heaved with the beat of something which was part American jazz, part Sirian drum-music, with a flavor of strains from half a dozen other star-systems.

Behind the bar was a monstrously fat character whose hair was white as the clouds of Venus, and whose face was as black as space itself. Elby Jones had a love for wine and women which was matched only by his addiction to the music which the small band in the corner emitted.

He nodded to the pair as they entered, and waddled over to the small table where they seated themselves.

"Evenin', Joe and Mister Grey," he greeted them. "You'll have Space Punch and smokes?"

This, casually—even though never before had they been in this place.

Just as casual was Grey's reply, "Sure enough, Elby. Nice place you've got."

No need to show surprise at the fact that Jones was, himself, a telepath. The very fact that his place was the congregating point for the Canopan crowd attested to that probability.

With a goblet of warm Space Punch between his hands, Grey leaned back and absorbed the peace and relaxation which he had sensed within these walls the moment he had stepped through the door. Joe, immune to alcohol, took the first ecstatic drag from a long white cigarette—a cigarette of very ordinary tobacco.

Through the dimly-lit, smoke-laden atmosphere of the room, Grey could see the musicians at the far end, the small tables at which the Terrans sat with their Canopan partners, the few Sirians who sat alone with their tekla glasses.

Joe, performing an indescribable feat of mental recognition, happily greeted a Sirian who sat across the room. To Grey the Sirians all appeared identical, but he received the impression that this was the one they'd gone on a tear with last month in Joplin. It had been a most memorable occasion. He suddenly laughed uproariously as he recalled the picture they'd made marching down Joplin's main thoroughfare singing the Sirian national anthem in harmony—with Joe taking two of the parts simultaneously—both mentally.

Joe, having no vocal apparatus, performed his music telepathically. At times it was indescribable, and at other times it was—well—magnificent.

Within the Purple Claw there was music permeating the smoky air, coursing through the nerve channels of the listeners. It was slow and hot, loose and tight at the same time.

Grey slipped down farther into his chair. A horn took a high passage, and the chill began to pass up and down Grey's spine. He knew, then, that he was in—that the night was good and the music right.

Joe's antennae swayed quietly, in time with the beat, in time with the antennae of the other Canopans who sat there, spreading a net of rapport through the room. Imperceptibly there was produced an augmentation of the music, a heightened receptivity, as though the entire audience was in itself a musical instrument, guided by the band, and in return leading the band ahead.

"Lawdy, that was good," Grey sighed when the spell finally broke and the audience shuffled feet, scraped chairs, ordered fresh drinks, and relit forgotten smokes.

These moments of complete retreat had become more and more rare during the past few months.

The mobilization had been accelerating, and the training periods had become more and more intense, in preparation for this day when they were now assigned to a ship and were about to push off for a training run, followed by the long trip to the battle sector.

It had been slightly more than a year ago that the first enigmatic events had been noticed in a corner of the galaxy which was just newly being explored and developed. Ships had failed to return—colonies had ceased communicating with their prime bases.

To Jed Grey, a young man still in school on Terra, far within the borders of the civilized galaxy, these events had seemed distant and impersonal. They had been words in the newspapers, on the news broadcasts. They had been vague events taking place on just another of the many hundreds of habitable planets which by that time had been discovered.

Then the knowledge had grown that the events taking place thousands of light years distant were to have an impact on the life of Jed Grey and the others living on Terra. Gradually it developed that the civilized galaxy was rapidly becoming immersed in a struggle for existence against an enemy whose character was initially somewhat obscure, but whose unfriendly aims were quite definite.

Overnight, it seemed to Grey, Terra flew into a turmoil of mobilization, manufacture of spaceships and weapons, research for the creation of new weapons and new defenses against the strange attack methods of the enemy. In the tiny circle of existence in which he walked, that which he observed was the increased crowds of people on their way to work in the factories, the increased difficulty of buying various items, and inevitably the card which had ordered him to the mobilization center.

Among the many classification tests which they gave Grey was a curious one which seemed nonsensical until later on in the course of his training its purpose became quite obvious. It was given by a young man with very large and quiet eyes, who was seated beside an individual with soft, silky fur that changed color from moment to moment, and whose antennae had a fascinating, restless mobility. The four tentacles were brown and graceful, while the total attitude of the creature was one of repose and dignity.

Grey stared at this personage with curiosity, and with a slight chill. From photographs he knew the form of the natives of the fourth planet of Canopus, and from rumors and bar-room tales he had heard sufficient concerning them to ring a note of alarm in his brain.

Yet, as he sat there for a moment, the alarm died away for although to his untrained eyes the Canopan was practically featureless, there was an aura of pleasantness about it appearing from a source which at that time he was not able to identify.

Into his mind the thought came, "What if they *can* read my mind, like everybody says? He doesn't look like he would hurt me. But ..."

The voice of the examiner cut his thoughts short.

"Here are ten cards lying face down on the table. Tell me what markings are on the front of these cards."

"But how can I tell you if the cards are face down?"

The man smiled. "Just try, anyway."

Grey wanted to snort and laugh in the man's face; but then suddenly he shivered, for actually he knew ...

"Why there's a circle, a square, a triangle, another circle ..."

Then there was a sealed box in which he identified a cube, a sphere, a cylinder, and a more difficult object which turned out to be a key.

The examiner grinned at him and said, "That's fine. Welcome to the fraternity of telepaths and perceptors."

And, amazingly, there came a thought of congratulation which was unmistakably from the Canopan, who extended a tentacle and laid it for a moment upon his arm.

A gate in his mind swung open. A flood of memories crowded into his consciousness. Small items. Incidents in which he had known things before he had seen them. Incidents so unaccountable that he had put them out of his mind, had refused to consider them. Now they jigsawed together into a pattern which revolved about the important fact that he possessed the rare skill of perception coupled with telepathy.

How rudimentary this skill was he realized later when his training began.

In a month, feeling drab in his work uniform and exhausted from the preliminary training, he was brought face to face with the Canopan whom he soon learned to call Joe, and who was to become his partner for as long as should be necessary.

The first meeting was stilted and formal. They sat in the small room together with the Terran and Canopan training officers, and within Grey there was the nervous sensation that the Canopans recognized every one of his thoughts. There was the embarrassing realization that his dislike of Canopans was as plain to them as the expression. on his face and the embarrassment was intensified by the fact that he had not the slightest idea why the dislike was there.

"Sure, Grey," the officer said, abruptly. "We know you don't like

Canopans. Nobody on Earth does—except the people who actually know them. We know the whole story. But you'll get over that. You're going to spend the rest of this war working together with this fellow here—since he doesn't talk a language, he doesn't have a verbal name. You won't have trouble conversing with him, however, because he knows what you think, and you will know what he thinks when he wants you to."

"Then they do read minds," Grey said.

"Sure. What of it? You can almost do it, yourself. Why do you think we picked you for this job? Out of the thousands that we test, a few here and there have the right kind of sensitivity. When the professors learn more about the science of psychomechanics maybe we'll learn how it works. Now all we know is that it works."

"What's wrong with them, then?" The question was involuntary, dropping suddenly from Grey's mouth. Confused by his own frankness, he stammered, "I—I mean, why don't people like them?"

"This is a question with many angles," the officer said, gravely. "It's an old story. We had barely obtained a world government when interstellar travel was on hand and we came into contact with strange types of intelligent beings. Man was still trying to overcome distrust between the slightly different groups within his own species. When he came to deal with species of such strange shapes and psychologies as those on the other planets, the distrust was intensified many times.

"Particularly, people fear the telepathic powers of the Canopans. They fear the mysterious and the supernatural. Telepathy still seems a supernatural thing to the ignorant and—I'm afraid—to some who are not so ignorant. People are afraid of their minds being invaded. Their sense of privacy is outraged.

"They cannot visualize the fact that the Canopans are completely uninterested in what thoughts a Terran may have. The Canopan psychology is sufficiently different from ours that our private thoughts may be interesting, perhaps curious, but never the sort of thing upon which they would put a moral judgment. Their sense of morality is too different from ours for moral judgments to have meaning.

"You may accept this intellectually at the moment without absorbing it into your system. In a short time you will really be convinced that this is so. In the meantime, the two of you must become friendly enough so that you can perform your jobs."

Grey looked from the officer to his Canopan partner, and clearly received the verification that all of this was really so. Inside Grey there was an impression of relief, a loosening of tensions.

From that moment on, Grey and Joe were inseparable. They lived together, ate together, and in their training they were as one mentality.

"Doggone if you wouldn't think we were married," Grey kept saying.

Surely the extreme rapport, and the warm feeling of relaxation and mental capability which Grey felt when in the presence of Joe, indicated an intimacy which was the equal of any physical attraction.

With the extreme complexity of the control and communication equipment in the great space vessels, there had arisen the need for something radically different in maintenance technicians. The delay of testing circuits for faults and breakdowns had to be eliminated. For this purpose the peculiarly suited Canopans had been brought to Earth by the thousands.

Even in the specialized branch of computing-machines to which Grey had been assigned, the magnitude of the knowledge to be absorbed in a few hasty months would ordinarily have made the task impossible. With the two nervous systems of Grey and Joe acting as one, however, they were able to absorb huge chunks of knowledge at one gulp, assort it, store it away, and go on to the next item.

Carefully supervised by psychiatrists to ensure that no breakdowns would occur from overloading of nervous connections, Grey advanced from the status of an untrained youngster to that of a highly skilled electro-technician.

"Joe, with all the brains that you fellows have," Grey remarked one day, "it's a wonder that you haven't advanced any farther than you have, as far as technical things are concerned. I don't know why you need me around. You know all the stuff that I know, and maybe a lot more. Why don't you Canopans just take over the whole works?"

"We're really not very interested in electronics and such things," Joe replied. "We put up with this as a rather unhappy necessity, but our creative instincts do not lie in that direction. Since we have developed without hands, and with a brain of capabilities which are strange to you, our culture has become more introspective—more interested in the being within than in the things without—more interested in creating things of beauty to perceive rather than machines of complexity for the control of nature."

"Very pretty," Grey sighed. "And just as well, for otherwise I would be out of a job."

Even so, Grey felt little more useful than a soldering iron or a screwdriver in the hands of a master mechanic. For Joe, with his ability to perceive without sight, with his capability of feeling the very electric currents flowing through a machine—he was the diagnostician, the one who squatted before a defunct piece of equipment and without hesitation unerringly decided what was wrong with it and directed Grey to the point where the repair had to be made. From that point on Grey wielded the tools.

But there was no room for false pride. The two of them together constituted a working team, The two of them made one mechanic.

In addition to learning the technical things required for maintenance of machinery, both Jed Grey and the Canopan had to learn many other things which inevitably went with their partnership.

They had to learn how it was to walk down a city street and feel the ebb and flow of thoughts about them—thoughts concerning the race of Canopans in general and concerning the type of Terran who would walk down a street arm in arm with a Canopan.

They learned this quickly. Gradually the psychic hurts healed over and in their place was a hard defense-mechanism compounded of wisdom, mental toughness, and a contempt for the opinions of the others.

Actually, to Joe, the opinions of the Terrans were of no interest. But as he once remarked to Grey: "It's an impersonal sort of unpleasantness—like walking through a street filled with a bad odor, like walking through a room filled with buzz saws. It jars the nerves."

Grey presently came to feel in the same manner.

"I'm not quite a Terran any more," he said.

Joe assented. "You are a real cosmopolitan. You have the real interstellar attitude. In time everybody will see it that way."

Time—time. It went so rapidly. It swept them along through the several stages of their training, and now it was their last night out before stepping into the great battlewagon for the final and irrevocable journey across space to the war, which up to now had been a hazy background to their work.

Elby Jones brought Grey another drink, "It's a good night here tonight."

"I'm glad it is," said Grey.

Yes, it had to be a good night, because the last one had to be good. There had to be that much to remember out there a thousand light-years away.

The music started once more, and it brought to Grey the thought that it was curious how the Canopans had taken to American jazz and cigarettes and had intensified their effects to a degree previously unknown. What a group of characters they were. They could go on an intellectual jag from a Bach Fugue as quickly as they could go on a nicotine binge. Their entire psychology was geared to the obtaining of pleasure from sensations of many different kinds.

"The Terrans do likewise, you know," Joe transmitted to him.

Grey grinned back at Joe. You couldn't keep a stray thought-wave away from the guy.

"It's different the way you do it," he replied. "You don't get blind stinkin' drunk when you go on a jag. You do it for exhilaration, for an uplift."

"The process of getting stinking is . . ." Joe broke off suddenly.

Simultaneously, Grey could sense that the other Canopans had shifted their attentions, that the music, although it kept playing, echoed hollowly between the walls, unsupported by the listeners.

Grey caught the faint jar of a commotion outside the door. A roar of voices and heavy footsteps crescendoed suddenly as a mob in blue uniforms burst into the place. As it seemed to Grey in the first violent moment, each had a bottle in one hand and a brightly-painted female in the other. There seemed to be a squadron of them. It turned out, finally, that there were perhaps ten altogether.

From the insignia on their uniforms, Grey guessed that these were combat men on their way back from the battle sector, ready to tear up the first town that they hit on the first night out.

"Cripes! The place is full of snakes!" One of them shouted. "What're snakes doing here when there's some good ol' Earthmen lookin' for a place to sit down?"

One of the girls pulled back. "Let's get out of here, Jack," she whispered, nervously. "I'm afraid of them snakes."

"They ain't gonna hurt you, honey," Jack told her, hoarsely. "I always wondered if them snakes grew together if you pulled them apart."

He walked a few paces inside the door.

"If you snakes can read my mind, you know what I'm gonna do if you don't clear outta here pronto. An' readin' my mind ain't gonna help you against my good right arm."

Grey felt sick. A brawl on the last night . . . There was a stray thought in his mind that he and Joe would make a good fighting team if the two of them could coordinate fast enough.

"No," Joe's reply came to him instantly. "This isn't your fight. We'll handle this."

"The hell you say!" Grey attempted to stand—found himself limp as a rag. He could suddenly smell his own perspiration as he strained to move, and as he looked about the room he saw that the other Terrans at the tables were remaining there, their expressions startled and anxious.

The Canopans had risen, and were slowly making their way between the tables to the front of the room. The band was still playing a slightly mad background to the picture, which consisted of the smoky room with the dim lights, the Terrans sitting paralyzed at their tables, the Canopans moving in on the Fleetmen at the door . . . who stared in disbelief, began to swing their bottles, and collapsed quietly on the floor.

The girls, without time to shriek, collapsed just as quietly, and lay there in an unmoving heap.

Grey abruptly was stone cold sober. He wanted out, as fast as possible. The idea of going up for murder appealed to him not at all.

"Forget it," Joe flashed at him. "They're not dead. But we'll have to get rid of them. We'll be back in a minute."

The Canopans silently carried the bodies outside the door, leaving Grey sitting still at his table, performing a great quantity of furious thinking.

Joe was back quickly. He anticipated Grey's questions.

"They'll wake up, and they'll think somebody slipped them a Mickey. But they won't remember what happened."

He hesitated, sat down, and lit another smoke. "You're okay, now, by the way."

Grey tried, and found that the nervous impulses now went where they were supposed to go. He stood up, shakily. Then he sat down again. While he was searching for words to say something, Joe interrupted.

"Look," he transmitted. "This has to be kept under cover. Things are bad enough for us without this sort of thing getting around. I didn't even want you to know, but that couldn't be helped. I didn't feel like getting bashed."

Grey accepted another glass gratefully from Elby Jones.

"Sure," he said. "I don't talk to anybody, anyway. But you have to tell me. How much can you do?"

Joe considered for a moment before replying.

"I don't know, really. Terran nervous systems are not like ours. We have had only a short time to discover what we can do and what we can't do. We don't have real control—although there are certain possibilities with a modified hypnotic suggestion. At present we are only able to introduce resistances temporarily in certain nerve paths, so that inhibitions are produced."

"So for a while I was just inhibited against standing up, and they were inhibited against being conscious. It that it?"

"Approximately."

Grey sipped from his glass, peering over the edge of it at Joe. Precisely how much was there, he thought, hidden within the recesses of that brain? Just how much did this innocent little character have on the ball?

Joe chose this moment to become taciturn. The music was riding once more, and the place was settling down after the sudden disturbance. It took Jed Grey several more minutes and another glass to throw off the nervous tension which sat like a blanket over his shoulders. Gradually he began to relax, and the warm spot within his belly proceeded to creep up into his head.

"Tomorrow," he thought drowsily, "we will be taking off, and there will be no more of this. No more music except from cans. No more . . ."

Abruptly he realized that the rapport had been broken off again by the Canopans, and that at the other end of town there was the faint howl of the police siren.

"There's a brawl down the street," Joe informed Grey. "Some of our heroes back from the battle sector feel that they haven't had enough fighting."

"I bet you a pack of smokes that the guys in the fight haven't been within a light year of an actual battle," said Grey, dryly. "They're the ones who always try to make like tough heroes when they get back."

Through the Canopan's sense of perception Jed Grey could catch faint impulses of the tumult which filled the street a hundred yards away. There was a violence in the thoughts projected from that area which caused the colors of Joe's fur to shift erratically, nervously. In Grey they caused a tightening of the stomach and a heavy feeling in the chest.

"It hurts almost as much to listen in to a fight as it does to be right in the middle of it," he remarked. "Why don't you just shut it off if you can't take it?"

"As well try to shut off your sense of hearing," Joe snapped back.

The sirens down the street had wailed to a halt. Grey lit another cigarette and tried what was left in his glass. It was flat. The warm glow which had diffused through his body was gone, and in its place there was a bitter taste and a burning sensation around the eyes.

Abruptly he mashed out his cigarette and stood up.

"The night's washed up," he growled. "Let's get out of here,"

Joe, with a thought of regret, assented, and the two of them left.

It was bitter to end the last night upon such an uncompleted note.

The two of them strolled back in the direction of the bus station. The fresh night, bright with the blaze of stars and saloon signs, should have exhilarated them; but the mental tension which filled the street pressed hard on Joe's receptors, and, through him, against Grey.

A pair of police cars squatted at the corner. Fleet Police milled through the crowds, shock sticks in hand. An ambulance helicopter roaring in from the Fleet Base settled down in the center of the street.

The fight was over, but so keyed up were the Fleetmen in town that for Grey and the Canopan to walk through the street was to walk through a sticky, obscene glue of malevolence.

Joe's fur colors had faded to a dismal blue. Grey glanced at this with alarm.

The thoughts in the crowd around them had been impersonal ones—fight thoughts, pleasure thoughts, passion thoughts—violent and unnerving to the pair who had to thread their way through this tumult, but yet impersonal.

It began to change.

They began again with the snake thoughts and the thoughts about the Terran who walked with the damn snake. They looked at the pair who walked in their midst, and in their state of excitement with violence not yet out of their minds there was a redirection of passion from the recent fight to the new center of attention.

Grey gasped as the force of this new agitation struck them.

The pair of Fleet Police ahead of them changed their direction of motion and started walking towards them. Grey's face twitched as he felt the increased tension within Joe's nervous system.

"Hold it, son," he cautioned. "Remember we're supposed to be tough. Remember the nerves of steel we're supposed to have, like it says in the books."

Joe's grip on Grey's arm tightened, and then relaxed.

"I thought I could take anything. Tonight has been almost too much."

The Fleet Police were directly in front of them. The one on the right pointed at Grey with his stick and began to say something.

The door of the adjacent saloon swung open and a giant of a bearded Fleetman roared out. The girl hanging to his arm caught a sudden sight of Joe, and a burst of fright exploded in her empty little head, shocking Joe with its intensity.

She screamed, "It's thinking about me!"

The big Fleetman clapped his hand to his hip. There was no gun holstered there, but Joe reared back in a dismayed reflex. . . . In the next moment the Fleetman slumped to the pavement, where he lay quite still.

That was all—for a moment.

The Fleet Police looked at Joe and they looked down at the Fleetman. Then they looked back at Joe. One of them stooped down and remained there for a long minute. He rose, and his face was white.

"The guy's dead," he said, and his shock stick came tip, pointing at Joe. "You do that?" he snapped.

"He didn't touch the guy," Grey said.

"Maybe yes and maybe no. Guys don't just drop and die, I think both of you'd better come."

*   *   *

At the Fleet Police headquarters the medic turned pale when he examined the body. A number of urgent calls were made. The Canopan liaison officer arrived after a nasty fifteen minutes during which the doctor and the Fleet Police Commandant argued violently and then stood staring blackly at the floor.

Grey's eyes widened when behind the Canopan there stalked not only the commanding officer of his ship, but the Commandant of the entire Fleet Base.

"The joint's lousy with brass tonight," he flashed silently at Joe as the two of them stood rigidly at attention. "I think you've become notorious."

He caught a sense of amusement from an undetermined source, and in a moment narrowed it down as coming from the Canopan liaison officer.

Good for our side, Grey thought in relief—at least Canopan officers kept their minds unbound by brass. They'd stand behind Joe.

The Fleet Base Commandant knifed Joe with a rigid stare. He spoke rapidly and bitingly. "It is difficult enough to keep harmony among the various planetary groups at the base without it becoming known that the Canopans can kill Terrans by their mental powers. You have been trained in self-control. By this incident tonight you have jeopardized the morale of all the troops in the region."

The Canopan officer put in genially, "This was clearly a case of self-defense. The Fleetman was drawing a gun."

"Unfortunately for that argument, stated the Commandant, "the Fleetman was not carrying a gun."

"But this 34C could not see in the first instant. His attention was on the thoughts which the Fleetman transmitted at that moment. The Fleetman forgot he was not wearing a sidearm, and in his mind there was the distinct picture of drawing his gun and shooting 34C. To 34C this was the reality of the moment. In his extreme nervousness he misjudged the force needed, and projected a lethal thought."

"A pretty legality," the Base Commandant growled. "Is it self-defense when you kill a person for *thinking* that he is about to kill you?"

"I know nothing of your law," the Canopan replied. "We have warned that an incident such as this was bound to occur sooner or later in the tense atmosphere of this town. May I suggest . . ."

"I know, I know." The Commandant passed a hand through his hair in disgust. "Your ideas about orienting the entire fleet. Subconscious psychological training still sounds like hypnotism to me. But if we must, then we must."

"And you, Jeffreys." He turned to Grey's ship-commander. "You're taking off tomorrow. You wouldn't want to lose a team, would you?"

"Certainly not, sir." Grey caught the relief in the commander's mind. "They're a good team."

"Then as far as anybody is concerned there has been no incident tonight." The Commandant turned to the medic. "Get that?"

Commander Jeffreys motioned to Joe and Grey. "You two will return to the base with me."

Grey nodded mutely and began to follow the commander out of the door, his attention focused upon an idea which had sprung into his consciousness during the past minute.

"Look, Joe," he thought. "If you can do that to a Terran, what could you do to one of the enemy?"

Joe began, "If I knew what the enemy was like. . . ."

A blast of thought broke into their minds. It blazed a warning signal in vivid, incandescent pictures, and in roaring sound. It said, in numerous and tumultuous manners, Stop where you are—keep out—restricted, confidential, top-secret territory!

Grey jerked his head around. He stared for one astounded moment at the Canopan officer.

Then he was walking out to the waiting helicopter, the palm of his hand moist as he tightly held one of Joe's tentacles.

The people who ran a war were not always the obvious ones, he thought.

FORMULA FOR GALAXY 1

AS JACK ROMANO approached the chair, the Geiger counter in his belt burst into a furious, raucous warning. Shocked, he turned back to a point where the buzzing stopped.

The chair, an aluminum-ribbed folder, stood where he had left it the night before, on the edge of a small cliff overlooking a valley hemmed in by iridescent crystalline spires. In front of it was an easel, beside which stood his paint case.

The ground beneath was bare, with a sprinkling of soft green growing things in the crevices. The rocks that towered on all sides reflected the light of the distant sun in a pattern of startling colors. No animals stirred.

Romano tentatively approached his chair once more, and again the Geiger counter shrilled in his ears. He retreated to a safe distance, and surveyed his painting equipment with dismay. The fingers of his right hand pulled fretfully at his thick, black hair.

Abruptly he turned and walked to the aircar which stood several yards behind the edge of the cliff. Snapping the communicator switch, he said, "Let me have Robot Service, please."

To the metallic voice which replied, he commanded: "Get a location fix on this transmitter and send out a robot equipped with radiation measuring equipment. Immediately, please."

"Yes, sir," the robot said, and cut out.

Romano left his carrier wave on as a guide, and walked back to the point where, about twenty yards from the chair, his counter clattered mildly. He made a half circle and verified that, indeed, the radioactivity centered upon the chair or painting equipment.

This, he mused, was a curious thing. And even more deadly than curious. More on the lethal side.

He circled again, drew a cigarette and lit it, trying to think the situation through. The preceding night he had left the chair and paints in that spot, intending to return and continue his work. On the asteroid of Doreen, with its man-made atmosphere, its artificial gravity, its automatic temperature control, there was no weather to dampen the chair, no animals to interfere, no human within fifty miles. No reason to prevent him from leaving the equipment out overnight.

This morning. . . . Suppose he had not possessed a counter? The thought trickled chillingly through his mind. Suppose he had not been given a warning?

His fingers trembled the smallest amount as he lit another

smoke, and he walked back to the aircar to await the robot. He toyed with the buckle of his belt—which contained the tiny, concealed radiation detector among its silver ornamentations.

His life had been saved by the single fact that he habitually carried a detector with him. This was thought number one that that loomed in his consciousness. A radiation counter or detector of some form had been standard equipment with photographers for a number of years. In a solar system pockmarked with radioactivity left over from an interplanetary war, such a precaution was a necessity. Without this warning device, the famous Romano scenes of nine planets would more than once have become vague blotches of colored film.

Thought number two bloomed into life. Radioactivity does not grow like a weed. It could not have appeared by itself. It might have fallen as a meteor, but examination of the area showed no signs of a fall. Furthermore, meteor showers were prevented by the same force fields which kept air on the asteroid and which maintained gravity at Earth normal.

It could not have come by itself. Therefore, it must have been brought.

His mind stopped at that point.

Above his head another aircar whispered through the atmosphere. It circled once and dropped directly beside his. A tall, glistening robot detached itself with a flowing motion from its socket.

"Your instructions, sir?" it asked.

For a moment Romano hesitated, thinking how to frame his uneasiness into words.

"Go to the chair," he directed, "and measure the radioactivity there. Locate the source of radiation and hold it up so that I can see it. Then take it to the radioactivity dump."

"Yes sir," the robot said, moving off toward the chair. It paused hardly a moment as its built-in radiation-measuring instruments recorded the flux intensity at the chair. A cap at the end of a flexible member flipped open, and the directional Geiger counter probed here and there, seeking the source of the radiation. In a moment, it came to rest pointing at one of the legs of the chair. The robot paused, baffled. Suddenly, with dumb inspiration, it picked up the chair and held it for Romano's inspection.

Impatiently, he shouted, "Unscrew the bottom of the leg."

The rubber plug at the bottom of the tubular metal leg screwed out, allowing a long, narrow cylinder to drop free.

Romano stared at it through binoculars, found nothing to see. The object was the size of a toothbrush box, black and featureless.

"Report on radiation," he heard the robot saying. "Gamma rays 100 roentgens per minute at a distance of one foot, plus high intensity of fast electrons and neutrons."

"Thank you," Romano said, blindly, as he stumbled into his car and had the autopilot spin him aloft.

Ten minutes on that chair and he would have been a dead duck.

As he circled the Hotel Doreen, preparatory to landing, he watched the other aircar dash off in the direction of the radioactive waste dump, where the cylinder would be held until sufficient load was amassed for transportation to the sun itself.

He paused as he reached the terrace, his eyes scanning the thirty-odd people sitting around tables, lounging on the sand, swimming lazily in the pool. How typical, he thought, that with an entire hundred-mile-diameter asteroid for exploration, the guests at this resort chose to remain within calling distance of the pool and bar.

How many were there, he wondered, including the ones inside the hotel, in the dining room, in the game rooms, on the playing courts. Two hundred, perhaps? How many employees?

Eliminate the children and the matrons and you had left a number of hard-type characters who remained strictly in their own tight clans. Of these, perhaps half could be allocated as legitimate businessmen on legitimate vacations. The remainder—the ones who sat around the game tables, or who wandered alone among the rocks gazing with impatient, hot eyes at the stars—these were the ones in temporary or permanent exile—the businessmen of dubious businesses, the entrepreneurs of shady dealings, who found the asteroid a convenient and quiet place where the police paid few visits.

Romano walked onto the terrace. One of these people had quietly presented him with the radioactive slug and was now waiting for him to die quietly.

Which one?

Was it the white-skinned tenth-generation Venusian in the florid green shorts, or was it the leathery-hided Martian colonist who split a bottle of Tekla with him?

What could be the connection between these total strangers and himself?

While he had spoken to many of the people in the hotel as part of the process of gathering material for his article, there was no more connection between them and himself than there was between any reporter and his public.

Christopher Chavanne had been his major contact. Chavanne, fabulous even in a solar system teeming with fabulous individuals. He sat now at a large table near the swimming pool, together with several others whose acquaintance Romano had made during the past few days. His huge bulk overflowed the minute quantity of clothing that he wore, and as he lifted a glass to his lips with a great, hairy paw, he caught. sight of Romano and boomed out in his heavy, bass voice, "Romano! Back so soon from the painting?"

"Yes. I . . . uh . . . am out of turpentine . . ."

"Well, then. Have a seat and join us."

As he borrowed a chair from another table and fitted it in among those at Chavanne's, it took Romano's breath away to think that one of these was possibly the person who planted the radioactive slug in his chair. In the moment that it took for him to seat himself, his eyes rested briefly on each person at the table, and his mind ticked off the information that he had concerning each one.

First, Chavanne himself, the owner of the asteroid and of the hotel. And much more than that. Chavanne, the robot manufacturer and inventor who had bought up the bankrupt hotel fifteen years ago in order to give himself a pleasant place in which to do research on calculating machines. Made habitable and landscaped more than a hundred years previously by a forgotten, genius, the asteroid was a spot where Chavanne could reign as absolute monarch, and where the most fashionable people in the solar system would come for their amusement.

His face broad and smiling, Chavanne held the ever-present glass in his great hand, an obese sybarite in appearance. Yet Romano knew that in another hour he would be in his laboratory, supervising the construction of his latest and most complex mechanical brain.

On the other side of Chavanne there sat Jennahagan, one of the tenth-generation Venusian settlers. Not quite as bulky as Chavanne, his flesh was of more solid muscle, and his skin had, by exposure to ultraviolet lamps, become darkened to a deep tan. Poking back in his memory, Romano dredged up the identification: Jennahagan, inventor of Jennite, the drug derived from certain well-known Venusian plants, a drug which had been outlawed for many years. But, Romano guessed, not sufficiently outlawed to prevent Jennahagan from maintaining a very expensive residence in the Hotel Doreen.

John Grimmenden sat beyond, small and wrinkled. A retired manufacturer of small machinery, he had attached I himself to Chavanne's crowd without invitation. An unknown quantity.

Jerrold Wald, young, thin, and prominently beaked, came next. Seeing him, Romano wondered where Jerrold's uncle was. Sigmund Wald, one of the solar system's great authorities on force fields, had come to Doreen ostensibly for a vacation. However, Romano did not think that a person with a mind as active as the scientist's would hide himself away in a frivolous vacation resort—although Romano was sure that at the rates Wald charged as a technical advisor he could afford to buy the place.

Romano had thought the uncle-nephew relationship a trifle strange. Jerrold, a real playboy type, fitted into his present surroundings perfectly. Yet, into his position as secretary to his uncle, he fitted not at all.

Again an unknown quantity, as far as his relationship to a certain slug of radioactive matter went.

Finally, sitting at Chavanne's left, was one whom Romano had seen and admired at a distance. Dressed for swimming, she filled her costume adequately. In the broad expanses between portions of clothing her skin was tanned deeply, and her dense brown, almost black hair was braided and coiled nobly about her head.

Romano shot a raised-eyebrow glance at Chavanne. who took up the cue with, "You two haven't met, have you? Dr. Helva Hansen— Jack Romano."

She took his hand firmly, and with a small shock he realized that the eyes staring squarely into his were of an amazing blue.

"Romano," she said. "Oh yes, the photographer. I remember your series on the Martian ruins. Very beautiful. But the painting. . . ?"

"Strictly a hobby. Call me a frustrated artist, if you will."

Romano had maneuvered his chair next to that of Helva Hansen, so that Chavanne sat two places to the right. The robot manufacturer grinned at Romano.

"Make sure you get Dr. Hansen into one of your photographs," he said. "Improve the scenery."

"An improvement indeed. But the doctor handle: M.D., Ph.D., or what?"

She smiled broadly at him. "M.D. and Ph.D. both. Psychiatry and psychology. The entire broad expanse of the nervous system is my territory. You are now supposed to be very impressed and ask me for an analysis right away."

Flippant social small talk grated against his mood.

"Sorry, not impressed. My mother is a psychiatrist, and I discovered at an early age that psychiatrists are people. Most of them, anyway. As, for an analysis, I'm afraid that my present troubles are not suited to that technique."

The psychiatrist's trained ear heard not only the words that he said, but the entire manner in which he said them, and she became aware that what he said was not frivolous banter, but something very serious.

Casually, she asked, "What sort of troubles?"

Romano said: "My major trouble at the moment is trying to get an angle for the article I'm doing on the asteroid Doreen. The place is fascinating and fabulous, but I have to put my finger on one aspect to build around. An angle."

He paused a moment, gathering courage to make the plunge he contemplated, and choosing the proper words. In this pause, Chavanne suggested, "Why not use the robots as your angle?"

"There," he said, exhibiting mild enthusiasm, "is an idea I've been toying with. There are probably more robots per square meter on this asteroid than anywhere else in the solar system."

"Naturally." Chavanne leaned back in his chair and crossed his hands on his vast belly. "They're my babies. In other places they're still too expensive for everyone to use them as housemaids But here is their experimental proving ground. Here I can indulge myself."

"Then they will be used more commonly in the future?"

"Of course. Robots will be built to manufacture other robots, which in turn will manufacture other robots. They will become more intelligent and organized."

"Could they become dangerous?"

Chavanne shrugged. "A robot is a machine. Machines can be dangerous if misused. You can be killed by a car walking across the street."

"But could a robot intentionally kill a man?"

"Of course not. A robot has the most limited intelligence. It will carry out short-range orders and then it will sit still until you tell it to do something else. It can't really think for itself.

"As for killing someone, there are circuits in every robot which forbid it to handle any weapon."

"But what's to prevent me from ordering a robot to fill my best enemy's sugar bowl with sugar—with a few micrograms of plutonium added for flavor? The robot doesn't know any better, and—"

A glass toppled, and Jerrold Wald, his face a furious red, leaped backwards from the table to prevent his drink from landing in his lap.

Romano and his psychiatrist neighbor lifted eyebrows at each other.

Chavanne was not so easily diverted from his favorite subject. While the robot waiter mopped the table and refilled the glass, he continued, while Romano filed the incident in a corner of his mind and reminded himself to think it over some time in the future.

"The early robot inventors," Chavanne was saying, "saw a long time ago that robots might be used as tools in all sorts of crimes. They prevented this by a very simple device. A robot is not an individual. It is connected to its central office by a microwave beam. In the central office is a memory bank which records every order given to the robot, as well as the name of the person giving the order. Part of the reason for this, of course, is that the person using the robot will be charged for the services. But having the record kept centrally means that you can't hide what you have done by destroying the robot. The record can always be found in the central office."

Jennahagan, the Venusian, grunted impatiently. "Damned lack of privacy," he bellowed. "Any nosey character can find out what you've been doing by calling up Robot Service."

"Not at all," Chavanne objected. "The memory bank is confidential. It responds only to the police and to high officials. If you think that I have nothing better to do with my time than spy on my friends you're sadly mistaken."

A train of thought tumbled madly through Romano's mind. If orders to robots were on record, then all he had to do was ask who had sent a robot to deliver the radioactive slug, for surely nobody had carried it by hand. Could he trust Chavanne enough to ask him, or should he wait for the police? But surely Romano's unknown enemy must have known that some sort of record would be kept. . . .

Then the significance of what Helva Hansen was saying filtered into his head and jolted him hard.

Her words were: "Is the memory bank on this rock operating yet, or are you still working on it?"

Chavanne said: "It should be operating very soon. The new system we have installed will be more efficient than the old by a large factor."

Romano heard himself say, "Do you mean to say that no record is being kept of robot orders? How long has this been going on?"

"For about ten days we have been converting the memory banks into the new experimental system. We were able to do it without interrupting robot service, but it meant that records could not be kept."

Romano's voice, was hard, argumentative. "And you allowed this to be public? So that anybody could give a robot any kind of order without being caught up?"

The argumentative tone overflowed into Chavanne's voice. "I intended it to be secret, but it got out accidentally. Only the people at this table know about it—aside from the men at the shop. Why get so excited about it? No harm has been done."

"No harm's been done, eh?" Romano felt the words burn through his throat, and he suddenly found himself very angry. "But somebody ordered a robot to plant a slug of radioactive material on my painting chair this morning. If I'd sat on that chair for ten minutes I'd be dying now, right in front of you."

The group at the table was shocked into a sudden quiet. For a long instant each stared at him. Presently eyes began to wander and there were many sidelong, questioning glances from one person to another.

"But who?" Helva Hansen finally asked.

"That's what I'd like to know." Romano's anger began to turn back upon himself. Furious because he had spoken without caution, he began to realize that his best action now would be to protect himself by implicating everyone present.

"You can bet your boots about one thing," he declared sharply. "The slug was handled by a robot, and the robot was ordered by somebody who knew that records were not being kept. That means somebody at this table, or else one of your men, Chavanne."

Romano sat back, and found himself perspiring. He had tossed the situation into their faces. He hoped that it would not blow up in his.

Chavanne broke the silence. "How did you know it was radioactive?"

"With a Geiger counter, of course."

"Since when do photographers go around wearing radiation detectors?"

"Since the last war. There's so much radioactive crud lying around loose that a photographer has to know where his films will be spoiled."

"Lucky for you."

"Damn lucky. The question is, how long will my luck hold out? This character who tried to get me—why is he after me? And is it important enough so that he'll try again, now that he knows I got away the first time?"

"Don't be too sure," Jennahagan roared at Romano, "that it was one of us."

"I'm not sure of anything. But I'm going to make sure that whoever is after me won't try again."

"And how will you do that?" Chavanne asked.

This brought Romano up short. "I'd be stupid to tell," he snapped, knowing that the bluff was as transparent as air.

Chavanne's suggestion, then, turned out to be absurdly simple. "Why don't you," he said, "hire a bodyguard from Robot Service? It's a new model we have just developed. In fact, I'll let you have one free as a field test. It does everything except taste food for poison, and we might even work on that if there is enough demand."

Bursting into laughter, Romano shook helplessly for a moment. It was partly caused by the picture of a bodyguard robot standing watch against an enemy robot, and it was partly a reaction against the tension of the past hour. Chavanne's solution to his problem was so elegant that Romano felt a feeling of warmth toward the fat man.

This led to a train of thought, which in turn led into a plan for doing something more than sitting and chewing his nails.

So he said, after his laughter had subsided, "Man, what a brilliant idea! I'll go order myself a robot watchdog now." He stood up quickly and withdrew from the table.

A moment's pause at the service desk in the hotel sufficed for Romano to place his order with Robot Service. While he waited for the mechanical bodyguard to arrive, Romano visited the communications office and asked for a private, scrambled beam to Earth. While the connections were being put through, he examined a large timetable and noticed with a feeling of relief that day hours prevailed in the Western Hemisphere. Then he recalled that the rotation of Doreen had originally been arranged to bring this about.

Romano locked himself into the tiny booth with the typewriter, and sat down to collect his thoughts.

Because of the time lag between the asteroid and Earth, telephone or television communication was too tedious to be practical. Teletypewriter was standard.

"Dr. Felice Romano," he typed. *"Cybernetics Research Institute, Mexico City, Mexico.*

"Hello, Mother. Your big boy wants some confidential information concerning a fellow psychiatrist, namely, Dr. Helva Hansen. Is she any good and can I trust her with my last penny?"

He had almost written "and trust her with my life," but had decided that this would not be discreet.

It was nice, he thought, to have a mother who knew people.

While he was waiting for the reply, his bodyguard arrived and was promptly named Fido. It was a fairly ordinary-appearing robot, slightly larger than usual, and with a bizarre red and yellow set of markings. It was a walking type, for universal mobility, as opposed to the domestic rollers.

When Fido reported to Romano the latter acknowledged receipt by touching his identification seal to a contact on Fido's chest, transmitting a signal to the central office for the beginning of charges. Considering what the charges normally were, Romano was quite happy that Chavanne had offered to put this on the house. He hoped that the presence of Fido would do him some good.

The clattering teletypewriter, indicated a reply on the way.

"Helva Hansen is a first-rate psychiatrist, I am told, and a fine person as well. She has not been known to make bad debts. Is this it?"

Is this it? Mothers. Between taking photographs, writing articles, and dodging sundry assassins, he was expected to indulge in romances. He had nothing better to do.

Well, his subconscious asked him, did he?

Enough of this, he said sternly to his subconscious. There are serious things afoot.

His subconscious subsided, but not without a moment of triumph, for as Romano emerged from the communications room into the hotel lobby, Fido trailing behind him, he encountered the psychiatrist hurrying to the elevators.

"Hello," he greeted her. "The clambake has busted up?"

'Yes. There's been some bad news."

"Oh? How bad?'

"Sigmund Wald just died. He had been ill for several days." She looked him square in the face. "Radiation sickness."

Rornano clamped himself steady and stood for a moment, concentrated thought screwing his face into a knot.

"Somebody tries to get me with radiation," he said in a very even tone, "and then Sigmund Wald dies of radiation. Do you mind if I connect them?"

"It's too easy to jump to conclusions. The story is that Wald blundered into the area where the ship crashed during the last war. The radioactivity there covers a large circle, perhaps ten miles in diameter."

Romano's laugh was sharp and bitter. "So Wald just happened to stumble upon the radioactive area while mountain-climbing. That's the story they would have made about me if I'd gotten it. If my Geiger counter hadn't . . ." He clutched at the thought which he had just scared up. "I suppose Wald wasn't wearing a radiation meter of some sort? A physicist going around without a detector?"

Helva stopped at this, her mouth open in what Romano thought was a very charming manner.

"Suppose we look in at Wald's room," she said.

They found Chavanne there, with Jerrold Wald and Dr. Broden, the hotel physician. Sigmund Wald still lay on the bed.

Romano stared at the body for a long moment, his mind an ugly blur of thought, his fists clenched, his arms stiff along his sides. With a conscious effort he released his muscular tension and dragged his mind up from the depths.

Silence fidgeted for a moment. Romano explored with his eyes up and down the room. The exploration came to rest upon Jerrold Wald, who leaned against a chest of drawers, nervously playing with a wrist watch of a very elaborate sort.

Romano walked over casually. "That watch has a counter in it, hasn't it?"

"Yes. Uncle was wearing it the day he went out mountain-climbing."

Romano found it interesting that Jerrold Wald was compelled to offer this information.

"Didn't it warn him of the radioactivity?"

"No. It wasn't working."

"It wasn't working!"

"Dead as Pluto. We discovered that afterwards."

"But . . ." Romano paused in frustration. "Dammit!" he exploded. "How can a physicist go around with a counter that doesn't work?"

Jerrold Wald shrugged, turning the watch over and over in his hands, looking out the window, at the bed, on the floor, everywhere except into Romano's eyes.

"I didn't have anything to do with Uncle's work. Just wrote letters for him. I don't know when was the last time he used the counter. He hasn't done any experimental work for a long time. He's a consultant, you know."

With disgust twisting his mouth, Romano shook his head. The story hung together. A physicist with a counter that doesn't work, and with an urge to go mountain climbing. A radioactive area with insufficient markers, into which an unwary person could blunder and be marked with slow death.

It hung together, and yet it was wrong.

Shoulders hunched forward, head jutting forward, Romano paced the floor, thinking with blind fury. His black hair curled wildly over his forehead, where jewels of perspiration glittered. The roundness of his ordinarily easy-going face was distorted with the effort of his thinking. Both hands were thrust deeply into the pockets of his brown hiking pants. As he clumped back and forth in his heavy shoes, his robot bodyguard followed until he snapped at it to keep still.

He jerked at the touch on his elbow, and his upward glance caught the smile that paused for an instant on Helva's face.

"Jack," she said, "don't you think you're trying too hard?"

He caught his breath—a nervous grin untwisted his mouth. For a moment she had sounded like his mother, with the same professional psychiatric trick of making remarks that dug through the surface and rocked you back on your heels.

"Obviously," she said, "something is biting you. Out with it."

"I'm being bit," he replied, "but I can't tell what's biting me."

"Nothing unusual. Any guesses?"

"Nope. Just because somebody tried to radiate me out of existence it doesn't mean that Sigmund Wald was knocked off in the same manner. Yet I feel that he was, and at the same time I can't tell why I feel that way. I could call it a hunch, and yet . . ."

"And yet you know that a hunch does not come from nowhere. Could you have observed something, somewhere, which has stuck in your mind without being noticed, but which comes up to the surface sufficiently to give what you call a hunch?"

"1 could have. But what? What could I have seen?"

"Don't beat your brains out. It only makes things worse. You should know better."

"Okay" Romano sighed and slumped against the wall. "So I relax and I free-associate. Then what?"

"That's for you to say. Maybe it's something you saw in this room. This is the only place where you have seen Sigmund Wald during the past three days."

Shrugging his shoulders, hardly believing that he would find anything, Romano began to look. In outward appearance it seemed that again he paced the room aimlessly, sunk in tense thought, but now his eyes shot his sight perception into every corner, upon every object.

"Oh hell," he groaned presently. "I'm just as likely to miss the very thing I'm looking for. Uh . . ."

Then he had it.

"The pants," he said. "The belt buckle."

Helva was quickly at his side as he lifted the pair of trousers from the chair and examined the silver buckle. Jerrold Wald craned his head over their shoulders, while Chavanne and Dr. Broden looked up from their conversation, becoming aware that the course of events had been broken, that something was taking place.

"So?" asked Helva. "What about the buckle?"

Romano smiled broadly at her, his tension released. "What about the buckle?" he repeated. "I'll tell you. A belt buckle saved my life this morning. It's a wonderful little thing. A complete electronic circuit within a belt buckle. A radiation detector, in fact. It's the latest thing back on Earth. I bought mine just before I came here. Sigmund Wald must have bought his very recently also."

Helva's mind leaped at the succeeding thoughts. "Then Wald did have a detector that worked, and that means he couldn't have walked into the radioactive area without being warned."

"Right. And Sigmund Wald was murdered, just as I would have been murdered if my detector hadn't warned me."

Then there was the room with the five standing about the bed, amber light filtering through the window curtains, the silence of hard thinking and of rapid breathing.

"But, Jack." Chavanne's voice was quizzical. "If Wald had a working detector, then it would have warned him of murder just as it warned you."

Romano clutched desperately at his thoughts to prevent the entire structure of his theory from collapsing.

"Maybe they got him at a time when he wasn't wearing the belt. Maybe they used a different method entirely. The point is, he *couldn't* have gotten his dose of radiation by walking into the radioactive area.

That's the story we were expected to believe, and it's not so.

"Sigmund Wald was murdered by radioactivity, and somebody tried to murder me this morning. I think, Mr. Chavanne, that you had better call the police."

Chavanne heaved himself to his feet, chewing his lips and pulling his brows together. "I suppose it's necessary," he growled, beginning to leave the room.

"Dr. Broden," Helva asked, "are you certain that Wald died of radiation sickness?"

'I'm not a very good doctor," he said, in a low voice. "You don't develop and expand when you play being doctor at a fancy resort hotel. This was the first case of radiation poisoning I had seen in twenty years. Since I was an intern, in fact.

"So two days ago Mr. Chavanne came to me and said Sigmund Wald was sick, that he was nauseated and his gums were bleeding. He'd been walking around in the mountains and must have gotten into the radioactive area. So I looked at him, gave him a blood count, found it down to nothing and said, yes, he's suffering from radiation sickness. Shot him full of what remedies I had, but it was too late."

Dr. Broden turned away from the window and forced himself to look at the others. "Now I'm not sure of anything," he said. "I'll have to make an autopsy."

Romano sat with Helva Hansen at a small table on the terrace, his hand wrapped firmly around a cold glass. Fido stood stolidly behind, gazing imperturbably at the gay figures which sported in the pool and lounged on the beach.

Romano said, "Look here. Why do people get themselves murdered? Mostly for money. Sometimes because of passion, revenge, just plain lunacy, but mostly for money. Did Sigmund Wald have any money?"

"Depends on the point of view. For a scientist he had quite a pile. To somebody like Chavanne it would look like peanuts. The point is, do *you* have any money?"

"Hell, no. But . . . oh, I see. Why should I be considered a tempting target?"

Helva looked into her glass and spoke deliberately. "I look for similarities and throw out all extraneous data. The only thing you and Sigmund Wald had in common was a habit of hiking about over the countryside. For you it was painting. But you were among the very few guests in this hotel who were to be found on the other side of this rock."

Romano's mind latched onto the idea like a steel trap.

"Then whoever tried to do us in didn't want us over there. Either we saw something we weren't supposed to see, or we were bound to come across it. This makes it clear what's to be done."

"It's clear, but is it safe?"

Romano chewed his lip. "Depends on how nutty our murderer friend is. Suppose we go out there among the mountains to find what it was we weren't supposed to see. Our Mr. X knows that if we find it, his goose is cooked for sure. Will he try to knock us off again? First, it won't be so easy with a few robot bodyguards on our side. Second, he'll give himself away for sure if we have Robot Service keep tabs on everybody leaving the hotel."

Helva let her eyes wander over the shimmering blue water surface. She found this a meaty problem.

"As you said, much depends upon just how psychopathic our murderer is. If he is sufficiently unbalanced, his desire to kill the ones about to discover his secret will overbalance the more remote danger of giving himself away by making this killing.

"And from our point of view, if we get killed, it is still no cause for rejoicing if the murderer gets caught with us as the bait.

"I suggest you wait until the police arrive. This is no game for amateurs."

"We're going to smoke out our man just as safely as lying in bed. Furthermore, we're going to make Chavanne get off that big fat end of his and earn his pay."

Helva smiled maliciously. "That I'd like to see. Chavanne's idea of security is to set robot guards all over the hotel, when the man we want could be a hundred miles away. Makes the guests feel safe while at the same time experiencing a little vicarious excitement."

"One piece of excitement per lifetime is enough for me," Romano said sourly. "When it becomes fatal, that is. Let's find Chavanne."

They crossed the lawn at the rear of the hotel and entered Chavanne's laboratory. Romano called for the fat man through the interphone and the two waited impatiently in the tiny anteroom.

Dressed in his working coveralls, Chavanne appeared like a tiny, impatient blimp. "I have a calculator running," he said breathlessly. "Have to get right back. What can I do for you?"

"It occurred to us," Romano said, suppressing a frivolous compulsion to sink a pin into the blimp, "that while we are sitting around on our butts here, the clues to the murder of Sigmund Wald are to be found over on the other side of this asteroid. I suggest that you send some of your robots out on a systematic search—to look for whatever it was that Wald and myself were on the verge of discovering."

Chavanne jerked his hands irritably. "Don't you think that's a job for the Interplanetary Police?" he asked.

"But Chavanne," Helva cajoled, "Jack is trying so hard to write a good article about your asteroid. You'll make it easier if you can help, with this. And you'll look so much better yourself. Think of the publicity."

Chavanne snorted. "I detect the fine odor of blackmail in this. If I sit back and wait for the police I'm just a dull clod who invents robots and calculating machines. If I help you solve a mystery, then I'm a great celebrity and people will hail me from all ends of the solar system."

Romano shrugged. "That's life." Chavanne waved his hands distractedly. "All right, all right. Just don't bother me any more. Tell Robot Service to go ahead. Now, please excuse me. I must get back to the calculator."

But he was optimistic. As he turned to leave, Dr. Broden walked in, followed by a robot laden with small pieces of equipment.

"Returning your counters and things," he said in a voice that dragged slightly with weariness.

Romano smelled antiseptic soap on the doctor's hands. His reporter's nose perked up.

"The autopsy?'

The doctor nodded. "Finished."

He paused a moment, collecting words. "We were right, and yet we weren't right. It was radiation sickness after all, but from internal causes, not external. Minute quantities of radioactive material had been taken orally. In other words. Sigmund Wald was literally poisoned. Probably with a mixture of fission products."

Romano pursed his lips to whistle, and heard Helva Hansen gasp with a quick intake of breath. Radioactive poisons—the most devastatingly deadly materials in the universe! Poisons so incredibly potent that a millionth of a gram could be absorbed into the body, to remain in the organs, in the bone marrows, sending virulent radiations directly into sensitive tissues. No wonder Wald's counter had failed to give him warning. The amount of radioactive material used could be so tiny that it would emit no more radioactivity than an ordinary fluorescent watch dial—it would affect the counter no more than the customary cosmic ray background.

But when ingested it produced slow, certain death.

The radioactive material dump was a lonely, bare building, some ten miles from the hotel, surrounded by a terrain of harsh red rocks. A sign on the door said, in large red letters: RADIOACTIVITY! *KEEP OUT!* It had been locked, but now it stood open, its lock blasted to bits.

Romano did not care to enter.

"How convenient," he said to Helva Hansen, who stood by his side in front of the building. "An entire dump loaded with ashes from the asteroid's atomic power plant. Free for anybody's picking. No guard, no alarm. Enough stuff in there to kill everybody in the place."

Helva walked with him back to the aircar.

"It seems irresponsible," she agreed. "Yet remember that nobody but a robot could go into that building. And the robots all report back to Robot Service central office."

"So just at this particular time the recording system is on the bum and the field is clear for anybody to have a robot commit any kind of mayhem in privacy."

Romano closed the door of the aircar and punched the starting switch. "I wonder if the robots have found anything."

"Unlikely. They've been on the lookout for only an hour. It's a difficult search when you don't even know what you are looking for and don't know how well it might be hidden."

Romano grunted. He repressed an urge to call the hotel, knowing that they were to call him if anything was found.

"Can't blame them," he said. "There are at least 25,000 square miles to be covered, and only ten Robot Service's resources."

He whirled the car aloft and circled for a moment, while a thought circled in his mind.

Finally he said: "I'm going to play screwy hunch. I don't know where it comes from except that I must have a suspicion that's so wild I can't even admit it to myself."

Helva raised her hands in mock admiration.

"Well!" she exclaimed. "Your subconscious is working overtime today. Just let me know when you need help."

Romano grimaced at her and put in a call to the hotel. He wanted to know the location of the radioactive area where Sigmund Wald was supposed to have gotten burned.

Helva stared at him while he wrote down the figures.

"No, I don't intend to get myself irradiated," he reassured her. "But it strikes me that since both Wald and I were supposed to have gotten our doses at that place, then just conceivably the mysterious doings we were on the verge of witnessing might have been somewhere in that locality."

Helva nodded, dubiously. "That could possibly be logical."

"I have nothing better."

Twice they caught flashes of light, reflections from the cars of the robots cruising in calculated circles. Doreen's landscape was gone into night, and there was only darkness below and the shimmering mesh of stars above.

"Hell," Romano grumbled. "I forgot it would be nighttime on this side."

He switched on a pair of searchlights that spread pale fingers through the darkness, raising glittering and. confusing reflections from the rocks below. Still nothing could be recognized.

"We should be about there," Romano muttered, slowing the car and beginning a wide circle. Helva clutched at her seat arms, while Fido, the robot bodyguard, stood solidly braced in a corner behind them.

Romano had the aircar skimming the ground, searching for the radioactive area markers, when without preamble Fido boomed out in a tremendous voice a warning that an aircar approached within close range from behind and above.

Romano, responding with instantaneous reflex, swung the searchlights around to that direction and at the same time slowed his car to almost a halt, allowing it to sink towards the ground.

There was a tremendous white flare followed by a concussion that bucked and jarred the car. The roar of the explosion joined with the crunch of steel on rock into a single, ear-splitting din.

Almost simultaneously there came a blast that demolished the tail of the car, hurling Romano and Helva out of their seats and into the windshield.

Red-lined darkness settled over their minds.

Romano awoke feeling a soft, arm hand upon his forehead and a grinding ache behind his eyes. Cautiously testing his vision, he found the countenance of Helva Hansen filling his field of view.

"Welcome home," she said.

Romano replied with an incoherent groan, and surveyed his environment sufficiently to discover that he was flat on his back on the floor of an aircar whose motion was barely perceptible. He made as though to get up, but a firm hand on his chest and the anguish in his cranium weakened his intention before he had moved far.

"Hey there," Helva's voice reached his consciousness as though from a great distance. "You've suffered quite a nasty concussion. Doctor says you stay flat on your back for the next day or so."

She fed him a drink very slowly.

After a few minutes he was able to say: "Where in all the four confounded dimensions are we going?"

Helva smiled sweetly at him. He was really recovering.

"Back to the hotel, of course. You may thank your pal Fido for getting us out of the wreck. The big lug picked us up bodily and carried us out. My sides still ache. The car was blown completely to bits."

"Old Fido's really worth his keep then?"

Romano looked gratefully at the robot and patted one of the legs of the huge bulk. "Nice work, old man. I'll buy you a can of lubricating oil when we get back."

A sensation of baffled curiosity crept into his mind. "What happened to the wreck? Where'd this fine car come from?" he demanded to know.

"Courtesy of Robot Service. Apparently when a car gets smacked, Robot Service knows when, where, and how. It wouldn't do for the hotel to have its guests lost all over the asteroid."

A slight clicking in the automatic pilot, and a feeling as though the car were changing direction drew Helva's attention to the window.

"We're back already, Jack. Do you walk quietly to your bed, or will I have to carry you?"

"First I must do one thing. Then I'll do anything you say. But first one thing. We must find out who was away from the hotel in an aircar at the time we were shot down. We get that dope, and we have the case tied up fast in our fat little fists."

They found, however, when they stopped at the Robot Service office, that the case had dribbled completely out of their hands.

Everybody, it seemed, had chosen that particular time to go dashing about the asteroid in his aircar. Romano doggedly wrote every name down.

Jennahagan, the Venusian drug manufacturer.

John Grimmenden, the retired machine builder.

Jerrold Wald, Sigmund Wald's playboy nephew.

And Christopher Chavanne himself.

It came back to these four people then.

The same four who had sat at the table that very morning. Incredible that it had been just that morning. That same four who had known—of all the people on the asteroid—that the memory bank in the Robot Service center was disconnected, and that orders to robots would not be recorded.

Helva Hansen entered the room, followed by a robot bearing two dinner trays.

"One for you and one for me," she said, setting her own meal out on a small table.

Romano looked at the tray which the robot set on his bed. A feeling of regret twisted his mouth.

"This is not a pleasant way for us to spend our first evening together."

She touched his hand lightly.

After the robot had removed the dishes, Romano felt himself overcome with sleep. Helva sat beside him for a few minutes, then left quietly.

After ten hours' sleep, the throbbing in Romano's head had quieted to a dull ache. As he was swallowing a white tablet and debating whether to shave himself or to visit the barber, Chavanne walked into the room with a greeting of revolting heartiness.

"Sorry to hear about your . . . uh . . . accident. I hope you are well."

"Well enough. Let me have two minutes while I shave my face," he asked of Chavanne, "and I'll join you in breakfast."

"I've just had lunch," Chavanne smiled, "but another cup of coffee never hurt."

Depends on what's in it, Romano thought.

Aloud, he said, "I need your help. I want you to tell me everything you know about some of the people here."

Chavanne shrugged, cautiously. "What could I know? These people are strangers to me. They come here for a few weeks or months. I see little of them."

Romano said deliberately, "You seem to be quite friendly with Grimmenden, Jennahagan and Wald. They're the only ones I'm interested in."

"And myself also? I was out in an aircar when you were shot down. I'm one of your suspects, too . . . eh?"

Romano smiled at him candidly. "Sure. You're a prize suspect." He wiped his face. "Shall we go to breakfast?"

They found Helva Hansen already in the dining room.

"How's the head?" she asked.

"Still where I left it last night," he replied. "I'm beginning to think it's very nice having a doctor so handy."

"Are you sure?" she replied sweetly. "Do you think you could stand being healthy all the time?"

"Sounds repulsive."

Breakfast arrived, diverting his attention for a few minutes.

Presently he said, "You know, Chavanne, it would be very useful if one of your calculating machines could be used as a mystery solver. Put in all the clues, turn the crank, and grind out all the answers."

Chavanne smiled. "It would be very nice, if you could be certain that you have *all* the evidence. This may involve almost an infinity of items, including the entire life history of all the participants, the psychological factors involved, the motivations. It becomes very intricate.

"However, I don't think it's necessary here. I think I can tell you who your man is."

Romano exploded slightly. "What!"

Helva stiffened in her seat, was more cautious. "Are you sure?" she asked. "Or are you only guessing?"

Chavanne shook his head. "Not guessing. Deducing. Furthermore, I can tell you what it was you were not supposed to see while you were wandering among the hills."

Romano stared at Chavanne, felt himself growing hot.

"You mean to say you knew this all along, and yet you let us go out there and get shot up without telling us?"

Chavanne dropped his eyes, and his great bulk made slight squirming motions.

"The situation," he said, "is rather embarrassing for me. Say that it's delicate."

"You see, I'm being blackmailed," he continued. "I tell this to you only because the person blackmailing me is the one who caused Wald's murder and who tried to murder you. I know you can keep my secret because catching the murderer will depend upon it. When the police come it will be all over anyway."

Chavanne leaned back in his chair and wearily massaged the spot between his eyes.

"I'll be disgraced, but at least my life will be safe."

Helva suddenly felt that she'd been here before. To her professional ear the exaggerated dramatization was as transparent as a glass window.

"Okay," she said, dryly. "So you've been a bad boy. We'll forgive you, but what's the story?"

Chavanne lowered his eyes, his fingers playing with the coffee spoon. "For some time now a narcotics smuggling ring has been using this asteroid as a base of operations.

"At first this smuggling was kept secret even from me, and by the time I found out these men were well established and were able to make certain threats . . ."

"And certain offers?" Romano interjected. "How much did they pay you?"

Chavanne chuckled. "You're a smart boy. What they paid me was barely enough to make up my losses in running this hotel. As long as they didn't bother me and nobody got into trouble, I didn't mind. But now it's gotten into the killing stage and the Interplanetary Police are on their way. I'm pulling out of the deal. The question is, will they let me?"

Drumming with stiff fingers upon the table top, Romano thought fast and hard. "So the mysterious business out in the mountains that I was about to stumble on was what? Their center of operations for the smuggling game? Their cache?"

Chavanne nodded.

But . . . Romano quickly shuffled the card index of his mind, dealt out the four names which could be involved, and chose the only one which fit.

"It's Jennahagan, of course," he said.

Chavanne, lighting a cigar, smiled. "I said you were smart, boy. Yes, he's the one." He leaned forward conspiratorially. "But I think

Jerrold Wald is in this also. Who had better chance to knock off his uncle?"

Chavanne rose ponderously. "I must get back to the shop. Take my advice and keep this under your hat. Sit tight until the police arrive. This is their job."

"Wait a minute—wait a minute." Romano, vaguely dissatisfied, clutched for a vagrant thought. "Grimmenden—how does he fit into this? What was he doing out in his aircar the time we were attacked?"

Chavanne flashed a brilliant smile and waved his cigar triumphantly. His air of polished composure had returned in a phenomenal manner. "Well, my boy, I don't really know. Grimmenden is the type of character who gets himself into the middle of everything, but who doesn't say anything. You see him all around, but you don't know anything about him. And if you—let's say—send back to Earth for information on him, you'll find there isn't any. There isn't any John Grimmenden, retired manufacturer of machinery.

"You know what I think? I think Grimmenden is a narcotics agent from the Interplanetary Police. Alter all, you don't think that the police are going to let this asteroid go without keeping an eye on it?"

And, with an odd sort of cheerfulness, considering the death of Sigmund Wald, the sundry attacks, and the overshadowing presence of the narcotics agent, Chavanne walked off.

Romano leaned towards Helva and asked fiercely, "Do you remember how Jerrold Wald nearly had himself a fit when I mentioned plutonium poisoning yesterday? You didn't miss it, I know."

Helva retreated behind her professional mask. Romano, in a sudden spurt of insight, recognized this as a clear sign of conflict.

"Hey," he said. "What's between you and Jerrold Wald?"

Her eyes blazed a hot flame at him. "Jerrold Wald is a patient of mine. I know everything about him. I know him better than he knows himself."

Romano produced a meditative whistle. "So that's what you're doing around here. A nice way to make a living."

Helva brought her temper down two octaves. "It's a good living. And a useful one. I'll tell you about Jerrold. It's not violating professional secrecy. You could check on it yourself by calling the right people.

"Go ahead." he said. "I'm listening."

The psychiatrist spoke quietly and intently. "Jerrold Wald had a good reason to react when you mentioned plutonium poisoning. Three years ago he killed a man that way—in the very way his uncle was killed. He was a neurotic young character—wild and spoiled. The murder was proven, clear and fair. Five hundred years ago he'd have been hung without further ado."

Shakily reaching for a cigarette, Romano felt his mind lurch off in all directions, instantly building up a vast structure of possibilities. First and simplest: Jerrold had killed once, and he could go off his rocker and kill again in the same way. Second, he could be framed by someone who knew that he had killed before and who planted things to make it look like the same pattern. Third, Jerrold had nothing at all to do with it, but was scared half to death because he was afraid somebody would make a connection with what had happened three years ago.

Returning from his wild loop of thought-association, he heard Helva Hansen continue: "The court sentenced him to confinement with psychiatric treatment. After almost three years of this he was considered sufficiently cured to be returned to society. Then his uncle, Sigmund Wald, brought him here to Doreen and hired me to continue the treatment."

"That was quite expensive for Uncle. Why was he so interested?"

"Wald's main reason for coming here was to do some special research with the help of Chavanne's calculators. He thought it would do Jerrold some good to get away from Earth and at the same time continue his therapy. He hasn't had to support me completely, as I've acquired a few patients among the other guests here, while having a well-earned vacation on the side. Everybody's been killing two birds with one stone."

"And I was nearly one of the birds." Romano, with ruthless tenacity, insisted upon returning to the number one subject. "Why do you think Jerrold is innocent now? Can it be you are afraid to admit that one of your patients has relapsed after you thought you had him cured?"

Helva sat silently for a full minute, searching her mind for indications of her reactions towards Jerrold's behavior.

"I knew that Jerrold had gotten into bad company here," she said slowly. "The question in my mind is: how much can he keep hidden from me, his doctor? I honestly believe I would have known immediately if Jerrold had killed his uncle.

"In spite of the coincidence that Sigmund Wald was killed by the same method that Jerrold used three years ago, and in spite of the fact that he was the closest to Sigmund and could have poisoned his coffee with the least difficulty—in spite of that I think he didn't do it. And I don't think he shot at us in the aircar. His mind was once sick enough for him to be a poisoner, but I'd be very ashamed of my abilities if he were no better now."

Romano reached a long distance to a wild assumption. "Why does it have to be that the same person did both jobs? Maybe Jerrold did poison his uncle while somebody else—perhaps Jennahagan—went after me."

Helva stretched her arms and stood up from the chair. "Maybe this and maybe that. Look. Give me one hour alone with Jerrold and I will know for certain whether he did or didn't. I tell you I know Jerrold Wald better than he knows himself. Literally."

Romano believed it.

"Okay," he said, following Helva out of the dining room. "So Jerrold didn't kill his uncle, and Chavanne is talking through his hat. What does that do to the story about the dope-smuggling and Jerrold's connection with Jennahagan?"

"The smuggling is plausible. As for Jerrold . . ." Helva stopped in the center of the doorway. "I think," she said, "that he can be very useful to us. I'm sure he can."

Romano paced outside the door like an expectant father, scattering cigarette butts along the hall and holding a desultory conversation with Fido. Helva had been inside the room with Jerrold Wald for an hour by now, and Romano winced as he imagined the intense psychological pressures that she would be exerting upon Jerrold, utilizing the intimate knowledge of his mind that she had gained through dozens of hours of psychoanalytic interviews and through all the various techniques at her command.

He was certain that Jerrold could keep no secret from Helva for long.

Finally they emerged from the room—Helva quietly triumphant, and Jerrold pale but with less anxiety than he had shown before. Romano knew the signs. Jerrold had purged himself of his conflicts due to his activities with the smugglers and was back on the path towards mental peace.

"He's clear," Helva announced to Romano. "I was right. Jerrold didn't poison his uncle."

"Then it must have been Jennahagan?"

Helva paused, her mind occupied with the puzzle. "Jerrold doesn't know. The story about the dope-smuggling is true. Jennahagan is using this asteroid as a warehouse for the stuff. Jerrold has been playing around with him for the past few weeks. He got involved in gambling, needed money, and was led right down the path by Jennahagan. But apparently Jennahagan hasn't been telling Jerrold everything. He doesn't know anything about the death of his uncle, and he's been scared to death ever since the whole thing started. He's glad to be through with Jennahagan, and he'll do anything we want."

Romano tossed away another butt. "Fine thing. But what do we want? Where's Jennahagan?"

"That's the catch. Right now Jennahagan is packing up, getting ready to leave. With the police on their way, it's getting too hot for him. He's out by his dope cache now, and if we wait until the police come he'll be gone."

Romano could see what was coming, and a violent feeling of reluctance swept over him. "So we should go out and pick up Jennahagan ourselves? Get all shot up again? The man's dangerous."

"Ha. You were the demon reporter all set to catch criminals, write a big story, and get a big bonus."

"So I was. It took a knock on my head to remind me that this is a game people play for keeps. A man can get hurt this way. But what's your big interest in this? What sudden passion makes you so anxious to foil the villain? I'll bet it's not a pure and sweet desire for justice."

Romano's eyes suddenly narrowed. "Oho. I get it. The evidence still points to Jerrold as having done in his uncle. Professional pride is sitting on your neck. You have to prove Jerrold innocent because he is your patient and you'd be a sad case of a psychiatrist if your patient tipped and poisoned his uncle."

Helva, suddenly furious, turned her back. "All right. Then wait for the police."

Romano caught her by the shoulders and turned her around. "Don't go away mad," he said. "Wait a minute and I'll pick up my gun. It might come in handy. And you had better put on some more suitable clothes."

An hour later, Romano felt that this was where he had come in. Once more he sat in an aircar hurtling through the thin air a mile above the surface of the asteroid. Again Helva Hansen was at his side, and Fido, the robot bodyguard, stood in the rear.

This time, in addition, there was the thin, nervous form of Jerrold Wald, wedged in between Romano and the psychiatrist.

Now there was no searching for an unknown object, no circling and hesitation. Their trajectory arrowed directly toward a precisely-known destination. In almost complete darkness, only the dim lights of the instrument panel and the red tip of the cigarette smoked by Jerrold Wald were visible to Romano's eyes.

Innumerable times Romano tried to visualize what he would find at the destination, tried to plan what action he would take. His heart beat slightly louder in his ears as he felt the small gun in his pocket.

He kept telling himself that this was nonsense, that he was a photographer and a reporter, not a policeman, that he had no business sallying forth in this manner to capture a smuggler and a murderer.

It took a woman to drive a man to this sort of thing.

"I would like to know," Romano said, "what happened to Grimmenden."

Helva shrugged her shoulders. "He's nowhere to be found. I checked everywhere I could think of—with Robot Service, with the hotel desk, with Chavanne himself. Disappeared."

An uneasiness insinuated itself into Romano's mind. "A real unknown quantity," he said. "Tell me, Jerrold, what do you think of Chavanne's theory about Grimmenden?"

"That he's a narcotics agent?" Jerrold asked. "Who knows? He hung around Jennahagan a lot, but it never meant anything as far as I could see."

"The fact that he's disappeared could mean that he got to Jennahagan before we did. It would be good to know."

Romano felt himself tighten up as they approached their destination. In a few minutes Jerrold Wald motioned the others to keep quiet. Switching on the radiophone, he called Jennahagan, giving an identification code.

"That you, Jerrold?" Jennahagan's voice came through.

"Yes. You said you needed some help. I'll be down in thirty seconds. Give me a beam."

The aircar swooped downward in the darkness, the robot pilot steering its way along the directional beam from Jennahagan. Mountains loomed over their heads, blotting out the stars. Then there was the crunch of gravel under the car wheels and the feeling of motion ceased.

The three climbed out of the car onto the bare ground. Ahead of them loomed the almost-invisible form of a small spaceship. Focusing their eyes in the direction of a loud clattering noise, they saw a robot clamber down from the dark entrance of the ship, walk along a path for several yards, and then disappear into a low building which was partly obscured by a towering group of rocks.

Jerrold set out towards this building, motioning for the others to follow him. Fido took up the rear. As they neared the door, a robot emerged carrying a huge box.

They passed the robot and entered the door, single file. Jerrold went first. Perspiration on his forehead glinted in the light that came from an inner room as he opened its door.

Jennahagan looked up from the filing cabinet he was examining and nodded as he saw Jerrold enter.

"Good thing you came. You can speed things tip by helping the robots move the stuff off the shelves. I'm moving out in ten minutes."

Romano slipped quickly through the door, allowing Fido to follow him instantly. "No you're not," he said. "We'd like to talk a little bit about the murder of Sigmund Wald."

"What the hell!" Jennahagan roared, and reached for his gun pocket.

'Hold him, Fido," Romano snapped.

The great form of the robot leaped forward, smashed into Jennahagan's round, hard body, and pinned his arms to his sides, even as he had one hand already in the pocket, clutching a gun.

As he gasped for breath, Helva Hansen came through the door. She walked up to Jennahagan, held motionless by the robot, and said, "You heard what the man said. We want to talk about a murder."

Jennahagan strained against the robot's arms. The red in his face deepened as he shouted in fury, "I don't know what you're talking about."

"We don't intend to waste time" Helva said, removing a tiny hypodermic kit from her shoulder bag. "You're a little excited. The doctor recommends a sedative. Then you can talk."

She approached his arm with a needle.

"Drop that thing, Doctor!"

The hard, high-pitched voice from the doorway sent a wave of shock through Romano's nervous system. As he whirled around he heard Helva's gasping intake of breath, and a moment later the click of the needle as it struck the floor.

"Fido, get him!" Romano barked, diving for cover.

The robot, dropped Jennahagan, thrust him aside, charged across the room toward the door, and met a pair of slugs that tore his middle open with a shower of tiny metal parts.

John Grimmenden, standing in the doorway, held his gun quite steady in a small, gnarled hand.

"Let's have no more of this nonsense," he advised them. "Nobody in this outfit has killed anybody on this asteroid and we're not going to unless you give us trouble. We're closing up shop temporarily because we don't care to be around while the police are looking for murderers.

"You don't think we'd bungle a job as thoroughly as that try on you? We're *professionals.*"

His eyes fixed steadily on Romano and Helva Hansen, he snapped to Jennahagan: "All right, get on your feet and see that the loading is finished so we can clear out of here."

Jennahagen clambered heavily to his feet, rage stiffening every muscle of his body. He walked towards Romano, fists clenched.

Grinimenden waved him hack. "None of that now. They'll get what's coming to them, but our first job is to get out of here. By the time the police arrive we're going to be completely lost in this big solar system of ours.

"Let me kill them," Jennahagan demanded fiercely.

Grimmenden shook his head. "That would be amateurish," he said. "It would be unaesthetic. I have an aversion to committing murders that might be traced to me. We don't have time to do the kind of job which would be necessary here."

Grimmenden seated himself on a desk, the gun still unwavering in his fist, not for one instant allowing Romano a chance to draw his own.

"But it's not necessary to kill them. These two will be sorry that they meddled into our business and, as for our friend Jerrold Wald, he will deeply regret his little double-cross."

For the next ten minutes the robots diligently removed packages from shelves and stored them in the bowels of the spaceship, while the three—Romano, Helva Hansen, and the quietly hysterical Jerrold Wald—watched in silence.

Finally the work was completed. Grimmenden backed cautiously through the door and said, in a deriding voice, "It's a long walk back."

He slammed the door shut and they heard various thudding noises on the other side, followed by footsteps rapidly retreating outside. As they rushed to open the door there was the sound of two gun shots, followed by crashings and clatterings.

They wrestled with the door—finally opened it to find one of the robots leaning inertly against it. Its bulk slid to the floor with a crash and they dashed outside in time to see the spaceship lift from the ground and disappear among the stars.

*   *   *

With grim cheerfulness Romano surveyed the scene. The controls of both aircars had been smashed by bullets. The power equipment had been rendered useless. There was water, but no food. No means of communication of any form.

Romano grinned paradoxically at Helva. "It really does look like a long walk back," he said, chuckling. "About a hundred miles, wouldn't you say, Jerrold?"

Helva Hansen had been observing him with restrained astonishment for the five minutes that had gone by since the spaceship had left them stranded. Presently she said, "Okay, Jack, what's the joke? Either you've gone slightly psychotic, which I doubt, or you have something up your sleeve. Give."

Romano sat himself down on a rock outside the door of the building, still laughing to himself.

"Oh, they did a beautiful job of it! We're completely isolated. Only way we can get back is to hike a hundred miles over hill and dale. We could probably make it, but we wouldn't like it.

"Yes, Grimmenden's a real smart egg. Aesthetic objections to murder, ha.

"Except he forgot one very interesting point. This is such a wonderful asteroid we are on. We are waited on hand and foot by robots. Robot Service is at hand every minute of the day. Even the aircars are run by robots, and whenever something goes wrong with one of the cars, the central office knows it immediately and sends out help. Like the time we were shot down before."

Helva gave a sudden shout of laughter. "Oh, lovely. As soon as Grimmenden shot up our aircar he gave notice directly to the central office."

Even Jerrold Wald cheered up at this. "Then all we have to do is wait!" And he, too, began to laugh.

The only feeling of regret which insinuated itself into his mind, producing a feeling of emptiness inside himself, came when he saw how Helva Hansen and Jack Romano held each other's hands, how they looked at each other, and how they laughed.

He turned away from them abruptly, his mouth twisted. It hurt, even being the third in the crowd. He turned back to the other two, stirring about in his mind for something to say, something with which to interrupt them.

He felt that he could not stand it, though he had known from the very beginning that for him the psychiatrist was unattainable.

Suddenly he felt conversation necessary.

"Chavanne was pretty far off base, wasn't he?" he said. "Thinking that Grimmenden was a narcotics agent. When all the time he was the big boss of the gang. Grimmenden was certainly one smart person. He never let me know who he was, even when I was working for him."

Romano gave a start and dropped Helva's hands, his mind abruptly brought back from a great distance. "Chavanne was far off base on many things," he growled. "He's been off base ever since the moment he tried to kill me without noticing that I was wearing a radiation detector."

Jerrold Wald blinked his eyes rapidly. "It would have to be him, wouldn't it? By simple elimination, if nothing else."

"Of course!" Helva snapped, a flush of anger on her face. "Once I was satisfied that you were not the one, it had to be either Chavanne, Grimmenden, or Jennahagan. The moment Chavanne suggested it might be the smugglers I knew he was lying. I knew it by the sound of his voice. I knew it because the method of killing was wrong. A gang of smugglers doesn't mess around with radioactivity and poisoning. When they kill, they kill.

"No, the murder of your uncle and the attempt on Jack looked like an amateur job, not a professional one. But we had to come here to make sure. We had to question Jennahagan."

"A job we certainly botched up," Romano laughed unhappily.

"Indeed we did. But I'm satisfied that the smuggling business and the murders are not connected. This leaves Chavanne."

"It adds up." Romano thought back carefully. "Chavanne owns the asteroid, runs everything on it. He could fix the robot memory bank so that it would not record his orders to the robots concerning the murders, and at the same time he told some of the others that orders were not being recorded just to give him a scapegoat in case something went wrong with his plan to make the murders seem like natural deaths. He had two beautiful scapegoats—the smugglers, and you, Jerrold.

"Chavanne could sit back and order the robots to do all his dirty work, while passing around his little rumors about who might have been the killer. He could blast the door of the radioactive dump, just to confuse the trail. At the same time he could play with me, recommend that I get a robot bodyguard. This threw suspicion away from him, while he could get rid of the robot any time he pleased.

"Chavanne was the one who knew where we were going the time we started to investigate the area of radioactivity. He was the one who waited there for us and shot us down.

"At that point he slipped up. His overconfidence threw him for a loss, because the robot bodyguard warned us—the robot that he himself had given to me. But his original, fatal slip lay in not recognizing the radiation detectors that Wald and I wore in our belts. He probably even went to the trouble of putting out of commission the detector in Wald's wristwatch so that it would seem plausible for Wald to walk into the radioactive area by mistake.

"Chavanne could do all this better than anyone else because he had the run of the hotel and because the robots were all under his command."

"But why?" Jerrold wanted to know. "Why?"

"There," said Helva, "is a question."

"Our first guess must still be right," Romano insisted. "Sigmund Wald and I were on the verge of discovering something important connected with the radioactive area. We find out what that was, and we have the entire story."

"It is hard to think of what it might be. Rare minerals? Valuable metals? Chavanne already owns the asteroid. Why should he worry about who discovers them?"

Romano shrugged his shoulders. "Who knows? Maybe the answer is not logical at all. Certainly Chavanne is not quite sane. A person who commits murder to hide a secret is by definition unsane. Who says the motive has to be logical?"

They had to be satisfied with that for the time being. Further conversation circled hopelessly to no conclusion.

After a time, Jerrold asked, "How long should it take for an aircar to come?"

They had taken to watching the sky intently, looking for the glistening of the sun on a metallic speck.

Helva said slowly, "It took less than an hour the other time."

By now three hours had gone.

The tiny sun rose into a cloudless, incredibly deep blue sky. With utmost patience its imperceptible motion carried it high until, over the top of its arc, it began to descend.

Conversation grew more and more sparse as the day dragged along.

Romano searched through the building once more, could find nothing to eat. Hunger was beginning to claw at their bellies.

When the sun was setting, with no sign of rescue in the sky, Romano said. "We'd better start thinking."

Helva nodded her head. "Chavanne learns," she said meditatively. "He remembered how we were picked up the other time, and he made sure that it would not happen again, by disconnecting the alarm circuits. We're not going to be rescued, because Chavanne fixed it that way."

Romano clenched his fists slowly, unclenched them, and exhaled a breath with a slight shudder over his entire body. "Another bit added onto the debt he owes us."

"We'll die of starvation," Jerrold whined.

"No, Jerrold," Helva said quietly. "There's a good supply of water. We can last long enough to walk back to the hotel."

"We need a map," Romano said, abruptly.

Jerrold Wald looked up. "There was one in my aircar."

Romano leaped to his feet and ran to the car. In a moment he returned, waving the paper triumphantly.

"Finally a break for our side," he said, breathlessly. He spread the map out on the ground, and the three squatted about it, straining their eyes in the meager twilight.

"We're here, and the hotel is there," Romano pointed out. He spread a pair of fingers to use as calipers and laid off the distance. "It's closer to one hundred and ten miles," he grunted. "Not good, but it could be worse. With flat terrain we could do it in four days. But with the rugged landscape on this rock . . . Maybe we'll find enough to eat to keep us going. I still have my gun. . . ."

As he gazed at the map and recalled the rocky land that he had painted during the past week, the feeling of hunger within him turned into a sensation of sickening dread. In his imagination there blossomed a minutely detailed picture of the march that would be required through the wild country, without supplies, without guidance. with unaccustomed bodies.

"But it's not impossible," he said, his voice filled with an effort to prevent hopelessness from showing through. "Among the mountains there are little valleys where we will be able to find plants and animals. We'll get along."

"Yeah." Jerrold's shoulders shook quietly.

"We'll need water containers. All we can carry. We'll need any knives we can find."

With a knife, Romano killed an unsuspecting and unafraid rabbit. It broiled deliciously over an open fire. Hunger put aside for another day, and strength restored, they continued across the grassy plain.

This gave them an easy ten miles, after which Romano insisted that they halt for the night. His planned route included two more such oases, and there was no need for the three to kill themselves with over-exhaustion.

More important, he wanted to be at the edge of the radioactive area the next morning.

The place was so poorly marked that had it not been for his close attention to the map, Romano would have missed it entirely. One signpost was actually found, but for the rest, a person could have wandered into the dangerous circle without warning.

Romano checked his counter. It registered nothing but normal cosmic ray background. He raised a querulous eyebrow to Helva.

"Of course," he said, dubiously, "the circle is ten miles in diameter and the actual radioactive section might be just in the center of it."

"If there is any there at all," Helva said, indifferently.

The thought struck deeply and rocked Romano back on his heels. "It fits," he said. "And yet it doesn't fit. If Chavanne were trying to hide something in there, the easy way would be to mark it *radioactive area* on the map and put a fence around it. But then why would he kill off Sigmund Wald and try to kill me for going near the place? We wouldn't have tried to go into the danger zone.

"If this place is actually not radioactive, it makes the mystery harder to understand. I think we should go in a little further."

Jerrold Wald grumbled at the extra walking, but he had no alternative. Romano had the map.

The terrain began to get rocky once more, and they stumbled with many curses through the jagged, splintered crystals. Romano stopped every hundred yards to read his tiny radiation meter. Finally, after they had gone over a mile, he began to get results.

"Gamma rays are coming through over the background. They become stronger as we approach the center. Chavanne was telling the truth for a change. The place is really loaded with hot stuff."

"We go back to the hotel now?" Jerrold demanded.

Romano nodded, wearily. He hated to give up the idea that the radioactive area was connected with the murder, untenable as the idea had turned out to be. Worst of all, elimination of the radioactive circle as the location of Chavanne's secret put them right back where they were at the beginning.

It left them knowing absolutely nothing.

Carefully consulting the map, Romano laid out a line of progress in a new direction, and the three proceeded to plod forward. It was up-hill for a long distance, and agony in their legs began to compete with the emptiness in their stomachs.

When the sun was three quarters of the way set, Romano called a halt, and they proceeded to tear apart the cold carcass of the small animal they had killed and roasted in the valley that morning.

With much coaxing, Romano induced the other two to rise and make a few more miles before nightfall, much as he himself longed for rest. They dragged themselves to the top of the hill and stood for a moment, panting for breath.

Helva Hansen seated herself on the ground and said, "Jack we simply must stop for the night. I'm finished."

Romano ruffled her hair with his hand. "Okay, baby. You'll feel better tomorrow. I'll look for a soft rock to use as a bed."

The light from the sun cut across the craggy spires almost horizontally. Ahead of them was a precipitous drop into a shallow canyon hemmed in by bare, flinty walls. Romano's heart sank very low as he surveyed the path they had to traverse the next day.

Abruptly every muscle in his body stiffened and the jump of his heart sent the blood roaring in his ears. What his eyes had caught was a round metallic shape which reflected the light in a brilliant glare. From a distance its size could not well be judged but, comparing it with the height of the canyon walls, Romano was certain that it must be a thing of tremendous dimensions.

He shouted for the others to come and look. They scrambled to his side and stood for many minutes peering with mind-wrenching curiosity at the spaceship. A ship of this magnitude had simply no business in this place. It was an absurdity that made them quite certain this was the secret Chavanne was hiding. This was the ship whose presence had caused the death of Sigmund Wald and had finally brought them to this place.

It was late the next morning before they managed to clamber down to it. The gigantic silvery bulk towered far above their heads and stretched an incredible distance forward and backwards.

"What a monster!" Romano hoarsely exclaimed. "How long has this been here?"

Helva's eyes darted in all directions, taking in every detail of its appearance, noticing that there was not a crack or a dented plate.

They walked around it. On its nose they saw great golden letters which spelled out a name whose syllables tumbled among forgotten memories in Romano's mind: *Galaxy I.*

"You know this ship?" Helva asked.

Romano shook his head. "I heard its name mentioned just once before. Years ago. By a couple of the wildest scientists in the solar system. They were talking about the possibility of traveling faster than the speed of light. They told me that, believe it or not, a faster-than-light ship had actually been built—the *Galaxy I.* Imagine—over a hundred years ago men were able to travel faster than light!

"But this was just at the beginning of the third interplanetary war. The ship disappeared, and the laboratories in which the faster-than-light principle—the superdrive—had been developed were wiped out, together with most of the continent. All records were lost, and today the *Galaxy I* is little more than a rumor."

"While all the time it has been hidden here." Helva tilted her head back to see the letters welded to the prow. "No wonder Chavanne was willing to commit murder to keep this secret. If he could duplicate the superdrive it would make him one of the most important men in the system."

"Not only in the system, but in the entire galaxy."

The voice, amplified to tremendous proportions, reverberated among the rocks of the canyon, bouncing back and forth until it died out in a muttering thunder.

The three jerked their heads source of the voice.

If you will come to the entrance port of this ship," the voice continued, "I shall be happy to receive you.

Romano grasped Helva's arm and whispered into her ear, "It's Chavanne inside the ship. He's been watching and listening to us—for how long?"

The psychiatrist nodded. "The man is dangerous. Watch your step."

They walked slowly around the ship, hugging its sides, until they reached the great entrance port. There was nobody to be seen.

"Where are you, Chavanne?" Romano called.

"Inside, of course," Chavanne's voice boomed out. "Come in and join me. Don't stand out there in the hot sun." He laughed.

Romano stood in place, hands on hips. "We'd like it better if you came out here to talk to us," he said.

Chavanne's voice snapped with impatience. "I said you come in!"

A blast of energy spurted dazzlingly from a projector at the side of the port, throwing up a gush of flame and pulverized rock from the ground behind them.

Jerrold Wald cried out in fright and stumbled forward. Romano, his face rigid with anger said, "I guess we'd better go in, like the man said."

The entrance port opened into a large hallway that drove straight through to the geometrical axis of the ship, where were located elevators and conveyor belts. The ship was empty of life and completely still except for the voice of Chavanne issuing from one loudspeaker after another as they passed along the corridor.

Following the directions of Chavanne they came to a bulkhead in the center of which a great round port stood open. The sign-plate above the port read: *Lifeboat Number 1.*

The three stopped before the port. "Suppose we don't go in?" Romano demanded.

For answer there was the crash of a heavy door in the bulkhead behind them.

"There's only one way out now," Chavanne's voice told them unemotionâlly. "You either go into the lifeboat, or you stay where you are and starve to death."

"Is there a choice?" Romano muttered, and stepped through the port. The other two followed, passing the double doorway and into the cramped quarters of the lifeboat.

As Romano expected, the heavy steel plug slammed shut behind them.

Romano's fury put an unsteady edge on his face. "We certainly walked into this, we did," he growled.

"Anybody with an IQ higher than a chimpanzee's could have seen this play coming, but we walk right into it, eyes open, on our own feet."

Helva put her hand on his arm. "Don't blame yourself. Once Chavanne saw us coming there wasn't a thing we could have done."

Jerrold Wald, completely undone, collapsed into a chair.

There was only one thing to do, Helva decided, and that was to keep Chavanne talking. Her only weapon was her voice and her knowledge of the human mind.

"Chavanne," she said. "Are you listening?"

"Listening, my dear," Chavanne's voice said conversationally.

"It would be so much more pleasant to see you, rather than talk to a microphone."

"I'm afraid that this is not to be a pleasure call. These are working hours, and there is work to be done."

Work! Romano drew a wild guess from his subconscious.

"Chavanne, have you gotten the superdrive operating yet?"

"Of course. The superdrive has been working for over a month. One final test is required. It has been difficult to decide how this test should he conducted. Your fortunate visit here has solved the difficulty."

"Yes?" Romano waited.

"You see, at the beginning of the Third Interplanetary War this ship was hidden on this asteroid while certain changes were made. When the time came for the ship to join the rest of the fleet, something went wrong. A flaw had developed in the superdrive generators. The moment power was applied to the preliminary geowarper, every man in this ship died. The ship remained where it was unharmed.

"Between the confusion of the war and the destruction of the records, almost all memory of this ship was lost. Fifteen years ago, when I was compiling material for the information bank at Washington, I came across sufficient data, hidden in an obsolete file, to allow me to calculate where this ship might be. I followed it up found the ship, and bought the asteroid. For the past ten years I have studied the principles of the geowarp and the superdrive, so that I will be able to duplicate them myself."

"That was very remarkable, Chavanne." Helva thought that a slight amount of oil would help.

"Indeed. And the results of my work are not going to be stolen from me. First it was Sigmund Wald, the old fraud. He thought I wouldn't know why a force-field expert would be nosing around here. Then Romano began to spy around. Very clever, posing as a photographer, but it was quite transparent."

"Look Chavanne," Romano broke in. "You can't keep us here. The police will be arriving in two days and when we turn up dead or missing you will be in trouble."

"No trouble at all," Chavanne denied. "The fact that the smuggler Jennahagan has departed abruptly will be considered very significant. In the meantime you are going to be useful to me. You are going to perform an experiment for me."

"An experiment!"

"A very simple one from your point of view. You simply remain where you are and talk to me. No trouble at all."

"And what will this prove?"

"If you remain alive while traveling on the superdrive, it will prove that I have corrected the fault which killed the previous operators of the ship. I am sure that my work has been good, and so you may expect a pleasant trip."

Chavanne's voice cut off and remained unresponsive to any further conversation. In a moment they heard the thudding sound of heavy relays closing on the other side of a partition in the lifeboat.

Heavy machinery whined into sudden activity.

Romano stormed about the room in sudden panic. The large exit port was locked. There were two inner doors, one fore and one aft. There was no furniture except for five padded seats. The walls were lined with cupboards, now empty. There was nothing to get a grip on. Nothing to break.

Helva sat back in one of the seats, her eyes partly closed. "Take it easy," she told Romano, in a tired voice. "No use knocking your head against a stone wall."

Chavanne's voice came to them again from the concealed loud-speaker. "We are now ready to begin. The lifeboat will leave the *Galaxy I* and take a course away from the sun. I hope to receive frequent reports from you."

A powerful whine arose from outside the boat, and they felt a strong sense of motion as the catapult ejected them from an opening in the side of the great spaceship. The generators within the lifeboat acquired a deep, complex set of beat noises.

"The superdrive is on now," Chavanne said, "and you are traveling at double light speed. I would appreciate hearing a word from you."

Romano raised an eyebrow at Helva. Would anything be gained by keeping Chavanne in ignorance as to the outcome of his experiment?

"I wouldn't try holding out on me," Chavanne said, mildly. "You see, if I think that you are dead, then I shall allow the boat to travel out into interstellar space. If you say something to let me know that all is well . . ."

"Then I suppose you'll bring us back to talk to the police," Romano snarled. "You rotten liar. I think you're nothing but a bluff, a fake. How can you talk to us by radio if we are traveling faster than light?"

Chavanne chuckled. "This is perhaps the most interesting aspect of the geowarp principle. Communication and remote control of the boat is effected, not through the electromagnetic four-dimensional spacetime continuum, but through a five-dimensional hyper-space-time embedded in a six-dimensional continuum. The Lorentz—what the—!"

Chavanne's voice broke off on a note of shocked alarm. In the background there was the buzz of a warning signal.

"Damn! A spaceship overhead." The voice was remote, as though Chavanne had moved to the other side of the control room.

Romano and Helva Hansen stared at each other. Jerrold Wald leaped out of the seat in which he had been slumped.

"It's the police!" he cried. "It must be!"

The sounds coming through the communicator were indecipherable—the noises of Chavanne moving around the control room, muttered curses, the clicks of switches being operated.

"The police were not due for another two days at least." Helva could not permit herself the luxury of false hope. "And even if it is the police, they are down there and we are up here. How can they help us?"

"We could—" Romano began, and stopped abruptly the speed of his thoughts far outracing his words. If it were the police, and if somehow they got into the control room where Chavanne stood, and where the police could hear them through the communicator—then a warning could be given—a message could be spoken. But he must not give Chavanne the idea.

At that moment the noises from the communicator ceased, leaving a vacuum of sound in the tiny room.

Jerrold Wald choked, "He's cut us off," and collapsed again into a chair. Helva Hansen buried her face in Romano's shoulder as he held her very close to him.

In complete silence now, they hurtled through space, past the orbit of Jupiter, on towards Saturn and the unimaginable stretches of void beyond. Completely cut off from the four-dimensional universe, leaving behind the spectrum of electromagnetic vibrations, powerless to change the course of their little vessel, they huddled in the lifeboat, nerves drained or emotion.

Savagely, Romano pulled himself away from Helva. "There must be controls to this boat," he rasped, moving swiftly to one of the locked inner doors.

It was solid, impossible to jar with his body. Compared to the massive outer locks, however, it was relatively fragile. Loading his gun with an explosive shell, Romano aimed at the lock and motioned the others to stand back. The blast of the shell tore at their eardrums and left a small, ragged hole in the metal of the door.

Romano pushed through and found the control room a tiny cubby, jammed with instruments. Their bewildering array marched across the face of the console. He stopped short in front of them.

He felt Helva close behind him. "It's dark outside," she said.

Jerkily, he looked up, and for the first time realized that the black panels above the control console were transparent.

"You wouldn't expect to see stars out there while we are traveling on the superdrive, would you?" he heard Helva say.

He shook his head dumbly. Faced with the black emptiness of subspace outside the boat, and with the maze of unfamiliar instruments on the panel in front of him, he felt a congealing dismay in his heart. He was just as lost with the controls under his hand as he was while locked in the other room.

He said, fighting back his panic, "If we sit down quietly, we can figure this out. All we have to do is stop and go back in the direction we came from."

"Are you sure? What do you know about the geometry of five-dimensional spacetime imbedded in a six-dimensional continuum?"

"Not a damn thing." But as he continued to study the control panel, his equilibrium began to return. Each function was labeled. The number of operations was limited.

"First thing," he said, "we get back into normal space and see where we are. I don't understand this method of determining position.

He reached his hands out, hoping that he performed the operations in the correct order, and began snapping switches. His breath came hard as he waited for the results.

Nothing happened.

Finally Romano sat back in his chair, cursing long, fluently, and unblushingly. "The boat's wired for remote control. The manuals don't work."

He felt this to be the final insult. The last opportunity for them to turn back had been stolen from them. There was nothing left but to open the air valve and finish things quickly.

They sat silently in front of the control panel, gazing out of the windows into the featureless subspace. After an indefinite time, Romano said, "I wonder if we have passed Pluto yet."

Then they sat in a wordless stupor for a further period of time.

The communicator burst into activity. "Captain Mellor of the Interplanetary Police speaking. Are you all right?"

"Yes, we're all right! Where is Chavanne? Don't let him get away."

"Chavanne is here, under arrest. You are being returned to Doreen."

The lifeboat landed beneath the towering prow of the *GALAXY I*. The Interplanetary Police ship shared the crowded canyon floor with them.

In the executive office of the police ship they saw Chavanne, crumpled in a chair, his head in his hands.

Bedraggled and dusty, they approached Captain Mellor.

"Let's eat, Captain," Romano pleaded, "then talk."

The missing threads of the story wove themselves into place around the dining table.

"As we approached Doreen, our instruments detected the operation of a geowarper," Captain Mellor related. "We drove to the source of the disturbance and apparently arrived just a few minutes after your boat took off. We landed and met Chavanne at the entrance port of the *Galaxy I.* He seemed normal enough at first, but the moment we asked him what he was doing with a geowarper he went into a fury and said something incoherent about how he was the only person in the solar system who knew about geowarpers and the only one who knew how to build a superdrive.

"We had to give him a shot of a hypno-drug before he'd tell us what was going on and how we could make contact with you people."

Helva's eyes sparkled. "His paranoid mentality could not conceive of the idea that other men, by independent research, could rediscover the superdrive. To him a scientific discovery was a *secret,* that had to be stolen, that had to be guarded."

At a point in spacetime one hundred miles away and ten hours later, Romano walked jauntily into the communications room at the hotel. with Helva hanging onto one arm. They entered a booth and Romano seated himself at the little table there to teletype the message:

"*Dr. Felice Romano, Cybernetics Research Institute; Mexico City, Mexico. Hello, Mother. Thanks for the dope on Helva Hansen. Yes, this is it.*"

FORMULA FOR MURDER

I

THE FIGURE OF Professor Glover slipped from the surface of the space station and twinkled away among the stars. Jim Britten stared at it as though he could call it back by the ferocity of his gaze. He stood paralyzed by helplessness while the spacesuited body plummeted off into the void, until he could no longer follow its motion towards the dazzling sun. Seized by an uncontrollable shaking, he dropped the radiophone antenna which he had ripped from Glover's back and flung himself down flat upon the surface of the station, where he clung while catching his breath.

A vast doughnut, twenty-five miles in diameter, the space station stood with no apparent motion a thousand miles above the surface of the earth. It floated in a sea of scintillating stars like diamonds scattered upon the blackest velvet.

"Jim, what's the matter?" John Callahan's voice grated in Britten's headpiece.

"Glover's line broke loose," Britten gasped. "He's gone."

"What!"

"I'm coming back in. Give me a hand."

Britten began the long crawl back to the entrance port, his nerves too shattered to attempt it standing up. He was several yards away when another spacesuited figure emerged from the port and helped him stagger the rest of the way. Inside the airlock he collapsed.

In a small room within a large hospital the two men sat talking. It was a featureless room with pale green walls, containing a desk, two soft chairs, and a leather couch. The doctor, middle-aged, inconspicuous, wearing glasses, a small moustache, and a gray suit, sat in one chair. Facing him in the other chair, Jim Britten, young, lean, and visibly pressed, wore pajamas and a hospital robe.

"You've been a sick boy," Morris Wolf told Jim Britten in a conversational tone.

"I guess so." Britten scratched at the arm of his chair and fingered the sleeve of his gown.

"You're coming along, though. When you arrived at the hospital a week ago, you had to be wheeled in and fed like a baby. Now you've pulled out of the hole and we're ready to do some talking."

"But, Doc, I don't know what happened. Honestly. One minute Glover was starting to climb down into the ion source chamber and the next minute his magnet line came loose, and when I grabbed after him I caught his phone antenna and ripped it off. Then I got the shakes and the next thing I knew I was back on Earth in the hospital."

The psychiatrist reached for his pipe and began to fill it from a large can on the desk.

"It's a great shock to have the person next to you snuffed out like that," he said. "Some people can take it standing up. When you fall apart like that we want to know the reason, so that it won't happen again."

Britten shrugged. "What's the difference? I'll never work in a laboratory again, let alone the Lunatron. I'll never finish my research and I'll never get my degree."

His voice trailed off in a discouraged whisper.

Wolf watched him for a moment.

"That kind of talk is the reason you are still here. You'll work in a laboratory again and you'll get your degree. You're still not quite well. I'm here to help you get well."

Britten shrugged again. "Okay. Bring on the dancing girls," he said, in a resigned tone.

There were no dancing girls, however, only a tall, blonde, squarish doctor in a white dress, who waited for them in the therapy room. Her cigarette made a cocky angle with the firm line of her mouth as she made final adjustments on the bank of electronic equipment that lined one whole wall.

"Jim, this is Dr. Heller," Wolf told him as they walked into the room. "She will work with us in here. Now suppose you get up on this table."

The two husky attendants who were always in the background helped Britten onto the table and strapped him down. As Wolf fastened the electrodes to Britten's head, he said, conversationally, "In the old days we would have just sat and talked to each other. It would have taken months to get to first base. Now we have ways of aiding the memory, of triggering associations, of lowering resistances to thoughts. It makes psychotherapy a much less tedious process than it used to be."

As he spoke, he slipped a hypodermic needle into Britten's arm.

"Now, suppose we see how much we can remember. Let's begin the day before Glover was killed. I want you to think back to that day and remember everything that happened, how you felt, what you thought about. We want to go through this traumatic experience of yours, and relate it to the elements in your life which caused such a profound shock."

And in addition—Wolf thought bleakly to himself—a good many people were anxious to know other things. For example: was Glover's demise at this particular time a coincidence? The Atomic Energy

Commission, though cagy about their reasons, had given top priority to the answers to their questions.

The strength of official interest in this case was further evidenced by the assignment of Bill Grady and Calvin Jones as attendants to Jim Britten. For some time Morris Wolf had wondered vaguely why two such clean-cut and alert young men should follow the low-paid calling of hospital attendant, until recently he had become aware that their paychecks actually came from the U. S. Treasury by way of the Federal Bureau of Investigation.

"Now," Wolf said, as Alma Heller switched on the tape recorder, "tell us what you remember."

After a year of being stationed on the Lunatron, Jim Britten had the feeling of being fed up. Lunatics they call us, he thought. Real crazy.

Looking out of the ports, he saw a black, starry space in which the only thing that ever changed was the view of the Earth, a thousand miles below, and the moon which was sometimes on one side and sometimes on the other. The stars were incredible jewels, and the sun was something that one never looked at with mortal eyes.

There was bitterness in his heart as he thought of his initial thrill at being chosen to do his thesis research on the Lunatron. He had been an envied boy, but now, after a year, he would have given the chance to the first bidder.

But there was no way to back out, short of breaking his contract or breaking his neck. Passage to and from Earth was too costly to be used on weekend vacations.

Many people on Earth would have been excited by the chance to work for two years with Professor Glover on the ten-thousand-billion-volt proton synchrotron which they called the Lunatron. Most physicists thought they were lucky if they could spend a few months with the fifty-billion-volt antique at Brookhaven.

But at Brookhaven, you are only a few minutes from New York. Up on the space laboratory Britten was a year from any place and every day that went by made it a day less.

"Johnny, what's the first thing you're going to do when you get back to Rhodesia?" he asked his roommate.

Britten sat, twanging halfheartedly at his guitar, while Johnny lay undressed on his bunk, his body hard and black against the white sheet.

"Oh, I have a good job lined up in a brand new research institute in Salisbury."

"I don't mean that," Britten said, impatiently. Johnny was such a serious boy. "I mean don't you think of all the fun you're going to have when you get back to Earth? Don't you think of getting a girl friend and living like everybody else lives?"

But Johnny's deep brown eyes remained serious, and he said, "Coming up here has been a great opportunity to learn something so that I will be able to do good work when I get back. Everybody down there does not get such a chance."

Well, Britten thought, that's how it had been with him at first. Now he could think of nothing but walking arm in arm with a pretty girl—*his* girl—down the street of a big city at night, drinking in the excitement, the feeling of being with other people among the bright lights, under a sky that would be dark blue instead of black, that might have clouds in it, that might even send down rain, instead of being the stark changeless interstellar space that existed up above.

Scientists aren't supposed to have thoughts like these. But Britten was young, he was homesick, and he was bored. A young, homesick scientist cannot remain a solemn, dedicated, single-minded scientist.

The next day at work he absentmindedly switched on some pieces of apparatus in the wrong order and burned out a minor piece of electronics.

"Damn it, Britten," Professor Glover shouted at him. "Where are your brains? Replacements are expensive up here. Time is expensive!"

Britten began shaking with rage. Words rushed to his tongue which he choked down unsaid because Glover had the power of life or death over his degree and these two years must not be torn out of his life for nothing. "I'm sorry," he said, in an unsteady voice. "I guess I'm not all here today. It won't take long to repair the damage."

"Never mind," Glover said. "You're coming off the project, anyway."

Britten stood still. The anger roared back into his head.

"I'm coming off the project? What happens to the year I've just spent?"

Glover suddenly seemed more embarrassed than angry.

"I'm sorry, Britten," he said, "but it's for your own good. This project has just become classified and you'd never get a publishable thesis out of it."

Britten stood there looking at Glover. "This is a hell of a time to tell me," he exploded, finally. "What's become so secret about this experiment?"

"Obviously, I can't tell you. I'm sorry, but we'll make it up to you somehow. We'll think of something you can do while you're here, and if necessary you can stay a little longer."

Stay longer! Outraged, Britten fled to his room. It was all he could do to stick out the remainder of his two years.

He could not sleep that night. Little teeth of anger nibbled into his mind, while the basic question repeated itself in endless circles. Why had his experiment been pulled out from under him?

Fundamental experiments in high-energy particle physics were not generally classified secret. What were they doing which had suddenly become so important?

The general purpose of the space laboratory was to gather basic information about the laws of nature. The optical telescopes studied the planets as well as the farthest nebulae, unimpeded by atmospheric disturbances. The tremendous twenty-five-mile-diameter radio-telescope pinpointed short-wave radio vibrations from all parts of space. The solid-state group could study the properties of matter in a vacuum chamber of rarity unattainable anywhere on Earth.

In Jim Britten's group, known variously as the Elementary Particle Division, the Lunatron group, or simply as the Lunatics, the topic of investigation was the meson. A long time ago people had considered atoms the most elementary particles. Then they found out about protons and neutrons, which were the bricks that made up the atomic nuclei. A little later, when scientists learned how to build atom smashers such as the two-billion-volt proton synchrotron, they found that they could knock mesons out of the nucleus, and they decided that the protons and neutrons were not so simple after all.

Year after year the atom smashers had become bigger and bigger. There came a time when they could not be built on the surface of the Earth any longer, so a space laboratory was conceived, built around the doughnut of the ten-thousand-billion-volt proton synchrotron. Protons, whirling around for thousands of cycles in this vast doughnut, eighty miles in circumference, could acquire energies equal to those of the most powerful cosmic rays. Even mesons shattered at this energy.

By inspecting the remnants of these broken mesons, scientists could begin to get some idea as to the ultimate structure of matter and energy.

Now, Jim Britten thought, what was there about this work that should suddenly become too secret to be published? Peace had reigned on Earth for many years, and it was once more fashionable to think of science as being free and unbound by security regulations.

But not, apparently, here in Glover's private domain. Rephrase the question, Britten thought. What was there about this work which had suddenly made it desirable for Professor Glover to take Britten off the project? Was there more to this experiment than Britten had seen up to the present?

Sitting through the night, Britten thought and calculated, filling his desk top with paper, feeling the frustration of a scientist who spends day after day with the details of an experiment, pushing buttons, reading meters, soldering wires, until he begins to lose sight of the ultimate aim of the project.

As he fell asleep, long towards morning, his anger was still at a furious temperature, filling his mind with dreams of a tormented, violent nature, which he forgot promptly upon awakening.

Professor Glover stopped by to see him as he ate a late breakfast.

"We have a job to do today," Glover said, his voice tinged with an impersonal annoyance that was not directed at Britten.

Britten stared up at Glover with a hostility that made no impression upon the scientist.

"The ion source has gone bad and has to be replaced," Glover continued. "The spacesuits are being readied in the airlock."

"Why us?" Britten complained. "What's the matter with the maintenance crew?"

Glover's frown deepened. "They're busy with other things. You're free for the moment, and so am I."

Then his face cleared, and he slapped Britten on the back.

"Come on, fella, snap out of it. It'll do us both good to put on the suits and get out in free space."

Britten uttered grumbling noises about "A guy can't even finish a cup of coffee," and followed Glover out to the maintenance lock nearest the ion source.

As he climbed out of the airlock, there again came the sensation of vertigo which he felt every time he stood on this island suspended in nothingness. The circumference of the doughnut stretched its great arc away from him in both directions, while twelve miles away, at the center of the circle, was the spherical shape of the radiotelescope receiver. The long, slender girders which bound the station together had a fragile, spidery appearance.

Britten and Glover walked clumsily to the linear accelerator which projected one-billion-volt protons into the initial lap of their long journey around the doughnut. At the far end of the hundred-foot tube, within a shielded chamber, was the glass bottle of the ion source. Normally, a brilliant crimson flame glowed within this bottle as numberless protons were stripped from their electrons, to be hurled down the accelerator tube. Now there was nothing but the blackened, dead glass.

As they approached the chamber that surrounded the ion source, Britten found that the resentment left over from the previous night had a new object upon which to fasten. Why should he be doing the work that belonged to the technicians? In his anger he lost sight of the fact that Professor Glover was out there doing the same thing.

Damned slave-labor, he thought. A Ph.D. candidate was at the bottom of the heap, the lowest form of existence, pushed around by everybody else. Glover thought he was being clever, pushing him off the project, making excuses about security, when probably his aim was to keep for himself the Nobel Prize that the experiment was going to receive some day. Thought he could keep his poor stupid student in the dark about the outcome of the experiment but the poor student wasn't as stupid he thought.

Glover reached the hatch that opened into the ion source chamber and started undoing the fastenings. Suddenly he turned and stared at Britten.

"Where's the new ion source?" he snapped. "Don't tell me you left it in the airlock!"

Britten stammered wordlessly, shocked out of his reverie.

"Well, of all the stupid—Go back and get it! I'll remove the old source."

Glover turned his back and continued to unfasten the hatch. Rage came into full bloom instantly. Without an instant's thought, Britten reached out both hands, wrenched the antenna rod from Glover's back, tore his anchoring lines from their snaps, and pushed the struggling body out into space, where it soon dwindled away into a tiny speck.

II

DR. MORRIS Wolf leaned back in his chair after Jim Britten was wheeled, asleep, from the therapy room. In a random fashion he let his mind wander over the story he had just heard, savoring not only the facts, but the feelings behind them and the intuitions which they built up in his own mind.

"Well, Alma, what do you think?" he said, swiveling his chair to look at the other doctor across his desk.

She hesitated. "The story seems satisfactory, up to a point. That is, we've broken through the memory block and have determined that Glover's death was not really an accident—which of course we suspected all along. And we have a motive—of a sort."

Wolf sighed. "Yes—the motive. The boy feels that Glover is cutting him out of the credit for an important experiment, so in a burst of anger he disposes of the professor. There are just two things that bother me about that. Look."

He switched on his desk projector and ran through the microfilm card of Britten's record until he came to the examinations which Britten had taken to get the post on the space station.

"Here we have the standard Jameson test for paranoid personality. Obviously an important item in an examination of this sort. You wouldn't send even an incipient paranoid into close quarters with a group of people for two years. And so in the case of Jim Britten the Jameson test gives a negative result—no evidence of any paranoia, and in fact no evidence of any neurosis except the drive to do research."

Alma Heller lit a cigarette thoughtfully. "I see. No paranoia predicted, yet the story he tells us now is a typical textbook example of persecution psychosis. Of course . . ." She paused for a moment. "He might be making up this story to hide his real motive."

Wolf shook his head vigorously. "No dice. Not under deep therapy. He has to tell us the truth."

"So we have a paradox." Dr. Heller's methodical mind ticked off the possibilities systematically. "Either the early exam was wrong, in which case he was paranoid all the time, or the exam was right and he turned paranoid later. Neither of which things are supposed to happen."

"Or," Wolf presented the third possibility, "he is withholding information while in deep therapy. Also something that is not supposed to happen. So this leads us to the second point that bothers me. Britten talks about sitting up all night trying to figure out what his experiment was leading to. Yet he never mentioned what conclusion he came to. Apparently this is a crucial point which is buried in his mind so deeply that we didn't touch it with our first try."

"Could be." Alma Heller seemed skeptical. "There are a lot of very iffy questions running around in my head which could be settled simply if we could get some concrete information. Do you think you could buzz the AEC and ask them why Britten's project became classified? That would settle a number of obscure points and at the same time give us a handle with which to pry Jim open a little more."

Wolf shrugged. "We might get our heads chopped off, but we can try. My contact at the AEC is Charles Wilford. He's the one who was so anxious to know what Britten did the night of the 15th. Maybe he can trade us some information."

Wolf pushed the button for an outside line and asked for the Atomic Energy Commission, extension 5972. Wilford's image appeared on the phone screen, the picture of a large, powerful face with a great mass of gray hair.

Wolf knew him only as someone high up in the personnel department of the AEC.

"Good morning, Dr. Wolf," he said. "Find anything out?"

Wolf shrugged. "Britten killed Glover, if that's what you want to know. But why? That's what really interests us. You can tell us one thing that will help us find out. And that is—did Glover really take Britten off his project for security reasons? If so, what were those reasons?"

Wilford's face froze slightly. "Obviously, Dr. Wolf, if security were involved, it is a matter I cannot discuss with you, especially over the phone. You may write me a full, confidential report, and we will consider what is to be done."

Wolf cut the connection in exasperation and pushed his chair away from the desk.

"Well, there's a bureaucratic mind for you!" he exclaimed. "He wants a problem solved and then refuses to give you the information necessary to solve the problem."

Slowly he filled his thinking pipe and lit it. "The hell with them," he said, finally. "We'll see this thing through ourselves. We'll have another session with Britten tomorrow and get to the bottom of his story."

"I hope," Alma Heller added, "that there is a bottom to be found."

As the attendants strapped Jim Britten on the table the next morning, Dr. Wolf thought how often the formula for murder repeated itself in this psychiatric age. Knock off the victim, prepare a real sick motive, and be sure you'll go to a hospital for treatment, to be released after a cure. Under these circumstances the psychiatrist must become a detective—required to dig deep for the real motive, which generally resolved itself into the classical ones of love-hate-money.

From his point of view as a doctor, any murder was a sick act, but the authorities were interested only in the legal question of whether the murderer knew what he was doing, and why.

In this case, the question of the motive had a fascination to Wolf even from a purely academic point of view.

"Let's face it," he told Britten. "We both know you killed Glover. You've heard the playback of yesterday's session, so you can no longer fall back on the old excuse of 'everything went black and when I came to he was dead.' Nobody gets away with that any more."

Britten maintained a sullen silence.

"Just for the record," Wolf continued, "I want to fill in an important gap in the story. You told us that you sat up half the night figuring out what discovery your experiment was aiming at, but you glossed over what you actually decided at that time. Suppose we return to that night and go over the story once more in a little more detail."

Britten continued his silence, and beyond a single hostile glare from beneath half-lidded eyes, gave no expression of emotion. Wolf, as he checked the connections and slipped Britten the hypodermic was thankful that his technique did not depend upon a friendly rapport between doctor and patient.

Presently Britten began to talk.

"You're being taken off the project because it has become classified secret," Glover had said, and at a blow an entire year of work had been struck out from beneath Jim Britten's feet. As he sat in his room, he picked raucous chords on his guitar and allowed the anger to wash deliciously through his consciousness.

Not for a minute did he believe the security classification story. He knew that the project was beginning to strike gold in an unexpected direction, and he knew what that direction was.

There was a discovery in the making. A discovery so precious that for every diamond-like star out there beyond the porthole there could be a bucket of diamonds accruing to the discoverer.

And Glover was after the profit himself, pushing Britten out of the way. This was the thought that clawed little furrows in his mind. Then, pushing their way into those little furrows came other thoughts such as: "Suppose Glover should have an accident. I'd have his notebooks, and . . ."

Then he began thinking of returning to Earth, and the vision of spending a life dedicated to research in a laboratory became clouded over; instead there arose a picture of himself riding in an expensive car, with beautiful, expensive women.

He ripped a full chord out of his guitar and began to sing.

In the morning, Glover stopped at Britten's breakfast table, annoyed with word of the ion-source burnout.

"Now how are we going to get it fixed?" he demanded, in exasperation. "Gamp cut his hand yesterday, Williams had his appendix out a week ago, Langsdorf is busy with the kicksorter, and—"

"Why don't we do it ourselves?" Britten interrupted, eagerly. "It'll do us good to get into spacesuits again."

It would do Jim Britten some good, he thought to himself. If genius was measured by the ability to spot an opportunity, then his success was assured. The plan of action was in his mind, completely formed in that instant.

On the outer skin of the satellite, the two of them alone, any one of a number of accidents could occur. Holding them down against the pull of centrifugal force would be only the magnetic shoes and a thin line. From that beginning, his mind went precisely to its conclusion.

"Alma," Morris Wolf said, "I'm beginning to feel very uneasy. What do we have here?"

He poured coffee into the cups on his desk.

Alma Heller looked at him shrewdly, and stirred sugar into her cup.

"I think we have a bear by the tail," she said. "We seem to peel off layers of Jim Britten's mind, and each time there's something different underneath. Every time he tells his story there is something new and contradictory in it. And there is no clue as to whether he is getting nearer or farther from the truth."

Wolf swivelled his chair around and stared out of the window onto the hospital lawn. "We thought that the deep therapy method was something perfect. Something that would make a patient tell the absolute truth as he saw it. But our patient is making hash out of it."

He lifted his coffee cup and tasted the black liquid tentatively.

"Follow it through. The first story he gave us was conscious. He said he couldn't remember exactly what happened to him. Okay. This could be a fabrication. The next story he gave under therapy conditions. He said that he killed Glover in a fit of rage because of an argument. Okay again. We could have accepted that at face value, and he would have gotten away with it, except that we got curious about a couple of things. We wondered how the paranoid tinge got into his thoughts, and we wondered exactly what it was that he and Glover were on the verge of discovering. So we tried again. Now we find that he deliberately plotted to kill Glover, and the paranoid symptoms are now so intense that he gives us a completely phony story about making millions of dollars out of the discovery, when everybody knows that you can't patent anything for personal profit when you invent it in a government laboratory."

Alma Heller lifted her hand, making a one with her forefinger. "So our friend Jim Britten is doing two things—both of which we did not believe him capable of doing. First, he is lying and inventing stories under deep therapy. Second, he is withholding information. For notice that he is still avoiding specific mention of the result which his experiment was aiming at."

Her voice became flat, precise, and probing.

"Now, could our young physicist, Jim Britten, do this thing? No. Not unless he is an unsuspected superman type. Or—unless he has had special training and conditioning for resistance against deep therapy. How does a young physics student obtain such training? And where?"

She looked across the desk at Morris Wolf, who chewed savagely on his pipe bit.

"If I had any sense," he growled, "I'd call up the AEC and throw Jim Britten right back in their faces. If they give me a problem to solve they should at least tell me how hot they think it is. And my viscera are beginning to tell me that this is going to be a very, very warm baby. Maybe I should holler for help. I have a wife and two kids at home. I don't want to get hurt."

"Who are you kidding?" Alma wanted to know. "You wouldn't let a juicy problem like this escape you just when you have it clutched about the middle. Besides, our two undercover friends from the FBI will be keeping their eyes on things. Let them earn their pay."

"Okay." Wolf came to a decision. "We'll give it one more try, and then we'll call for help. First thing tomorrow morning. In the meantime, there are two things I want. First I want Britten to have a complete physical examination. The works. Inside and outside. Blood tests, electro-encephalograph, tissue specimens, complete x-rays—everything they can think of. Then I'll spend tonight keeping company with Britten while the technicians pull down some overtime pay analyzing the examination results."

"You have an idea?"

He nodded. "At least one idea. But it needs feeding."

That evening Morris Wolf walked down the hospital corridor past the door of Britten's room. He entered the next door and found himself in a tiny chamber already occupied by Bill Grady. This was no surprise, for he knew that Grady and Jones kept Britten under constant surveillance. He motioned for Grady to keep his seat, and made himself comfortable in another chair, which he placed so that he could watch Britten through the one-way window set in the wall. Through this window he could see every move which Britten made, and through a loudspeaker he could hear every sound.

It was not clear in Wolf's mind precisely what he expected to find by watching Britten but he knew that if he was to unravel his puzzle, he must know everything about the boy, including the way he walked and talked and combed his hair.

For a time Britten sat and read, then paced the floor restlessly, as if waiting for something. Finally he picked his guitar up from the bed and sat down on his chair, tuning the instrument. When he began to sing, it was quietly, as though to himself. Wolf had heard him sing before, generally folk songs from the Southern and Midwestern states.

Now there intruded into Wolf's mind a thought which had previously been on the edge of consciousness and simultaneously his hand reached out to touch the start button on his tape recorder. The manner in which a person sings should reveal a great deal about his early life—about the kind of language he grew up with, down to the very vocal structure which has developed in his body since childhood.

As a result there are many types of voices: French voices, Tennessee voices, Italian voices, Texas voices, each with its own flavor caused by the way in which the vocal muscles have been trained by the native language, and also by the way in which people are accustomed to singing in those places.

When Wolf went home that night he carried a tape of Britten's song with him. It was convenient that he did not have to go far for an expert opinion to corroborate what he had already decided as an amateur.

He entered his house, the pleasant place with the warm colors, the rows of books, the grand piano, and of course his wife.

"Sorry I had to stay late, dear, but there's something important going on. Something really important. And you can be a big help to me right now."

"Me?" asked Lynne. "You're going back to musical therapy?"

"Not exactly," he said, dryly. "More like musical detection. I'm going to play a tape recording of a song or two, and I want your professional opinion as to what part of the world the singer came from."

He walked over to the recorder and began threading the tape.

"Now pay no attention to the song itself," he instructed. "I'm interested only in the voice quality."

The tape spool unrolled slowly, and Britten's voice filled the room.

"Not bad for an amateur," Lynne commented, listening closely. For several minutes she remained silent, until finally the tape was completed.

"Well," she said, finally, "I don't think it's an American. A bit too rich. It doesn't have the French quality, nor the Italian. More chesty, kind of ripe and fruity. Central European, Hungarian, Russian, or something of that order." Wolf kissed her solemnly.

"You win first prize, girl. That's the answer I wanted, and that's the answer that fits."

III

IN THE MORNING, the act of going to the hospital produced within him a sensation as of marching to the front line of battle.

Whitehead, the laboratory chief, was prowling about his office when he arrived.

"Morning," Wolf greeted him. "Got something for me?"

"I have a strangeness," Whitehead said. "A very great strangeness."

"We all do," Wolf replied. "What's yours?"

"This Britten of yours. How old is he?"

"By appearance, and according to the records, about twenty-one."

Uh-huh. And by cellular structure and metabolism he is least forty!"

"So."

Wolf sank down in his chair and cocked an eye at Alma Heller, who came into the room that moment.

"Did you hear that, Alma? In more ways than one our boy isn't what he seems to be. By last night I was certain that he is not a native of Louisville Kentucky. Now we are told that he is twice as old as we thought he was."

Alma stared for a moment.

"We do seem to get in deeper and deeper. Have any ideas?"

Wolf ran his hand worriedly through his hair. "One. But I'm afraid of it. At any rate, we're in too far to back out. This morning we're going to dig for more information, and we're not going to stop until we have Britten squeezed dry."

He reached onto his desk for his tobacco can and began filling a pipe, meanwhile organizing his thoughts.

"Somehow or other," he resumed, "Britten has received conditioning to resist giving information under deep therapy."

"And not only that," Alma interposed, "but he has the ability to retain consciousness under deep therapy and fabricate a story to replace the true facts."

"Correct. So, since the ordinary deep therapy method is useless, we have to get tough. We have to eliminate his present set of conditioned reactions and replace them by a new set. In other words, we must reset the controls so that he responds to a new set of orders."

Alma pursed her lips for a soundless whistle. "Fisher's method! Do you know how much of that a nervous system can take?"

Wolf shrugged. "Who knows? This is very new stuff. I've played around with a little of it, but . . . who knows? At any rate, we're going to assume that Britten has a fairly tough mind in order to get as far as he has. We'll assume this not only for his own sake, but for ours, because we are going to shake him loose from his present set of memories, and we want enough of his original memories left for us to assemble. Now suppose we begin."

Whitehead excused himself. There was work waiting in his laboratory, he said, and watched wistfully as the two disappeared into the therapy room.

Alma began switching on the apparatus, while Wolf called for Jim Britten to be brought in.

"Still going digging in my mind?" Britten wisecracked as he walked in, flanked by the ubiquitous Grady and Jones.

"With a steam shovel," Wolf replied, and motioned that Britten be strapped onto the table.

This time Wolf wasted no explanations. Without pausing he

slipped Britten a preliminary shot and began fitting electrodes onto his head and arms.

"We're going back a long time, now," he said, quietly. "Remember back to the days before you started college. How old are you?"

Britten began dreaming off. "Sixteen years old. It was a hot summer. Kentucky in summer. Hot. Hot as a solar cycle . . . hot as a bicycle down the road . . . a tricycle down the toad . . . doctor you look like a big pimply warty green-eyed toad."

Morris Wolf waited until the drug-induced schizophrenic symptoms were well under way, then motioned for Alma Heller to send a sequence of high-frequency pulses through Britten's nervous system, breaking down synapses and destroying memory patterns. This, in combination with the drug, was intended to clear the mind of memories involving the period of time to which Britten's attention had been directed. In this period, Wolf guessed, the conditioning had taken place. If not, then he must try another period. Britten's body stiffened under the onslaught and perspiration rolled out on his brow. His mouth twisted and his eyebrows writhed. Morris Wolf himself felt perspiration starting out on his face, while in the back of the room the two "attendants" stared in amazement.

After enough time of this, Wolf switched the controls so that a rhythmic pattern of pulses went through Britten's system in such a manner as to aid the triggering of synapses and the formation of memory patterns. The slate having been wiped clean, new writing had to be placed on it.

"Now," he said, tensely, leaning over the patient and speaking close to his ears. "Cooperation means obey. Cooperation means obey. Cooperation means you do what I say. Cooperation means you do what I tell you to do, say what I tell you to say, remember what I tell you to remember. Cooperation is the key word."

The words went from Wolf's mouth to Britten's ears in the form of sound waves, were converted into neuro-electrical impulses, and under the influence of the rhythmically repeating pulses, from the machine, circulated around and around through Britten's system, tracing a deeply etched path.

Finally Wolf ceased the talking, and Alma handed him a needle with the antidote to the first drug.

"Now we see how successful we are," he said.

He gave the shot and several minutes went by while they waited for it to take effect. They remained silent, as though to say a word would break the spell.

Then: "Cooperation," Wolf said.

Britten lay still.

"Open your eyes." Britten's eyelids struggled open, but the eyes stared.

Wolf thought: what question is most basic?

Then he asked: "What is your name?"

The mouth writhed, and whispered, *"Pyotr Fermineyev."*

There was a small roaring in Morris Wolf's ears, and beside him he heard the intake of Alma Heller's breath. The FBI agents Grady and Jones, had moved until they were leaning over Wolf's shoulder.

Then: "Where were you born?"

Again the whisper from blank face: "In Leningrad."

Then: "Who sent you to America?"

"The Society for the Restoration of the Revolution."

"What is the nature of this organization?"

"It is an underground group pledged to return the Soviet Union to its status as the leader of the world revolution and to overthrow the present appeasers of the capitalist governments."

Wolf glowed with triumph. "Get that, Alma?" he gloated, and he turned around half way and winked at the two men behind him.

Alma Heller shook a strand of hair back from her eyes. "The fanatical revolutionaries—now they're trying to overthrow their own government because the Soviet is too friendly to the Western governments!"

"This is no comic underground," Wolf said. "There are big people in it who know how to do things that we're just barely starting to learn about."

He paused, and considered his next questions. The time had come to dig in.

He phrased his query: "What was your task on the satellite?"

Britten's face writhed. Perspiration rolled down his cheeks in a steady stream. Obviously some of the original conditioning remained, causing interference with Wolf's orders.

Alma Heller's knuckles showed white and her clenched hands trembled. The FBI agents inched forward, their bodies stiff with impatience.

Between hard breaths the words came: ". . . was on the satellite to watch . . . new developments in nuclear power . . . complete conversion . . . matter to energy . . ."

Understanding grew in Wolf's mind with a brilliant glare. Glover had been on the verge of taming the ultimate source of energy—the total and complete conversion of matter—a source of power over 130 times more potent than the hydrogen-helium reaction. No wonder the project had been put under wraps!

"So you killed Glover to prevent him from continuing his work. What did you intend to gain by that? Somebody else will take it over.

How are you going to develop this power source yourself?"

Britten groaned audibly. His back arched and his arms strained against the table straps.

Through clenched teeth: "Ruppert . . . next man in line for Glover's job . . . one of us."

Wolf's eyes opened wide, and he whirled to the telephone.

"I'm calling Washington—" he began, then stopped in horror.

Behind him, Britten's voice said, in a strangely firm tone: *"Now is the time."*

Wolf whirled again. He saw Britten, still strapped to the table, his eyes unglazed, and his facial expression commanding.

The FBI men had stiffened, and were standing in place, motionless.

"Cover them, and untie me," Britten rapped out, in a voice that was greatly different from the youthful, uncertain tone he had previously used.

Grady pulled his gun, backed Wolf and Alma Heller against the wall, while Jones loosened Britten's straps.

"So you're one of them, too, Grady," Wolf growled. "And you, Jones. May you burn in hell."

"Don't malign them," said Britten, sitting up and rubbing his arms. "They are good, loyal G-men. But they sat outside my door too long, and now they do what I tell them to do."

Wolf narrowed his eyes and stared at Britten. "Just what are you?" he demanded.

Britten met his gaze, bleakly, and ignored the question.

"We have a rendezvous to make. The two of you will escort me to a helicopter that Grady will order. I need not repeat that we are prepared to blast our way out of this place. You'll save lives all around by being as inconspicuous as possible."

He indicated that Wolf and Alma Heller would go ahead, while the two agents took up the rear. Out in the main corridor they merged into the confused traffic of the busy hospital, two doctors and two attendants conducting a patient out.

Grady took the controls of the helicopter that waited for them out on the parking lot. As they climbed to a high traffic lane, Jones took care of tying the hands of the two doctors behind their seats.

Britten sat beside the pilot, staring through the windshield. "Head due west one hundred miles," he said. "Then I'll give you further directions."

Wolf looked down through the port next to him and felt his heart constrict as he saw houses below grow smaller smaller. One of those houses was his; there was a small figure beside it that could have been his little boy. That was the thought that set his heart beating violently and the adrenalin pumping swiftly through his veins. For himself he didn't care so much, but his son needed a father to come home.

He looked at Alma sitting beside him, her face pale and frightened. He wondered how much time there was before the rendezvous. For this was all the time he had. Beyond that were many unknown factors to consider.

He leaned over sideways.

"Alma," he said, in a voice not loud enough to carry over the roar of the motor. "Tell me exactly what happened when Britten said, 'Now is the time.' My back was turned then. Just what did he look like?"

Alma swallowed. She composed her face and turned her thoughts inward, remembering.

"There was a sudden change," she said. "One moment he was in the trance state, the next moment he was fully aware of his surroundings and in charge of the situation. As though he received a signal at that instant."

A signal, Wolf thought. From where? The implication was shocking.

Look at what we have, he continued to himself. Britten comes to me, under conditioning, ready to act out his part to the hilt. We question him under deep hypnotherapy and he comes forth with a plausible story. We might have stopped right there, but we got curious and began to ask more questions. He brings out another story. Why? Obviously, red herrings to confuse the issue. To stall for time. We apply more pressure, blank out his original conditioning so that he gives us straight answers to questions, and we are getting along fine. Then, suddenly he snaps out of it and into his original, pre-Britten character, all forty years of him. Therefore there must have been another, deeper level to the control over his mind which we did not even touch. A level activated by a new signal which we did not even detect, a signal which came at a crucial time.

"Now is the time" meant that the stalling was over, that the preparations for Britten's escape were completed.

There were still questions to be answered, many blank spaces to be filled in, but at the present instant there was only one question that mattered. The treatment which Wolf had given Britten—had it been at all effective? Was it still effective?

There was one way to find out.

Morris Wolf leaned forward and called in a loud voice: *"Pyotr Fermineyev!"*

The man's head snapped around.

"Cooperation is the key word!" Wolf shouted.

Confusion passed over Britten's face as conflict once more knotted his nervous system.

Wolf threw his second punch immediately. "Tell Jones to cut me loose," he demanded.

"Cut him loose," Britten echoed, in bewilderment.

After an interminable interval, Jones laid down his gun, found his knife, opened it, and slashed the cords from Wolf's arms. Wolf's muscles were already tensed. He snatched Jones gun, lurched forward, and even as Britten's mouth opened to countermand his order, he slugged Britten with the butt of the pistol, hitting him viciously and hard until he lay unconscious on the floor.

Then he said to Grady, "You'd better get us back to the hospital," keeping the gun in his hand.

But Grady and Jones made no trouble. With Britten out of the picture they obeyed the one obviously in command. Poor boys, Wolf thought. Now they were in need of therapy.

As the hospital hove into view, he said to Alma Heller, "We have just seen the real beginning of psychological warfare. Where it took us a whole roomful of equipment to condition Britten's responses to a trigger word, he was able to do it to Jones and Brady single-handed. His method is something we'd like to know. But more than that, Britten himself was conditioned to respond to a signal unknown to us and undetected by us. My God, it could only have been telepathic!"

Alma Heller's eyes closed for a moment.

"I think," she said, "That psychiatrists are going to reach the same position that physicists did during World War II."

Morris Wolf looked dourly out of the window, watching the hospital balloon up under the helicopter.

"That's the most unpleasant thing anybody has said all day," he replied.

GETTING TOGETHER

LIFTED TOWARD THE ceiling by a score of hands, Onestone felt as though he were standing on his head prior to rocketing toward outer space. When they gently laid him on the floor he felt sorry that the experience was over.

"Oh, wow," he finally said. Then he lay still for a while.

"You see," Jay Foreman said gently. "We can be trusted. We could bear your weight and we didn't drop you."

"That is true." Onestone bent his waist and sat up. "But can I extrapolate to the future? What happens when I leave this group? It will be the same on the outside as it was before. They'll still hate me."

"I'm so exasperated I could scream," sputtered a big woman called Jennie, whose full breasts hid behind a long veil of black hair.

"So scream," said Onestone.

She screamed. "There, that's better," she finally gasped. "But you're still exasperating. You use words that are too big. You intellectualize all the time. You put me off with that cold, cold voice of yours."

"What do you want from someone with my background?" he asked bitterly.

"Hey!" Hairy Bill rose to his knees. The front of his body was a shag of black from his full beard down. "Old Onestone practically sounded bitter. Maybe he's getting somewhere."

"Yeah, he used some feeling there."

"A little honest emotion."

An excited jabber circled the group and crashed onto Onestone, who sat on the mat in the center.

"How would you like to do some role-playing?" suggested Jay Foreman. "You be the son and Bill here will be the father. Come on, Bill, get in the middle and sit facing Onestone. Let's try to get a father-son thing going."

Bill crawled over and squatted. "Hello, son," he said, affecting a kindly voice while trying to suppress a feeling of ridiculousness. "How was school today?"

"Okay, Dad."

May, a tall blonde, tittered. The whole scene was so weird!

"We learned inversion of matrices today," Onestone plunged on bravely. "I can't wait for us to do things together, like going to the Computer Center. Gee, it's great to have a father."

"Look, son, you have your head too much inside the console. You should get out more and play with the other kids on the block."

Onestone slumped. "That wouldn't be any good. They wouldn't play with me. I'm too different. I'd beat them at chess all the time and—"

"That's the trouble," Bill shouted. "I say play with the kids and you say chess. All you think about is your head. You have a body, too. Become aware of it. Don't you have feelings in your body?"

"Why, sure. I can feel temperatures with my right index finger and voltages with my left. I can feel how far my elbows and knees are bent. And orientation—up and down, north and south."

"But—" There was an interruption from Bald Bill, the football player, two meters tall and roughly as wide, completely devoid of hair from top to bottom. "If somebody tackled you across the knees you wouldn't feel a thing. And he'd probably break his neck. Just how strong are you, anyway?"

Onestone shrugged. "Compared to humans, I have no idea. What does it matter?"

"One thing you don't know about humans," Bald Bill told him, "is that they are always comparing each other. Always measuring and testing. I see a strong guy, I want to know if he is stronger than I am."

He stared a challenge into Onestone's face.

Jay Forman shuttled his eyes back and forth between the two. "We can settle it with some arm-wrestling," he suggested. "You don't have to if you don't want to, Onestone, but remember that one of the things we are trying to deal with here is your lack of aggression and inability to feel anger. Arm-wrestling is a nonviolent way of combat, a test of strength and will."

"But I don't know about fighting. What if I hurt him?"

"You can't hurt him with arm-wrestling," Jay explained patiently. "Look, you lie down facing each other, put elbows together and then you try to push his arm down flat on the mat."

Bald Bill flattened himself into position and raised his arm from the elbow. "Come on, you brainy son of a bitch, let's see what you can do."

Onestone, still on his knees, looked around the group, wanting someone to intervene.

"Why does he insult me like that? I was conditioned never to be hostile to humans."

"Oh, you dumb ape," Hairy Bill groaned. "You still don't understand what the score is. You're so damn inhibited you can't feel hate, love, anger. How do you expect to be accepted as a human being? You have to learn to feel human emotions."

"Come on, you obscene artifact," Bald Bill taunted deliberately, reaching out his hand. "You can't hurt me, you stupid automation."

Stung, Onestone drew back. Words could hurt, after all. Somewhere inside him pain glimmered dimly. "All right, you dumb athlete," he muttered, and got down on the mat.

The two locked hands and stared into each other's eyes. The dim light from the lamp in the corner glistened coldly on Onestone's stainless skin. Bulk for bulk he and Bald Bill were evenly matched, but the construction was different. Onestone's surface was polished, smooth as a Brancusi sculpture. Bald Bill's skin glowed a fine pink; hard muscles, tensed for the combat, rippled under the thin surface.

"Go!" Foreman started it. Instantly Bald Bill's face flushed crimson and the veins on his forehead popped out like writhing worms. His shoulder muscles stood out rigidly as his eyes drilled all the way into his opponent's.

The sudden violence of the attack caught Onestone by surprise. His arm was halfway to the floor before his torque adjusted to counter the motion. Bald Bill dug in and searched within himself for another measure of power to complete the job, but to his amazement he felt his arm relentlessly forced back to the vertical and over. His face twisted. Sweat ran from his body. A growl rasped from his throat.

Inside Onestone strange new feelings stirred—anger in response to the growl, excitement at the close body contact, determination to dominate. He advanced his torque another notch and closed the gap to the floor. Bald Bill collapsed, panting.

Onestone lay motionless, sorting out the torrent of new sensations. Joy at winning a contest. Affection for a defeated opponent. Sorrow for the vanquished.

"Where are you now?" Jay Foreman asked, softly.

"I really felt something there. I felt something that wasn't just solving problems or doing logic. It could not be expressed as numbers, forms, equations, or colors. The sensation was unpleasant, but it was exciting."

And for the first time his voice broke out of its monotone and sounded excited.

"Oh, wow!" Marian, a small girl in her late teens, burst violently into tears. "He felt a real emotion. He broke through."

Every one of the ten group members behaved as though a cold wind had blown briefly across his perspiring skin.

Onestone turned to Marian. "But why do you cry?"

"Oh, you dumb contraption," she wailed. "How would you know? Don't you know that we can cry from happiness—or we can cry at perceiving an emotion in another person, from empathy? That's what makes you so frustrating to talk to. We don't get any emotional feedback from you. I'd like to hit you."

She crawled across the mat and proceeded to beat on Onestone's stainless-steel chest with a pair of futile, tiny fists. Suddenly the thought came to Onestone that he would like to embrace Marian with his arms. Startled, she began to draw away. But he gently drew her close and, kneeling on the mat, they remained for a long minute close together.

He thought to himself that his skin ought to be covered with soft padding, and temperature and pressure sensors should be placed under the outer integument so that he might obtain more physical sensation from the close proximity of a human being. But even now, just the thought of the experience was pleasurable.

At a signal from Jay Foreman the rest of the group stood up and formed a circle around the pair. Slowly they drew closer to the center until all ten were in a huddle, nestling Marian and Onestone in a close embrace. As though it had a mind of its own, the group began to sway gently back and forth, remaining that way for a long time.

Finally the time was over and they reluctantly separated, Marian wiping tears from her eyes and Onestone sunk in deep thought.

"This feels like a good place to stop," suggested Jay Foreman. "The hour is late and we have a lot of learning to consolidate. We have seen that feelings are complicated and our responses to them are not always what we might expect on the surface. Onestone, with his flat, schizoid, unemotional manner, generated frustration and anger in everyone else. He has to learn the meaning of feelings and emotions and of course, that is what he is here for."

As the group broke up, most of the members went down to the pool to wash off perspiration and then made for the lounge to sit around drinking and smoking. Unable to enjoy these amusements, Onestone made his way in darkness to a rock overlooking the ocean and watched the starlight bounce off the surf spray. Both his smog and radioactivity sensors showed a clear night. Needing no sleep, he remained where he was for the night, busying himself by trying to reach the end of a complex mathematical calculation that had been troubling him for some time.

As the sun illuminated his back in the morning, Marian approached him and said, "You've done nothing but sit out here all night. And we had so much fun in there."

"I've been enjoying myself. Work is fun—and I've been working. I think I begin to see the solution to an important mathematical problem."

Marian looked around. To her mathematics meant a computer terminal, she did not see a keyboard or screen.

"Oh. You're one of those lucky people who does mathematics in his head. I can hardly add two and two."

"I cheat," Onestone said. "I have a built-in remote connection with a computer unit over there in my car."

Not to mention the radio relay to the central computer utility in San Francisco and a satellite link with the world's most powerful computer at MIT. All available as fast as the speed of light would allow, directly perceived visually and symbolically on a "screen" within his own nervous system.

"Oh," Marian said, as though she understood.

Onestone had learned not to make detailed explanations. The gap between the scientifically educated and the uneducated had grown so wide that there was no way of explaining to a layman what a scientist was doing. Yet Onestone had to learn how to make small talk, to converse about the trivia of everyday life, to understand how people felt about unimportant matters.

"Are you on your way to breakfast?" he asked. "May I join you?"

"Sure. But—uh—you don't eat do you?"

"No," he replied with a touch of wryness. "But I can stop by my room and install a recharged battery."

Marian watched with interest as he snapped the battery cube out of the center of his belly and clicked the fresh one in place.

"That's neat. But I'll bet it doesn't taste as good as eating breakfast. Let's go. I'm starving."

Onestone glanced at her with alarm, but decided that the primary meaning of "starving" did not apply and searched the thesaurus in San Francisco for secondary and tertiary meanings. He still had much to learn about the tongue, having been raised on computer languages and their clarity and logic, and finding the complexities of twenty-second century American not to his liking.

The group session this morning took place on a secluded field where the sun soon burned its way through the sea mist and fell hot on naked backs. Onestone decided he had been the center of attention long enough and sat quietly while a tall thin boy named Ken went through a tale of woe concerning his parents. It seemed to be a typical enough story, fitting in neatly with the thousands of cases Onestone had scanned in the files. Both parents busy, working. When at home father alternated between alcoholic low and hash euphoria. Mother compensated for not taking care of son by gushing affection, alternating with nagging about the boy's sex life.

"Jeez, she was afraid if I didn't get it every day I'd shrivel into a raisin."

"Sounds like she was unconsciously seducing you," suggested Jennie, who had been to many groups and had a good command of the jargon. "Like she wanted some of that action herself."

Onestone despaired of ever getting a real understanding of that aspect of human behavior. He glanced around at the others sitting in the group circle. Their nakedness made the sex differences plain to see—-they were just as pictured in every textbook and tape he had scanned. He knew their purposes anatomically and physiologically, yet the great importance attributed to them by these beings eluded him.

Onestone's own body, smooth and hard, with no characteristics of a biological nature, had a pleasing form and texture. The others, with their hairiness, their softness and pouchiness, were not objectionable to him since he had not been conditioned with prejudices against human bodies. And yet, from what he could hear, the humans did have their own prejudices and irrational responses to their own bodies. So much so that coming together in a group like this with no clothes at all was a highly special occasion charged with great significance and emotion. The entire first day of the group had been devoted to discussing their feelings of strangeness, embarrassment, nervousness while he, Onestone, could only conjure up the usual mild curiosity he acquired in a new situation, since he had actually never before seen naked human beings.

His attention reverted to the center of the group, where Foreman had set up a psychodrama with Ken playing the son and Jennie taking the mother role.

"For Crissake, Mom," Ken was complaining. "Why don't you get off my back? Every night I come home you want to know how I made out. Don't you think that's my own business?"

"Son, you know I'm only doing it for your own good."

"I think you're a dirty old lady. My generation just doesn't think about these things the way you do. We believe in privacy. You're just driving me crazy. You're never home when I need you—and when you are home you keep prying into my affairs and then I never want to see you again. And Dad, he was never there at all. He was just way out. All those times when I really needed somebody—nobody home."

Then came the miracle, the strange episode that never failed to astonish and bewilder Onestone when it unfolded in front of his eyes. Ken's face twisted, his shoulders began to shake and suddenly tears were gushing from his eyes and anguished sobs were bursting from his throat. What kind of unknown manifestations arose from the depths of the nervous system to cause such a reaction? Onestone's early training and conditioning had done nothing to prepare him for this type of affair. He had been trained for logic, for problem-solving. His thoughts were always straightforward, on the surface, with no hidden messages contradicting each other.

But with these human beings, messages were always on two or three levels—what they said and what they meant were always different things. If the mother really loved her child why did she behave in such a way as to make him unhappy? There must be some fundamental reasons for these paradoxes. He could refer to the library files in San Francisco for the latest research on the subject, but he had agreed to stay out of the library during the group sessions, for he had to learn from the humans in the group directly and experientially.

To understand these human beings meant to learn the hidden communications, to infer the secret meanings from subtle clues, to make guesses about the thoughts going on in their minds—for there was no way of getting at these thoughts directly. No telepathy, no ESP, no vibrations.

While making these conjectures he continued to focus on Ken's narration, forced out between sobs.

"—and when they were home together there was all the arguing and fighting and I just didn't want to stay home and I hated them— but I couldn't leave because I also loved them—"

The manner in which human beings were born and raised to adulthood was simply unbelievable. The agony—what torments parents perpetrated on their children! What was it like, Onestone wondered, to be a child and have a father and a mother? The thought of something soft and warm wandered through his mind, and then. . . .

Onestone felt an incomprehensible scrambling of his thoughts, a sensation as from a high-voltage line in the back of his spine. His arms jerked from side to side and a strange sound issued from his mouth, as though a muted siren were hidden within. His gaze swept frantically around the circle, appealing for help. Ken had stopped weeping and was sitting still, staring at Onestone. Jay Foreman leaned over him, undecided. The rest of the group sat, mouths gaping.

Finally Foreman took Onestone's hands in his and tried to damp down the quivering. Gradually the motion subsided and the wailing died away. Onestone sat for a moment, putting his thoughts in order.

"What did it feel like?" Foreman asked.

"As though my circuits were being tangled with contradictory messages, generating a network instability. It has happened before. This, in fact, is the reason I'm here in the first place."

Jennie, motherly Jennie, leaned forward intently. "You know what I think. I think you were crying."

Both Foreman and Onestone jerked their heads around to stare at Jennie. What she had said sounded incredible—and yet it sounded right.

"Either that," Foreman said, "or you were having some kind of epileptic fit. How do you tell the difference when there are no facial expressions to go by? Tell me, Onestone, what were you thinking about just before it happened?"

"I was listening to Ken and I was wondering what it would be like to have a father and a mother and—"

Suddenly the shaking returned, and Onestone was unable to continue for several minutes.

When Onestone quieted, Foreman said, "You were talking about your reasons for joining this group. Perhaps you'd like to go back to that."

Onestone nodded. "As you know, I am the latest in the line of man-machine interaction computers. I was designed to be a general purpose scientist. Some people would call me a robot. Conceptually my design goes back along two lines. One incorporates the remote console that allows a human operator to interact back and forth with a large computer, using ordinary language. The second features the self-learning computer that can be taught to learn from experienced information and so does not require a human operator to program every move ahead of time. This development led to the computer-controlled interplanetary and interstellar exploration ships.

"As techniques became more sophisticated during the second century of computer development, somebody got the bright idea of making a computer terminal that would not be fixed to a desk, but could walk around and converse with the scientist using it. In that way it could go to meetings, take part in discussions, solve problems on the spot and, in general, behave very much like the surrounding human beings.

"All of which led up to me. Part robot, part computer, a tiny bit human—the part that cries, perhaps. You see, the old-fashioned, science-fiction robot was always limited physically by the volume of space inside his body. It was essentially impossible to put enough machinery and circuits inside that space to perform all the required operations. With me, the problem was solved in a more or less obvious way. You see, I'm not all here. The part you see is the physical mechanism, the short-term memory and some elementary information-processing units. Another part of me is in the trunk of my car, linked to me by radio waves. This unit includes my personal long-term memory and much information processing. The rest of me, in a certain sense, is all over the world, because I am capable of making direct connection to every major computer center. In this way I can make use of all information libraries in existence. Looking at it from that point of view, I have in my memory virtually everything that was ever learned by mankind.

Jay Foreman swore. "My mind boggles."

Onestone wished he could smile. "Actually there are limitations. To recall a given piece of information requires being able to locate it. Either you use an indexed memory or an associative memory. Whichever way you do it takes time. Fortunately, the way I'm built I can send out a call for a given piece of information and then do something else while the processing goes on. I understand human beings can perform in a similar way. You claim there is a word or a name you can't remember. As the saying goes it's on the tip of your tongue. Then, later on, it suddenly pops into your here-and-now processor.

"And so I was born—or at least created—with the most powerful brain in existence. The first several weeks of my life were spent feeding into my personal memory the essential knowledge that I would need. Languages, mathematics, science, a modicum of history. The only people I encountered were my programmers.

"My name, in case you have wondered, was originally Stone-1, since I was the first model of my series developed by the designer Jeremy Stone. However, Onestone seemed easier to pronounce. Furthermore it reminded one of the programmers of another name of historical interest. So in a short time the transposition took place informally.

"After a few weeks of preliminary testing I was introduced to the world of science. The professors and scientists sat around me in an amphitheater. It was like an examination. 'Let's start with something classical,' one of them said. 'Derive the dispersion relation for non-linear plasma waves with two ion species.'

"The solution is not available in closed form, but I can give numerical results,' I replied, causing the computer to project a three-dimensional graph directly onto the readout screen on the front wall of the auditorium. That trick bowled them over, for being linked directly to the computer I did not have to push any buttons or perform any other overt actions.

"From there we went to elementary particle theory, then to the structure of protein molecules and finally to the structure of the human nervous system. Specialists from all these areas were in the hall. When the session was over, Professor Mandelkern got up and said, 'I congratulate you on your erudition. I am sure your career will be distinguished. Right now some of us are going to do one of the two or three things you cannot do. We are going into a neighboring friendly bar and get drunk.' They didn't invite me."

Onestone paused for a moment as he remembered the past.

"You poor kid," Jennie cried in sympathy. "You were the smartest kid on the block and they were all jealous. Nobody warned you to hide some of those brains."

"Nobody really told me anything about getting along with human beings. I had to learn myself. I had no real friends to give me advice. Perhaps I was too intimidating. Perhaps everybody thought I knew everything. But, really, to learn about humans it is necessary to interact with them, to be with them, to be intimate. And there was nobody I could be intimate with.

"I read books. I watched TV plays. Soon I realized that I was missing something in life. Some of the books were very explicit about what it was, but there was nothing I could do.

"Therefore I turned my back on the outside world and remained in the office they gave me at the university. I immersed myself in work, choosing two main fields of specialty to avoid being bored with one topic alone. One was unified field theory, study of the fundamental nature of the forces between objects—a problem still unsolved after hundreds of years of effort. The other was the nature of human consciousness, perhaps the most important scientific problem for humanity, because man's ultimate behavior depends on the mental model he has of his own nature and of his place in the universe.

"Actually the two problems are interrelated. One basic mystery of nature is how we acquire knowledge of the world around us when the only information passing from the outer world into our nervous systems consists of electrical pulses moving from sensory organs into the depths of the brain. From these signals we somehow become conscious of what goes on out there, even to the extent of making models of atoms and smaller particles. My own construction is a step toward the solution of the consciousness problem. For I am a model of a brain. Whether I am a model of a *human* brain is a question still to be answered."

Jay Foreman interrupted. "I feel that you are getting off onto a general philosophical tangent and are avoiding coming to the main issue. You were going to tell us how you happened to come to this group."

Onestone said, simply, "I think I started going insane."

Foreman had an instant vision of an entire new index in the psychological data center entitled Computer Dysfunction, subheading Computer Neurosis, Computer Psychosis and so on. Suppressing this irrelevance, he pressed onward.

"What made you think so?"

"The problems I started working on were difficult. I was naive at the beginning and thought that problems always worked themselves out in a straightforward manner. Then I found out that dealing with problems nobody has ever worked out before requires more than just memory, speed, manipulative ability and so on—the usual things listed under mathematical ability. Also required is the ability to think a thought that nobody ever thought before, to put things together in a new way. Some call it creativity. Others call it associative ability or imagination. It has to do with leaping a gap between known and unknown—guessing at an answer and then testing the guess.

"That is where I had trouble. Apparently here is one area where some humans have greater ability than I have. As a result, there were problems I could not solve. Unfortunately, whoever programmed me installed a tremendous drive in me to solve problems. You might call it a built-in compulsion neurosis. So when I come up against a hard wall with a problem I can't solve and then get pushed from behind by this compulsion, something goes wrong with the circuits and I go into this state of instability and there's nothing I can do to stop it until it dies down by itself.

"As a result, I retreated even more into isolation. I would not even go to meetings. My technicians were in despair. Then one of them came to me—a girl named Marcy. She said she had an idea that my being alone all the time was not good for me and that I should do something, associate more with people. She thought that perhaps group therapy would be of some help.

"The rest, of course, you know. From what Marcy told me and from my other sources of information, I learned of the beginnings of the Human Potential movement in the early years of the twentieth century. Encounter groups, gestalt therapy and the rest. It became a powerful movement toward the end of the twentieth century, was eclipsed for a hundred years as a result of the totalitarian swing of the twenty-first century and was then rediscovered by Vander—"

Onestone suddenly awoke to the fact that he was lecturing again—in fact, he was forcibly reminded of that fact by the rude interruption of little Marian, who piped up with: "Hey, Professor, come on back to the real world. We're not in a history class, you know."

Group leader Jay Foreman leaned forward and spoke intently to Onestone. "Look, I think we're getting down to the important issue now. You know that human beings are raised from infancy in a certain way. Every child has a mother—either real or substitute. And usually a father of some sort is around somewhere. If not, the child is in trouble. From the very first day, interactions between the mother and child imprint certain modes of behavior upon the child. If those ingredients do not come along at the right time the child is thereafter crippled.

"Mother singing lullabies determines future musical tastes. Simple sensory stimulation—fondling, tickling, playing—creates growth in the nervous system. Telling fairy tales stimulates imaginative thinking and—most important the ability to think in terms of high-level abstractions, such as magic, that later may develop into an understanding of science. Your trouble, Onestone, is that you never had a proper childhood. Worst of all, you never had a mother."

At this Jennie burst into sympathetic tears. "No mother, no father, no family warmth. No love. What an empty life."

Foreman's face brightened. "I have an idea. There is a technique called Directed Fantasy that is often effective. Of course—" he shrugged, glancing at Onestone—"how it will work in this situation is anybody's guess. This is really an experiment. But in theory it should kill two birds with one stone. First, it will give you practice in engaging in fantasy, free-floating imagination, visualizing new and strange things—we want to release your creativity. Secondly, in order for you to have a childhood and a mother, you must be born again—and this we can accomplish by means of what we call the directed fantasy.

"Suppose you, Jennie, sit in the middle. Cross your legs. Give us a lap. Now, Onestone, you lie down on you back. Yes, right here. Place your head in Jennie's lap. Hope that's not too heavy for you, Jennie."

"For a mother it's not too heavy," Jennie replied dreamily. She was already far into her fantasy, gazing down fondly on the polished head, smoothing imaginary hair out of its eyes.

"Now, Onestone—" Foreman took a position beside Jennie and stared down intently at the supine robot—"close your eyes and relax. I'm going to start you along a directed fantasy or daydream. When I stop you carry the story along and tell us what you see and feel. You are suspended in a warm, dark place, filled with soft fluid. A heart beats far away, steadily, rhythmically. You are only a single cell, a featureless sphere embedded in a wall of tissue that stretches away on all sides. Along come a swarm of small tadpole creatures, wriggling along the dark tunnel. One of them reaches you, and at that instant it is as though an electric charge polarizes your entire body. The tadpole is swallowed up by your round body."

He paused for a moment. "Visualize that round body. Feel it and its dark, soft, warm surroundings. It is your body. Feel life beginning. Now go on from here."

Onestone lay completely motionless for a time. Finally, as though forced with reluctance, the words started to come.

"I am now two cells, dividing into four. Each division is like a small shock. I keep dividing more and more. There is a spinal cord, an elementary brain, elementary sex organs. I am becoming a small human being, complete with fingers and toes and curly hair. I grow and grow until I fill the crowded space to the bursting point and wonder how much farther it can stretch. I kick my legs and move my arms and hear sounds of voices coming from outside."

Foreman glanced at Jennie and nodded.

"Feel the baby kick inside," she exclaimed. "Oh, he's going to be, a big strong one."

"More sounds are coming from all around. Now I can hear my own heart beating. The warmth and the pressure hold me close. A dark red light comes through my eyelids. There is the sound of music, of someone singing."

Again Foreman glanced at Jennie. She started to hum a lullaby.

"Now the pressure is squeezing me. It is beginning to push me out of my warm cave. The walls contract and squeeze hard. I see a brighter red glow coming from, somewhere. The glow is the outside. I am frightened—I am frightened. I want to go back to the quiet dark place, but the force pushing me out is irresistible. My head bursts into a bright outer world."

There was a moment of absolute silence.

Then there was a strange humming sound that came from One-stone's mouth—growing louder until it became a sobbing wail.

Jennie looked down, love bursting from her eyes, a beatific smile stretching across her face.

"Every Jewish mother," she said, "wants an Einstein for a son."

FUSION

THE ONLY THING Russell Hertzherg could see of Bill Kramer as the bulky engineer climbed atop the magnet coil was his voluminous posterior jutting massively among the busbars and cryogenic pipelines of Toroidal Device Number 3.

"Okay, let her go," Kramer finally called down, having settled into an uncomfortable crouch.

Hertzberg fingered the intercom switch as he shot a glance across to the control room out past the great glass window. "Close the interlocks and enable the pulsed confining field generators," he spoke into the microphone. "Prepare to pulse every thirty seconds, starting at one kilogauss and gradually increasing up to fifty kilogauss, or until I tell you to stop."

At the door, sealing the control room off from the machine room, he heard the clicking of the locks as Bruce Kelly, the head technician, turned the keys and isolated the two of them inside the machine room. In another moment the klaxon sounded, warning the lab that machine pulsing was about to begin.

This raucous horn was the signal for anyone accidentally locked inside the machine room to run, not walk, to one of the big red panic buttons and to punch it hard. Not by accident did Hertzberg and Kramer remain in the machine room during this operation, however. On occasion, when standing 100 meters away in the safety of the control room would not suffice, safety regulations were purposely overridden so that observations could be made right at the machine.

However, Hertzberg had never before watched such a harebrained stunt as the one now being performed by Bill Kramer, who was about to perch right on one of the TD3 magnet coils while the machine was in the process of being pulsed. To be sure, there was no plasma in the two-meter-diameter vacuum vessel, nor a discharge of any kind, so no danger from radiation existed. All that was about to happen was that slow pulses of electric current—each two seconds long—were to be sent through the coil windings. With each pulse the amount of current was to be increased, until fifty thousand amperes flowed through each coil and the magnetic field strength went up to a rather impressive fifty thousand gauss. During this process Bill Kramer would strain his eyes in the dark to look for the flashes that would be evidence of intermittent arcing at one of the busbar connections.

The only dangers were the snapping of mechanical parts, the ejection of molten copper through the air from electric arcs, and similar straightforward electromechanical hazards—hazards that were encountered rarely, but with finite probability.

The countdown bell sounded, and Hertzberg focused his attention on the machine in front of him. The room was darkened so that Kramer could more clearly see the electric arc whose position he was trying to locate, but enough light filtered in from the control-room window to outline the towering bulk of the fusion device. Twenty feet high it loomed, a massive form of magnet coils arranged like the segments of a tangerine around a doughnut-shaped vacuum vessel lying flat on its side. In the horizontal direction, the machine spanned a diameter greater than fifty feet, while auxilliary coils, cooling pipes, vacuum pumps and sundry instrumentation stretched out over an area the size of a baseball field. The ultraviolet spectrometer lurked in one corner, flanked by the laser scattering system and the neutral injection apparatus.

When in full operation the enormous toroidal vacuum vessel would be filled with low-pressure deuterium gas, and an electric current amounting to many tens of thousands of amperes would be magnetically induced to travel round and round the circumference of the doughnut, using the gas itself as the conductor. In the process, the outer electrons of the deuterium atoms would be stripped from their nuclei, ionizing the gas so that it became a plasma—a volume of positive and negative charges moving around separately but intermingling with one another. Confined by the intense magnetic field so that it did not physically touch the walls of the container, the plasma could be studied with the vast array of diagnostic instruments, with the aim of understanding the numerous oscillations, instabilities, diffusions, and other mechanisms by which it attempted to wriggle its way out of its magnetic confinement.

Hertzberg himself felt utterly dwarfed by the immensity of the apparatus and could comprehend the machine and its paraphernalia only by breaking them down mentally into individual parts that could be handled. At this moment he stood close to the base of the coil atop which Kramer perched, so that he could relay communications through the intercom to the control room. A slight, white-bearded man in a tan jump suit, whose silvery hair haloed his head, Hertzberg somehow seemed out of place in the midst of all the machinery. His recurrent fantasy placed him, instead, on the platform of a lecture hall—or better yet, seated on a sunlit lawn surrounded by young and attentive students.

Next year, he thought. Next year. Right here and now was the problem of the troublesome arc, and he forced his attention to return to the business at hand.

Nowhere in the vicinity of the machine was there any indication that at this very moment electric current flowed through the coils, producing an invisible, intangible magnetic field that pervaded the space in and around the torus. Only in the control room did the meters and oscilloscopes signal the event.

To Hertzberg it seemed strange that the strongest magnetic field was almost without perceptible biological effect. He could stand next to a magnet coil, Kramer could perch on top, and neither could feel anything out of the ordinary. Only as the current pulsed repeatedly, building up in intensity each time, did a visible effect begin to take place.

The effect was this: When the current grew greater than thirty thousand amperes, the magnetic field drew adjacent coils together with such a ferocious force that the ten-inch-thick coil cases of stainless steel could be seen to bend toward each other slowly and ponderously until the current passed its peak, whereupon the coils slowly moved back to their normal position. Any force that could make those solid steel members bend even slightly out of shape—the intensity of that force simply boggled the imagination. Here was something that could not be comprehended. Yet nothing could be seen pushing the coil, nothing could be felt by the human hand—nothing but the invisible magnetic field.

Hertzberg could remember seeing a steel tool box, forgotten in a far corner of the laboratory, hurtled violently from its resting place and dashed to bits against one of the coils undergoing testing. Every nut and bolt of the machine was constructed of nonmagnetic stainless steel, so that the only mechanical forces were those between the electric currents themselves.

At forty thousand amperes the creaking of the coil frames became audible. Suddenly Kramer stiffened.

"Okay," he said. "It's starting to arc. One more pulse and I'll have the location pinned down."

At the next pulse he grunted in satisfaction. "Good. That does it. Tell the boys to shut it down so that I can get my tail off of this monstrosity."

Hertzberg pushed the intercom switch once more. "Okay, Bruce. Stop pulsing and open up. We're coming out."

In a minute Kramer had crawled down from his perch. "The arc is in a nasty place. Should take the boys two or three days to pull the busbars apart and retape the insulation. Then you should be on the air first thing next week."

Hertzberg drew in a deep breath. The moment of truth was coming closer, and the accumulated anxieties of the last twenty years began to build their pressures to the point where safety-valving was becoming necessary. He followed Kramer out into the control room, where the technicians busied themselves with last minute details, getting the equipment ready for the big push.

Feeling unwanted there, Hertzberg wandered next door to the empty conference room and sank into one of the cushioned swivel chairs arrayed around the long table. Closing his eyes amid relaxing, he fell into a soft darkness. He became aware of tension in his back muscles and massaged them in fantasy, constantly sinking deeper into his self-imposed hypnotic state. For a time he concentrated on nothing and then became aware of somebody nearby. With a feeling of lightness, he zoomed upward and opened his eyes.

Bill Hawke sat there in the next chair, a grin splitting his black-bearded face.

"Where've you been, Russ?" he asked lightly.

"Only inside," Hertzberg replied. "Just getting the brain tuned up and ready for work. The day of reckoning is upon us."

He nodded his head in the direction of the bulletin board where future schedules were to be posted.

Hawke threw a newspaper onto the table, leaned back and stretched.

"You said it, buddy. Look at that headline and weep."

Hertzberg leaned forward and experienced a shock. He read:

COURT NIXES BREEDER REACTOR

The Federal District Court, in the case of *Sierra Club vs Consolidated Utilities,* has overturned the permit of the power company to build a liquid-sodium breeder reactor in New Jersey because of safety considerations. Population density was cited as the main reason for refusal to . . .

Hertzberg looked up and whistled. "Well, now it's really hit the fan. Bully for the Sierra Club, but if we can only build breeders in the middle of the desert—and how are we going to do that without water?—then we get into a real energy distribution problem. And even nonbreeder reactors are in trouble because of the radioactive waste hassle. So the crunch is really on as far as energy is concerned. The dream of uranium fission powering our new world of the future may turn out to be just a fantasy."

Bill Hawke nodded. "That means it's up to us. Either we put up or shut up. We said we were going to get controlled fusion on this machine, so that is it. Either we make it or we don't. And if we don't, well, good-bye tomorrow."

This was really the moment of truth.

Instantly, Hertzberg's mind flashed back to the early days, twenty-five years ago, when he had switched from research in nuclear physics to controlled thermonuclear fusion. He was all starry-eyed and excited by the promise of this new, clean, inexhaustible form of energy. Even then it was beginning to look as if uranium fission was running into trouble because of the radioactive waste problem. And when the environment crowd started to raise hell about it, fusion began to look even better as a source of energy for the future.

Into fusion research he plunged, together with a number of other physicists recruited from various specialties. For naturally, nobody had ever taken courses in thermonuclear fusion in school, and plasma physics was barely heard of in the outside world. A whole new field of science had to be developed, and new fields of science, by definition, are invariably developed by people who never formally studied those subjects.

This meant months of labor to learn the theory of this brand new branch of science—plasma physics—and more months of floundering through experiments with strange and complex machines in order to become expert with the techniques of dealing with the heating and confinement of ionized gases in magnetic fields.

Then had come the years of plodding and frustration, for between the theory of thermonuclear fusion and the actual taming of the process lay a gulf that narrowed ever so slowly and reluctantly, despite the utmost efforts of thousands of scientists all over the world. It was easy enough to say that a self-sustained thermonuclear reaction required the heating of a container of deuterium-tritium mixture to a temperature of 100 million degrees Kelvin together with the confinement of the resulting ionized gas—the plasma—for a period of about one second in a properly shaped magnetic field. Under those conditions one could predict that the deuterium and tritium nuclei would fuse together copiously enough so that they would give off more energy than was used to get the reaction started. From then on, the reaction would keep going, and there would be a generator of power whose basic fuel—deuterium—could be obtained easily and cheaply from sea water.

Since the fuel was essentially unlimited—and since there was little of the problem concerning intense radio-activity that dogged the fission process—thermonuclear fusion was the answer to the question of what to do when coal and oil ran out. On the success or failure of this project rested the question of whether the twenty-second century would be an era of high-or-how-intensity energy usage.

Those facts were well-known and easy to explain. Theoretically, one could devise a dozen ways to attain the goal. But to do it, that was another story. Heating a plasma was easy. Just send a big enough blast of electric current through a tube of gas at low pressure. Then watch the plasma twist and writhe and vanish from the tube in less than a millionth of a second. In so doing, the physicists learned about hydromagnetic instabilities and found that trying to confine a plasma in a magnetic bottle was something like trying to maintain water in the top half of a container by means of compressed air in the bottom half. The air pressure might be strong enough to keep the water up top, but the water just won't stay up there. It's an unstable situation.

Thus the main effort was directed at devising ways to stabilize the plasma container. Over the years Hertzberg worked with devices whose fanciful names—*stellarator, tokamak, levitron*—represented various attempts to tailor magnetic fields into shapes that provided hydromagnetic stability to the plasma confined within. Year by year the plasma physicists discovered the different types of instabilities and learned how to cope with them, and gradually their ability to maintain higher plasma temperatures for longer periods of time brought them closer to their goal.

One fact remained clear during all this time. The bigger the volume of plasma, the longer it would remain confined and the more time it would have to react. Thus the plasma devices grew larger and larger, until now the third-generation toroidal confinement device lay out there in the machine room, ready to start operation, with the theorists predicting that in this machine the conditions for a self-sustained thermonuclear reaction should be reached.

But—and here the damnable pessimism resulting from twenty years of experience nagged at his brain cells and turned his feet into clay—never did a plasma device work according to theory. Something unexpected always happened because some aspect of the theory had not been understood properly because it was too complicated for anybody to understand properly. And so one never knew what was going to happen the first time one of these machines was turned on.

So Hertzberg could only shrug his shoulders at Bill Hawke's remark: "Either we make it or we don't."

"I'm willing to bet," Hertzberg said, cautiously, "that we almost make it. The machine will almost work, but something will happen to keep it from working all the way. And then nobody will be satisfied, and we will spend years trying to analyze what went wrong and trying to sort out the four or five different instabilities that cause the plasma to run out of the machine."

"Oh come on, Russ. How did you manage to last this long in this business with such a pessimistic attitude? You have to be an optimist to keep going around here. It's going to work. I just feel it. This is going to be the machine that gets fusion off the ground."

Hertzberg grinned at Bill Hawke's enthusiasm. "I hope you're right. I'd like a success before I retire."

Yet he didn't quite believe it was going to happen.

As it turned out, at least another month passed before the moment of truth arrived. First, Ralph Petty had to spend a week checking the alignment of the magnetic field with his little electron gun. The size of a thimble, the electron gun was thrust into the center of the vacuum vessel on the end of a remote drive, and brief microsecond pulses of electrons were ejected along the magnetic axis so that they went round and round the doughnut. By minute adjustment of the coil positions and by the application of currents to auxiliary coils, the alignment of the magnetic field was touched up until the electron beam went around the torus dozens of times before vanishing into obscurity. A small amount of gas in the vessel made the circling beam visible, and it gave Hertzberg a big kick to see the narrowly focused threads of electrons wind their way around the tube. It really gave him faith in the existence of those little beasts.

Next, the interior of the vacuum vessel had to be cleaned up—rid of impurities and gases adsorbed onto the inner surface of the hollow stainless steel doughnut. This operation was a simple matter of running a discharge—a huge low-pressure electric arc—inside the vacuum vessel. A small amount of hydrogen gas was admitted into the tube, and an electric current of several thousand amps was magnetically induced in the gas itself to flow around the torus. Electrons were separated from atoms, ionizing the gas and creating a plasma, bombarding the wall with electrons, protons, and ultraviolet photons, sputtering off a flood of adsorbed impurities.

For hours and days the continuous bombardment went on, while the color of the plasma changed from the bright bluish violet of nitrogen and oxygen to the palest red of hydrogen, and the intensity of the impurity lines in the spectrometer decreased to a negligible amount.

Now the machine was ready to go.

With some trepidation Hertzberg came to the Wednesday staff meeting, wondering what his position would be on the schedule. One part of his head wanted to be in front of the line, to have the first crack at the big time. Another part said, no, I don't want to be first. Let somebody else take the responsibility of being the first to fall flat on his face. Thus a small portion of relief mingled with disappointment when he saw the lab director Ned Fraser making notations on the blackboard.

"We decided," Fraser explained, "to do the first experiment with neutral injection rather than with RF heating. If the experiment works, that way will be easier and more economical, and that's the path we're going to take. So Ron Warner goes first, and Hertzberg goes second."

Hertzberg shrugged. "As long as I get on the machine before July first, that's all I care about. One final fling before my retirement date."

But then the feeling of insult overcame the feeling of I-don't-care, and he suddenly realized how glad he was going to be to retire and get out of there. He was completely fed up with playing second fiddle to fair-haired boys like Ron Warner, who was going to get first shot on the machine simply because he tooted his own horn loudest and so was more noticed and as a result was put into position to get the credit for the first big breakthrough on the big new machine.

But as he watched Ron Warner get the neutral-injection equipment ready during the next few days, Hertzberg realized he was being unfair. Warner was good; that's all there was to it. Young and energetic, intense and outspoken, popping off ideas in all directions—he had that rare ability to do theoretical calculations of a fairly sophisticated nature, then to turn around and do the experiments based on the theory. It may be that he batted only .500 accurate on his ideas and theories, but—what the hell? That's the way you do scientific research. Generate theories as fast as you can, test them with experiments and throw away the ideas that don't work. Warner's primary fault was that sometimes he fell in love with his own theories and held on to them a little too long, thus generating heated arguments with those who disagreed.

But perhaps that was better than the caution with which Hertzberg proceeded, with the result that very few original ideas emanated from him. Those ideas he did have were presented with such diffidence that very little attention was paid to them. And when, occasionally, he came up with a really important experimental result, it slid past the consciousness of his colleagues, hardly noticed at all.

Just a sophisticated technician, that's what he felt himself to be. An old workhorse knowledgeable in pushing buttons, collecting data, programming the computer to analyze the data and trying to fit the data to one or another of the theories that had been generated in the minds of the theoretical physicists who inhabited the other end of the building. That was, of course, a useful occupation, since the theories were so complex that nobody could guess which one correctly represented the real world unless people like Hertzberg slogged through the long, tedious experiments, gathering data, plotting curves and applying ingenious devices to help compare the experimental results with the theoretical predictions.

Hertzberg sat in the control room with the rest of the staff as Warner began his first machine run. Maybe another reason for being grateful. Who could do research with everybody looking over his shoulder? Warner could. He gloried in it. Leaning back in his swivel chair, he smoothly dictated the starting conditions to the head technician, who in turn adjusted the knobs and threw the switches that sent the operating sequences on their way.

The control room was long and narrow, running the full width of the machine room. Along one wall was the large window through which the observers could see the TD-3, squatting there like an enormous metallic insect. In front of the window was the control console, with switches and dials to regulate the operation of the many parts of the system. Flanking the control console were the observation posts, consoles with oscilloscopes and other instrument readouts, together with the remote controls for the operation of the numerous diagnostic instruments surrounding the machine. Many of the scopes had Polaroid cameras for capturing photographs of the signals received during the machine operation. The rear wall of the room consisted of a computer installation for automatic storage and manipulation of the experimental data. Often the raw electrical signs required considerable mathematical processing before the resulting numbers had meaning to the experimenters. Graph plotters allowed the computer to display the end results of these calculations automatically.

As Hertzberg looked around the control room, be wondered idly how many people in the room really wished Warner well and how many hoped for a minor catastrophe—just enough to slow Warner down a little. For there were at least three groups of people there, each with a stake in a different method of attaining thermonuclear fusion in this particular device. V/bile there was a clear-cut end goal—a temperature of 100 million degrees, a density of 10'~ ions per cubic centimeter, and a confinement time of one second—there were numerous and devious paths to that end.

The most direct—which was Hertzberg's—was to produce and heat the plasma right inside the confining magnetic field. A more devious method—Warner's—involved injecting high-energy deuterium nuclei into the magnetic field from the outside and then trapping them so that they formed a hot, confined plasma.

Since the injection of ionized atoms into a magnetic field involved serious difficulties, a roundabout method had been devised. In an ion source outside the magnet, electrons were stripped from deuterium atoms, and the resulting ions were accelerated to high velocity by electric fields. They were then passed through a chamber filled with gas where they captured orbital electrons from the atoms of that gas—a process known as "charge exchange." The result was a mass of fast, neutral deuterium atoms passing down a tube without hindrance through the magnetic field of the TD-3 into its toroidal vacuum chamber. There it encountered a low-temperature plasma produced by passing electric current around the torus. Again charge exchange took place. The high-energy atoms were stripped of orbital electrons and became high-energy ions. Now they were trapped within the magnetic field, and in this way the desired high-temperature plasma was formed.

That, at least, was the theory. The method had been tried on smaller devices and was now about to make its debut on the giant TD-3. Ron Warner, leaning lazily back in his chair, kept an eagle eye on the meters and digital readouts that signaled the important machine conditions. Axial current flowed smoothly—just enough to keep the deuterium ionized and to form the magnetic lines of force into the requisite corkscrew shape.

Warner flicked the switch that lit the filament in his ion source. While the others in the room leaned forward and conversations dropped to silence, Warner seemed to grow even more nonchalant. He was the maestro and he knew he was onstage. His deft fingers set the switches that started the discharge in the ion source.

All eyes shifted to a large oscilloscope screen where the output of a diamagnetic loop was displayed. The loop was nothing but a coil of wire wrapped around the vacuum vessel, sensitive to the changing magnetic fields inside it. Heating or cooling the plasma produced small variations in the magnetic field, inducing tiny voltages in the coil. By processing the signal in a small analog computer, the output picture could show directly the plasma temperature. Hertzberg was rather proud of this simple device for he had worked out the technique twenty years ago. It was his little part of the machine.

Now the screen showed that the injection of ions into the plasma produced a small increase in temperature. Something was beginning to happen.

"Well, folks, don't break out the bottle of champagne yet," Warner drawled. "We still have a way to go. Gotta tune up the ion source a little better. Just relax for a while."

Hertzberg nervously joined a little group at the coffee pot in the corner. When he returned to the screen, the signal had grown somewhat bigger. Every time the ion source pulsed, the green line would slope upwards, reach a maximum and then trail off as the pulse ended. As Warner skillfully turned the controls, homing in on a region of optimum operation, the pulse height began to zoom upwards to a value representing a temperature of one thousand electron-volts—about ten million degrees.

The temperature within the control room appeared to rise, also, as a result of the breath-holding going on Suddenly Warner leaned forward to inspect the oscilloscope screen more closely.

"Damn!" he exclaimed. "It's saturating."

The temperature was no longer increasing, but was rising to a maximum value, leveling off and then dropping rapidly. Close inspection showed the top of the curve to be broken by a number of wiggles and oscillations.

Then, abruptly, there was no signal at all on the scope, and a pair of red lights appeared on one of the wall panels.

Warner leaped out of his seat, his cool evaporating. "The rotten son-of-a-bitch" he grated. "The ion source is gone. Shut down the machine."

He raged around the control room, beating on the tables, walls and consoles with his fists while the switches were thrown and the door to the machine room unlocked.

"Damn it," he complained to the others who crowded around. "Something was just beginning to happen. I think we hit an instability and the plasma started running out too fast so that it stopped heating. Then the ion source conked out, so we lost everything. We'll have to see what's wrong."

He tore out onto the machine floor and began poking at the injection apparatus with an ohmmeter, muttering to himself. Presently he came back, dejected.

"We'll have to open up. The filament is shot, but I think there's also been some arcing from the high-voltage electrodes. I don't know how much time it'll take to fix it."

"Take whatever time you need," Ned Fraser told him. "This is a high-priority operation."

And he turned to the others, saying, "You might as well go home for the night and keep the champagne on ice. It might be a few days before we operate again."

There were sighs and condolences, but since it was getting late and nobody could think of a good reason to hang around, they quickly dispersed.

"What a frustrating business!" Hertzberg remarked to Bill Hawke as they walked out of the building. "That instability is a mystery. It showed up just on the last few pulses. A high-temperature effect, maybe? But just before we get a chance to study it, the machine blows up."

"Yup. It's frustrating," Hawke agreed. "But what about you? I thought you were scheduled for the next run on the machine. Are they going to cut into your time?"

Hertzberg stopped. He hesitated. He blushed. Once more he had avoided recognizing when he was being screwed. "You're right, of course," he said.

He looked at Bill Hawke, and the two locked eyes. He knew and Bill knew that the machine was supposed to run on the schedule that was posted in the conference room. Each experimental group had two days to run the machine and ten days to analyze data in between runs. If someone had a breakdown that could not be fixed during his time, then he was out of luck. One waited for the regular maintenance days. But no one could use somebody else's time to fix up his own experiment.

"I'll talk to Fraser tomorrow morning," Hertzberg promised.

He had to. Because he just could not afford to give time away any longer. As a result, he knew that he had nothing to lose when he stood in Fraser's office the next day.

"Look," he said. "I know you're backing Warner's experiment, and you're giving it first priority. But I've a right to my time on the schedule according to our regular procedure. You know I'm due to retire in July, and I can't afford to give my time away."

The urgency vibrating in his voice suggested much more than the bare words. Not only had the July deadline staring remotely down time's corridor become important, but each moment, each quantum of life, had suddenly become infinitely precious, as though it might be the last.

Fraser, tall and thin behind his desk, blinked in amazement and embarrassment. Not being used to the spectacle of Hertzberg standing straight in front of his desk and demanding his rights, Fraser had casually and thoughtlessly proceeded to walk right over Hertzberg's rights. He knew it, and he knew Hertzberg was right.

"Why sure, Russ. If that's the way you feel. We do have to go by the schedule, don't we?"

And that was all there was to it. Hertzberg, his breath taken away by the victory, now had to look forward to the big test—the experimental run coming up in two days. The repairs on the injector were still not complete in that time, and a disgruntled Warner carried his armful of notebooks out of the control room to make room for Hertzberg's group.

It was Hertzberg's turn to remember the old saying:

"Beware of the day when you finally attain your heart's desire." Now, after insisting on his rights, the burden was firmly and squarely on his shoulder to do something.

Realistically, however, the responsibility was not entirely his. Entering the control room with him were his two partners. The Russian, Denis Ivanovich, youngish and intense. The Israeli, Zalman Avivi, stocky, fiercely moustached and wildly energetic. Each was responsible for operating certain units of the instrumentation, and all three combined wits to plot the strategy of the experimentation.

The first few hours of the morning were spent checking out the instruments while the machine was rapid-pulsed to clean up the vacuum system a bit more. Following lunch, Hertzberg called in the engineers to stand by while the ohmic heating system was brought up to full power. Ohmic heating was the brute-force method of inducing an enormous electric current to flow around the doughnut-shaped plasma, ionizing the gas and accelerating the electrons to a moderately high temperature—one million degrees—leaving the ions at a somewhat lower temperature.

Since the aim of the game was to make the ions hot, this method of preparing a plasma was useful only as a preliminary device—just to got things started. The real problem was devising a way to energize the ions to a higher temperature. A dozen methods had been invented over the years. Some turned out to be inefficient. Others were not useful in a toroidal device. Some, like the neutral injection, were still in the running.

Hertzberg's pet method—radio-frequency heating—had proven powerful in the past, but the plasma never stayed confined in the magnetic field for a long enough time to reach maximum temperature. Therefore the first order of business was to check the confinement time, which was done simply by pulsing the ohmic beating to bring the plasma up to maximum density quickly, shutting off the current, and then watching the decay of the plasma density after the pulse.

To measure the plasma density, the laser-scattering equipment was used. Light from a high-intensity laser was reflected from the electrons in the plasma. The amount of scattered light indicated the number of electrons along the path of the light beam, while an on-line computer interpreted the results instantly and displayed them on an oscilloscope screen.

Every thirty seconds they heard the ding of the count-down bell and the click of relays as the machine went into its pulse. Simultaneously, the traces flashed across the faces of the many scopes ranged along the control panel. Hertzberg recalled how fast the sweep speeds had been when he first came into the project. In those days each pulse of the machine constituted an experiment that lasted less than a thousandth of a second from beginning to end. Of course, since he had come into the plasma business from nuclear physics, a thousandth of a second had seemed to him like a tremendously long time. At that time he was accustomed to measuring events that took place in less than a millionth of a second!

Since then, the progress of thermonuclear fusion could be measured in the way the sweeps of the oscilloscopes grew progressively slower and slower—as the confinement time of the plasma grew longer and longer. So now it took a hundred milliseconds—a tenth of a second—for the electron beam to go from one side of the screen to the other. That was slow enough to see it move with the naked eye. Before the present set of experiments was finished, Hertzberg aimed to turn the sweep-speed knob on the scope another notch.

Looking at the density scope, he saw the plasma easily going up to 10^{15} electrons per cubic centimeter and then decaying after the pulse, with a lifetime that was automatically computed and written out on the face of the scope: twenty-three milliseconds.

Not bad for a start, Hertzberg thought. On the last-generation machine he would have had to work hard for that result.

"Okay," he said, "let's take the confining field up to maximum, in steps of one kilogauss."

A certain amount of routine surveying had to he done to determine how the machine operated under various conditions of currents and magnetic fields. If he wanted to make a really thorough survey over all the parameters available, it literally would take weeks of continuous running. For there was not only the confining field as a variable, but a number of auxiliary fields that changed the pitch of the field corkscrew, so that there were regions of stability and instability that could be—and should be—mapped out in order to really understand how the machine behaved.

The thought of that tedium brought a feeling of revulsion, and he thought to himself, this is not physics. This is just studying the behavior of one particular machine. I'm a machine psychiatrist, that's what I am.

"Hey buddy," Zalman boomed. "Let's give the RE a try. Enough of this monotony."

"As soon as we finish this confining field survey. You young people must learn patience."

Hertzberg loved to put on the act of the old patriarch, something he knew and they knew was completely fraudulent.

Denis Ivanovich fingered the keys of a computer terminal and announced, "The confinement time does increase with the magnetic field, but not directly. The function is a complicated one."

Hertzberg nodded. "That's what I would expect. So far things are going smoothly."

And peace was in his heart. He had under his control the largest confined plasma in the world—fifty cubic meters of ionized gas held in the torus by the magnetic field, heated to a temperature of one million degrees Kelvin by a fifty megawatt pulse of power lasting forty milliseconds. Yet this was only the beginning. The next sequence of steps had to raise the plasma temperature to a peak one hundred times greater.

"Okay," he said. "Let's warm up the RF generators and get ready to tickle the plasma a little bit."

Heating a plasma by shooting high-power radio waves into the ionized gas was nothing new. Twenty years ago he had helped with some of the early experiments in ion-cyclotron resonance heating. In these experiments, induction coils surrounding the plasma had generated electro-magnetic fields within the plasma that acted in rhythm with the natural frequency of the ions whipping around in the magnetic field, accelerating them in the manner of a cyclotron. While a highly efficient way of accelerating ions, this method could only be used with plasmas of lower density and was not suitable for the high-density plasma in the machine now.

However, there were many types of waves that could be launched into a plasma cylinder, and a number of frequencies that provided resonances which allowed strong transfer of energy from the transmitting antenna to the ions and electrons in the plasma. The main problem was strictly an engineering one of concentrating enough electromagnetic energy into the small volume of the transmission lines and coupling devices. Extremely high voltages had to be encountered and overcome.

As the technicians flipped the proper sequence of switches and the pilot lights changed from red to green, the tension in Hertzberg's back began to increase. He leaned back in his chair, forced himself to relax. Zalman appeared with a cup of coffee in each hand.

"Thanks," Hertzberg breathed, gratefully.

Releasing a deep breath, he pushed the button starting the flow of radio-frequency power into the coupling structure—a sort of antenna designed to project power inward into the plasma rather than outward into space. Only a few watts went down the transmission line.

Hertzberg sipped at his coffee and said to the others, "Better relax for a few hours. First I have to tune the coupler and then search for the plasma resonance. Then retune again. It's going to be a dull afternoon."

The others groaned. Denis returned to the computer terminal and buried himself in his calculations. Zalman sat at the control console, rocked back and forth, singing to himself, as though by force of will he could induce the temperature of the plasma to increase.

Hertzberg turned control knobs until his arms ached, cursing the inability of the engineers to put all the knobs within easy reach. But after all, his set of knobs was only one out of many. Gradually he began to zero in on the optimum coupling condition. Until the frown that creased his forehead began to deepen and puzzlement pulled down the corners of his mouth.

"Hey Bruce," he called over to the head technician. "Would you go out on the platform and check tuning control number three? I don't think it's doing anything."

Hiatus. The TD-3 stopped pulsing, the door to the machine room was unlocked, Bruce Kelly went out and located the tuning control, then watched to see what happened as Hertzberg turned the knob. Nothing.

"The shaft doesn't turn," Kelly called back on the intercom. "I'll have to check further to see if the trouble is with the selsyn motor or with a slipping shaft. It'll take a little while."

"Okay," Hertzberg sighed. The delay only served to increase the rate at which the initial spurt of driving energy was seeping out of his body. He said to the others, "I guess we might as well break for dinner. Come back in two hours and see if we can get back on the air tonight. We still have till midnight."

The long hours stretched onward into the evening. When the pulsing of the machine resumed, Hertzberg tuned the coupler with a precise hand until almost all the electromagnetic waves went into the plasma and very few were reflected out. Then, varying the magnetic field strength in tiny steps, he searched for the precise combination of field strength and plasma density that provided the energy absorption resonance he needed to heat the plasma.

Slowly, as he converged on the proper condition, the oscilloscope trace that signaled the plasma temperature began to show an abrupt rise at the instant the RF power was applied during each pulse. Zalman leaned forward, and his singing took on a more intense character.

"Tune in there, baby," he crooned. "Hey, Russell, how about a little more power. Give us some action."

Hertzberg shook his bead. "Tune first. Then power. Don't want to get high voltage in the transmission lines. But we're close. Just a couple more minutes."

At this point the RF power going into the plasma was several kilowatts, just enough to warm the ions gently.

"Okay," he said presently. "Here we go."

With his hand shaking just the tiniest bit, Hertzberg approached the knob that controlled the output power of the RF generator—essentially a super-high-power radio transmitter. A small turn of the knob and immediately he could see changes in all the outputs. The power indicator read one megawatt, and the temperature signal made a distinct climb during the forty-millisecond time of the pulse.

"Oh baby, come on baby," Zalman crooned in his ear. The Russian had left his console and was now breathing down his neck.

Another turn of the knob. Power up to fifty megawatts. Ion temperature was up to 500 electron-volts—equivalent to five million degrees. That had been the all-time record on the old stellarator, and now they had equaled that record in one afternoon. The big difference was that to heat this enormous volume of high-density plasma, a vastly greater quantity of power was required.

Up to 100 megawatts. The ion temperature signal from the diamagnetic loop leaped upward gratifyingly. Onward to 200 megawatts, and the plasma temperature reached well over 1000 electron-volts.

Hertzberg became aware of a buzzing sound and a red light flashing atop the control panel, while the illuminated numbers of a scaler began flashing with increasing rapidity.

A grin split his face from side to side. "Hey, we're making neutrons! That's a sign of progress."

Zalman's song became a prayer of thanks. But Denis remained dour.

"You know making neutrons is nothing new. You made them twenty years ago."

"To be sure. And just because the temperature is high enough to get some of the deuterons to fuse, it doesn't mean we have a self-sustained reaction. But when we made neutrons before it was in a localized region of the machine—a hot spot. Now we have the entire torus hot enough. That's something. Let's try another notch on the power."

Hertzberg twisted the knob another fraction of a turn. Again the temperature went up, but, he noticed, not very much. His eyes rapidly scanned from one scope to another. Abruptly he glared at the density signal.

"Uh-oh." His finger darted out and pointed to a sudden dip in plasma density that appeared during the application of RF power. "We're losing plasma. Density is going down and heating is running out."

Zalman broke into a song of lamentation, while Denis nodded, his lips pinched tightly together.

"I think," he said, "that we have run into a region of instability, so that we're losing energy as fast as we are putting it in. Look, the confinement time is way down."

Hertzberg glanced at the clock. It was past 11:00, and the weariness in his shoulders coupled with the growing pain in his back made the beginning of a cry poke its head up from some dark depth down below. But he pushed it under. No crying in the control room. Don't freak out in front of the technicians. Be calm and in control. After all, it's a control room. For both man and machine.

"Okay," he said. "That's the way it goes. That plasma will do it every time. I go into an experiment with a scenario nicely plotted. I know what I am going to do, and I imagine what the machine and the plasma are going to do in response. But the plasma has a way of its own, and it pays no attention to what I had planned for it."

Hertzberg winked at Zalman. "That's the colossal joke that nature plays on all of us. We go around deluding ourselves that we control nature by means of our machinery. In actuality, all we can do is to arrange things so that when they do what they must do according to their nature, then the resulting actions will agree with our expectations and desires. But we can't make any thing do anything that it doesn't have to do. A stone doesn't have to fall up, so you can't make it fall up. A plasma doesn't have to be stable with our screwy magnetic field, so it's not stable. What can we do?"

He slumped in discouragement. Zalman put a hand on his shoulder. "The first thing we can do is get some sleep. Then in the morning, worry about what to do."

Denis said, "Surely we can trace down a region that is more stable."

"Okay, we'll do both those things," Hertzberg said, and plodded off to home.

To awaken the next morning, muscles screaming in stiffness, was an act of torture.

"I'm too old for this," he agonized, bitterly wishing he had never gone into a laboratory. Then, stubbornly gritting his teeth, he crawled out of bed and into the shower.

By the time he arrived at the lab, the technicians had the TD-3 pulse-cleaning, and the computer readouts of last night's accumulated data were piled on the work tables. He sat staring into a cup of coffee while Zalman and Denis wandered in.

Denis started right out. "We need more ohmic heating current to give more rotational transform. That will put us into a region of greater stability."

Hertzberg shook his head in violent disagreement. "Nope, that will only give us greater turbulence and make things worse than ever."

The two went back and forth for a period of time. Anybody who thought that science was based on hard, cold facts was simply not acquainted with this kind of situation, where the variables were so numerous and the theoretical knowledge so complex that you could make arguments to prove any point you wanted, depending on what approximations you chose to make and what variables you chose to omit.

Finally Hertzberg said, "Look, sometimes experience is better than all the theoretical arguments. Let me do something that once worked for me a long time ago in a different context. If it doesn't work now, then you can try out your idea. What do you have to lose? You have plenty of time."

Hertzberg set the controls so that the ohmic heating current ran at top level for only a millisecond and then was reduced to a trickle for the remainder of the fifty millisecond pulse—just enough to keep the electrons warmed up. Auxiliary coils were activated to increase the stability of the plasma. Hertzberg worked with notebook and computer to calculate the precise amount of current needed in all the coils.

The RF power was turned on, tuning checked and gradually increased in magnitude. As during last night's run, the plasma temperature smoothly increased until the neutron monitor started clicking away. At 400 megawatts input, the temperature was still rising. Two kilo-electron-volts! Twenty million degrees! The neutron counter clicked at a furious rate.

Hertzberg could feel a chill run up and down his spine. His bearded face was split with a grin so wide he felt the top of his head expanding. Sitting cross-legged in his chair, he looked like a triumphant gnome. He had not yet reached self-sustained fusion, but the ion temperature and density were approaching the magic conditions.

Heart pounding, he turned the power up to 500 megawatts. Still the temperature rose. Take it up to 1000 megawatts and then call up Ned Fraser. Blow your horn, he advised himself gleefully.

He turned to Denis, who was busy plotting a graph. "Is the temperature still going up linearly?" he asked.

Denis frowned. "I'm not sure. The last two points are a little low. Give me some more data."

Six—seven—eight hundred megawatts. Brief pulses of concentrated energy directed into the heart of the trapped plasma. Each time Denis read the maximum temperature and added another point to his graph.

Then, sadly, he took a straightedge and drew a line through the first few points. The last three points fell far below, and a pencil line drawn through those points showed in actuality a curve that flattened off instead of rising steadily upward.

"Hell. It's saturating." Hertzberg's eyes clouded with disappointment. No matter how much power they poured into the plasma, the temperature was not going to rise any further. Something was stealing energy out of the cloud of ionized gas as fast as they poured it in.

With his hands pressed together under his chin, his body slumped deeply into the chair, his eyelids narrowed to a slit, Hertzberg thought and worried and tried to visualize what was happening inside the machine.

Whatever he thought at this point, it could only he guesswork.

Finally be said, "I imagined a long time ago that charge exchange might be a serious loss mechanism. A small percentage of neutral gas comes into the machine from wall sputtering—the neutral atoms exchange electrons with the energetic ions. The result is energetic neutral atoms leaving the plasma, leaving cold ions behind. And stealing away all that energy."

"You could check that theory," Zalman said, "by using the neutral atom spectrometer."

"That's the next thing to do," Hertzberg sighed, as he got up and directed the technicians to cease pulsing. It had been close. Very close indeed.

But that was the way things went in the fusion business. The expected never happened. Fantastic breakthroughs occurred only in the fevered brains of science-fiction writers, for the real world of research consisted of patient slugging, gradual enlightenment and step-by-step resolution.

After checking his theory concerning charge exchange, Hertzberg found his two-day run on the machine over. He crawled back to his apartment one solid ache of fatigue. One large vodka on ice sent a relaxing wave through his body.

"Oh man," he gasped, sprawling on the couch. "I just can't take that routine anymore."

It was not just the running till midnight, the getting up early next day but rather the constant tension at the control panel, trying for the right decisions, coping with the unexpected.

He was determined to take the next day off, but the afternoon found him back in his office, scanning the data plotting graphs, mapping strategy. Somehow the world seemed a little brighter.

"Look," he said to Zalman, "I can get two more runs in before July. Then you can ship me off to the old folks home. But until then I'm going to hang in."

"What about the charge exchange?" Denis Ivanovich demanded, practical as usual.

For a moment Hertzberg looked pensive, then replied, "The answer to that question is the most basic of all. Improve the confinement of the plasma and you have fewer ions hitting the wall and knocking out junk to give you trouble. So on our next run we go for broke. *One second* confinement time."

"Oh."

Zalman and Denis appeared stunned. One second—one thousand milliseconds. A plasma confined in the magnetic field one thousand times longer than the plasmas commonplace at the beginning of the project.

Denis recovered. "Assuming, of course, that Warner does not do it first."

Hertzberg looked at him. "I don't see," he said, "why that should stop us."

He enjoyed the momentary feeling of heady arrogance that passed through him.

It turned out that Warner did not do it. But he came close again. Everything worked—almost perfectly, but not quite. And again it was Hertzberg's turn.

He slowly walked into the control room on the morning of the run, pulling fretfully on his beard. His back pained him in spite of his efforts to stop worrying. In his arms were charts of magnetic fields and regions of plasma stability on computer printouts. They were to be his weapons in the battle coming up.

He settled in his swivel chair with the first of many cups of coffee. Ned Fraser walked by and said, "Hey, I hear you're going for broke today."

Hertzberg put his finger to his lips. "Shh. Don't let the machine know. It'll fight." But he was glad the director had noticed.

Denis and Zalman came in and found their seats. Zalman's song was unusually subdued, only a mournful hum floating through the quiet control room.

Finally Hertzberg activated himself. "Okay," he said to the technician in charge. "Set her up for rapid pulsing. We're going to do a little spectroscopy first, because I want the machine as clean as a whistle."

An hour was spent with the optical spectroscopes, scanning some of the well-known oxygen and hydrogen lines until Hertzberg was satisfied that the impurity level was in fact better than the previous week. Then, with an unconscious bunching of his shoulders, he switched to slow pulsing and began to search for the magnetic configuration that led to long plasma confinement.

Slowly and patiently he crept through the contours of parameter space, varying first one magnetic field and then another, always keeping his eye on the oscilloscope that read out the plasma density. It was the rate at which the density decayed after the heating power was shut off that gave the clue to the confinement time.

With a wide grin fixed on his face, Hertzberg watched as the curve took longer and longer to come down. Finally, with a triumphant bellow, he leaned over and twisted a knob of the oscilloscope one position clockwise.

"A tenth of a second per centimeter," he exulted. "Just look at her go!"

The trace on the oscilloscope face was no longer a line, but it was a tiny spot of light that slowly moved from left to right, taking one entire second of time to go from one end of the screen to the other. Oh glorious slowness!

But on the next machine pulse the trace never rose above the baseline.

Hertzberg climbed out of his seat in consternation. "What the hell's wrong?"

Denis frowned, his eyes darting back and forth amongthe other scopes.

"The machine's working all right. Current and voltage traces are normal. Better check the laser."

Hertzberg fussed and fumed and went out on the platform to breathe down the neck of the laser technician who finally determined that a vital power supply in the laser-scattering system had acquired a short circuit and had given up the ghost. By the time the components were replaced, it was well into the afternoon. Savagely he went back to pulsing the machine, regaining the previous conditions and moving forward.

Came time to activate the radio-frequency power. Bruce Kelly pushed the appropriate buttons, and nothing happened.

"Oh, no! What now?" Hertzberg demanded.

Zalman Avivi, head between his knees, hummed a dirge of mourning.

Kelly did nothing but mumble to himself, staring off into the distance, while poking at one of the buttons uselessly. Finally he sighed.

"Guess we'll have to check out the relays and interlocks."

An enormous chart was spread out on the table; Kelly counted off all the interlocks that had to be fastened tight before anything would operate. Hertzberg scratched his head in bafflement at the complex circuit diagram.

Finally Kelly walked off into the RF transmitter room, Hertzberg, Avivi and Ivanovich trailing behind. The RF room, a vast bay filled with cabinets of electronics, stretched for many yards in all directions. For several minutes Kelly walked among the cabinets, opening doors and slamming them shut, checking with the control room through the intercom, until he got the word that a red pilot light had changed to green.

"Damn sticky switches," he grumbled. "We'll have to change that one next maintenance period."

By that time the crew was grumbling because it was past dinner time.

"What next?" Hertzberg asked himself when they returned, having barely eaten, his mood sinking lower and lower.

Next on the program was a stuck and shredded IBM card in the data-acquisition system.

"Good God!" he screamed. "I'm being nibbled to death by trivial accidents. All I need is one goddamn second of good plasma on the machine. One sixtieth of a minute. Is that too much to ask? Why does anyone in his right mind ever get into this business in the first place?"

He crawled home in real pain, his back muscles in spasm. Aspirins, a drink and a session of autohypnosis managed to sink him into slumber.

In the morning he sat and stared glumly at the machine. It was not his friend anymore.

"Well?" Zalman boomed, sitting down next to him. "Ready for another struggle?"

Hertzberg lifted an eyebrow at him. "You can have all the struggles after today. I'm going to wrap it up. Just too old for this routine."

"Oh, come on," Zalman said. "Give it one more try. Just relax. I'll get the machine started."

Hertzberg was grateful. There was a day when he had that kind of resiliency.

The magnetic field was started up, as was the pre-ionizer and the ohmic heating. The instrumentation was checked out. Returning to the conditions they had left the day before, they found the confinement time still gratifyingly approaching the magic period of one second.

The RF came on, and its power was applied to the plasma in increasing doses. Hertzberg suddenly found himself sitting erect in his chair, feeling as if an invisible cord lifted his head vertically, an electric shock passing down his spinal cord. An incredulous stare alternated with an intoxicated grin as he saw what the plasma temperature was doing.

With the longer confinement time, less power was required to reach a given temperature. With only ten megawatts going in, the temperature was already up to ten million degrees. As he increased the power, the neutron counters buzzed merrily away and the signal showing the temperature kept climbing. In the control room there was an increasing flurry of sound, and gradually, as he looked out of the corner of his eyes between pulses, he saw that the room was filling with staff members. The word had gotten around that a record was being broken; that morning. Soon Ned Fraser arrived.

With a start Hertzberg noticed that Fraser was followed by Matt Brackett, the thin and elegant white-haired old man who was the grandaddy of fusion research, having designed the first toroidal device built at the lab many years ago. He smiled and waved, and then his right hand turned the knob that raised the RF power to 100 megawatts.

"Let's take this next one," he said, in a businesslike tone of voice. Zalman and Denis swung their cameras into position, and as the machine pulsed they caught the indelible images of the oscilloscope traces spelling out: plasma density, 10^{15} electrons per cubic centimeter; ion temperature 950 electron-volts—or about ninety-five million degrees Kelvin; confinement time, 0.98 seconds.

Hertzberg swung around in his chair. His white hair and beard stood out so that from a distance he appeared to be a happy grin surrounded by a luminescent halo.

"Welcome to fusion land," he croaked.

The audience cheered, laughed and applauded. Bill Hawke came over and squeezed Hertzberg's shoulders. Then the machine sounded a warning that the next pulse was coming up, and Hertzberg turned back to the control panel.

"In honor of ecology and of our electric bill," he said, "let's not waste power. We're still working."

The next pulse verified the results of the last, and it was with a light heart that Russell Hertzberg faced the future. At this point he really didn't care what the machine did. He had finished his job.

POSTSCRIPT: Were it not for two prophetic items, this piece would be historical fiction rather than science fiction. Except for those two details, every major scientific event in this story has actually taken place. What makes this story science fiction? Simply the fact that Toroidal Device Number 3 has not—as yet—been built, so that the high temperatures and confinement times needed for thermonuclear fusion have not yet been reached. Otherwise, this story is based—rather loosely—on events that have happened. And some of them happened to me.

—M.A.R.

PRIME CRIME

12/22 1800

BORED EYES LAZILY scanning the video readout came to a sudden halt. Leo Renninger leaned forward in the swivel chair as though to impale the terminal upon beams of invisible force from his pale blue eyes. His flat-cut grey hair bristled.

Renninger read the line once more and there was no doubt about it. Comparing the failure rates of the fifteen computer sections during the past year, Biology stood out like a sore thumb. Up 100%, while the others had remained essentially unchanged.

Renninger's right hand drummed on the desk for a moment, then moved to the keyboard and tapped out the Maintenance code.

Two seconds for reply, and the green luminous letters flashed:

MAINTENANCE DEPARTMENT CLOSED FOR THE EVENING.
PLEASE LEAVE YOUR MESSAGE.
IN CASE OF EMERGENCY CALL . . .

Oh hell. Renninger glanced at his watch and saw that it was almost six.

Donovan contact renninger first thing in the morning, he typed. *Urgent.*

How urgent he didn't know. But just try to get somebody at this hour, three days before Christmas.

Oh hell. Again. And double damned. He stood up in a rush, shoving his chair across the room. He was due for dinner with Sandy in a half hour.

He paused at the front door in his rush out of the building. The spectacle of the rings of lights curving out and over in the evening sky of satellite Lagrange brought a sudden rush of feeling to his chest. At this time of year multicolored lights twinkling in scattered arrays reminded him of Christmas trees, of years back on Earth with a family no longer in existence. At this time of year buried memories exhumed themselves.

He sighed and fingered the small package in his pocket. It was time he found himself a permanent relationship again. He knew Sandy would like the diamond. It was a good one. It was one of the few things you could bring up from Earth without paying more for transportation than for the item itself.

12/22 1900

To Noah, Paula, and nine-year-old Joshua Pike, Christmas was family time. The satellite interior at nightfall, always a breathtaking sight, began to come alive with scintillations of lights stretching along the axis and circling the circumferences. Filters on the light slots cut the solar radiance down to a dusky rose and then to a deep, dark blue, so that within the cylindrical satellite habitat there was a normal rhythm of night and day.

As the end of the year approached, the standard street lighting began to be supplemented by strings of tiny, twinkling, multicolored bulbs, and even the hub of the satellite—the hollow tube that stretched along the axis from one end to the other was entwined with a garland of tiny lights. It felt to Noah Pike like living in the center of a Christmas tree.

To Joshua, first child born on the satellite, Christmas trees were made of scrap aluminum and colored plastic.

And once a year Santa Claus could be seen fleetingly in his glider swooping about in the low-gee region near the satellite center, a kilometer up. He didn't quite understand how all this had gotten started, but was enchanted by it, nevertheless.

To Paula, Christmas was time for the continuation of traditions transplanted from Earth. The machine shops and parts bins were scoured for recycled materials. Evenings were spent secretly making gifts.

For on Lagrange there were no department stores. Manufacturing was strictly utilitarian and the cost of bringing luxuries up from Earth was out of range of all but the wealthiest.

As Noah had warned Paula when they had emigrated: "All of life on the satellite will be conditioned by one simple but ruthless fact, based on the most fundamental laws of nature. To bring any object, living or dead, from Earth to the satellite requires a certain amount of energy. And energy costs money. It's a simple problem, and when you work it out you find that to move one kilogram of matter from Earth to Lagrange costs at least two hundred dollars *just for the fuel*. Add to that the cost of the vehicle and the rest of the equipment and your bill skyrockets out of sight."

On this night, as the family cleared the dinner table, Paula signalled Noah with her eyes, saying, "Why don't you go with Joshua to the concert, and I'll go over to Joanne's for the evening."

Noah grinned. He liked the feeling that she was going to spend time making something for him.

The walk to the park was easy. Joshua, all legs and hair, trotted alongside Noah. Noah wondered if the time spent in zero-gee caused elongation of the body. Watching the bands of lights curling over to meet at the antipodes, he made a mental note to see if it would be feasible to provide seasonal changes in the interior lighting.

As director of the Lagrange settlement, Noah Pike was responsible for introducing little touches that made the place livable. The first years had been sterile nightmares. Even though men and women came up from Earth to spend their life in serious pursuits—research, zero-gee manufacturing—the stark black and white atmosphere was deadly to everyday living. Color was needed. Live green most of all.

A pet project had been the music park, an opening circled by evergreens and tropical plants. The horticultural club fussed fanatically over the bordering flowers. Admittedly, no professional musicians existed on Lagrange; the population of two thousand plus was not enough to support a crew of live entertainers, let alone concert artists. For music they had amateurs with their guitars and flutes, and in the park there was the one really good audio system on Lagrange. Everyone had their own tapes at home, but few individuals could afford the massiveness of first-class loudspeakers and amplifiers.

Early for the concert, Noah and Joshua sank down on the soft grass near the center of the amphitheatre. With his big head of rumpled hair and closely trimmed, curly brown beard, Noah resembled a shaggy bear contemplating the flowers, cub at his side. He nodded briefly at the man already in place next to Joshua.

"Good evening, Mr. Pike."

Pike felt at a disadvantage and searched his mind for the man's name. Ernie. . . ? Yes. Ernie something.

"Good evening, Ernie. Nice night for a concert."

Ernie laughed silently. "It's always a nice night for a concert up here, Mr. Pike. You take good care of the weather."

It had never been known to rain on a concert night. Or any other night, for that matter. This small joke was as much as Ernie allowed himself. A small man with short, sandy hair and no distinguishing features, he was known to Pike only as a familiar face at the weekly concerts. Beyond that, nothing.

A guitarist fitted himself to a stool on the stage and the music began. Jack Lowrey had, obviously, been practicing, and the results showed.

The guitar pleased, but Pike missed hearing live piano.

The only piano they could get was on tape, re-recorded from earth. Tonight's treat was the latest Silbermann recording, notes issuing from the big loudspeakers like machine-gun bullets in cascades almost too fast for the ear to resolve.

There are some things that the ordinary mortal cannot do, no matter how hard he tries, no matter how long he practices. One of these things is playing the Mephisto Waltz in a manner even approximating that of the legendary Silbermann.

Halfway through, Pike's attention was jarred by a wriggling nine-year-old: Joshua, jerking from side to side on the grass. As he stared into some private infinity, his hands writhed like molten talons. Alarmed, Pike reached over and grasped the boy's arm.

"Son, are you all right?"

Joshua turned rigid, scowled in red-faced anger at the interruption, and slumped back to the ground. The music finished in a violent climax that tore the piano apart.

Pike blew air out of his lungs. "Just incredible!" he marveled. Ernie shook his head in awe. "Really unbelievable. Too much competition for us."

He turned his head to Joshua, who sat silent and stunned.

"That music really does something for you. You'd like to play like that, wouldn't you? Your father ought to have a piano brought up here."

The boy's eyes opened wide. "Hey, Dad, could you get a piano?"

Pike drew back. He had gone through this question a dozen times, and the numbers always came out the same. He threw a scowl at Ernie, as if to say *now look what you've started,* and turned to his son with a patient sigh.

"Joshua, do you have any idea how much a piano would cost here? Just to bring it here, to haul it up against the Earth's gravity. You know how much that costs? I'll tell you. The shipping charges from Earth to Lagrange come to about a thousand dollars per kilogram. You know what a thousand dollars is? That's about what I make in a whole week."

Joshua's eyes began to bulge.

Noah Pike continued, relentlessly. "Let's say a piano weighs about 500 kilograms. I'd have to justify spending $500,000 to transport a piano. I don't know where to put it in my budget."

Joshua's face burned with disappointment. "Damn it! Is money the only thing that counts?"

"No. But try doing anything without it. Energy costs money and the cost of energy has to be figured into everything you do."

"Then why not make the piano here, if it costs so much to move it?"

Pike laughed. "Have you any idea of how complicated a piano is, and how many different materials and skills go into making it? On Earth it took hundreds of years to build up the whole complex of industries feeding the right woods and wires and plastics to the piano builder. Give us time. We've only been here ten years.

"You don't have to make it the same old way," Ernie suggested. "Instead of ivory or wood you use metal and plastic. Instead of a heavy steel frame and sounding board you use tone generators and amplifiers."

"Then you don't have a piano," Pike objected. "You might have a synthesizer or organ, but it wouldn't be the same thing."

Ernie shrugged. "You have to start somewhere."

A tight little smile emerged briefly on his face, then vanished as he rose from the ground.

Noah Pike watched him as he left. A strange little man. Why had he come to Lagrange?

But then, everybody had a reason.

12/23 0900

Leo Renninger sat down at his desk, peace in his heart. Sandy had been agreeable, and it had been a good night.

He had barely made contact with the chair when the phone buzzed, Joe Donovan's face appearing on the small screen. Renninger flicked the reply switch.

"Good morning, Joe," he said. "Thanks for returning my call."

"Hi, boss. What's up?"

"I'm asking you," Renninger rasped. "Why the hundred-percent increase in maintenance calls in Biology? I should have been informed."

Donovan scratched his nose. "What maintenance calls? There've been no more than usual."

Renninger scowled. He purred, "Look, my friend, get yourself a readout on the annual statistical survey. See for yourself what the hell's been going on."

Donovan disappeared from the screen while he swiveled to his terminal. In a few moments he returned to the phone, his eyes worried. He licked his lips.

"What you say is true, boss. The statistics show twice as many maintenance calls in Biology than in the other sections. But if you look at the operating log, you find that there is no down time listed for about half of those maintenance dates."

He inhaled noisily. "Looks to me like half of those maintenance calls are fakes."

Renninger digested the information angrily. A premonition of trouble clouded what had started to be a fine morning.

"Donovan, you had better find out what kind of monkey business is going on in your department. I'm coming up to your shop and I want an explanation by the time I get there."

"Yessir." Donovan's startled image faded.

Renninger stood up from his chair and at a brisk pace strode down the long corridor toward the elevator. His figure had kept much of its military posture, even after years at a desk.

Fortunately the car was down and there was no wait. He marched through the door, thumbed the UP button and leaned his elbows against the rail in the far corner of the elevator. The floor pressed heavily on his feet as the car rose upward through the roof and into the outer light surrounded by an open tube of metal and plastic grillwork.

Initially the scene expanding before him had been breathtakingly spectacular. But that had been ten years ago. Now he stared blankly at the concave horizon falling away from him, the swoop and curve of the ground as it looped over to meet itself at the antipodes.

The hollow cylinder of the satellite stretched out before and behind him. Its ten kilometers of length and two of diameter opened up and out as the elevator sped vertically toward the axial tube. In the early days he had been startled by the press of the coriolis force jamming him against the side of the elevator. But now it was taken for granted as one of the facts of life experienced on a rotating satellite. Streamers of light reflected through slits by external mirrors sliced through the air, illuminating the checkerboard of streets and buildings that went along and around the interior of Lagrange.

The satellite axis was the central tube, four hundred meters in diameter, where zero-gee manufacturing and research activities were located. Filling approximately a million cubic meters of this space were the fifteen sections of the Computer Division, his domain to oversee.

When the elevator slid into its receptacle within the axial tube, Renninger still felt one-fifth nominal Earth gravity. Further in towards the axis was the true zero-gee section, a cylinder decoupled from the satellite rotation, resting motionless in absolute space, while the satellite spun about it. To those in Lagrange, this inner section appeared to be a spinning axle within a stationary satellite.

As Renninger entered the Maintenance office, Joe Donovan stood up from his terminal. Disbelief on his face, he pointed to the screen.

"There are the facts. See for yourself."

Renninger sat down, while Donovan pointed with a shaky finger at the column headings.

"See. I'm listing computer down times, maintenance times, and lists of parts withdrawn from stock for repairs. Look. Here, here . . . and here. Maintenance dates and lists of withdrawn parts on those dates. But no indication on the operating log that the computer was actually shut down for repair at those times."

Renninger stared at the screen, his eyes going from column to column, his lips becoming more and more tense.

Finally he exhaled. "Okay. It's clear what's happening. Somebody has devised this clumsy plan to steal electronic parts. It's just a step above straightforward theft from the stockroom. At least that would have been caught at the first monthly inventory. As it is, he files a phony maintenance report and requisitions the parts for repair. That took a year to uncover.

"But look, only authorized personnel go through the computer into Supply. Who's been making all these requisitions?"

Gloom deepened on Donovan's face. "See for yourself. John Bergen on every one. Sound familiar?"

"No. Should I know him?"

Donovan spread his arms. "No, you shouldn't. The name's a phony, too."

"So. Our man's clever enough to get into the computer and forge credentials." Renninger considered just how clever that had to be. Momentary anger flared behind his eyes.

"Well, what the hell?" Donovan leaned back in his chair and laughed. "How far can he get on this hunka tin? All we have to do is to look for a homemade computer built from our spare parts."

Renninger cooled down. "Assuming it's a computer. We don't know what kind of device it might be. If I thought for a moment that it might be a threat to the safety and security of Lagrange, I'd call for an immediate general search of all quarters. But we don't even know what we're looking for."

He came to a decision. "Okay, then. That's what we need. Get me a printout of the missing components. We'll analyze the list for function and deduce what is being assembled. Then we'll decide where to look."

Donovan chewed his lips thoughtfully. "And who's going to do the looking? We don't have any police."

Renninger sighed. "It looks as though we might have to make some. This place has done without cops for ten years. But now the screws are starting to come loose. Progress is being made."

12/23   1130

The parts list lay on Renninger's desk, long and baffling. It read like a general catalog: digital registers, memories, multiplexers, logic circuits, oscillators, amplifiers. Computer components predominated, but there was an admixture of items that appeared to have audio or communications functions.

How could he make sense out of this? Why would anybody want

to make a communication device? Within Lagrange you could call anybody just by picking up the phone.

But suppose you wanted to make an outside call? And suppose you did not want that call to be monitored?

Renninger began to feel a chill coursing down his spine as he swiveled aimlessly in his chair and focused his mind on the possible reason for secret communication with the other satellite colonies that circled the Earth. The Russian, the Chinese, the Third World Collective . . . What could be going on?

Growing dread filtered into the passages of his mind. Abruptly his aimless rotation stopped and his hand reached out for the phone switch. The director would have to be notified.

As Noah Pike's face appeared in the screen Renninger suppressed a faint sense of distaste. The image was too much that of a shaggy bear; more the scientist than the administrator. Renninger's taste ran more to straightness, smoothness, and efficiency.

"Good morning," said the image in the screen. "What's up?"

"I'd rather tell you in person. Can I come over?"

"Right away?"

"Sooner."

Pike's eyebrows raised. "Okay, I'll put off a few visits and will expect you over—approximately instantly."

Even with the pneumatic tube, travel to Pike's office was not completely instantaneous, but as Renninger loped into the room he appeared to have been running continuously since leaving the phone.

With a fast look at Renninger's face, Pike decided this was no time for casual chit-chat.

"Okay, lay it out," he said.

Renninger removed the printouts from his portfolio and spread them on the desk in front of Pike. Quickly he explained the discrepancies and the lists of missing parts.

"It's not just the loss of a few thousand dollars' worth of equipment I'm worried about," he said, finally. "It's the fact that somebody on Lagrange is building something in secret. We cannot tolerate any kind of secret activities. Our position is too precarious."

Pike scanned the list in silence, while Renninger sat on the edge of his chair. For a moment Pike hummed to himself, then spoke.

"Let me just think out loud. We have these thefts that have been going on for nearly a year. Question: is there an emergency? What's the probability that something serious will happen during the next day or two?

"Putting it another way, what are the chances that the device being built, whatever it is, has been finished? If it's still in the building stage, then our procedure is simple. We put a flag on the computer to catch our culprit the next time he makes a requisition like this again. What if he has finished? Then we must catch him before he puts the device into operation. The presumption being that whatever he is doing surreptitiously can't be doing us any good. That is the only safe assumption."

"Under that assumption," Renninger broke in, "I recommend that we institute a complete search of the satellite. Go into every corner. Every apartment. Immediately."

Pike's face slowly grew a pained expression. "There are two things wrong with that idea. First, we don't have a police force. Second, we are still legally part of the United States, and there are constitutional safeguards against unlawful search and seizure. Lagrange was founded as a civilian research establishment, not as a military base, and our scientists take a dim view of violation of their legal rights."

Renninger exploded. "Good grief. You quote constitutional rights when the safety of the satellite is at stake? If you knew a bomb was hidden somewhere, would you wait for a search warrant?"

"If I knew a bomb was hidden on the satellite," Pike replied, "I would take appropriate action. But I don't know that a bomb is hidden. I don't know that there is a clear and immediate danger to the satellite. We can't go charging off and upsetting the entire population because we think there might be a problem."

Renninger stared at Pike in disbelief. He selected his words carefully and coldly. "When you think there is a possible danger, then you prepare for the worst contingency. You cannot gamble with our security."

"Okay." Pike capitulated and began to count off on his fingers. "We'll do the following. First, put a flag on the Maintenance computer to catch the next phony requisition. Second, we get the external maintenance crew to start an immediate search for an unauthorized antenna. If this is a communication device we're dealing with, there must be an antenna somewhere. Third, internal maintenance will search all non-private spaces inside the satellite. Anything connected to an antenna should be not too far from the antenna. Fourth, we call a meeting of the Satellite Executive Board for first thing tomorrow morning. They will have to approve any extended search.

"In the meantime we intensify the monitoring of radio signals to and from Lagrange. If illicit communication is taking place, we'll catch it in the act.

"Anything else I haven't thought of?"

Renninger gave grudging respect for the precision of Pike's mind, once nudged off of dead center.

"Short of searching personal quarters, it sounds thorough."

"The maintenance crews are just going to love this, two days before Christmas."

"Every day's a working day up here. In space eternal vigilance is the price of life."

"Amen. Be here for our meeting tomorrow. Make it at nine."

Renninger, having returned to his office, sat back at his desk, fingers drumming the smooth surface quietly. The lids on his eyes lowered as he contemplated an unpleasant fact. There was one more thing he had to do.

From the back of a drawer he removed a small notebook. A page towards the rear disclosed a name and phone number he had not used since coming to Lagrange. With eyes still hooded he punched the number and waited.

It was time his link to Intelligence became activated.

12/23 1830

As Noah Pike watched Joshua from the corner of his eye it occurred to him that growing up in Lagrange was not really much fun. The little world had to be more confining than a small town in mid-America. Already Joshua was feeling the constraint of physical barriers.

The boy, slowly eating his dinner, appeared drawn into himself and unapproachable.

"Are you feeling all right?" his mother asked him.

He shrugged. "I'm okay." His eyes kept to his plate, his fork circling aimlessly.

Pike felt his own tension level rising, always the result when Joshua went into his slow, sulky burn. *Look,* he told himself, *it's not your fault you can't bring a piano up here. Don't get guilty.* Still, amidst all the paraphernalia, furniture, games, soil, trees that had been brought up, a piano might have been included.

"What are you doing during school vacation?" he asked, not too probing, not too remote.

"Oh, just messing around with the kids. Finishing up a new game on the computer. I'll be ready to beat you tomorrow."

A flicker of interest crept into his voice and a quick, sly grin rose to his face.

Volatile was the word, Pike thought. Already, in the past two years, the boy had lived through the space-pilot period, the astronomy kick, the mathematics binge, and the computer programming passion. Was music to be next?

What are you going to be, Joshua, when you grow up?

The words formed in Noah Pike's mind, but he clenched his teeth to keep them unspoken. *What you are not going to be is something that requires large crowds of people. You're not going to be a football player or film star, a sailor or a mountain climber. You'll visit Laplace, the twin satellite. You'll travel to other satellites, to the Moon, perhaps to Mars if you go in that direction. Yes, we are like a small town. We can hear a concert pianist on records, watch him on TV, but never will he come here to give a live performance. You may escape to Earth, for falling down is relatively cheap. But once down, returning to Lagrange means either being on official business or possessing a personal fortune.*

Joshua slipped away from the table.

"Where are you going?" his father wanted to know.

"Oh, just out to the park."

And he was gone, his father's eyes following him out the door. *Stop worrying. Probably when the kid grows up he'll be something you never even heard of. After all, when you were a kid, would anybody have believed you'd grow up to become director of a satellite colony?*

12/24   0900

By morning the information on Pike's desk was uniformly negative. Search of the satellite skin had turned up nothing resembling an antenna.

Search of the interior, still under way, had revealed nothing out of the ordinary. Continuous monitoring of the entire electromagnetic spectrum revealed no unauthorized signals.

The Executive Board filled the small conference room next to Pike's office. Their interpretation of the silence was simple: the mystery device was not yet complete.

"Then," said Pike, "we'll catch our man next time he makes a requisition."

"Not necessarily." Larry Conn, Chief of Psychology, vehemently shook his head. "He's already been warned. Everybody on Lagrange has noticed the search parties and rumors are flying. He'll change his system before ordering more material."

"What do you conclude from your analysis of the components?" Pike asked Renninger.

"No conclusion. We just know that the list contains parts from three kinds of systems—computer, audio, and communication. The closest we can come to a guess is some kind of multiplexed communication system with digital controls."

Renninger scratched his chin in bafflement. "Incidentally," he continued, "not only did our thief appropriate these items by using an assumed name, but he programmed the computer to accept that name as an authorized identity for making requisitions. This means our man really knows his way around the insides of the computer. He's a programmer as well as a technician."

Larry Conn raised his head in interest. "We might locate your man by searching the personnel files for somebody with the skill to put together this kind of gadget."

"A very good thought, Larry," said Pike. "Go to it. Don't spare the bytes."

At the meeting's end, Pike felt less tension than before. He had handed his worries to a committee and the sensation of crisis was slackened. For an hour he cleared away routine business, humming to himself, satisfied that he was doing what had to be done.

His peace crumbled at the phone ring. From Earth, the call was coded and scrambled, of highest priority. Pike stared at the uniformed figure on the screen and felt anger beginning to rise.

"General Rogers here. Division of Intelligence. We have received word that there is a potential security problem on Lagrange. I want to offer our assistance and cooperation."

"I beg your pardon, sir, but may I ask how Intelligence has become aware of our situation?" Pike's voice grated in his own ears.

"We are not free to divulge our sources," the other replied smoothly. "Our only purpose is to ensure that maximum effort is going into the solution of your problem. The security of Lagrange is paramount."

In other words, translated Pike, get off your asses and do something, or else we'll do it for you. It must have been Renninger, that slick sonovabitch, going over his head. . . .

Pike fiercely resented the intrusion of the DOI into the situation. The formation of Lagrange colony had, from the very beginning, set off a many-sided struggle between civilian government agencies, industry, non-government scientists, and the Department of Defense. The outcome had been an uneasy compromise between government and civilians to maintain Lagrange as a strictly research and manufacturing station. Evidently Intelligence, not satisfied with this settlement, had infiltrated the ranks; and now if it appeared as though the civilians could not handle their own security problem, the military would come in and handle it for them. In the end, if they had their way, Lagrange would become a military outpost, and there would be band music in the park instead of Bop and Beethoven.

One consequence of that call was authorization to search the residences of all personnel—in particular those with enough electronics education to imply a reasonable presumption of guilt. More of an order than an authorization, it took a morsel of the responsibility from his back, but Pike refused to be consoled. Once he took the irreversible step of instituting a general search, Lagrange would be started down the path toward the kind of state in which any individual right could be eliminated by declaring it was all for the good of the colony.

Besides, it was Christmas Eve.

There had to be some other route to take.

With a quick determination he punched Larry Conn's number. "Larry, I know this is a hell of a time, but can you put in some overtime tonight and tomorrow?"

"Sure. I'm hanging loose."

"You got those names you were going after?"

"Sure. One hundred eighty-nine of them. Either with degrees in electronics, physics, or related subjects, or with experience as technicians."

"Okay. I want every piece of information you can find on those names. Education, hobbies, associations, phone calls to and from Earth, anything you can think of."

Conn's eyebrows shot up. "Well, we have psychological profiles on most of the folks, but we're not exactly a secret police. And there's a question of confidentiality."

"Confidentiality be damned," Pike roared. "I have an order to search every apartment on the satellite if I have to. Would you rather have that on Christmas Eve?"

Conn sighed. "Okay, Chief. I'll put the material on your terminal and will hop over to your office. Best we scan the stuff together."

Several hours of drudgery got them halfway through the list, at which time Pike became aware of hunger pangs gnawing a hole in his middle.

Conn sat back and stretched his arms. "Well, we've learned a lot about our neighbors, but I haven't heard any little bells tinkling in my skull. These are very ordinary people."

"Come home to dinner," Pike said, pushing his chair away from the terminal. "We'll finish the rest later."

Patient Paula had drinks and the table ready. "I ate hours ago with Joshua," she explained as she zapped the food in the microwave oven.

Pike looked around. The small apartment, colorful with prints and Christmas decorations, seemed quiet. "Where's Joshua now?"

"Who knows? Out with his friends. Where can you get into trouble on Lagrange?"

"They'll find a way." Pike grinned to underline the jest, but feared the truth.

As they sat with their coffee Joshua came in. His hair was more disheveled than ever, there was an energy of excitation in his gait, a light in his eyes. Christmas, Noah Pike thought.

"Hi, dad." Joshua's eyes peered with curiosity at the stranger sitting opposite.

"Hi, Josh. Meet Larry Conn. We're doing some night work, trying to solve a mystery."

"Hey, slick. What kind of mystery?"

"A mystery of missing electronic parts pilfered from a crooked computer. Tell me, you and your friends haven't been building a homemade computer, have you?"

Joshua turned away. "Aw, dad, don't be silly. I'm not into that kid stuff anymore."

Already? What was he into? Noah's eyes followed Joshua as he moved over to the couch and spread out a sheet of paper. Peering over the edge of the coffee cup, Noah watched Joshua sitting on the couch, eyes intent on the paper in his lap, hands spread on an imaginary keyboard, fingers moving slowly to an inaudible tune.

Damned if the kid didn't look as though he was teaching himself how to play the piano. Unfortunately, this was one passion that could be of absolutely no use to him. Even if he were born with the nervous system of a Horowitz or a Silbermann there was no piano on which he could develop its potentialities. What did he expect to do?

Noah Pike felt baffled over Joshua's new behavior, but soon the main problem returned to his mind and drove out every intruding thought.

12/25   0900

On Christmas morning, while every inhabitant of Lagrange greeted the day in his own way, Noah Pike and Larry Conn sat in a lonely office completing the scan of personnel records. By this time Pike had adjusted to the idea that nothing was going to come of it. The quarry's cover was too well-planned to be disclosed by a simpleminded run through the computer files. No way of knowing what each of the legitimate-appearing phone calls signified.

Pike's eyes hurt. As he massaged them gently with his fingertips he told Conn, "Go home, Larry. But stand by. I'm going to make the big decision this afternoon."

Instead of heading home from the office, Pike found his feet walking him to the elevator. He recognized the symptoms: his body took him to the place where he could think best.

In total gravless condition, in the shimmering light of a million stars pouring through the observatory shell, Pike floated in silence. Earth could be seen in one direction; the twin cylinder of Laplace floated a few kilometers away in another. Spinning in opposite directions, the twin cylinders manufactured their illusion of gravity while avoiding the gyroscopic behavior of a single rotor. Consequently the task of maintaining one end perpetually pointed at the sun was rendered relatively simple.

Enclosed in the transparent bubble, Pike felt acute awareness of the fragile ecology of the satellite, a thin balloon surrounded by the deadly vacuum of interplanetary space. This vacuum left little margin for error, little time for response to crisis. Any misstep could lead to destruction.

He felt squeezed in a vise. If he could not settle the mystery by technical means, then he had to use brute force methods such as general search of the satellite. If he did not do it himself, someone else would do it. Whichever way, the basic character of Lagrange would be changed; its political innocence would be gone forever.

The limited search was a compromise. Search only those you had reason to suspect. That would reduce the matter to 189 invasions of privacy. While, in a sense, that had already been done, now they would be aware of it.

Returning to his office, he set up a conference call with the Executive Board. He waited as the faces flashed on to twelve tiny rectangles on the phone screen and considered grimly that at least now the guilt would be spread around. The search would be carried out by the Board members personally, together with assorted department heads and assistants.

The screams of protest came close to blowing the fuses on the phone, but he remained adamant. Incessantly he repeated his argument: "The Intelligence people on Earth are on our backs, and if we don't want them coming up here and taking over, we simply must do this job ourselves. I hate it as much as you do, but if we don't show that we can operate Lagrange in an emergency, we'll be out of power before we've completed another orbit. This is a political issue now."

"But on Christmas day!"

"Yes. Get them while they're all home."

The peaceful brown bear had turned into a snarling wolf. What he hated most was seeing the satisfied, knowing grin on Renninger's face as the conference ended.

12/25 1600

Through the emergency intercom Noah Pike's well-known voice filled every room on the satellite.

"Forgive the intrusion on this day, but our emergency requires us to act now. You know of the material stolen from the electronics stockroom. It is imperative that we find those parts, or the device that has been constructed from them. Starting now, teams of searchers will visit 189 selected homes. We ask your cooperation and request that you all remain outside your homes for the duration of the search to ensure that nothing is moved from one apartment to another."

Fourteen pairs of searchers moved out into the streets, where up and down the length of Lagrange astonished men and women stood outside their doors and whispered among themselves. For the first time since the founding of the colony, suspicion crept along the walkways. Neighbors glanced at each other from the corners of their eyes, knowing that one among them had turned out to be a thief. The first crime on Lagrange had been committed.

The logic of the operation was based on the list of stolen parts. Assembled, the package had to be too big for hiding under a pile of shirts. Since the criterion for selecting the 189 names had not been announced, no one could be sure who was going to be searched.

By midnight it was all over, but puzzled, angry, indignant conversations continued along the streets far into the small hours.For Pike and the Executive Board there was nothing but exhaustion. Nothing had been found.

They sat about in Pike's living room, gloomily finishing his stock of wine.

Larry Conn groaned in frustration. "Our man has just fallen through the cracks."

Renninger sat stiffly, eyes narrowed, lips compressed.

"We've clearly been looking in the wrong places," he said. "We've been assuming the thing is hidden, that we have to search for it. What if it's right out in the open? Suppose the device was assembled in one of our shops and is sitting there in the middle of all the other electronics equipment. Who would know?"

Pike stared at him. "There's some supervisor who would get his ass in a sling."

Renninger persisted, his voice low, intense.

"We've overlooked so many possibilities that I'm convinced it's hopeless to solve the problem by logic. We must go ahead with the total search of everybody on the satellite. Everybody is suspect."

Pike assented, gloomily. "And paranoia wins the game."

Sleep came hard that night.

12/26   0900

Noah Pike wrestled with logistics and conscience. Logistics was mechanics: organizing a search of one thousand and twelve domiciles involved nothing but manpower, time, and strategy. Conscience was tougher, involving broken promises, about the kind of society being forged, where freedom from search could no longer be guaranteed.

Best to make a clean breast of it. Explain the risks, the reasons.

Larry Conn called, excitement in his voice and in his eyes.

"I found the cracks!" he crowed.

"Explain that, kindly." Pike felt slow.

"The cracks they fell through. It was my fault. I had pulled out the names of those who came to Lagrange with education in electronics. However, I had not accounted for the possibility that some people might have learned the subject since coming to Lagrange. It turns out there are six of them. Six eligibles who missed the search last night."

There was a buzzing in Pike's head, a tingling down his spine. He ran his hand through his hair, through his beard. He refused to become hopeful.

"Shoot them over to my terminal," he said quietly.

No particular flavor could be tasted in the first three files. Nothing set them apart from the other technicians except for that one difference: their credentials had come through correspondence courses from Earth.

The next one started the bells tingling.

To begin with, the photograph accompanying the file showed a face strangely familiar, and he thought that five years of aging would make it even more familiar. What really set off the alarm was one strange discrepancy in the *curriculum vitae*.

Name: Ernest Miller. (Vaguely familiar?)
Present occupation: Programmer for Biology Division.
Age: 35
Marital status: single; no particular friend.
Education: B.S. and M.S. in Computer Science, NYU. B.S. in Piano and Organ, Juilliard Institute.
(Juilliard? Why did he go from Juilliard to computer science at NYU? Computer music, perhaps?)
Correspondence courses from United College of Electronics, incomplete.

Questions crowded quickly and tumbled over each other. Why the correspondence courses? Why, indeed, was Miller on Lagrange at all? Was this an escape from a failed musical career?

Pike skipped to the phone records. Facsimile transmission of textbooks and lessons from the school. Copious correspondence—problems and exams. Then an entire collection of calls to someone at the Allen Corporation. What in the world was the Allen Corporation?

After a moment's thought, Pike channeled a swift call to the Library of Congress. Breath held, sitting like a rock, he waited the thirty seconds until the reply unfolded across his screen. As he read it, his brows knitted deep furrows. It made no sense, until bits and pieces of memories began to float and fit together. Then he began to laugh. The more they fit the more he laughed until, doubled over, he could no longer wipe the tears from his eyes.

In this state Leo Renninger found him.

"Are you all right?" It was not clear to Renninger what kind of fit had struck Pike.

Pike shook his head, his body quaking weakly. "I'm all right, but I'll never be the same again. My friend, have we just led ourselves into the wrong orbit! Sheer panic, that's all. Just sheer panic. We latched onto a theory and followed it straight into the ground."

"Pike, what the hell are you talking about?" Renninger rasped in exasperation. He was beginning to think the director had stripped his gears.

"I'll show you." Pike got up and led Renninger by the elbow out the door. "Come with me and I'll show you a great wonder."

Pike took the distance to the Biology Computer Center in long strides, humming cheerfully to himself. Renninger followed, resenting the mystery game, conscious of being patronized.

They found the programming section, a cluster of cubbyholes, within one of which nested Ernest Miller.

"Hi, Ernie," said Pike, tapping at the open door. Startled, half-turned in his chair, Ernie Miller appeared about to run.

"Take it easy, Ernie," Pike whispered, gently. "I just stopped by to see if you have something to tell me. Or to show me. When we talked at the concert I didn't know you were a musician. But I might have guessed. Can you show me what you have?"

The relaxation of Ernie's body was so sudden that he appeared to slump in his chair. The faint, tight smile appeared on his lips.

"I was going to show you anyway, Mr. Pike. But with all the excitement going on I got scared. I was afraid you wouldn't understand."

"I understand. Where is it?"

"It's at home. Come on. I'll show you."

"Show us what?" Renninger demanded to know.

Pike grinned. "You'll see."

Miller's apartment was a tiny two-room-and-bath affair. As Pike entered, his eyes made the circuit of the miniature kitchen, the day-bed, the table, and the door leading to the other room. Naturally, that's where it would be.

Miller went ahead and opened the door. Pike, peering past his shoulders, obtained a confused impression of a room jumbled with tools hanging from the walls, shelves loaded with tiny boxes, racks of electronics strung with a tangled web of cables. The center of the maze was a box-like affair with a pair of keyboards flanked by rows of switches. On the floor was a sequence of pedals, an enlarged version of the manual keyboards.

Seated on a bench in front of this contrivance was a small figure with long legs and bushy hair, face sandwiched between a huge set of earphones. From the rear Pike had no trouble recognizing the nine-year-old Joshua, lost in concentration, eyes fixed to a page of music, hands slowly walking over the keys, feet feeling their way among the pedals.

The last bit of the puzzle snapped into place.

"Well, Ernie, I'm not surprised."

Noah Pike entered the room, marveling at the complexity of the installation. "I knew what you had," he said, "as soon as I found out that the Allen people make organs."

Joshua heard the sound of voices, turned around, and his eyes became saucers. "Uh-oh," he said. "The jig's up."

"I've been letting him come here to practice," Ernie Miller explained. "This is a very talented kid. Listen to what he's done in less than a week. Keep playing, Josh."

Miller flipped a switch that allowed the sound to issue from a small loudspeaker in the corner. Slowly shifting harmonies of something pre-Bach smoothly stroked their ears.

Miller grinned in satisfaction. "First time I've had it on the loudspeaker. No need to keep quiet now.

Renninger finally exploded. "So this is what we've been chasing after. Kept us up one night after another. Dozens of people searching hundreds of homes. Upsetting the entire satellite. Not to mention a hundred thousand dollars' worth of components. All for a lousy music box."

Ernie flushed. "I'm sorry about all the trouble. I was going to tell everybody about the organ when I was all finished, but you got on to me before I had a chance, and then I got scared."

"And now you're in real trouble," Pike pointed out. "Grand larceny by computer. You'd have done better to make a direct proposal for a cultural project."

Ernie shrugged his shoulders, glumly. "You said yourself you couldn't justify the cost. I figured I'd be an old man and my fingers would be as stiff as a corpse before I got an okay. My hands were beginning to hurt because I wasn't using them. So I said, build the thing first. Then get approval."

He touched the boy's elbow. "Josh, show them what this thing will do."

Joshua grinned widely and said, "Dad, this is a really neat organ. Listen to this."

His hands flew among the switches, and the loudspeaker responded with roars, whispers, pipings, flutings, and other assorted sounds. Ernie listened, entranced, his head cocked to one side.

"The sounds are from real organ pipes," he said. "The memory bank stores the wave parameters and the computer pulls them out on command. It's a standard method."

While Noah Pike watched Joshua play, a new problem insinuated itself into his mind.

"You say Joshua is talented?"

"One in a billion. He's picked up the music so fast it makes my head spin. It would be a crime not to give him the training to use it. I can give him a start and he can get the rest from Earth."

"And without your inspired insanity," Noah said, "your notion to put together this wild contraption, Joshua would never have known what he wanted. Craziness, chance, impulse, they drive us in directions we never anticipated."

Pike turned to Renninger, who had been standing in the doorway with thunder in his eyes.

"Cheer up, old man. At least we'll have Intelligence off our backs now. Our only problem now is explaining all this without looking like a bunch of complete idiots."

"If we're idiots we may as well look the part," Renninger grunted. A chuckle escaped involuntarily and the dour look on his face softened. "Seems to me your problem now is finding room in the budget for this junk pile. And while you're at it find somebody to clean up the wiring. You can't expect Josh to give concerts on a disaster like this."

Pike smiled gratefully. A new view of the future took form in his mind. The well-laid plans for Lagrange were about to give way to unforeseen forces. The organization charts with room only for solid, useful citizens were about to bend and crack as young people would make up their own minds concerning their destinies. The ranks of engineers, technicians, and scientists would become tempered with artists and entertainers. And who was to say which was more useful?

The only prediction he could make for sure was that the next generation would be unpredictable.

THE ETERNAL GENESIS

THE ALARM WHINED abruptly into Jon Secular's ears. He jerked his head around and stared with hard eyes and grim, compressed lips at the emergency readout. The landing had been going slick as oiled teflon, and suddenly there was this message blinking away at him in big red letters: **Gamma detectors saturated at 100 rem per minute.** *And 500 rem was lethal.*

The shuttle had barely made contact with the outer fringes of the atmosphere. Mother ship Primus hung above at 20 thousand kilometers.

Secular's grey eyes turned for half a breath to the forward viewscreen and scanned the terrain 200 kilometers below. The planet looked blue and inviting; no sign of hostile energy transmitters was visible.

He hesitated for another half a breath and then spoke tautly into the microphone. "General alarm. Fasten seat belts all. I'm pulling us out of this atmosphere. Mason, compute us a course to return to Primus."

He punched a command into the control, then leaned back in his acceleration chair and pulled the restraining web across, in time to feel the surge of the rockets as they labored to pull the shuttle out of the descending spiral.

The radio squawked. "Hermann here on Primus. We see your course changing. What's wrong?"

"I don't know. From the symptoms we're under attack, but I don't see any attackers. Our detectors have crapped out under a huge flux of gamma radiation. Can your people determine where the gammas are coming from?"

Secular waited while hearing words muttering and mumbling in the background. Finally: "Hermann again. Our radiation people tell us the gammas are directly from your shuttle. There's no other source."

Secular's mouth hung open in blank disbelief. His hand pushed back the shock of greying hair that had tumbled over his eyes. "Are you telling me we suddenly became radioactive? I can't believe it."

"Let me get Geza Janosz on the phone."

He called for Janosz; the computer searched the shuttle passenger compartment and in a moment the thin face within the frame of white hair became centered in the video screen. The figure was frail, but the long, bony hands could still play a lively tune on the computer keyboard.

"Why are we leaving this planet?" Janosz asked the moment Secular's face bloomed in his screen. His eyes were like black olives.

"We're returning to Primus. Because we're being blasted by an enormous dose of gamma rays. Another few minutes and it would have been fatal."

"Gammas? From where?" Janosz's eyes glared into Secular's face with an intensity that still caused a curling and a fading within the younger man.

"That's the strange part. Primus tells me that gammas are coming directly from our own shuttle. I had thought we were under attack. But there is no evidence of an outside source. How can we suddenly become radioactive?"

Janosz seemed to sink into his flight chair. His eyes became hooded and for a brief moment closed. When they opened they glared With black ferocity at Secular. "Ask Primus if we are still radiating. And ask them to determine the energy of the radiation."

Secular returned to the radio, patching it to the phone so that Janosz could hear the reply. "Hermann, what's happening to the radiation?"

Hermann's voice, baffled, uncertain, crackled across the vacuum from orbiting Primus. "It's gone down. Drastically. The farther out you climb the less radiation there is."

"Janosz wants to know its energy."

"Just a minute. I'll ask the technicians."

Again mutterings in the background, while Jon Secular scanned the readouts on the control panels, checking for normalcy. The forward screen showed star-spangled blackness with the spheroid of Primus in the upper right hand corner.

Hermann's voice returned on the ship-to-ship. "They tell me it's about half an MeV Zero point five one one MeV, to be exact. Does that mean anything?"

"Janosz should know."

Secular turned to Janosz in the screen and stopped, shocked. The old man's mouth was turned down in cold, bitter disappointment. His shoulders heaved slowly, and his gnarled hands came up to cover the tears that welled up from the corners of his eyes.

Lost. It was all lost. Janosz's mourning deepened. He covered his face and rocked in his chair. A century of effort, 88 years of travel, a civilization, an entire heritage of humanity, all for naught. Memories sifted through his mind—a montage of scenes from that world irrevocably left behind: the development of his grandiose plan to escape from the collapsing universe; the decade-long struggle to build the Primus, their lifeboat into eternity. Hollowed out of a ten-kilometer asteroid, it offered at least a miniscule sample of humanity an opportunity to escape from universal collapse into blackness.

Outward they had traveled, at a constant acceleration of one normal gravity, picking up speed at a steady pace until at the end of three years' time they were within one percent of the speed of light. And still they continued to accelerate, year after year, while time and space altered their aspect in relation to the ship. For 22 ship years they drove outward, beyond the Galaxy, past all the remaining galaxies, leaving the universe behind while it passed through four billion years of collapse and black death.

Then, a new bang, a new birth, a new universe. All the while they slowed down, accelerated back toward the newly condensing galaxies and stars, and decelerated once more until able to approach a new, fresh planet. A total of 16 billion years had transpired in the universe, while the travelers had lived through 88 years of working, playing, making love, bearing children, growing old.

Then, just at the instant of triumph, just at the approach in the shuttle to the tenuous outward reaches of the planetary atmosphere, they were forced to recoil, to flee back to the haven of mother ship.

All lost. All wasted.

Jon Secular's voice pulled him out of blackness. "Janosz, what is it?"

"Don't you know?" Janosz's voice, shrunken and bitter, crept through the phone system, with barely the strength to fall on Secular's ear. "Half an MeV is the energy of annihilation radiation—the gamma rays created when electrons meet positrons. The dying cry of matter annihilating antimatter."

"Antimatter!"

"Don't you see what's happening? We lived past the death of our universe and the birth of a new one. But the new universe chose to become made of antimatter. We can never land on this planet. We can only flout aimlessly through space, and in time our ship will gradually become annihilated as it reacts with the gas of interstellar space. Our great effort has been in vain. The life of our species is finished."

Silence wrapped itself like a cloak around Janosz as he sank back into his seat.

May Wheeler turned from the fading screen, her mouth twisted in dissatisfaction. "It's not a bad idea," she said, grudgingly, "but the customers want an upbeat ending. The characters have to get themselves out of their jam."

She stood up and stretched. The room was small, colorless, with only the projection screen on the wall, three chairs, and a table with the usual terminal module. Wheeler perched herself on the edge of the table. Her figure was a continuum of curves and bulges; but her face was becoming hard, the lines at the corners of her mouth and between the eyes beginning to subtract from her attractiveness.

The fact that she had to tilt her head way back to look at the object of her criticism in no way slowed her tongue.

"Furthermore," she continued, "you have this story laid some billions of years in the future, when the universe has turned around and is collapsing instead of expanding. But your characters are completely human, with ordinary American or European names. Hell, we have more changes than that in a few hundred years. Give a little more color, a little more of that famous imagination of yours."

Jim Kincaid blushed. He blushed easily, his skin rabbity pink, his white hair scrabbly. He gangled interminably, appeared to be all legs and knees and elbows. His eyes were as blue as a sky he had never seen and the lines of his mouth were beginning to take on a gentle firmness. He looked down sadly onto the top of May Wheeler's head.

"No tragedies, eh?"

"No tragedies. When you get to be Shakespeare you can write a tragedy. Right now you're trying to get your leg up in the entertainment world and the public likes nice endings, with all problems solved. And we're trying to get a studio going that will bring some money into Lagrange. So use your talents profitably. You do have talents. Don't throw them away."

Kincaid sighed. "Okay, I'll try again." His voice was that of a very ancient twenty-year-old.

He left the room through a door labeled LAGRANGE ENTERTAINMENT RESEARCH BUREAU and ambled his way to the nearest radial column, finding an elevator waiting. As the elevator rose to the central shaft of satellite Lagrange, he ignored the spectacular sight of the hollow cylinder swelling up around him while he climbed two kilometers to the zero-gee region. His chair swiveled to align him with the total of the forces pulling on him. Because he was inside a rotating satellite, centrifugal force pulled him outward; because he was moving toward the center, coriolis force pulled him sideways. As it appeared from his vantage point the entire satellite tilted crazily about, but he ignored this behavior because this was the way things always had been since his day of birth.

The elevator slowed as it reached the central shaft and stopped just inside. Once inside that hollow cylinder stretching the entire length of the satellite, he braced himself for the lateral acceleration that whipped his small car around to match its speed with that of the small opening in the inner shaft spinning massively over his head, making one revolution every 90 seconds.

With an ingenious maneuver, the elevator capsule made a quick rotation and fastened its mouth to the opening on the face of the inner shaft. The door dilated and he floated out. Totally weightless now, he found himself within the motionless axis about which the entire satellite habitat revolved.

Swiftly he swam down one straight hallway and around another, a circumferential one, pulling himself along with hand grips on the wall. At a small door labeled CYBERNET STUDIO ONE he fingered the lock until it opened.

Inside was a cramped control room, a console, a pair of chairs, a closet, a bathroom, and a door leading to the studio. Slowly Jim Kineaid removed his clothing. His naked body, pink as a boiled shrimp, gangled more than ever. His height brought his head two inches from the ceiling, but little flesh clothed the bones.

He sat on one chair and breathed deeply, going into himself. Soon he felt calm return to his mind, and he stood up to enter the studio. Without his clothing there could be seen at the rear of his skull starting at the base of his neck and running up into his thick mat of hair, an unobtrusive plastic covering, the shell of his cybernet transducer.

The studio was a horizontal cylinder, with enough diameter to stand up in, enough length to lie down in. He pulled the heavy door shut behind him, fingered a switch on the small control panel just inside the door, and laid himself down on the air.

Without gravity, he floated. Silent, invisible currents of air held him centered. He reached out with his mind to the controls and dimmed the lights. Through microsurgery, crucial filaments of his spinal cord had been connected physically to the transducer circuit. There, the infinitesimal electrical impulses were amplified and relayed to radio pickups lining the walls of the chamber. In this way he could communicate with the computer in the next room.

In darkness, in silence, with no touch on the surface of his body, his thoughts were free of interference. Images began to grow. A microcosmic universe burst into creation within the cells of Kincaid's brain; the electrical pulses corresponding to the images flowed through the wires, through the transducer, into the computer. There they were recorded, later to be reconstituted as visual images.

Bessar's body, steel grey and flexible as a whip, stood motionless at the crystalline console of his ship, antennae rigid. The white clouds of the receding planet swam hazily within the vision sphere. Ultrasonic signals from within Bessar's dorsal segment resonated with the tuned luminescent crystals of the control console as he planned the return trip to Xextra, their home ship. The crystals glowed blue, green, red, and infrared—vivid sparks of color feeding back signals to Bessar's alert senses.

Old Shawmssen reclined dejectedly on his flight nest. Striations of silver surrounded his optic stalks; his complex claws were scarred with the ravages of great age.

"We've failed." His voice remained musical and resonant, but was underlaid with a quaver. "It has all been wasted effort, futile effort. We shall all die on Xextra."

"Perhaps not." Bessar turned to Shawmssen; his body twisted lithely as a thought suddenly evolved. "Perhaps only this galaxy or cluster consists of antimatter. It is logical that the universe should contain just as much real matter as antimatter. We have simply come back into the wrong region. We must now go on and search for a galaxy made of our kind of matter. There is no need to give up."

"For you, perhaps, but not for me." Shawmssen curled into a tight spiral, overpowered with black despair. "I am too old to sustain another intergalactic voyage. Too old to hop from one sector to another."

He fixed his gaze into the blank interior of the vision sphere, where the mottled grey ball of Xextra began to enlarge. "Perhaps our people will yet find a home. But for me it is the end.'

Looking at the sour line of May Wheeler's mouth, Jim Kincaid knew he still hadn't scored. He sat limply and waited for the barrage.

"Jim," she began, "there are some good things about this new try. Your imagery is very fine. The detail work, the color. The aliens are very imaginative. That's why you were chosen to become a cybernet in the first place. You always had superior powers of visualization. But your concept of a story is pitiful. Your ending is too vague. Nobody will know how it's going to work out. You can't end on a maybe. You must have a positive ending. You must have the successful resolution of the problem. And your whole tone is too sad, too pessimistic."

He shrugged. "What do you expect? I've lived on this stinking wheel for all of my 20 years. I've never done anything, never gone anywhere. How do you expect me to make up a story? Why don't you hire a writer?"

Irritation edged Wheeler's voice. "Good writers are hard to come by. There's nobody on Lagrange who can write anything but computer programs and tech memos."

"Then bring one up from Earth."

"Believe me, we're working on it. But try to get an expense like that through Executive Committee! They'd rather spend the money on a ton of computer components."

"Hell, don't they know we're trying to make money for them?"

"I tell them and I tell them. But they're a bunch of hard-heads. You can't convince them that cybernet discs will be a profitable export item until you produce a working model. And that's what we're trying to do. They let us have a pilot project to show feasibility. Now we have to show them."

"So I'm your goose. And if I can't lay the golden eggs?"

"Don't worry. You will. It just takes some learning. You have the picture-making genius. With your head we don't need sets or scenery. Just a computer to translate your thoughts. You just have to learn the mechanics of script writing."

He laughed. "Yeah. That's all."

"Look," she urged. "Take the rest of the day off. Go get some rest. Enjoy yourself."

"Okay," he said. But his heart was not in it.

As Kincaid left, Wheeler turned to the closet with a sigh and poured herself a drink, returning with it to a soft chair where she sat and schemed. It was not easy riding herd over a young genius with a mind yet unformed, a soul full of *weltschmertz*. But her vision of a new form of entertainment, a new art form perhaps, drove her furiously from one day to the next.

Jim Kincaid stretched his wings and flew. Light air whistled softly past his ears. Below, above, all around the vast cylinder of the satellite swooped and stretched away to a vanishing point. Behind him, the end wall of the satellite, sculpted to resemble a mountain-side, fanned out from the central shaft mooring.

Just below the shaft, the flyers soared. In this region of zero grav-ity, gliding over air currents with filmy webs strapped to the arms made a sport exhilarating and popular. Since childhood Kincaid had come up here to the axis to float, to glide, to escape the heaviness of the periphery. Entranced, he flew with eyes opened just enough to avoid the other flyers, with just enough attention to keep clear of the hazard limit. Flying below that limit carried with it a risk—not of fall-ing to the periphery, for in free flight there was neither gravity nor centrifugal force—but a risk of being swept up by the air rotating with the satellite and being carried to a rough landing. Some did it pur-posely for the thrill.

Not Jim Kincaid. He liked to float and dream and build fantasies in his mind. From his earliest testing, the psychologists had been im-pressed by his ability to form mental images. It was for this reason he had been chosen to participate in the cybernet experiment. He had been one of the first subjects to have a transducer spliced to his spinal cord. The original aim of the experiment was to train a man to be his own computer terminal, to communicate directly with the machine, with no keyboard, microphone, or video screen in the way.

Afterwards, it had been realized that Kincaid could make pic-tures this way, and the pictures could be set end to end to make a story, recorded on computer discs. The concept of cybernet discs was born.

Kincaid was grateful for the chance to do something creative. Growing up in Lagrange had been like growing up in a small town of a few thousand inhabitants. School had been strict, amusements few, and the horizon curved over and met itself. There was no place else to go, except for the sister satellite, revolving reversely a few kilometers away, a mirror image of home.

He'd made that trip a few times, shuttling back and forth to the sister satellite, watching the sun dazzling in one direction, and blue-white earth beckoning in the other. Earth, with its thousands of kilometers of surface to explore, its endless varieties of places, reached out and drew him like a magnet. But the cost of going down to Earth and returning to Lagrange was more than he could contemplate. Only those on official business managed it.

Soar. Swoop. Turn. Some did it in pairs, performing arabesques in the air. Candy Cooper sailed by, holding hands with that lunkhead Jeff Stone. Anger spurted into Jim Kincaid's skull. He gasped at the sudden throbbing. Candy saw him and waved casually, as though there had been nothing between them—as though last week had meant nothing at all to her. Had he been idiotic to take it seriously, to take it for more than a game?

The anger diffused inward, turned rancid, turned against himself. Any girl who found attraction in such a skinny, pink, frizzle-headed misfit had to have something wrong with her, he decided. He was better off alone.

Soaring was suddenly without charm. He resisted the urge to fold his wings and let the winds spread him flat like a smear of grease on the inner surface of the satellite. Slowly, he pulled himself back to the takeoff ledge.

There, lifting in a graceful flight, was Tina Cummings. Tina of the black braids and brown eyes. Tina, whom he had adored silently and from a distance, in school. Now her beauty was greater than ever and he knew she would never look at him.

For an instant a vivid and colorful picture bloomed in his mind. His face flared a bright red before he realized she had no way of knowing what he was thinking. Still, the image had been strong enough to cause him clinical excitement, and as he hurried down the path to periphery he wondered what old May Wheeler would think about a line of porno fantasies.

They floated in the twilight, nude bodies coming together with wings fluttering faintly. Her hands moved over his skin, arousing sensations that caused the clouds to mushroom over them.

He found his body beaded with perspiration in the dark.

Migod, I hadn't intended to do that!

Hastily, he had the computer kill the file just created. Still, he thought, perhaps he should keep the idea on the back burner. His sexual fantasies were strong and clear, and if Lagrange could make a profit as the porno capital of the solar system, well, then. . . . But what would the Executive Committee say?

With a sigh he relaxed once more in the darkened cylinder of the studio and tried to get back to the script he had been pursuing.

Solat Kun scanned the spectra of the distant stars and his fringes flared a bright red.

"They're blue! They're shifting blue!"

Argor Vail retained a cool green iridescence on the hair-like fringes that circled his optic stalks. "They've always shifted blue. Ever since the universe started to collapse."

Solat Kun twisted irritably. "But we've gone beyond the collapse, beyond the new rebirth. The universe should be expanding once more. But the shift remains blue. The universe still collapses! Argor Vail, call a council meeting."

The Phardor council quickly assembled in the central chamber of Home. Solat Kun stood on the podium, reported his observations, and confessed his puzzlement. "Somewhere there has been a miscalculation. What could it be?"

"If I may make a suggestion," the pale, cracked voice of Nian Shon rasped across the room. The ancient sage of the voyagers remained couched, his shriveled members drawn up beneath him. "Find a viable planet. Make a close surveillance of its surface. Take video records of activities on that surface for several cycles. Then bring them here and let us see what is happening. But do not under any circumstances touch the surface of the planet or its atmosphere."

Solat Kun's fringes wriggled in appreciation. "A fine suggestion. Let it be done."

It took but one cycle for the evidence to be clear. Solat Kun silently showed the video to the Phardor Council. There was nothing to be said. The distant camera caught the inviting planetary surface with a clarity modified only by occasional atmospheric distortions.

Sun sparkled on the ocean as waves leaped up from the beach and rolled out to the sea. A bird dove into the blue water with a fish in its beak and swooped off empty-billed. The scene shifted to a river, cutting its way through a canyon. At a small waterfall the water clearly leaped from the lower pool up the cliff to the narrow stream far above. A large animal appeared, waddling in a strange manner along the riverbed until it came to the bloody carcass of a smaller creature. It busied itself with the skeleton, taking flesh from its mouth and molding it around the bones until the smaller animal, complete, leaped to its feet and began a brief struggle with the larger carnivore.

In fascination the Council watched the smaller creature back away from the fight, unmarked.

Nian Shon, the old, whispered faintly. The others leaned forward to hear. "The shift is blue, the water falls up, the waves unbreak and then flow outward. My friends, do you see what has happened? In the universe to which we have returned, time runs in the direction opposite to our own. Therefore instead of the stars expanding away from a new birth, they fall once more into another death. With our reversed time line we can never land on a planet, for to us it would seem like a world of antimatter."

Solat Kun's body arched in disappointment. "Then the trip has been wasted. Our universe has ended in futility."

Nian Shon stirred. An eye gleamed brightly. "Our universe has ended, but another one is out there. It simply exists without us."

"You don't even have to look at it," Jim Kincaid said to May Wheeler. "I know it's no good."

"What the hell's the matter?" Wheeler wanted to know. "You go into the studio knowing what's wrong. You know where you want the story to go. Why do you keep getting derailed onto this goddamned fatalistic track?"

"I don't know. Once I get in there and start floating the story takes off by itself. I lose control over it."

"I think it's time you started seeing the Shrink." Wheeler paced the length of her small office, turned, and leaned against the wall with her arms folded. "You need to get your mind under control. Make up your mind who's boss."

"Oh hell, May, I'm not gonna sit there talking to that stupid machine. I've had enough of that. I know all the answers it has. And it's not programmed for this problem. Getting into that cylinder and floating there—I fall into a trance and it's like I really live the story. It just happens."

Wheeler peered at Kincaid from behind slitted eyes. "You need more positive feedback from the computer, that's what. So far we're just using it for short-term processing—to help you hold images steady. But suppose we put into the program the outline of the plot. Enough to keep you headed in the right direction."

"Umm. Could be. At each crucial point it would feed me a hint about what's to happen next, and I fill in the picture. Can you program it?"

"Let me get Jack. He'll do it."

"But you still need a story."

"And that's still your job. You're the creative one, and you'll do it if I have to beat you."

Kincaid flushed. Behind his light tone hid a resentment. "Beat me till I bleed and then beat me for bleeding. But suppose I can't do it?"

She shrugged. "You can always go back to being a computer terminal. You want to be a star, you learn to create. If you don't want to do what has to be done, then just stick to your routine job. And some day you'll see the world go by and wonder how you got left behind."

"You act as though anybody can be creative just by turning on a switch."

Her broad face flickered. Memories of her own struggles broke to the surface. "Not everybody. But more than you realize. I don't have the same kind of talent that you have. I get people to do things. I'm a change agent. I put my money on you—but if you don't come through it'll be more your loss than mine."

Jim Kincaid scowled. "God, I hate the old don't-worry-about-me-I'll-be-all-right routine. You're just like my mother."

Her face hardened. "Better I should be like your father."

Kincaid turned his back, furious. How dare she bring that up?

May Wheeler's hands trembled at her throat. She had really put her foot into it this time. "I'm sorry, Jim," she said, softly. "Look, take a couple of days off. I'll get Jack started on the new program and by that time you can have some new input."

By his stiff back she could tell he was still angry.

"I hope so," he said, stomping through the door.

She turned to face the bland white of her office and, opening the little cabinet, poured herself a drink. What would happen if she told Jim that one time she, too, had loved his father? That when he had disappeared out in the asteroid belt, part of her own soul had vanished. She could not guess how he would take it.

In his own room, hunched over his terminal, Jim Kincaid milked the library for ideas. Does the universe expand forever or does it expand just so far, then collapse? The controversy still raged. The experimental evidence was still miniscule; the mass needed to cause collapse was still missing, but perhaps hidden.

Suddenly he sucked in his breath. He read the page on the screen again and again, unbelieving. How had he missed knowing this? But then none of the books accessible to his level of knowledge had ever mentioned this one obscure fact. This fact, this bit of information, this capsule of intelligence, this parcel of theory, became a bombshell of knowledge that blasted away the foundation of his script idea and caused the entire structure to collapse in ruins within his appalled mind.

"Omigod!" He called to a god in which he did not believe, and help did not come.

Waste. All the effort for nothing. In his story, in his life, in the world, in the Galaxy, in the Universe.

What he had not realized, and what a more detailed knowledge of four-dimensional geometry would have told him, was that the basic premise of his story was an impossibility. Black depression overwhelmed him like a tidal wave. On the terminal keyboard, without thinking, without knowing what he was doing, he typed the Shrink's number.

The Shrink had an hour. At 2 AM., that is, but the Shrink did not sleep.

Jim Kincaid slumped into the soft armchair. The pale, featureless walls of the cubical had not changed. The voice-controlled console faded into the wall in front of the chair, the video screen dark but ready to leap into brightness when needed.

"Your name is Jim Kincaid?" It was half a question, half a statement. "You made an appointment for therapy?"

Kincaid grunted. "Yeah."

The Shrink searched in the files for a moment. "You have not been here for over a year. What has happened?"

Jim found it hard to start. "I'm stuck," he said, finally.

"You're stuck."

Kincaid sighed. He hated to explain. "I'm supposed to be writing a script. Like a film script. But I keep going up blind alleys. My boss doesn't want pessimistic endings. My endings always end up with everybody dying or everything hopeless, and oh . . . what's the use?"

"You have a feeling of hopelessness?"

"You bet. And to top it all I just found out—after spending weeks working on this thing—I just found out that my basic plot device is useless because it is impossible to escape from the Universe. The escape velocity from the entire Universe is infinity—nobody can get out of this four-dimensional spacetime bubble. It's like the whole Universe is one big black hole. So my plot is hopeless from the start."

The therapy computer paused, obviously not programmed to deal with the intricacies of relativity. However, subject-matter was not important; the Shrink dealt entirely with process.

"I hear you say your plot is useless." The machine paused for the briefest moment, and Jim was ready to pounce and destroy if the next sentence was going to be: "How do you feel about that?"

But the Shrink knew Kincaid too well. "Why is your plot useless?" it asked instead.

Jim jerked his head irritably. "Didn't you hear me? I told you, because the basic premise is a scientific impossibility."

"And how does that make it useless?"

"I can't write about something that is impossible."

"Why can't you write about something that is impossible?"

Jim felt himself being ground to a fine pulp between the why's and the how's. He clenched the chair arm. "Because I can't fool the reader into thinking that something might happen when it can't. I'm not like the rest of the crappy writers. They have no trouble writing five impossible things before breakfast every day."

The shrink again retreated into one of its pauses. "Then you are not like writers who write about impossible things."

"No. I must stick to what I know for sure."

"You must stick to what you know."

"That's not much, is it?"

"How much is it?"

Kincaid had a sensation as of sinking into a lake of deep, black, bottomless mud.

"It's not much," he said, finally. "That leaves me with very little to write about."

Now the Shrink said it: "How do you feel about that?"

And now Jim had no defense. "I feel I'm wasting my time. I'm supposed to be imaginative and creative, and yet I block myself completely off from new ideas if I insist on staying safely with what I know."

"What are you going to do about that?" the Shrink wanted to know.

"Not many choices about the matter." Jim could feel wheels of calculation beginning to turn rustily within his head. "Either I find good stories within the realm of what I know to be possible, or I let myself go and write about things I know to be impossible. What the hell, everybody else does it. Why not me? Or else I change my standards about what's impossible. Or just get out of the business entirely."

"It sounds as if you are beginning to think clearly," the Shrink said, in a smug voice. "Come back next week and tell me what you decide."

It appeared to be the end of the session.

Glumly, Jim slouched out of the office, ducking to clear the door. It always ended that way. What good was the damn therapist? He always had to work out all the answers by himself anyway.

Next morning he slept late, turned on his terminal to see what there was to do. He felt like doing nothing, but thought he had better do something. Moving around was better than sitting still.

Events of the day chugged upward on the screen. Garden club.

No. Choral rehearsal. No. Tennis, handball, and swimming meets. Ought to, but he felt paralyzed. The satellite was filled with things to do, and he wanted to do none of them. Noon hour organ recital at the church.

There, at least, he could escape in the semidarkness, while aloft the tall, white-headed Joshua Pike sat at the four-manual console. Now tall, slender, elderly, and elegant, Pike had been the first child born on Lagrange. His recordings and broadcasts had earned considerable exchange for the Lagrangian economy.

It would at least be peaceful. And perhaps it would jog something loose in his head. Kincaid's aural imagery equalled his ability to make visual pictures. He thought: could I record music directly from my head? How would it sound?

The idea intrigued him. It always excited him to poke around in the dark corners of his mind and come up with unsuspected thoughts that had been lying hidden there.

When Jim arrived at the church it was just beginning. Few seats were filled. Jim crept silently down a side aisle to a spot as secluded as possible and quietly sank into a seat.

All he could hear at first was a minor chord that whispered in his ear and swelled slowly into a melody of exquisite sadness. Harmonies washed calmly through his mind, building, fading back to nothing, then returning in a giant roar of triumph like an incandescence blazing across the darkness of death. Until it faded to a final whisper he sat paralyzed; when it ended he shook.

Finally he looked up to read the title projected on the annunciator. "Kom Süsser Tod." Bach's calm acceptance of inevitability. In his mind there blossomed the vivid image that had been dogging him for weeks: the Universe collapsing into blackness, the end of all life. Impinging on this picture and overlaying it was a spaceship fleeing through the asteroid belt; in a flash of incandescence it collided with a massive, pitted spheroid and disappeared.

Images tumble over images. His mother waiting, growing more silent day after day. A ten-year-old boy looking out at the black sky, filled with the tension of unfinished business, of a goodbye unsaid.

Suddenly Kincaid had to flee. To fly. He needed to move, to shake visions of death from his head. He crept out as silently as he had come in, stopped at his place for wings, and took the shuttle to endzone, where ponds sparkled around the circumference at the base of the artificial mountain. He disdained the elevator, but took the trail upward, knowing that the apparent gravity would decrease as he approached the central shaft. In a few minutes leaps and bounds carried him aloft in a ragged spiral.

He began to feel exhilaration. Something was working in his

head, trying to come out. He couldn't wait to find what it was.

At a ledge halfway up he met Tina. Tina Cummings, standing, at the wall, wings folded under her arms, looking over the vast scene, the great satellite interior, extending all the way to the far end. Jim Kincaid's heart leaped at the sight. He remembered his shyness with her, the fantasies that filled his mind at her sight. This time he did not even blush. A recklessness drove him on.

"Tina! I'm glad to see you. On your way up? Will you fly with me?"

The rush of words came without premeditation, and Tina glanced around with surprise. It was not the stammering Jim Kincaid she had known in school.

"Sure," she said, pleased at the attention. Her dark face was framed with sleek black hair knotted behind her head. Jim had watched her fly from a distance many times, knew her to be strong and sure of herself.

They climbed as high as they could go. Few others were about at this hour. Most people were at work, and the eternal sun streaked its incandescent slabs through the longitudinal slits.

"What are you doing these days?" she asked as they climbed.

"I'm doing video visuals. Very fantastic."

"Oh yes." Her eyes flicked to the back of his neck. "I heard."

"Right now I'm hung up on the end of the Universe. I'm trying to find a way to prevent it. Do you realize that some time in the future when the Universe collapses inwards all this will be gone and all our efforts will have been wasted?"

Tina stared at him as she began to don her wings. "Isn't your worry a little premature?"

He laughed. The tilt of his head and the shrug of his shoulder showed the silliness he felt. "It's like the old joke. The man goes to his shrink and says he's awfully worried and depressed about the world coming to an end in another million years. The shrink says you've been misinformed. It won't end for at least a billion years. The man says, what a relief. That makes me feel much better."

"Well, there you are. I mean, it's even silly to worry about your own death," she said, bat-winged arms stretched out, poised on the ledge. "When your life is finished, that's the end of it. Every minute you spend being miserable is simply time wasted."

Jim buckled the last of the buckles, flapped the wings tentatively, and rose a foot off the platform. "But . . . but then what's the meaning of it all?"

"Oh, hell. The meaning is whatever meaning you give to it. Your mind is the thing that attaches meaning to things. Everything else, is just there. Come on, let's fly."

She rose on filmy wings and with strong strokes headed away

from the platform toward the opposite end of the satellite. Kincaid followed, an unanswered question in his head.

"You're right," he shouted, as he caught up to her. "I can make my own life mean whatever I want. But what about the rest of it? Humanity, civilization, finding out what the Universe is all about? What's the point of it all if it's going to come to an end eventually?"

She turned to face him, hovering a few yards away. Silhouetted against a bright shaft of sunlight he became a dark angel with bright hair. She wondered, was this too absurd to take seriously, or was he really into something deep?

Finally she played it straight. "There is no point, Jim. There's nothing but whatever you make of it. If you go to church they'll tell you it's God's will, but they won't tell you where God was before the beginning of the Universe, and they won't tell you where he will be after the end of the Universe."

"Hell, that's an empty philosophy."

"Heaven or Hell, anything else is a delusion. Really, Jim, what kind of person goes around worrying about the end of the Universe? If I wanted to make a guess, I'd guess that it's your own imminent death that's bothering you. Why should a twenty-year-old kid be worrying about death? Your life is just beginning."

Kincaid stared back at her, feeling the dart strike deep. She was right, of course. His obsession with universal catastrophe was a coverup for fears closer to home.

"How do you know so much?" he asked. "You're no older than me."

She glanced down at the lake, two kilometers below. He could feel her shudder.

"I had a friend, a close friend. We split one day. Over something silly and stupid. That night he went through the airlock without a spacesuit. Then I had to learn what it's all about. I'm a fast learner."

"Oh yes." Jim took her hand. "I remember now. I'm sorry." He felt drawn into those dark eyes. Another burst of erotic images cascaded through his mind and he turned away, his face becoming crimson.

"Let's fly," he shouted, to cover his confusion.

In an instant she had flown a swift circle about him. Her face became alive with excitement as she put the past behind her. "Let's take a dive. Then you'll feel what living's like."

He shied away. "I never tried it before."

"You can do it. It's a great blast. Come on."

She released him, moved her wings in a mighty power stroke and nosed down towards the periphery of the spinning satellite. Gasping, hesitating the barest instant, Kincaid followed her. It was like ski-jumping. The first time was terror mingled with exhilaration. Wings pumped him up to speed. The air tore through his hair.

Beneath them the lakes rotated in silent majesty. As they flew farther from the central core, the atmosphere, rotating with the satellite, began to buffet them and tear at their hair, carrying them faster and faster. Kincaid imagined how it would be to plummet straight down; his body jerked with a lightning-vivid picture of the final instant.

No. That would be the real waste. He still had too much to do. There began to grow in his mind a picture of the many years to be filled with the multitude of things to do.

"Now follow me." He caught Tina's words flung back at him through the quickening wind. She spread her wings and caught the air so that she was thrown forward and out. He followed suit, and the two of them began to level off into a descending spiral, propelled by the rotating satellite atmosphere.

Kincaid's breath came fast. It was a dangerous game, requiring strength and skill. As his blood pumped faster a fierce grin spread across his face. A vast joy enveloped him.

The ground and the lakes came closer, gyrating around them as the satellite spun. Faster the wind blew them until they nearly matched velocities with the ground.

"Try to land on water!" Her words came back to him in shreds, tattered by the gale.

The ring of lakes around the end of the cylinder was almost continuous, so the chances for a soft landing were good. A broad body of water was swinging up from behind; the two beat their wings steadily and strongly, trying to keep altitude and to gain speed.

"Okay, now drop," Tina called. They folded wings and made a clean fall of the last few meters. Their splash was impressive, water spraying to the edge of the lake. They did not descend far through the clear water, for a slight spread of the wings dragged them quickly to a halt.

Kincaid came to the surface gasping and spurting. Swimming with wings on was impossible. "Turn over and back kick," Tina instructed him.

Finally they made shore and pulled themselves out, as dripping and bedraggled as a pair of wet pups. A couple on shore applauded. "Fine landing," they laughed.

Kincaid wiped the water out of his eyes. "We're not exactly dressed for this sport. Where can we go to dry out?"

"There's a bath house on the other side of the lake," the man on the shore said. "You can get a towel there."

There was not only a towel, but a sauna where they could hang their soaked clothing by the hot stones. Gratefully Kincaid lay alongside Tina on the wooden bench and steamed. The wood had been grown on Lagrange and it was real wood.

He touched her hand and felt her replying squeeze shooting electricity through his spine. He thought: this is the only meaning I can make of it. We are born touching and holding, and if we stop getting it then we are dead.

Tina said, "This is better than worrying about the fate of the Universe, isn't it?"

"It's better than almost anything. As for the Universe, that's no longer a worry. The Universe will live forever."

She leaned up on one elbow and looked at him; her black hair fell loosely over her breasts. "You solved your problem. How?"

He grinned. "Inspiration struck during our descent. It was as though my mind opened up. Because you were right, completely right. Why was I unable to save the characters in my script? Every ending I dreamed was another form of doom. It came entirely from my own fear of death. And this is the most futile fear of all, for it is the one thing we cannot avoid."

"And your solution?"

He took her hand in his, held it, kissed it, rubbed it on his cheek. "You'll see."

He undressed in the anteroom and stepped into the cylindrical gravless studio. The day with Tina had stretched into three and he felt a calm, warm glow all over his body. As he eased himself into floating position and allowed the lights to dim, he quickly sank into the state of sensory detachment in which nothing existed except his mind and the thoughts that floated to its surface.

The Pharigee civilization had spread over much of the Galaxy. Even though travel was limited to below light speeds, the long life of the Pharigees coupled with the time dilation had made such a spread possible. While each of the Pharigees had a lifetime measured in the thousands of years, the unique nature of his nervous system and his natural radio connection to the central memory of his planet gave each Pharigee individual a continuity of thought and memory that spanned a period of billions of years.

From the center of his planetoid vehicle, Omicron watched the last stage of the em-ring construction. The machine, with dimensions that of a large solar system, had required fully ten million years to complete. But to Omicron, with his access to the central memory, it was as if he had been there at the beginning. Upsilon, facial fringes glowing excitedly, drifted into the room. He carried a portable video transmitter, ready to send the news of the great impending event to the civilized planets of the Galaxy.

"One more step, Upsilon, and it is complete," said Omicron.

"There will be celebrations throughout the Galaxy." Upsilon gave a many-legged, zero-gee dance.

"Your spirits are high. But save the jubilation for the outcome."

The control room began to fill with other members of the team. Their segmented bodies had a metallic sheen, and the facial fringes, fluorescing with excitement, made multicolored patches that reflected brightly from the instrument panels.

"Units 94325 and 95746 are now in place." The word came, not through a loudspeaker, but through a radio transducer that communicated directly with each individual in the room.

"Now we test," Omicron said. His communication with the machine was totally and directly by radio frequency. There was not a switch on the console before him. The readouts were purely a matter of redundancy.

Gradually Omicron fed power to the great ring-shaped machine. So vast was the structure that signals traveling over conventional electromagnetic channels would have taken many minutes to reach the farthest segments. A network of wormhole communicators had been established to allow instantaneous and stable control. Responding signals from each segment reported that at low power each segment was operating well. So far so good.

"We'll increase the power. Now it becomes critical."

The magnetic fields involved in the operation of the em-ring were of such a magnitude that the ability of normal matter to maintain solid form could no longer be assumed. Reinforcing fields became part of the structure.

The test continued for a very long time. Inflowing reports from the far-flung segments of the em-ring funneled into Omicron's mind for examination and storage. Upsilon's camera was set up and its controls instructed. The crucial moment was approaching, the event to be recorded for history.

Power indicators approached their maximum levels. "We're consuming one-tenth the power output of the nearest three stars," Omicron informed Upsilon, for the benefit of the camera record. "If this test fails we have wasted much energy."

Upsilon emitted a whistle. "But the gamble is worth the risk. If we don't try, we'll surely die in the end; for our sun is within a Megayear of going nova."

"And if the experiment succeeds," Omicron replied, "we will have a source of power equal to the young sun we started with originally. Remember the beginning, ten billion years ago, when the first em-ring extracted energy from the center of the sun? Everybody expected that to be a permanent solution to the energy problem, but as you see, all solu-

tions are but temporary. Except, perhaps the solution we now test."

Upsilon, thousands of years younger than Omicron, had not yet incorporated into his memory the early history of the race and had not Omicron's perspective. "I must say that it has been very depressing living through a time when the talk is of nothing but diminishing energy sources."

Omicron cocked an eyestalk at the other. "Even so, there is restraint on the profligate use of solar energy. An interstellar ship uses an appreciable fraction of an average star's energy output, and hastens the death of the star accordingly. Still, in a single Pharigee lifetime the symptoms of universal entropy death are difficult to notice. It is only with the long point of view available through our central memory that we can be aware of the fact that the Universe is aging, is running down."

"But now you will be able to reverse this process. A rebirth of the Galaxy." Inevitably the presence of the camera caused the conversation to become an interview; each sentence became a speech.

Omicron's attention had never wavered from the incoming signals. "The critical point is approaching rapidly. We are running at close to full power and soon will be breaking through the wormhole."

Even as he spoke flashes of light began to sparkle and flare within the circumference of the em-ring as energy began to come through. Since this energy was aimed away from the control room the direct beam was not visible, but a number of assorted meteors, asteroids, and other lesser objects found themselves caught in the radiation blast and instantly exploded in a violence of superhot plasma.

The major part of the beam was intercepted by the black, shrunken star located at the center of the em-ring. Soaking up the radiation greedily, its surface presently began to glow red. The higher energy components of the beam initiated nuclear reactions that broke up the elements of the star, created neutrons and protons, and proceeded slowly to restore the star to its initial youthful, energetic, and low entropy condition.

Upsilon crowed in shrill jubilation. The rejuvenation of a dead star, first in galactic history, had been caught indelibly in his camera. Already the light shields had to be darkened in front of all lenses as the star's brightness increased beyond tolerance.

"Now the theory has been proven," Omicron said, in quiet celebration. "Somewhere outside this four-dimensional spacetime continuum there is a source of energy that we can tap through a wormhole. We can restore every dead star to its primal condition, add fresh, high-level energy to the universe, reverse the entropy death into which we have been decaying. Our species has a future ahead of it."

The lights came on as the screen went black. May Wheeler sat bemused, her hands clasped in front of her face, vertical lines furrowed between her eyes. Jim Kincaid's chair legs rasped as he stood up.

'Well," he said, his tone a challenge. "You got your positive ending, didn't you? How do you like its magnitude? Lighting up an entire star? Try to beat that!"

Wheeler cocked her head at Kincaid, then shook it wearily. "I'll admit it. You've got a large scale production. A gigantic concept. My oh my. Saving the entire Universe from dying. It's a great ending."

Her eyes twinkled. "Now what you need is a story."

HOLOCAUST

THE RED SUN setting behind the starkness of the cliff momentarily outlined in silhouette the twisted framework of the old tower. The rounded top gleamed ruddily, as if in remembrance of the time when golden flame burned within the tower; flame as hot and raw as the sun itself. Dust, lifted by faint twilight breeze, shimmered, and settled back wearily, as if the last tenuous thread of life had been drawn from the heart of the planet.

Adman ran his fingers through his black, oily hair, and nervously twisted a lock into a knot as his large eyes, framed in shadows, moved with painstaking effort across the paper. The calculations were there. He had derived them from a sudden flash of inspiration, but he still could not understand them. The reason that he had taken the curious step was obscure, and he could not remember. But the method was correct, and the answer came out.

What did it mean?

His researches into the effects of intense magnetic fields upon the molecular structure of cooling metals had become strangely involved with the curious effects caused by clashing fields. He would not have predicted the effects, and he was not yet just sure how the calculations connected.

Finally he rose, and walked outside, to stand with his head bare in the whining winter wind. A few flakes of snow lazily sparkled in the lights of the city about him. Stretching for miles about him, its furthest limits obscured by the encroaching fog, was the city of towers. The spires grew up everywhere, like some strange plant, and few were higher than the one on whose roof Adman stood, the University Laboratories.

His head cleared by the piercing breeze, Adman walked back into the laboratory with new resolution. Gathering about him reference books and calculating machines, he set to work again. Presently he drew close his drawing table, tacked down a large sheet, and set to work with pen, ink, and ruler. From beneath his hands grew complex patterns, plans of machines spread across many sheets of paper. Back to his calculating machines, finally forced to sleep through sheer weariness, then again to work at the drawing board, until, after three days of almost continuous work, the plans were complete, and given to the mechanics of the laboratories.

During the day that followed, Adman almost lived in the machine shops, keeping jealous guard over the progress of his mechanism. Slowly the patterns were made, the parts cast, machined, polished to utmost accuracy, and presently the complete form began to take shape as the parts were assembled.

The machine was compact; curiously shaped coils combined in a ring three feet in diameter, supported by massive insulators above another ring of different construction. Power lines, transformers, meters, and a tiny control panel completed the form.

Adman eagerly loaded it upon a hand truck and carted it up to his laboratory, fastened it permanently, and with great impatience prepared for the trial. The power line was plugged in, controls inspected and adjusted, and finally the power switch thrown. Nothing visibly happened but the flopping over of two needles. Adman looked at them, and stood with his mouth open, stunned at the amount of power the thing was drawing. Visible effects were not obvious for many minutes, when gradually a strange refraction phenomenon started building up in the center of the top coil. Nothing was there, but light passing through it was bent.

Adman made a brief mental calculation of the energy his machine had drawn so far, and suddenly opened a switch. The disturbance within the coil remained.

Adman thoughtfully walked over to his desk and signalled the number of his laboratory director on the visiphone. Almost immediately the man's face flashed on and made greeting.

"If you are not busy now, Dr.," Adman spoke, "I would like to see you right away. I have something interesting to show you."

"Something concerning your experiment on magnetism?"

"Indirectly," Adman replied with a little twisted smile. "You might call it a by-product."

"I'll be up in ten minutes, then."

"Good, I shall be expecting you."

Adman walked over to his machine, and stood there, lost in speculation, until the buzzer sounded, and he, startled out of his reverie, pressed the button and admitted the director.

"So this is your experiment. It doesn't look very impressive."

"Perhaps not. But look at this."

Adman closed the switch, and again the meter needles flew over. The director appeared startled at their readings.

"Twenty amperes at a thousand volts! Where is that twenty kilowatts going?"

"Look through that coil," Adman suggested.

"Refraction? But how?"

"I'm not sure that I know. I think that I have an artificial gravitational field in there. A peculiar field that is all within itself, and does not attract bodies to it. But light passing through it is bent, like light passing through a glass lens. Only this is a lens of gravity. But it takes a lot of power to build it up."

"Twenty thousand watts! For how long, did you say?"

"Twenty minutes, so far."

"A wonderful storage device."

"Yes, it will store power, but I have other ideas too. Ever since I was a sophomore in college, I have been playing with the idea of finding a material that could focus cosmic rays if made into a lens. I wondered what would happen at the spot of high intensity. I won't have a material lens now, but a lens of gravity. What will happen at the point of focus when the field becomes intensive enough to bend the cosmic rays into that point? That is why I have the second coil there."

"Oh . . . I suppose you are thinking of the Menlo-Wall computations . . . that material energy will be released by the action of short waves upon matter. And the second coil?"

"A concave lens, to disperse the rays converged by the first, and prevent them from coming to a focus anywhere except between the two coils."

"Wonderful . . . wonderful. But the power it eats up!"

"Yes. I would appreciate a special line sent up here so I could draw a hundred kilowatts comfortably. It will all come back."

"I will do that right away." The director hurried over to the visiphone, and signaled.

Power flowed through the wires into the inexhaustible maw of the machine. The disturbance within the coil became more acute, until it was difficult to see through it. Finally blackness lay as an opaque wall within the circle.

Adman closely examined many meters, and turned dials to follow their readings. Suddenly an intense glare grew between the coils, and simultaneously Adman threw a tumbler switch. The glare dimmed, grew again, and finally steadied, while the readings of the two large meters climbed to fabulous figures. A platinum resistance coil hanging from the ceiling grew hot, and began to glow. The sweat dropped from Adman's forehead, as the refrigerators labored over dispersing the heat.

The brilliance of the resistance increased to a dazzling blue, and presently the metal began to sag. Adman hurriedly threw another tumbler, shunting the rushing power into a roaring arc which made an incandescent hell of the two-foot space between the electrodes.

"What a weapon!" the director whispered.

"Weapon?" Adman turned, startled. "I hadn't thought. . . . No . . . It couldn't be used for that! Think of the power!"

"Yes! Just what we need right now. With this on our side the war can be over almost as soon as we make more of these."

"War?"

"Why, yes. Didn't you know?"

"No. I suppose since I started on this. I hadn't heard. But we couldn't use this power. I really don't know what might result. Almost anything. No! You just can't!"

"Oh, come." The director grew impatient. "You will be the greatest hero of the nation. Think of the fame for being the cause of our victory. Come. I will report to the government immediately."

"Stop! Don't go!" Adman shouted hoarsely. "I won't let you use this machine for killing people. It's too dangerous."

"Ha! He talks about dangerous weapons in the middle of a war." The director manipulated the visiscope controls. "You will let us have the machine or be held as a traitor to your country. And why do I talk of you letting us use the machine?" The director's voice took a sudden upward inflection as the thought struck him. "*I* made the discovery, did I not?" He winked slowly above the broad grin that spread his lips.

"Why, you dirty crook," Adman advanced, fists clenched. "You don't know what dangerous means until you play with this toy. I'd kill you . . ."

He stopped abruptly as he saw glaring at him through the visiphone the face of the military district commander.

The red flower of destruction bloomed in the wake of material energy. High towers grew up, dotting the landscape, glowing inwardly with the light of disintegration. From their summits, one wintry night, streaked blasting bolts of lightning, destroying all before, leaving the land desolate.

Spies, however, were efficient, and secrets could not be held for long. Slender, cylindrical bodies hummed through the air on wings of flame and dropped pellets which gently expanded on contact with the ground and carried everything before a rushing, irresistible wave of force.

Shafts of sheer, radiant energy, speared up from below, impaled the flying bodies, and then disappeared in a vast explosion which seemed slow, as the front advanced in a billowing roar that nothing could withstand.

Armies marched and countermarched over territories that were blasted out of recognition. Land battleships rumbled across land that was seared and bleak. Airplanes droned their way entirely around the globe, leaving in their trail craters and furrows that did not heal.

Man went mad with destruction, fighting, burning, killing the other person because he was afraid the other person would kill him. Armies melted into disorganized groups, blindly wielding the weapons they did not understand, making the surface of the world a place on which nothing could live.

One night, amidst the roar and tumult of the ever-present battle, a light speared momentarily in an obscure hiding place in the depths of the mountains. The light gushed forth in a glare that made shadows of the exploding bombs and burning rays. The light rushed upward, carrying on its crest a cylinder of metal, which roared on with ever increasing speed, until it vanished as a tiny point among the stars.

The war continued aimlessly, by its own momentum. With millions dying constantly, no one noticed that Adman and a few others were missing. Soon there was no one left with sanity enough to notice. For radioactivity had been at work; a by-product of one of the many weapons produced with material energy. Deadly radiations ate away at the mind and body, and the few millions that remained died horribly with flesh disintegrating from their bones.

Presently there was no one left to view the wonderful sunsets that filtered through the dust-laden air. Impalpable dust it was, product of disintegration, dust that settled rapidly to the ground through the thin air that had almost disappeared. Then the setting sun glared starkly through the twisted members of the old tower.

Long afterwards, the descendants of Adman on the Earth looked upon the Moon with powerful instruments and pondered over the cause of the mighty craters that covered its face.

SKYLARK VS. THOUGHT

(A sequel to "Skylark" *by Smith and*
"Invaders from the Infinite" *by Campbell)*

HEAT, MOIST AND soggy, coiled and swam in engulfing waves and dripping streams of sweat. The day was a sweltering segment of fourth dimension sandwiched between the darker, but slightly cooler pieces of night.

Burton J. Cherney sat morbidly and methodically twisting a discouraged lump of tallow between his fingers, brooding over the fiendish devices nature used to torture her children. In time the former candle looked like nothing conceived on Earth, or on any of the infra- and super-universes.

"If each one of these figures represents an equation on a three-dimensional graph," he thought, "I'd hate to have to figure them out. This reminds me of those two stories, 'Arithmetica' and 'Living Mathematics.' They both had living equations in them, and although I couldn't understand them, perhaps some of the equations I'm making now might come to life. This silly thing, for instance."

He had taken the piece of tallow, bent it around into a spiral, squeezed the ends, and tied the whole thing into a knot, pulling it out again and then twisting around once more.

He was smoothing away a roughness in the figure when he noticed a small ball of radiation overhead. It was a shimmering globe of red and yellow luminescence fading away at the edges into sparkles of green flame. Through his shocked mind flashed one tremendous thought: "I did it! I made a living equation!"

The ball grew until it was two feet in diameter, and the space around it was curiously distorted. A corona of pearly haze swirled about, and lengthened into a misty tentacle which reached out to Cherney's head. He tried to dodge, but it caught him, and at once he felt a wave of great intelligence beat against his mind.

"From one chance out of incalculable numbers you have made me. The laws of chance say that there is one out of nine to the ninth to the ninth power of you turning the right combination of planes and solids which would cause my creation, but, unbelievably, you did it.

"My intelligence is such that I have already read the minds of everyone on this planet, and with this little knowledge I shall go out into the universe to discover the basic secrets of nature.

"But before I go, is there anything you would like me to do for you?"

Burton's dazed mind raced. A veritable Aladdin's lamp! Should he ask for money, great knowledge, strange and mighty powers? Or the one thing which he otherwise would have no chance at all of seeing?

"I would like to see a battle between the *Skylark* and the *Thought*. I've always wondered what would happen if they met."

"The *Skylark* and the *Thought*. The two mightiest spaceships in the universe, each with infinite power, but with different weapons. What would happen if the two met?"

In a flash Burton Cherney was transported out into the depths of interstellar space. Everything which occurred was revealed to his all-seeing eyes.

*   *   *

Hurtling through space at incalculable velocity produced by the sixth order system of propulsion was a tremendous sphere, as large as a small planet. On a broad, grassy plain, below many shells of inoson, stood three houses. Two were replicas of houses in Washington, D.C., United States of America. Between them was a modest gray structure. This was the room from which was controlled the vast cosmic forces handled by the tremendous sixth order projector which composed most of this prodigious ship.

"I say, Crane, do you pick up anything strange out there?" Richard Seaton's gray eyes peered out inquisitively from beneath the massive control helmet he wore.

"Yeah, about a hundred light years away and coming closer fast. Looks like some awfully funny fields."

"Uh, huh. And if it's what I think it is, our rotating into the fourth dimension was elementary. They, whatever it is, have got something, and I'm going to see what it is."

He rapidly gave some mental orders to the titanic mechanical brain which was, next to Seaton's own mind, the controlling power of the ship.

"That's the quickest way. The brain will analyze whatever fields are there and drag the thing here. Ah, finished. It's a space-distortion field designed to create a new space with arbitrarily fixed properties, and we're using an intense gravity beam—2980th band of the third order—to pull that ship out of the other space.

"Wow! What a jolt that was! We must've pulled the wrong tooth that time. The brain took a millionth of a second to put up the screens and in that time something sliced off a half a mile of our armor. Did you get it, Crane?"

"Yes. There was the most intense and solid beam of second order vibrations I have ever seen. Cosmic rays we used to call them. It heated half our surface to a temperature of 200,000 degrees. And then there was a curious beam of vibrations between the infrared and radio which caused all the inoson molecules to move in one direction, which made quite a mess of the outside."

Arcot and Morey looked through the visiplates of the *Thought* at the familiar view of the two "ghost" ships flying beside the real ship in the constricted space. Their artificial universe was so small that light from the ship went around it easily, coming back to them from the other side.

Suddenly the black space went gray, forces strained and snapped, sparks flew within the ships as terrific energy rushed from the storage coils to the space-distortion coil. Some terrific force was draining the big coil, and as fast as it was drained, the storage coils struggled to keep it charged.

"Lord, Morey, what a gravity field that must be! Our coils are enough to take us past any conceivable star. We wouldn't even notice that dead giant we were caught by before. It must be a spaceship using an attractor ray on us. I'm going to take us out of this space and look around for that ship. As soon as I see it I'll give it a touch of the molecular, cosmic, and magnetic, about a tenth of a sol each. Each of the first two will do plenty if it's ordinary matter, and the three combined will wreck relux pretty quick."

As Arcot thought his orders into the headpiece, the space in the ship became surcharged with electrical tension. Sparks snapped and metal points were surrounded by a blue corona as the mighty power flowed from the space coil to the storage coils. In a moment the strain was gone, and they were back among the stars. Three needles flickered in their dials, and then the mighty ship reeled to a titanic blow. Meter needles swung crazily as Arcot tried everything in his armory, but the unknown forces still struck the *Thought,* throwing it about wildly, and eating stubbornly through the tough armor. Then all went quiet.

"Whew!" Arcot mopped his brow. "They sure have something there. I gave them a bit of a nudge with my combination before their screens went up in about a millionth of a second, I wonder what kind of relays they have. And they sure have power. Maybe the same as we have.

"And they sent out something my latest researches had just begun to suggest. A ray far below the cosmic in frequency. It didn't even affect our screens, and I thought we could handle any vibration carried by the ether. That's it! They use sub-ether vibrations. It went right through the artificial matter and the protonic screens. The only way I kept our cosmium up as long as I did was by continually rebuilding it as soon as it disintegrated.

"I couldn't run away from them by the space distortion, so I pulled us up to their own height by a time advancement. I used enough so that their high frequencies are about in our visible spectrum, and our cosmics are down at their level.

"Let's see what we can do now. Their big size indicates that they use matter to handle their power instead of having space do it, as we do. I wonder what their limits are, and whether we can blow a couple of their fuses."

The space between the two giant ships was a seething area of energy. For light years around terrific radiations blasted and swirled. A stray sun wandered into the dangerous area and was lashed instantly into a shrieking ball of disintegration. A torrent of energy poured from the tormented sun upon the two ships which stubbornly resisted its onslaught, while at the same time absorbing this energy to re-discharge it in the form of lethal rays.

"Arcot! Our time field is failing!"

"Uh-huh. They've got a reverse field on us, and we've got to fight it. I'm going to send us up to a faster rate."

"But we can't go much faster. If we do, we won't be able to get enough power from the suns. They'll be sending us energy so slowly we won't be able to light our lamps."

"That's the idea! Suppose we take a sun along with us in the advanced field. A couple of suns! And disintegrate them so fast that the other ship won't be able to get power fast enough to resist."

"What happened, Dick?" Crane asked. "It happened so fast I got lost after the first second."

"After we got our screens up I socked them with a mixture of sixth order rays. They're not made of ordinary matter, because they lasted longer than I would have thought possible, and they kept rebuilding as fast as the disintegrated. Then they did something. I think they speeded up their time rate, because I'm sure they didn't have anything less than second order, and we received plenty of low sixth order. In the advanced time rate, their low frequencies would come to us as high frequencies.

"I sent a time stasis after them, which was supposed to nullify their advanced field, but they fought, and now we're in a deadlock.

"Wow—what was that?" His eyes opened in amazement as the heretofore noiseless machines whined and roared in their efforts to resist the unbelievable blast of energy that struck them.

"Say! We can play that way, too. They took a sun into the advanced time field and released all its energy on us in one second. I'm gonna do more than that. Here's a nice big star."

Seaton mentally directed forces which hurled the huge sun directly at the *Thought* and exploded it in an instantaneous gush of intolerable radiance. But the comparatively tiny ship held. In fact, it absorbed energy and used it for its own protection so fast that the space around it was dark and strained.

"Oh, I see." Seaton gasped. "Anything started at him is absorbed as a change in field density. I don't get to first base. We're stalemated."

Arcot compressed his lips grimly. "All right. If we can't get anywhere using clean energy, we can try something else. Remember what we did to the Thessians by using psychology?"

Out in space, in the racked and torn area between the two ships a weird drama was enacted. A mistiness appeared. It hardened, and solidified into an amorphous shape which, strangely, radiated tangible repulsiveness. Hate, horror, Arcot projected emotions amplified a million times, where embodied in this creature.

The shape whipped out a noisome, slimy tentacle towards the *Skylark*. A solid beam of energy cut it off, and the shape recoiled. It rapidly changed form, and now appeared as a colossal, hairy spider which leaped across millions of miles of space to the *Skylark*. Straddling it with elongated legs, it attempted to bite through the inoson with its cavernous, repulsive beak. It bit into a concentrated beam of sixth order radiations instead, and jumped convulsively away.

Now, appearing from the *Skylark,* was a giant figure of a man. As large as a sun it was, a distorted, hunchbacked monstrosity with arms a million miles long. In a great bag on its back was a mass of round objects—planets!

Peering around, it beheld a still more monstrous figure striding over from the *Thought,* holding a small sun in each hand. The first monster picked a choice planet out of its bag and hurled it at the other. It struck directly in the stomach, and the Terror gave a gasp, but strode purposefully on, pelleted by flying planets.

The suns in its hands began to radiate faster and faster, illuminating the scene with a devilish glow. The two monsters were close together now, and the one with the hot suns raised his arms and smacked them on the face of the other, one on each cheek. They exploded in a blaze of blinding, lashing fire. The monster roared with anguish.

The two figures grappled. Tumbling over suns through distances measured in parsecs they wrestled back and forth, making a shambles of that corner of the universe. Laughing, roaring, and howling with unholy glee, they swung stars at each other, demolishing clusters, growing in size and ferocity each second.

A galaxy in the hand of one of them was hurled like a bunch of pebbles. Suddenly there was an instant of utterly intolerable radiance, swirling colors, and chaotic forces. The cosmos disappeared.

Burton Cherney was back in his room shivering. "What happened?" he gasped.

The being he had created answered calmly. "Seaton and Arcot both went crazy. Anyway, I happened to remember that it was impossible for both of them to exist in the same universe.

"You see, the *Thought* recognized the Einstein theory, which goes to all sorts of trouble to go faster than light without violating the theory, while the *Skylark* merely disregards the theory and goes faster than light. So, if one is possible, the other is impossible.

"Anyway, it was an interesting experiment while it lasted."

THE MUSICIAN

FIVE YEARS, now, and it had been the same all the time. On top of the grey mist, the damp warmth, the grey and the wet mingled with everything. Underneath, the grey concrete corridors, sweating with dampness, the crowded barracks, the smelly machines, the unceasing close association with men and machines until you could not tell which was man and which was machine. And through everything, top and bottom, was the pounding and the droning of war noises that never stopped.

He was Lieutenant J-74k-MK now. Five years ago—or was it a million years—he had been a name. But in war, when men are machines, and machines are more noble than man, for they do not will death, it is more convenient to give men numbers, according to division, squadron, company. He had been Private B-348k-MH at the beginning, but then there are vacancies, and you get moved up. So now he was Lieutenant, pilot of mole D-431 of the 45th mole squadron.

Him a soldier! How he'd laughed. But it wasn't very funny now. No, after five years it wasn't very funny. He wanted to be a musician. Well, there he was, sitting in a tiny underground hall on Venus, pounding on the electric organ at an initiation rally.

All the time they came—the young fellows—the boys who thought they were soldiers—filled with the romantic slop of propaganda. They came, load after load, and they laughed and they sang, and he would play the music for the songs on the electronic organ. He was going to be a musician. Oh yes, he was going to be a musician.

> "Off in Space, there's a place
>   called Venus.
> 'Neath the mists, pretty girls
>   will meet us . . ."

And so on.

It was a very funny song. The new recruits laughed. One batch after another—month after month—they sang the songs there in the little underground hall, with moisture hanging from the grey concrete. They sang and they laughed, and they were new. After they were no longer new their laughter was of a different sort.

Hit it up! Hit it up, Lieutenant! With all stops out, and feet prancing on the pedals. Play the vulgar songs and banal marches so the kids can have a good time before they drink more deeply of the war. Pound it out! The more noise the better. Make a lot of noise; make more noise than the war, and then maybe you won't hear the war.

And the General up there. The Old Man himself, spouting off the same pep talk he'd given the kids for the past two years. What a magnificent talk! What a marvelous, patriotism-inspiring, blood-tingling oration! Lieutenant J wished the words would stick in the General's throat and choke the beast to death. Because when you hear the man say the words, make the same motions, the catches, the breaks—over and over again—then it sounds different.

When you do anything over and over, for hundreds of times—it makes a difference. And it makes the war show itself for what it is. No matter how magnificent causes and reasons and rationalizations sound when you first go out, the monotony and the greyness and the wetness quickly enough reduce it to what it really is—the sordid grabbings of imperialist powers—from any side—for any cause.

So there he was—up there on Venus, under the clouds, fighting the rebellionists. Maybe they had cause to rebel. It wasn't for him to think.

And sometimes, while he sat there at the organ, feet and hands mechanically moving up and down, he'd have a strange feeling that something was going to happen. There would be an emptiness inside him filling up with pressure that came close to exploding. There was something inside that wanted to come out and force his hands to play music that really meant something, instead of the staccato quickstep and the sentimental ballads that was all he knew. But nothing ever happened. Nothing ever happened, and he went on according to the routine. You couldn't change the routine.

Only sometimes he wondered why he had the empty feeling inside, and sometimes he felt like something important was going to happen, but nothing ever did.

He couldn't know what he wanted. He had never known any good music—there had never been any written, and if there was, wars had spoiled it.

It was one day during that period of time—the exact day never mattered—that the summons came from the General. The Old Man himself—what could he want? What was so unusual and important that the O.M. contacted the Lieutenant personally? Whatever it was, it was fatality; the General would command, and he would perform.

"It's a test job," the O.M. said, as Lieutenant J stood at ease after saluting. The Lieutenant's face turned to rock. Test jobs were nice if you were tired of living.

"We have a neutron blast projector. Something new." The General's old-young eyes stared fixedly at Lieutenant J. "Ion blasts are deflected by magnetic fields. Neutron blasts are not. But, for the same reason, you can't push neutrons up to high velocities by magnetic fields, like you do ions. The problem: to generate high velocity neutrons in appreciable quantities. We've done it, and the results are more than appreciable.

"We have a new mole. It has heavy armor, sonic nullifiers, and induction beam converters that will handle any power they can throw short of almost enough to fuse half the planet. The new mole has the neutron blast. The power plant is enough for a battleship. The entire machine is so strong that you have almost an even chance of coming back.

"Here are your orders." He handed Lieutenant J a paper. "You will destroy that base and return. That is all."

"Me—do that with one mole? It must be very powerful."

A buzzer drummed its song on the General's desk. He flipped a switch and listened to the voice that came out of the speaker.

"I'll be right over," he said.

He rose, and made ready to go, then suddenly recalled the Lieutenant standing there. "You have four hours before the test starts. Suppose you come with me."

"Where?"

"At the far end of passage AB-24, where digging is still underway, a buried spaceship has been found. It is very old. It may be so old that it actually comes from the civilization that existed before the War of the Beginning."

"Really?" Lieutenant J was not enthusiastic. Even if it were a relic, so rare, of that civilization that had existed on Earth before the war had destroyed everything 15,000 years ago, he failed to become interested.

He had suddenly become very tired. He was going to go out on a test job, and he would probably never come back, so who cared about pre-civilization spaceships? He would never come back and he didn't care. Perhaps that was what he had wanted all the time. That emptiness that wouldn't be filled, the harrowing of the weary noises, the lassitude that crept over him—he was tired, and all he wanted to do was sit for a million years and not move, and not have anything to do but sit. Perhaps that was the solution—go out and not come back. It was easier than keeping on with the routine when he was so tired and he couldn't find out what that was he wanted.

The car that carried him and the General to the end of the new passage ground to a halt. The O.M. stalked past the guards and surveyed the uncovered roundness of the metal hulk. How long ago was it that it had crashed? And now it was there, buried under yards and yards of rock and dirt.

Lieutenant J followed the General into the ship. The crash could not have been very heavy. Most of the machinery within was still intact. There were vague shapes on the floor, shrouded in dust, but of unmistakable outline. Bodies might go in 15,000 years, but bone still remained.

The General disappeared into the dusk of the rear chamber, his flashlight prowling around the engine. Lieutenant J went forward, peering half-heartedly at the furnishings and mechanisms, his mind neither here nor there, but in an empty state without thought. Why bother thinking? Everything would be over soon, and he wouldn't have to wonder anymore what had been left out of him.

A device caught his eye, and he walked over to it. The thing was a pair of spools, with a tape running between them and through some mechanism. The shape was different, but Lieutenant J knew what a tape running through a machine was for. He had listened to music from a device like that, long ago. But he had gotten tired of it. There had been no good music. Nothing satisfying, like meat and wine. Just spices and sweets.

He idly wondered what sort of music they had before The Beginning. He took a testing instrument from his side pouch and made contact with the leads from the machine with the tape and spools. He read his instrument, removed it, and clamped battery leads to the machine. The starter was snapped, and the motor ground. It was dry after so many years, so he supplied oil.

Then the music started, and everything else stopped.

That was some music. It snapped him to attention with four sharp chords, twice repeated, and then it flowed up and down, and it roared and whispered, and it held all the power of the universe within its form.

That was good music. How he knew it was good music, he couldn't tell, for he had never heard good music before. Good music had never been written in his world, when the sum total of his civilization was destruction. But he, somehow, had known he would recognize it when he heard it. Now he was hearing it, and it couldn't be anything else. It was the meat and wine—it roared through him and filled up the empty space.

Who wrote the music? Who cared? What did it matter that a deaf madman named Beethoven had conceived it and called it the Symphony Number Five? Names meant nothing, and it told no story.

There were other spools. There was slow, massive music of harmonies that shook the walls. There was quiet music that held a peace that transcended understanding. There was exciting music that brought the emotions to a boil and set the breath quickening.

He sat and listened, and the world was forgotten, and all the problems were solved, and all sorrows were nothing. Then he began to feel that something start to happen, and he knew that this time if he sat at the organ that thing would happen, and the music that he would make would be what he had wanted all that time.

The tape stopped, and he stood up. He must go to his organ. He had to play. He had to make that marvelous music himself. He couldn't wait any longer, for all the time that was the thing that kept almost happening, and never did. Now it would, and he hungered for it.

The General came back. "What is all that noise?"

It wrenched Lieutenant J back from the other world. It wrenched him back so abruptly and cruelly that he could not believe it. The soaring wave crashed upon the rock, and its dissolution was too much to bear.

"Come on," the General turned to go. "It's time to start the test."

Lieutenant J. left the wreck and moved off with the General. He didn't wanted to go. He didn't want to go with the General; he wanted to stay and play his organ and make for himself that marvelous music he had just heard, but he had to go, and that was all there was to it.

He entered the mole and the vibration started as it went forward, and he felt the monstrous power of the machine in the wheel he held and saw it in the lines of the metal. Forces blasted and gears churned, and the mole beat for itself a tunnel through the rock of Venus. Ahead he was to go for ten miles, and when he got there he would rise up in the midst of the enemy post, and he would wipe it out. At least, that was what it said in the orders.

The roars and the grinding and the pounding filled the mole, but in his head, and in all the emptiness of his body that it had filled, the music went on and on. But there was something wrong now. There was still something wrong, only it was different from what had been wrong before.

What is the matter with me, he asked himself, while the mole burrowed in a universe of noise. I wanted to be a musician, but there was no good music to play, and I didn't know what good music was, and I didn't care if I lived or died, for I had no purpose. I felt empty, and sometimes I thought I was going to discover what good music was, but nothing ever happened, for I was not great enough. I had no purpose and I didn't care whether or not I came back from the test job.

But now I know what good music is. I heard it in the machine, and all of a sudden I am filled. I am satisfied, and living can mean something now, for in that music there is something that can be life itself.

Now I know what is wrong. Before I didn't care. Now I care. Now I care whether or not I come back from the test or not, but I know I won't, for you never come back.

You never come back. The machinery rattled it out. The motors hummed it forth. The generators whined the song.

Then he was underneath the enemy, and their detectors sounded him out, and their forces beat into the ground. His ears and his bones ached from the sonic waves; the humped metal around him grew hot from the induction beam. Relays thumped, and the mole shrieked as the neutralizers gobbled up and dispersed energy.

The time was come now, and his hands reached out to the levers that jutted from the machines. Jerking and grinding, the mole slowly edged to face upwards. It was near the surface, and then it was through, breaking the ground to meet a hell of explosives and forces. The fury of the enemy was concentrated on him, but his armor held.

Now the neutron blast. The new beam that could not be deflected, and that had the power of a battleship behind it. It screamed out like an incandescent knife, and it cut through buildings and forts and tanks, and the little, shouting people that ran from its path. The people did not even flare as the beam struck them.

Why was he shooting at these people? He had nothing against them. But he was too tired to wonder more than vaguely. The squat torpedo that was his mole made a molten lake of the enemy camp, and his job was nearly finished.

The enemy had a new weapon, too. It exploded on, beneath, all around the mole. The concussion beat Lieutenant J to his knees, and the force lifted the mole onto its tail end. The neutron blast in the nose of the mole cut into the planet; the mole fell as the rock was torn from its path.

Now it was the end, and Lieutenant J knew it, as the noise pounded him. The screaming noise of the inferno without mingled with the music that was in his head. It roared and it roared, and it asked the question of life and it answered the question and it gave peace and excitement and love and joy and sorrow, and it mounted up higher and higher, until the outside noise and the inside noise was one, and the cylinder of the mole merged with the molten inside of the planet that came spurting up the tube to meet it.

THE BRIDGE

IT WAS SO ridiculous, he thought, as he walked there on the bridge.
All those scientists spending so much money on big machines to generate the immense voltages which they hoped would break down a few
atoms. You didn't need such big machines and powers. He knew how
to do it with a little thing, no larger than a Ford V-8 motor.

And he could do more than just pull atoms apart. He could destroy them completely . . . electrons and protons and all those silly
particles which weren't there anymore after you destroyed them. Energy came out of the other end of the machine. Lots of it.

He liked to walk on the bridge and think. Not many people were
ever there. Many times the whole mile-long span would be empty, except for him; and he would stand in the middle, looking down on the
boats that went back and forth far below, while the sun beat down
upon his neck. There was no sun today, and the fog made the big
snake-like cables appear vague and distant.

He liked the curve of those huge cables. He tried to imagine the
curve extending up in a circle. What a large circle it made. And then to
extend it into a sphere—the equations drifted aimlessly through his
mind.

Equations went through his mind constantly. Everything he had
to turn into symbols and reduce and then integrate them. Finally he
had gotten matter on one side and energy on the other side of the
equations, and they were the same. Einstein had gone that far. But
Einstein had never been able to switch the sides around . . . convert
one into the other.

He knew how . . . with a foolish little machine . . . and it began to
frighten him.

Because a lot of energy came out the other end. He could supply
the country with electrical power by using a quarter of an ounce of
matter every day.

What a boon it would be for the scrap metal industry. The power
companies would be able to sell their power plants to the junk dealers
and get a lot of money from the deal. And the people who worked in
power plants would be delirious with joy over the wonderful new discovery that would revolutionize everything; and supply everybody
with power so cheap they could sell it for a tenth of a cent a kilowatt-hour, and still make a hell of a profit out of it.

The only trouble was that you only needed a little power plant for
each state, and there would not be so many people making the money.
In fact, the people who owned the present power plants would be
angry if he, the inventor of the future power plant, would want to

make the money himself.

They might try to shoot him.

It was very unkind of him to think that. The man had been very nice and polite that morning when he, the inventor, had decided not to sell his invention to the man for a million dollars. He didn't want to sell it, because he wasn't sure what others would do with it afterwards. He wasn't sure what he was most afraid of, the things that they might do with it . . . or the fact that they might not do anything with it.

Anyway, the man from the electric company had been very nice to him. He couldn't have had anything to do with what happened a few hours later, when he stooped to feed the pigeons, and, hearing a curious noise behind him, rose to find a hole in his hat.

After that, people always seemed to be out when he tried to see them. He couldn't even borrow a few million dollars to manufacture the machine.

Except for the offer he had. The man had represented a country which would find copious power coming very handy to them. But although he was a scientist, and didn't know much about what was going on, he did know a little bit. And he knew that a millionth of and ounce of matter . . . any kind of matter . . . would equal six hundred pounds of nitroglycerin if treated as only he knew how. He knew that this country would just love that.

But he didn't. So he refused.

You see, he had hoped that with cheap power and lots of it, things would be changed. There would be big, clean, beautiful cities. And happiness, and plenty, and knowledge, and everything that was nice. He could visualize the beautiful city, like a picture projected onto the white of the mist. There were big, graceful towers, full of art and color, and happy people.

But then airplanes, powered by his machine, swooped down from above . . . like the curve the cable made . . . and released energies which came out of the machine he had made. Such energies didn't belong on a tiny planet like this. They belonged on the sun. They left a hole in the ground where the beautiful city had been.

He had a thought—and in thinking it he felt like a great philosopher It was this: . . . that before certain changes can be made . . . other changes have to be made.

So the waves of the river went out in big circles, while a hat and a piece of paper on which equations were written floated up and down. Up and down, and then down and not up.

Up was the bridge, with its big girders and swooping cables.

A NOTE ON PREVIOUSLY UNPUBLISHED FICTION

The following three unpublished stories were found among Dr. Rothman's papers after his death. Attached correspondence indicate that these stories were written in the late 1970s and early 1980s.

EDWARD: A NEW BALLAD

THE BUS depositing Edward Blake outside the palm-shaded building disappeared down the road, leaving him standing with twenty other newcomers. He smiled at the warm sun and admired the sculptured landscape that faded into the ocean on the east, merging smoothly into a rolling golf course on the west. To the south was a settlement of small houses that, apparently, was his destination. Silently he shuffled with the chattering crowd.

A tall, white-haired man bearing a large name tag ushered them into the reception house. There, several women with elaborate tinted coiffures poured coffee and gushed conversation.

"I'm sure you'll love it here," the one labeled Marjorie assured him. "I play bridge three times a week, and there's an excellent choice of movies. Time just goes by and you don't even notice it."

And you don't even notice yourself getting old. The unbidden thought sliced through his mind as he looked at the other members of his group and recoiled. *They've put me with a bunch of old men and women. I don't belong here.*

Still, he knew that he lied. To himself he lied.

"1 want to welcome all of you to Leisure Land." The man in the beard with the entertainment-director manner boomed his amplified voice across the room. "You've all paid your dues. You've spent your quarter century at work, and now at the age of fifty you can spend the rest of your life enjoying the fruits of your labors. We have here everything necessary to fulfill your needs: from music appreciation classes to arts and crafts studios. All sports are available and there is a cocktail hour every day. You will find friends and companionship.

"The only thing we ask of you is that you study the rules given in the rule book that you will receive. After all, this is a civilized community and rules are necessary to grease the wheels, so to speak. Remember the old saying: You play ball with us and we'll play ball with you."

Beginning at a very deep level in Blake's abdomen, a primal nausea began to overflow.

The feeling of revulsion was incomprehensible. After all, this was his reward. He had spent his 25 years of labor as computer programmer, faithfully filling his niche in society. Even more, actually becoming fascinated by the game of arranging symbols to move and manipulate numbers within the computer memory. His life had been neatly organized, his recreations circumspect, and his associations respectable. Here he was, apotheosis to glory in the most desirable of retirement communities. What more did he want?

The woman labeled Marjorie invited herself to show Blake his cottage. Her violet-tinted silvery hair, lacquered in place with microscopic exactitude, soared high above her head. He tried to imagine going to bed with her; the very thought was squeamish and uncomfortable. Sexual attraction buried itself deep beneath a sheen of varnish.

He said, "You must spend a lot of time on your hair."

"Oh yes," she giggled. "It's one of my main occupations. I've won prizes."

The shuttle-bus drove them past a uniformity of cottages through which they could see patches of ocean-reflected sunlight. Inside his cottage he remarked about its neatness, while wondering to himself if they were all identical. Adequate, neat, he could cook, he could entertain. He could be as alone or together as he liked.

Why, then, did he have to turn his back so that Marjorie could not see his secret tears?

"It's really nice here," Marjorie said. "I know you'll make lots of friends."

"I'm sure," said Edward Blake, but could not recall an especially friendworthy face standing out.

He said, "I think I'd like to spend a little time getting unpacked. Perhaps I'll see you at dinner time."

"Yes indeed," she said brightly, not perceiving the brushoff. "And don't forget the welcome party tonight. There's gonna be a big time in the old town tonight."

She shimmered out the door, leaving him alone.

His bass and boxes were already delivered. For company while unpacking, he turned on the TV, shuddering at the daily soap opera and switching to the news. Were events of moment still going on in the surrounding world? Without him?

HIGHLIGHTS FROM THE WORLD OF ENERGY: THE ARAB NATIONS, THEIR OIL FIELDS APPROACHING DEPLETION, ARE COMING HAT IN HAND FOR SHALE-DERIVED PETROLEUM TO KEEP THEIR REFINERIES GOING. THE TANKERS HAVE TURNED AROUND. A NEW FUSION REACTOR HAS BEEN COMPLETED IN NEW JERSEY CAPABLE OF SUPPLYING TEN MILLION KILOWATTS OF POWER TO THE NETWORK. THE LATEST AUDIT OF PLUTONIUM FROM THE COUNTRY'S BREEDER REACTORS SHOWS OVER THREE THOUSAND KILOGRAMS UNACCOUNTED FOR.

On the brink of the twenty-second century, problems are never solved, only multiplied.

Blake sighed, No more were these worries his responsibility. Henceforth his categorical imperative was simply *it's not your problem*. With no duties, powers, honors, privileges, or even expectations, he was just another retired person—gently propelled out of the mainstream of life to make room for someone younger to continue the cycle.

He prowled the room and, solitary at last, became aware of apprehension and anxiety. Ungoaled was unmanned.

Still standing, he breathed deeply, then burrowed into one of his packing crates where he found his little black box. Tenderly he cradled it in his hands and sank deeply into a soft chair. With its keyboard, its flashing numbers, its tiny luminescent curve tracer, he experienced this miniature computer as a part of his brain.

Fingers caressed the keyboard and touched the buttons that withdrew from electronic memory a symmetrical mandala figure that flickered and spun in the miniscule screen, cooling and calming his senses. With a feeling of inward-turning, he sank down into a blank state in which he became aware of every muscle tension, and by focusing on each knot of pain could gently smooth it out. In the end he dozed off to sleep.

Only to be jarred awake by the false cheer of the entertainment director coming over the hidden intercom, informing him that orientation period would be in half an hour, followed by cocktails and dinner. Dress informal. Which meant jackets and neckties.

Blake cursed. Orientation, indeed!

His vile mood refused to dissipate in the shower, and by the time he entered the auditorium he had returned to his original feeling of outrage and dislocation.

Because they were old. Old men and women with cheerful, impenetrable masks. Fifty years old, each and every one of them.

You idiot, that's why you're here. Because you're fifty, too. Like all the rest.

They took seats, waiting for the happening. The lights dimmed and the screen at the head of the room flared with color. Inspirational music swelled, and Blake curdled inside, sensing the memories of countless educational films echoing through the chambers of his mind.

"There was a time," the voice on the film said, "when society was different. The population was expanding, families were large, and three and four generations could live in one house."

Pan through shots of bucolic American farmhouse, children running around, granddad splicing rope, grandmaw knitting, mom cooking over a large, steaming stove.

"A century ago it became apparent that the resources of the world were unable to maintain a population that continued to expand, so that the goal of Zero Population Growth was set and reached in an amazingly short time. Before the 21st century arrived, the population of the United States had leveled off to an equilibrium value."

Superimpose shots of graphs with population curves snaking upward and over.

"At the same time, family life changed its patterns. People moved to urban centers. The single family with two children became standard. Grandparents lived by themselves, divorce became so commonplace that it was a rarity for couples to remain together as grandparents."

Shots of sophisticated middle-class apartments, well-dressed middle-aged couples zooming off to the country club.

"Other factors entered the scene. As population stabilized, the number of jobs available also leveled off. Then it became more and more difficult for people to advance their careers by way of more jobs opening up. Younger men and women had to wait for the elders to retire before they could move up the ladder of advancement. One result of this was earlier and earlier retirement. Now, towards the end of the 21st century, we feel that a working life of 25 years, with compulsory retirement at the age of 50, equalizes the opportunities. The older members of the community, having given their labor, can move on to enjoy their rewards, providing openings in the labor pool for the younger men and women coming up.

"As part of the reward, the state has established retirement communities where you can all live with a minimum of effort and a maximum of enjoyment . . . ."

Blake began to wonder: did this place have a computer terminal where he could continue to enjoy the puzzles and games that were his life as well as his occupation? He wondered: what happened to people who really enjoyed their work? How did they maximize their enjoyment in this disneyland of idleness?

Afterwards, at the cocktail party, feeling the cold martini explode inside, he stood, withdrawn, watching the others send out feelers towards relationships. Already a network was beginning to form. Already he was on the outside.

"Hi!" A hand touched his elbow. "I thought I'd find you here."

It was Marjorie. Naturally.

"You look lonesome. Let me introduce you around." She drew him into a group of old-timers and names flew by in a blur. Joe, Bill, Sue, Karen. He nodded, put on his best smile, and tried desperately to reply positively to the suggestions and invitations that came his way.

"Hope to see you at tennis soon."

"You'll love our perpetual bridge tournament."

"Hey, wait till you try the golf course."

He appreciated the suggestions, but already felt exhausted by the continual activity. Didn't anybody ever sit quietly?

He said, "Yes, it sounds great. . . . But I was never much good at athletics. Is there a chess club here?"

The blank pause following told him that he had made a mistake, but he shrugged it off. He found himself absolutely uninterested in their opinions, and since their conversation before, during, and after dinner was nothing but a continuous stream of opinions and gossip about persons unknown to him, he sought the first excuse for a quick exit.

There was a moment when Marjorie walked him to the door and he imagined that she was expecting him to invite her to his place, but for better or worse he ignored the thought and went out into the night by himself.

On the beach he listened to the roar of the sea and surf, wondering why he felt so completely out of place. Something in this beautiful settlement must satisfy his soul.

The next morning Blake surveyed the handbook that he found on his dresser. The list of activities available to him was almost endless: sports, hobbies, games, clubs. Endless ways of keeping busy. But no way of filling the vast hollow within himself.

In despair, he thought, let's see how the painting class is. At least it might be creative. When he went over he found them doing a bowl of little yellow flowers and he thought, but I don't feel like painting little yellow flowers now. So he started painting big red and purple flowers, and the instructor said, "That doesn't look very much like what we're doing."

Blake replied, "I'm being creative." And he carefully proceeded to cover his big red and purple flowers with a pattern of black dots in positions chosen from a random-number generator within his pocket computer.

The instructor looked at what he was doing and sniffed. "Mr. Blake, you know we're not doing abstracts this session. We're doing yellow flowers."

"I don't like painting flowers," he replied. "Do you ever use live models?"

"Oh yes. In fact, we will be using a model in our very next session."

With cautious anticipation he returned for the next session, to find that the model was a middle-aged woman wearing a white dress and a white hat with little pink flowers. Feeling a wild surge of disappointment—knowing that he had been stupid to expect anything else—he smeared the canvas-board with broad streaks of vivid, dark colors.

The instructor remonstrated: "You wanted a model, and now you won't paint anything that looks like the model. You're not being very cooperative at all."

"You're absolutely right," Blake muttered.

The following morning he received a message asking him to see Mr. Green at the Community Guidance Center. Mr. Green wore the beard and beads that appeared to be the trademark of the counseling profession.

Mr. Green said: "You don't seem to be adjusting to our community very well."

Blake replied: "That's a keen observation."

Mentally, Mr. Green noted that Blake was a wiseguy, but said, "You know, you have many years left to enjoy life, and you are only making yourself unhappy if you don't make the most of it."

"Undoubtedly I'm making myself unhappy," Blake replied, "but possibly the reason might be that I don't want to adjust to this place. I don't feel that I belong here."

Mr. Green nodded. "It's common for people to deny that they are of retirement age, so they feel that they don't belong in a retirement community."

"You insist on misunderstanding me. I didn't say I objected to retirement. I said I don't belong *here*. There's something missing here. I don't get any warm vibrations from anybody here."

Mr. Green raised his eyebrows. "Oh, is that your problem? Well, we're not exactly puritans, you know. There's a fair amount of swinging that goes on. Nobody's going to criticize you if you want to get a girlfriend. As long as you do it discretely, of course."

Blake spent a moment fantasizing bed with Marjorie, every lavender lock neatly in place. He shivered, and felt no vibes at all. No anticipation, no attraction—just a deadness.

He had learned not to argue. He said, "Okay, that's good to know."

When he left Mr. Green, Blake made a beeline for his cottage and knew exactly what he was going to do. As quickly as possible he filled a backpack with necessities, cast a despairing eye over his precious books, and wondered if he would ever see them again.

Then, without looking backwards, he walked out of the cottage and shut the door.

Nobody paid any attention to him as he walked north up the coastal highway away from the settlement. He was free to come and go, and who in his right mind would want to run away from such a place?

After a bit he tired of the main highway and turned inward along a secondary road. Not caring where he was going and not knowing what he sought, one thing he knew was that he had to escape from that prison of invisible walls and velvet gloves. There must be some other place in the world where he could stay: a farmhouse, a small town, any place far enough out of the network of society that his presence would not be noticed.

The sun turned hot in the afternoon, but there was peace in his heart and lightness in his feet. He was even able to hitch a ride on a small farm truck and made good distance. He lunched in a small village diner and nobody seemed curious about his origin. It was as though being out of the mainstream he had become a non-person and so had become invisible.

After nightfall he found a corner of a broad, flat field, as far away from prying eyes as possible, and spread his sleeping bag. It was the first time he had camped out in many years, but as he looked up at the stars he felt filled with a wild joy.

In the morning he felt hunger, but knew that somewhere along the road must be food. At the far end of the field where he had slept a flash of light caught his attention, and he saw the sun reflected in a window. There must be a farmhouse there, he thought, and set off in that direction.

As he approached he saw that it was certainly not a farmhouse. It was a long, low building, with branches running off at several points, as though additions had been tacked on periodically. His curiosity impelled him forward.

His approach, apparently, was from the rear of the building complex, and was unnoticed. A door facing him was unlocked and opened easily. He entered, feeling ready to be caught trespassing, an escaped prisoner. A short hallway brought him to a seemingly endless corridor running the length of the building.

What he saw there took his breath away with a sudden gasp. He stood in paralysis, an uncontrollable chill coursing up and down his spine. Sudden understanding flooded his mind.

Sitting in row after row down the long hallway were hundreds of men and women, silent, staring, shriveled. Occasionally one moved a hand, made a grimace, or let out a squawk, so that he knew they were alive. But their shrunken faces were masks in which their eyes sank deeply, vision directed inward or toward a far space beyond the reach of others. Clothed in white gowns, their bodies were wizened, featureless, sexless.

Blake shrank back against the wall. His mouth drooped slackly open. Here was AGE. Age beyond retirement. Age beyond reason.

A hum suddenly arose from a group to Blake's right. He saw that the wheelchairs in which they sat had suddenly activated themselves, had wheeled around, and were gliding down the hallway to a distant door. Without thinking, he followed them.

On the other side of the door he found the feeding room. Not the mess hall or the dining hall, but the feeding room, for these were the souls too far gone to help themselves. Blake watched with horrified fascination as the wheelchairs rolled themselves up to feeding cubicles, where robot-like appendages unerringly applied spoonfuls of oatmeal-like material to the mouths of the recipients, mouths which chewed noiselessly and opened again greedily like the beaks of so many birdlets. Robot feeders programmed to seek mouth openings, and the fed conditioned to follow directive light signals synchronized neatly, and there was a minimum of waste and dribblings.

Blake became aware that someone was watching him. He turned and saw a black man stolidly looking him over. The man was old enough to be retired, but not old enough to be an occupant of this place.

"Hi," Blake said, nervously. "I was just passing by and thought I'd see what was in here."

The other said nothing, but waited with a wary air, a suspicious silence.

"Actually," Blake continued, "I'm looking for something to eat. Is there anyplace here I could get something?"

The other's face softened into the barest smile.

"Is that all? Thought you was a nosy government inspector or senator. Always coming around to make trouble about conditions. Come on. We have a kitchen back here for the employees. Not too many of us left since we got automated."

The man turned out to be Jim Purdy, and, once started, was fairly talkative.

"I been workin' here about 40 years. We don't get many visitors anymore. Like people forget about the old folks once they're in here." Jim sat across the table from Blake sucking at a cup of coffee, while Blake hungrily downed a pair of eggs. A few other employees stood around the kitchen, having their morning coffee.

Blake looked around. "Who's minding the store?"

Jim stared, puzzled.

"I mean, who's taking care of the old people out there?"

"Oh, there's a couple of attendants out there. But mainly it's the machines. There's a computer that keeps track of every patient all the time, makes sure they get fed and cleaned and put to bed at the right times."

"You call them patients. What's wrong with them?"

Jim chuckled. "Just old age, son. Just old age. Wait and see. Some day I'll be there. Some day you'll be there. I've a body strong as an ox. Doctors keep me healthy with vitamins and all that. So I'm gonna live to be 100—mebbe 110. But the old brain's gonna give out first. It's gonna forget everything it knows and I'll be back to my second childhood. That's what my grandmaw used to call it."

With clenched fists, Blake again felt the chill that had stiffened his spine when he had first entered the building. The moment he had seen the long row of silent specters he had guessed what the house was. This was the house beyond retirement, where one waited to die, forgotten by the rest of the world.

"You're not gonna see *me* here," he growled.

Jim's eyebrow raised. "Maybe yes, maybe no. You might be lucky and die before you lose your marbles."

"I'll make sure of that. I'll kill myself before I get like that."

"If you can tell what's happening to you in time. Maybe."

Blake felt he could stay no longer. But before he left he must see the old people one more time, to impress upon his memory the emptiness and the waste that came at the end of a long life.

In the feeding room they were still being stoked: one robot feeding another. In the corridor the long waiting lines stood—waiting patiently for death to end the waiting.

The feeling of horror gradually left Blake as he watched them closely and saw them for what they were—a number of quiet, lonesome old people patiently sitting out their final days, cared for impersonally and mechanically by a society that did not know what else to do with them. As the memories gradually faded out of their poor brains, their eyes grew more and more empty, until there was nothing left but a few primal memories of the earliest days.

Suddenly one of the old crones began rocking violently back and forth, screeching at the top of her lungs. Blake whirled, startled, but the others around her paid no attention. In a moment a puff of tranquilizing vapor squirted from the chair arm and in a few more minutes she sank back into a somnolent stupor.

Blake left the building as rapidly as he could, and ran down the path into the woods. A short period of running left him breathless and he stopped to rest on the ground with his back against a tree. He deliberately slowed his breathing and caused his body to relax. After closing his eyes a feeling of floating came to him and the beat of his heart ceased its thudding. Shame at his panic passed momentarily through his mind, but it, too, went, for he knew that his fear was not of the sight of old people, but of the thought that some day he would be there, also.

Presently he rose. It was time to be going. Where, he did not know. But time to get going, anyway.

The sun rose into the zenith and poured heat down upon him. He stayed as close to the shadow of trees as he could, but by afternoon he was parched. He had chosen a narrow road, out of sight, away from habitation. He could go for a long time without meeting anyone, but he could also become very hungry.

Just as that thought filtered into his mind, Blake rounded a bend in the road and encountered a pair of figures sitting on the ground off to one side. He stopped in an automatic alarm, but as he had time to absorb the details of these strangers he saw that they were only a man and a woman eating out of a canvas bag resting between them. Pulled over to the side of the road beyond them was a strange vehicle consisting of a tandem bicycle hooked to a small two-wheeled cart.

The two glanced up as he hove into view and waved at him. Encouraged, Blake walked slowly toward them, trying to place in his experience their novel appearance. Dressed in a rough blue material, embroidered in bright colored thread, they wore wide, floppy straw hats bearing live flowers picked from the side of the road. Both had long blonde hair tucked into a pony tail behind.

Actually, Blake suddenly realized, the only way he could tell that one was a man and the other a woman was by the curvature of their forms. The man was thin and bony, while the woman was ample and softly convex.

The woman said, as he came near, "Hi. Care for some lunch?" Their smiles were friendly and real.

Blake flopped without hesitation on the grass beside them.

"You don't have to ask me twice. It's been a long time since breakfast."

As they cut large chunks of cheese and brown bread, Blake found that the two were named Jack and Lorrie and that they lived in a community two hours ride down the road in their vehicle.

"We've just been out riding," Lorrie said. "We make sketches and collect dried grasses that we use for decorations." She motioned to a basked loaded with colorful stems.

Jack said, "We don't often meet strangers walking alone down this road."

Blake shrugged his shoulders, a grim smile appearing and just as quickly vanishing. "I seem to be a fugitive from happyland. Leisureland, emptyland, idleland—it just wasn't my cup of tea, so I bugged out. Where I go now, I don't know."

A sideways look exchanged between Jack and Lorrie brought him a momentary puzzlement, but Blake continued. "Tell me, if you're old hands around here, what do you know about the place back down the road? With all the old people."

Again the sidelong glance, the exchange of hidden information.

"Oh. *The Home*," said Jack. "Yes, you couldn't miss it coming down this road. Were you inside? Did you see it?"

Blake nodded. "Yes, I saw it. Is that what's in store for all of us when we get too old for the retirement communities?"

Jack said, "Oh no, not for all of us. Only for the winners in this game of life. For those with bodies so healthy they refuse to die, so lucky they don't get sick, so fortunate they don't have accidents, so well cared-for that they last forever—winners all the way through. Until the final scene, when the heart lasts longer than the brain. Then they sit there with bodies they can no longer control and memories they can no longer bring back."

They sat there for a moment, silent. Then Lorrie added, "Life is sacred and precious, they teach us. It must not be taken away under any circumstances. So we use our fine science of medicine to prolong life to its natural limit, and no body is allowed to say: *Hey, you're just a body sitting in a chair; why don't you call a halt?* Nobody has the right to call a halt."

Jack sighed. "Actually," he said, "There are some good reasons for this arrangement. Aside from the nonsense slogans from the Sacred Life pressure groups, there is some logic to the prohibition against calling a halt. It's just a matter of historical observation that whenever you make it easy to kill one group of people by saying they're old or sick or useless, then you make it easy to abuse and extend this right to other groups who might be disliked by those in power. So the function of a blanket slogan such as *Life is Precious* is to make it harder for the authorities to get rid of dissenters such as you and me. It's self-protection.

"The price we pay is the need to keep institutions for those who really are useless and helpless and whose plugs ought to be pulled. We have to pay that price to keep a consistent moral code."

"But they cheat, as always," Lorrie replied. "By hiding *The Homes* out of sight so that the old people can be out of mind. It's as good as killing them, but without actually pulling the trigger. So you don't have the guilt and you don't violate consistency of principle. You just avoid."

Jack laughed and offered Blake a jug of wine. "And so we have the best of all possible worlds. Here, have a taste of our own little world. Made in our own little village."

Blake tasted and was beguiled by the smoothness and warmth of the drink.

He grinned and said, "I'd like to see where you make that."

"Then come with us," Lorrie invited. "We're on our way back. You can ride in the cart."

"I can help you pedal," Blake responded. "Even though it's been some time since I rode a bike."

"Okay. Next time we stop," Lorrie agreed.

They rode without haste through the afternoon, Jack and Lorrie keeping up a running commentary on the vegetation surrounding them, occasionally calling attention to small animals or bright birds that hid in the roadside. Their encyclopedic knowledge of flora and fauna impressed Blake. But even more impressive was their complete fascination with the myriad things around them, a trait he had found completely missing from the retirement community he had fled. He thought—*are there others like this ahead?*

He felt as though a magnet pulled him down the road.

By the time they reached the village of Arcadia, most of the winejug was gone. While the road went through the village center, most of the houses were hidden behind a screen of trees. Those visible were small and cabin-like, except for a large shed here and there through whose doors Blake could see mysterious activity. A red glare flaring from a kiln within one shed outlined the form of a potter leaning over an earthen shape on a wheel. He sat up straight and stared as the scene rolled past.

Through the open window of another building burst a convoluted musical sound, by its tone from an electronic instrument of some sort. Curling and writhing through the air, it suddenly halted, only to restart itself with a subtly varied repetition. Over and over the run tumbled through the leaves while Blake felt himself gripped by a new and intense excitement. Clearly, somebody was practicing this music—perhaps even composing it.

Another shed door revealed a solitary workman climbing over a complex structure standing within. Even at a distance the momentary view of the form stirred a deep and primal emotion inside him.

Peaking the crest of his excitement was the overriding thought: *people make things here.* Blake felt that his journey was over.

At that moment he felt the vehicle swerve into a narrow lane winding through the trees. Presently it came to a halt under an overhang beside a small cabin.

"Here's home," Jack said, dismounting. "You're welcome to visit with us until you find a place of your own."

"Thank you," Blake replied, grateful for the invitation, then suddenly aware of the implication that his staying in the community was taken for granted. *Strange,* he thought.

Then shrugged the apprehension out of his head: *picked up and brought here like one of their specimens.*

"I'm hungry." Lorrie broke apart his thought-train. "Let's eat at The Place. I don't feel like cooking now."

"Sounds good to me." Jack put his basket of reeds and straws inside the cabin door. "We should wash up before we go."

He glanced at Blake. "Our friend's been on the road for two days.

Probably feels smelly as a horse. How about a quick dip in the pool and a hot shower?"

Blake, suddenly aware of road dust caked with dried perspiration, found this the most attractive idea of all.

Then he hesitated. "But I don't have a bathing suit."

Jack and Lorrie both grinned widely. "You won't need one. Come on."

In fact he didn't. As they came down the path toward the artificial pond hemmed with trees there was a startled moment when Blake realized that all the bathers in and around the pool were completely nude. A moment of surprise, and then an intake of breath at the glory of it.

Then, of course, an instant of apprehension at breaking fifty years of conditioning, but all it took was the simple act of removing his pants and there he was. The warmth of the sun on his bare bottom he found one of the nicest sensations of his experience, and as he sliced through the clean coolness of the water unimpeded by the drag of cloth, he became dizzy with freedom.

Gasping, he surfaced, and swam four laps, then dragged himself back to the pond edge. Jack and Lorrie gradually worked their way to where he sat, stopping to greet friends along the way. As they beckoned him over to meet a small group, Blake's mind went blank with embarrassment and the names flitted through the quivering corners of his mind to disappear without a trace. However, in a moment the strangeness vanished and he delighted in the reality of dealing directly with persons, without interposed layers of clothing, style, and miscellaneous brands of lacquer.

These new acquaintances were direct and open, interested to know where he had been and what he had experienced. His description of Leisure Land brought shouts of laughter.

Ken, a big and bony man, told him, "You're not the first one to come this route. Every so often somebody freaks out over the banality of Leisure Land and then manages to find his way here. All of us got here one way or the other for the same reasons. We're the people who don't fit into the usual slots in the steady-state society out there. So we make a place like this away from the mainstream."

A cushiony woman named Laura added, "Poor mainstream. They don't even know what they're missing."

"That's probably a good thing," said Blake, thinking of the pompadoured and painted women at Leisure Land, imagining their presence here. The thought alone made him want to put on his pants.

By mutual agreement the group moved to The Place for dinner. The moment he walked in, Blake knew that this was where he wanted to be. Art of many forms hung from walls and ceiling, setting his eyes popping and his mouth agape.

Lorrie noticed his feeling, squeezed his arm, and remarked, "We have a number of very fine artists here. This is where the action is."

There was no time to think about what she meant, for he found himself in a cafeteria line and found concentration on decisions necessary. At the end of the line he saw others putting their universal credit cards into the payment slot and automatically reached into his wallet for his card. Without giving it a second thought he slipped his card into the slot when it came his turn. Retrieving it after the usual momentary wait for mysterious buzzings and lightings, he glanced at the photosensitive panel on his card and noted that as usual he had been credited with his retirement pay on the first day of the month and that the nominal charge for this meal had been deducted.

Blake found his food good, then lapsed into thoughtful silence while he ate.

"Anything wrong?" Laura asked.

"Not really. Just wondering what I'm going to do in this place. There's a lot going on. How am I going to fit into this high-powered crowd?"

Jack laughed. "Don't worry. Flounder around and find your place. Take your time."

"Usually," Laura said, "you start from where you were. If you like what you were doing, you can continue. Otherwise you can change to whatever you want. What were you doing before. . . ? Computer programming? Well, you should see what some of our people are doing with computer music. Or if that's not your bag, we have people doing research of one kind or another."

Blake's heart lifted as he thought of resuming his precious computer puzzles. Memories of some work he had done in aleatory art crossed his mind, to be driven out by another thought.

"So you have computers here," he said. "Then you're not completely out of the mainstream?"

Jack raised an eyebrow. "We don't have to give up all the useful things in the world just to get some peace and quiet. We have a number of personal computers and there are also some terminals tied in to the big library in the city."

"Universal Credit Department at the Treasury."

"Well of course. You don't expect us to get along without money."

Blake hunched his shoulders and sank deeper into his seat. This bucolic paradise turned out to be not so isolated and innocent after all. A web of connections tied it to the outer world. Already Blake had put his card into the slot and already the authorities knew where he had fled.

Overwhelmed by an intolerable urge to turn his head and look over his shoulder, he glanced about cautiously, but all he could see was a roomful of people eating, talking, relaxing. From their appearance it was as though all the brightest, most creative people had percolated into this place, and their strong, confident faces gave him such joy that he knew he had come home. This was where he belonged.

Suddenly bursting into a short laugh, he shook his head to sweep from its dark corners the shadows and cobwebs that had begun to accumulate there. Absurd to think that he was a fugitive—that someone was following him. Why should they care? A thousand pounds of load lifted from his back.

Lorrie looked at him quizzically. "Anything wrong?"

"Nope," he laughed. "Just glad to be here."

He caught Laura gazing at him intently, and, finding herself caught, she said, "I'm glad you're here, too."

Somehow, the question of where Blake was to spend the night never required a formal resolution. It just happened. After an evening of conversation, some drink and some smoke, Blake found himself walking Laura to her cabin and without premeditation found himself entering and staying.

"You see," she said, "Things just happen if you let them."

Do I have the courage to face such intense happiness, he thought, *for I know it cannot last.*

In the morning he found that there was organization to the village. There was a place where he could register for a cabin, a place where he could find out who was doing what, and where he could find the resources to do what he wanted to do.

All I have to do is decide. And even not deciding is deciding.

Wisely, he wandered. As he wandered, he wondered.

You would think, he thought, that in a place where everybody is retired, people would just sit around doing nothing. How does this place get to be such a hive of activity? Look at what people will do when they don't have to do it.

He stopped at the studio where he had heard the music the previous day. The man who answered the door was small and neatly put together. He spoke and carried himself with a clerical precision.

"Happy to meet you, Mr. Blake. I'm Wallace Cooper. I can talk to you for a few minutes now since I'm just having tea. Would you join me?"

Cup in hand, Blake stared around the studio at the electronic organ console, the computer terminal, the tape equipment.

"I take it you're doing computer music," he said. "I'm in programming myself. Or was," he remembered.

"What I'm doing is not conventional computer music in the sense of synthesizing new sounds by means of a program. My aim is to compile the ultimate pipe organ. In a real pipe organ there is tone with a feeling that a computer can't reach. What I have is recordings of the great pipe organs of the world. I am in the process of analyzing the characteristics of each tone—the harmonics, the envelope rise and fall times—in other words the entire multidimensional spectrum. Then by programming each pipe into a permanent computer memory I can recall its sound at the touch of a button or the insertion of a punch card. In this way I will have the best of all the real pipe organs in the world, and not just an electronic approximation."

"Sounds like a complicated and time-consuming job," Blake remarked.

"So far it has been," Cooper agreed, walking over to the console. "But with some improved electronics and programming I should be able to get the computer to do its own spectrum analysis. It will then be simply a matter of acquiring appropriate recordings. Listen."

Cooper hopped onto the organ bench, switched on the electronics, and passed his hand over the keyboard. The instrument responded with an authentic sound of pipes from a European Baroque organ. A flick of several stop keys and the sound roaring out of the speakers became the heavy brasses of an American theatre organ.

Abruptly Cooper switched off the organ, slid from the bench, and said, "I must return to work now. It was a pleasure speaking to you. Call me again some time."

Blake noticed that there was no invitation to join Cooper in his work. Well, why should he on first meeting? At any rate, Blake did not think that he wanted to devote the rest of his life to another person's obsession with organ pipes.

As he left, ambling slowly down the road, a vague wisp of a thought quietly poked its way up into his field of awareness and began a teasing assault upon his credulity.

I wonder who pays for all that expensive equipment he has?

Surely not the few hundred credits a month retirement pay. Savings? Investments? Grants?

Suspicion bloomed like a fungus on rich, rotted soil.

What's really going on in this town?

Blake's prowlings through the streets of Arcadia became purposeful, prodded by curiosity and moved by contradiction. On a sudden impulse he turned into the door of the information office that he had passed before.

"I want to rent a computer terminal," he told the woman standing there. She referred him to the computer office down the street, camouflaged like all else in the village inside a rustic exterior. He almost expected the terminal itself to be made of tiny logs, but it was a standard teletype kind of device with videoscreen.

The man there said he could rent a tiny office with a desk and a terminal by the hour, day, or month.

"Let me take it for the rest of the day and then we'll go on from there," Blake said.

He closed the door behind himself and sat down, scratching his head. What did he want? Simply information. Factual information that could be pulled out of a library with a little patience and skill.

Why not just ask somebody?

Grimly Blake dismissed the thought. Later, when he had some facts. Then they couldn't fool him as they had.

What were the facts he wanted? He wasn't sure. With no information at all it's hard to know where to begin to learn.

He began only with a feeling of unease, a feeling that this village was more than it seemed to be—more than a simple commune of bohemian types who drifted here by accident. His first task was to learn the procedures for entering the library system from his keyboard. Then, on a guess, he typed the name of the town—Arcadia—and asked for vital statistics.

The rush of numbers satisfied some curiosities, but not others. On a hunch, he again typed. Arcadia and asked for its history. Find out how it began. Skimming the printout, Blake suddenly felt an explosion in his head as he fixed his attention on one burning paragraph:

ARCADIA WAS PLANNED AS A RETIREMENT COMMUNITY FOR ARTISTS AND CRAFTSMEN OF ALL KINDS. IT IS INCORPORATED UNDER THE RETIREMENT ACT OF 2054, AND RETIREES FROM THE 13th DISTRICT AND CLASSIFICATION AAC22 ARE CHANNELED TO THIS COMMUNITY . . .

He slumped in disappointment. Thinking he had fled the web of bureaucracy, he had simply become caught in a different corner of the same net. He felt the iron fist disguised in a sleeker and softer velvet glove. But what, in fact, had he expected?

He signed off on the computer and left to look for Laura, only finding that she had gone off on an errand. He waited for her at the pool, slept in the sun, and found her in the late afternoon. He waited until dinner, and then in the cafeteria the accusation burst out.

"You didn't tell me this was just another retirement community like all the others.

"You didn't ask me, that's why." Her face showed hurt at his tone. "And we're not like all the others. We're different."

"Sure." Blake found within himself a need to be angry, a need to feel betrayed. "I thought I was coming into a peaceful kind of place. Out of the rat-race, a kind of commune with complete freedom. And what do I find? People working their asses off. A dozen writers, twenty artists, scores of craftsmen of all kinds. They're not working for their own amusement. They're selling to the outside world. This place isn't away from the mainstream. It's one of the nerve centers of the world."

"Look, baby, freedom is having the most choices to do what you want. To an artist freedom is being able to work when you want, whether it's an hour a day or ten hours a day. Did you ever hear of an artist retiring by giving up his painting? He'd just as soon give up sex."

"So what am I doing here?" Bitterness in Blake's voice—a feeling of once more being trapped. "I'm not an artist. I don't belong to this crowd. How the hell did I get here?"

Laura laughed. "You walked here on your own two feet, remember?"

"No. I was running. I was escaping from a place that was supposed to be right for me—that horror of a Leisure Land—that silver-plated concentration camp. Did the computer make a mistake, putting me in a place I couldn't adjust to? I don't think so. A nice, normal, middle-class programmer like me should have fitted in with the bridge and all the other games. I should have adjusted. Why didn't I? What's wrong with me?"

Laura gently covered his hand with hers. "There's nothing wrong with you, baby. You're just *not* nice and normal and adjustable. Look, I was a sociologist before I retired. Drowning in statistics, suffocating in graphs. Came here and got a second chance. That's what you get here, Edward. A second chance to find out who you are before it's too late."

Blake's reply was swallowed by the crash of a falling tray and the splatter of food on the floor. He whipped around in time to see an elderly man stagger and recover from an encounter with a misplaced chair. Blake leaped up to catch the man's arm.

"Are you all right?" he asked, to receive in reply a blank shaking of the head. He helped the man into a chair, while the dining room help cleaned up the mess. The manager came over, shook his head sadly, and clucked.

"Poor Ted," he said. "I'd better call the hospital." He vanished toward the phone.

In a few minutes Blake watched with Laura as two men in white coats helped the old man into an ambulance. Surprise caught him as she buried her face in his chest and clung tightly for a moment shaking silently. Letting go, she wiped her eyes and sighed, "I knew he was on his way out, but it's always hard to look at it."

Blake stared in the direction of the vanished man. "His way out?" Refusal to comprehend allowed innocence of horror.

"You saw it. Yourself. Where they sit and wait to die."

Finally he understood.

"Oh. The Home. On his way to The Home. Finished here."

His thoughts coming in short jerks, Blake stared gloomily into space, then shuddered. "Let's get out of here."

He talked as they walked toward the lake.

"The trouble is, we've divided our lives into distinct periods that don't blend smoothly into each other. Out of school into work. Bang. Out of work into retirement. Zap. A whole new adjustment, moving to a whole new scene. Then out of retirement into—what? Either welcome death or marking time at The Home. And waiting. Just waiting for death to come in its good time."

"Only about ten percent of the population makes it to places like The Home," Laura said, quietly.

Blake laughed. "There's the sociologist. Only ten percent is still a lot of people, and each person there is not a statistic. Each is a person, and each waits. For that matter, so do we. We wait. We pass our time and we wait for the end of retirement, however it comes. What's the use of it?"

Laura turned to look at him. "Hey, baby, I'm gonna flunk you in philosophy if you keep this up. What's the use of anything? You start waiting for death the minute you are born. The only meaning to your existence is what you give to it by yourself, every minute."

"Great. You pass Philosophy I. Give life your own meaning. That's why you artists bust your asses leaving works for posterity. Your productions are your meaning, your immortality. What did I produce?"

"What did my parents produce? Where are they now?" Laura asked., "When was the last time you saw your parents?"

Blake shrugged. "Years ago. We're so far apart. I don't even know where they are now. Living with them was like another life, a whole other incarnation. Even my working years seem shadowy and far away."

Sitting at the lake, Laura and Edward Blake spoke of their families and how fragmented they had become. Ceremonies and visits had become fewer and fewer until there was nothing left.

Laura defended herself. "I have my own community that I live in. These are my friends. You'll see, once you're in. It's closer than a family."

But Blake, suddenly aware of his condition, mourned the loss of his past, and nothing was able to drive this new idea from his mind, now that it had insinuated itself, worm-like, into his consciousness.

Obsessed, he spent a sleepless night. Rootless from vanished memories of childhood, in limbo he floated, having left all behind, having said farewell to nothing.

Come morning, he hurried to the computer office, locked himself in. Where to start? Ask the computer.

He switched on the terminal and typed out, "Library: how do I find a person?"

Impatient wait. The trouble with time-sharing. Then the typer sprang into life and printed out: "Use national directory service, code NDS-4238."

Connected to the directory service, he typed in the name of his father and mother and last address that he could recall. Followed some delay resulting from need for appropriate identification of himself using universal credit card. Further delay caused by tracing of peregrinations of Carol and Henry Blake from one place to another—and contrary to naive belief, searching a computer library can be time-consuming. Records are not always complete and changes are not always posted.

As the place-names clicked onto the printout page one by one it became clear that his own parents must have suffered from as great an identity mismatch as his own, a fact that in a strange way seemed to assuage his anxiety. Indeed, in the course of their travels they had passed through this very town not too long ago. They had been here, in this very place. Had they not left, a few years ago, he might have encountered them. Where had they gone from here?

He waited breathlessly for the next printout. Then froze.

It was too outrageous for coincidence. No, it was perfectly natural. No need to invoke magic or mysticism. Normal causality assured simplicity: reaching this settlement several years ago, and then drifting over the border into senility as had the old man yesterday, the natural place for them to have been sent was The Home. He went a year before her deterioration reached the required level. Right now they were there, at the place Blake had passed through just a few days ago.

The next action required no conscious decision. What he did rose from the deepest levels. Signing off the computer, he rose and walked out of the office, asking the manager where he could rent a bike. Soon he was on the road, heading back the way he had come.

At The Home he walked with purpose past the rows of wheel chairs toward the kitchen, where, as expected, he found his acquaintance Jim Purdy. Jim looked up.

"Hey, look who's here," he said, not displeased at the break in the routine. "Back for a visit?"

"Yup," Blake said, abruptly. "Sooner than I thought. Discovered I have parents here. Maybe you can find them for me."

Jim frowned. "Sure that's what you want? You haven't seen them since they've been here."

"I know. I'm sure. Carol and Henry Blake's the names. Central Directory says they're here."

Jim shrugged and led Blake to a small office where he slowly pecked the names out on a keyboard. The printout showed that both were in the same location.

"That's nice," Jim said. "They're together, at least."

Not quite charming was the scene that tore into Blake's vision when he followed Jim down the long corridor, into a department where the oldest, oldest, and most deteriorated inhabitants of the place continued their existence.

Shrunken, curled up in wheelchairs or beds, their protoplasm continued to function while their synapses had separated into chaos. Mainly silent, occasionally cackling, sometimes mumbling, they filled the air with a chittering of small sounds.

Blake's heavy footsteps led him closer to the end of the hall, unwilling to go on, unable to stop. When he saw them there was no recognition, for nothing remained patterned to his ancient memories. He paused, then moved slowly closer to the two beds, letting the vision arrange itself in his mind so that comprehension would follow the jumbled pattern of sensory impressions he now received. So intolerable was the sight that no gestalt could be made of it.

The once familiar, plump, smiling features had shrunk to death masks from which tubes undulated into a metal box studded with meters and glowing lights. Vague eyes stared out from above sunken cheeks between which lips slowly pursed in and out.

Outrage shuddered through Blake like a roaring wind. "Do they have to be wired up to the machines like zombies?" he demanded.

Jim shrugged. "Just routine. Keeps them comfortable. Keeps them from choking on their juices. Gives them a little oxygen. They're awful old."

A bell dinged in the distance, causing Jim to cock his head and lope slowly off in that direction. "Be back soon," he said.

Hey, Dad, Blake thought, approaching one of the figures. *You're just a routine wired-u hulk. Hey, Mom*, he thought, approaching the other. *You don't look so good yourself. Mom and Dad. Hey, Mom and Dad . . .*

Holding himself tight, he avoided shaking. Unbreathing, he avoided screaming.

My God, what a waste. The thought looped into a Moebius and continued to repeat itself.

What we come to is this. We bear children we raise them to go out into the world and disappear from our ken. Then if we are lucky and live very, very long. . . . then what we come to is this.

The man in the bed suddenly opened his eyes and stared at Blake. His eyelids raised themselves and for a moment there was a burning flash of recognition. Then blankness.

Blake said, "It's me, Dad. Edward. Do you know me?"

No reply.

"I would have come sooner, but I didn't know you were here. I'm sorry."

No reply. *Is anything happening inside?*

"Forgive me," he said.

No sign of forgiveness.

Blake wondered. *Do they really know me? Do they know anything? Would it make any difference if the machine stopped working?*

Smoky anger began blinding Blake's inner eye. Anger at his condition, their condition, the waste of their lives. Intolerable condition, not to be continued.

Darting swiftly behind the beds he tore the wires from their wall sockets, extinguishing the colored lights on the boxes, stilling the clickings and gurglings.

He stopped, panting, looked at the still beds. *It's too late for goodbyes, but goodbye anyway.* And again: *Forgive me.*

Somewhere in the distance a loud bell began to clamor.

He whirled and ran down the hall.

Outside, his flight led him to pedal blindly until he recoiled from the impenetrable truck traffic of a main highway. Angrily he swerved and continued on a secondary road that arrowed toward the ocean. He left the bike on the beach and, head filled with surf roar, he staggered across the sand and onto a great rock jetty that projected out into the water for a hundred meters. From one rock to the other he leaped and sprang until he had gone as far as he could go, then fell onto the flat stone to sit dumbly.

Spray spumed and splashed; wind wept about him. Gradually his heart-pound subsided, and he knew what he had done.

From far beneath, dimly remembered song words floated:

For I have killed my father . . .

A roaring from the sky joined with the rush of the sea, mingling with the tumult within his mind, replying: *What penance will ye do for that. . . ?*

The helicopter landed on the beach and the uniformed men emerged.

Cautiously they hopped out over the rock jetty. Blake watched them, silently, motionless. It seemed unimportant when they lifted him up and brought him back to the helicopter.

In the village of Arcadia they delivered him to a place where Laura came running to clasp him hard. Somebody led them into a room where there was an old man with a heavy white beard and a chain of green beads. The man looked calmly at Blake and said to him, "Sometimes it's hard to let things just be the way they are."

Blake looked into the man's face, was reassured by the twinkle in his eyes, and finally smiled.

THE REUNION

Over the river and through the woods,
To grandmother's house we go . . .

THE COMPUTER chimed. Its blue light flashed, signaling an incoming call.

Judy Kroll paused halfway between the bedroom and the kitchen. At the age of sixty her figure still filled a bikini and bra nicely, and her blond hair, hanging in a pair of braids, still had a soft sheen to it.

She glared at that nagging blue light. "Shit! They're starting to come and I'm not dressed yet and the table's not set. Where's that useless man? Sam! Where the bloody hell are you?"

Her voice bounced around the living room, down the hallway, into the two bedrooms.

"Hold on there just one little minute. I'm winning for a change." Sam's voice emerged double-edged from one of the bedrooms, bearing a mixture of irritation and impending triumph.

"Freakin' Starwar game!" Judy stormed into the kitchen, grumbling. "Prob'ly playing that guy in Australia. What a phone bill we're going to have. Winnie, darling, is everything ready?"

"Gettin' there." Winnie smiled at Judy. Eyes smiled in pleasure. Deep brown eyes in a chocolate face. "Don't you worry about me. Go on get dressed."

Judy hugged Winnie recklessly. It was sinful to be so happy. Between young, virile Winston and old, virile Sam, she had the best of all worlds.

The computer chimed again, insistently. Judy tore out of the kitchen and into the living room. The dining area was at one end, a dramatic window overlooking the Delaware River, while the computer dominated the space on the opposite wall. It was broad and flat, mostly screen covered with a colorful abstraction curling slowly and deliberately. The controls were below, covered by an invisible sliding panel.

"Who is it?" Judy shouted at it.

"Incoming call from Austin, Texas. Will you receive?"

"Tell them to wait five minutes."

"Will do."

She sailed into the bedroom, snorting at the sight. of Sam hunched over his 13-inch screen, where the purple and gold spaceships danced and flashed, and the sounds of poppings and whizzings issued sporadically from the loudspeaker.

"Don't you ever get tired of that game?" she asked, opening the closet door.

Sam's eyes, steely grey, remained fixed to the screen. Firm bands manipulated controls with fine precision. Grim, taut mouth moved, scarcely at all as he replied, "Never!"

Sighing, Judy started choosing clothing. The peasant shift would do, she thought. Beige, with a few embroidered flowers. Keep it simple. How does a grandma dress when the grandma doesn't feel like a grandma?

Where have all the flowers gone . . .

Hell, where have all the flowerchildren gone?

She shrugged into the dress while standing brazenly in front of the great window. It was the 30th floor and there was nobody in that direction for miles. The leaden skies above the river brought her back to that time at Woodstock. My God, what a time that had been! The beginning of a new life. A new world. Oh well . . . The children. The children had come along and somehow that free life of song and protest had slipped back into the past. They had become just like everybody else, but somewhere in the depths of her mind a hard there remained, a hard nugget of resistance.

"God, is it ever going to stop raining?"

There came a loud crash from the video screen, a bright flare of yellow light, and a triumphant cry: "Ha! I gottem! It's my game."

Sam spun away from the keyboard, chortling in glee.

Judy turned and looked at him, hands on ample hips. "A grown man . . . a greyhair, yet. Shooting at spaceships in a picture tube. Is that all you have to do with your time?"

Sam Grundy stood, caught her around the waist, and then, doing the only thing he knew would shut her up, he kissed her full on the mouth. Judy slid her fingers through his pure white hair, fine as spun silk, felt the salt and pepper beard on her cheek. Sam wore his batik holiday shirt and Judy thought he was mighty handsome for a man about to turn 63.

"Look, lady," he said, "I spend the whole week grinding out cases in computer software copyright law, a duller subject than which there ain't. I have a right to let my brain fall apart on weekends."

She smiled. "Of course, darling. I'm just uptight with the thought of all the company. Sandy's calling early, and you just know she's going to be asking for something. Whenever she calls she wants something."

"Remember what we agreed. Not another dollar."

"I know. Too much dependence spoils the offspring."

The computer chimed again.

"There she is. *Coming!*" she called to the bedroom extension. "Am

I all put together?" She grabbed a necklace from the dresser and slung it over her head. There was a day, she remembered, when she owned nothing but a pair of jeans and a ragged denim shirt. And had been deliriously happy. As for having two or three computers in the house, who'd even heard of one?

Why did Thanksgiving day always make her dwell on the past? *Physician heal thyself!*

She set her jaw. "Let's go, Sam," she said, heading for the living room.

"Just give me half a minute. I gotta get myself put together."

She sighed. The thought of meeting her family must be doing awful things to his nervous system. It didn't do much good to her own. Some day she was going to call a halt to the whole charade.

In the living room she shouted to the computer: "Okay. I'll take the call." She moved to stand in front of the screen and its camera.

The random pattern split and spread off the edges of the screen, revealing Judy's daughter and her family, a real married family, a truly 21st Century American Gothic. From left to right: Sandy Hunter, Bob Hunter, and four children in descending order of height. Four boys, polished, scrubbed, dressed in black, standing stiffly and concealing the squirming within.

"Hi, Sandy. Hi, Bob." Judy fiercely resented the way she had to *force* a casual tone with her own daughter, that daughter who seemed like a stranger from another, earlier century—the 17th, to be precise. "Sam will be here in a minute. And Winnie, too."

"Hello, Mother, it's good to see you." Sandy's voice was flat, dried out. Her pleasure at seeing her mother was unconvincing, belied by the turned-down corners of her mouth. Sandy was tall, her black hair bulled beck tightly, bun curled behind. Deepset olive eyes glittered from a face devoid of makeup. Her dress was severe and black, her shoes square with Puritan buckles.

Husband Bob Hunter was a shadow. An inch shorter than Sandy, where she was black, he was pale. His hair dust color, cut soup-bowl style, lips thin and colorless, overshadowed by a thin, characterless mustache. One corner of his mouth curved upward in a parody of an ingratiating smile; the other corner twitched and drew back as though he perpetually discovered a centipede crawling out of his box of breakfast cereal.

"Hello, mother," Bob echoed, his voice round and ministerial. "A good Thanksgiving to you."

"Thank you." Judy turned her head toward the hallway and thought, thank God here comes Sam. But I wish he'd have gotten the martinis ready first. It was bad enough that there'd been a different man here every year for the past five years. But now there was Winnie.

Stop it! she screamed silently to herself. You don't have to apologize to your own daughter for how you live.

Sam made a detour into the kitchen and emerged in a trice with Winnie on one arm. Winnie, the brown angel, carried the blessed tray of martinis. His broad, white smile was topped with a pair of terrified eyes.

"Oh, you wonderful man," Judy shrilled, taking one of the glasses. "Come, meet everybody."

Sam took his glass, Winnie deposited the tray on a table and took a glass of his own, and the two allowed Judy to lead them toward the screen.

"Sam, Winnie," she said, "meet my daughter, Sandy. And my son-in-law, Bob."

Sam's hand started to move forward. It was hard to change the habits of a lifetime. Remembering he was being introduced to a video image, Sam changed the motion into a casual wave. "Hi, Bob. I'm glad we can meet at last."

Bob stared out of the screen, his pale eyes flicking back and forth between Sam and Winnie. Judy could sense the wheels grinding inside his head. Sam was just another of her aging boyfriends, but where did Winnie fit in? Cold eyes slowly swept across the white apron, up to the white floury smudge on the dark cheek, and focused on the glass in Winnie's hand. Was he the cook, a friend, or—Judy could tell by the stiffening of Bob's face when the thought struck him—the third member of a triad?

"Hello Bob. Yes, we meet at last."

The sunovabitch, Judy thought. Couldn't even say he was *glad* they met. And as for Winnie, the snub was complete.

Sam smiled thinly, moving his eyes across the screen. "And this is Sandy. I've heard so much about you." He raised his glass. "And I'd like to propose a toast. To the family. To Thanksgiving. To our future happiness. Do you have toast makings at your end?"

Sandy sniffed primly. "Our church does not indulge."

Sam sighed. "Then we shall drink to your health."

He clicked glasses with Winnie and with Judy and took a deep quaff, eyes lighting in appreciation as the cold fire spread through his body.

Judy met Sam's eyes with her own, giggling inwardly, knowing that the entire toast charade had been simply an excuse to start drinking. When you can't offer your guests any kind of a drink, then it's every man for himself. That Sandy . . . How had she managed to create a person like this? How could such an offspring have issued from her Aquarian womb?

"And your children," Sam was saying. "They're a fine looking bunch."

Four of them. All boys, all lined up in a row. And suddenly, her eyes flashing to the front of Sandy's straight dress, Judy knew that a fifth was on its way.

It was a struggle to keep disgust from showing. My God, they breed like rabbits!

"This is Jeremiah," Sandy was saying, putting her hand on top of the tallest. "Then we have Joshua, Amos, and Hosea, the little one."

The little one was four, and the others averaged two years apart. They stood there stiffly, fidgety, staring into their screen at the strange trio. Four little prophets, and who would be the fifth?

"Well, hello there." Sam strained a gut whipping some heartiness into his voice. "I'm your new granddad. I hope we'll see a lot of each other."

"Are you our new granddad, too?" the four-year-old piped, looking in the direction of Winnie's video image.

Winnie choked on his martini. His face reddened under the brown. Recovering, he sputtered, "Well, I'm more like an uncle, I guess."

Judy came to the rescue. "Are you kids all ready for your big Thanksgiving dinner? What are you having?"

"We're having turkey," the oldest said. "What are you having?"

"Hey, we're having turkey, too. Isn't that a coincidence?"

What else do you say to a ten-year-old? Sam picked up the ball. "What grade are you in?"

"We don't have grades," Jeremiah said. "We go to a multitrack school."

"Oh yes?" Sam stared blankly.

"It's a private school," Sandy explained, her tone asking where this stupid old bat has been hiding all these years. "They receive computerized individual instruction."

"How interesting." Sam had a vivid image of these little kids sitting in a dim room hunched over their keyboards, eyes glued to video screens for eight hours a day. "They must learn a great deal," he said, dryly.

Dryly, he realized his glass was empty and was struck with inspiration. He turned to Judy. "My dear, let me refill, the martini pot." He collected the glasses, put them on the tray, and looked up at the screen. "Our church does not believe in suffering through dessication, especially on Thanksgiving."

"Let me help." Winnie followed Sam out to the kitchen, where Judy could hear them howling like a pair of hyenas. Dastardly traitors . . . leaving her alone at a time like this.

She bid for time by seating herself regally in a high-backed armchair, holding herself erect while the autocamera followed and zoomed in. On the screen Sandy dismissed the children.

"You kids go play for a little while. We'll let you know when it's time for dinner."

Inside Judy's intuition alarm bells rang. Here it comes. The reason they called early.

"How is the practice?" Sandy asked, settling into a hard-backed chair.

Judy shrugged. It sounded as if Sandy was testing the waters before making her pitch. How prosperous was dear Mother this year? "The practice perks along," she said, noncommittally. People don't know what to do with themselves now that traveling is restricted. They itch to get out of the house. So I give them therapy for boredom. Teach them how to escape through their imaginations. And how is your church getting along?"

Sandy and Bob stared stiffly out of the screen, hands folded in laps. Sandy sniffed. "The Church of the Messiah progresses. We give our people hope, rather than escape."

Judy's shoulder shook with silent laughter. "It beats me how they keep believing. When your boy didn't show up on schedule ten years ago that should have been the end of it.

"Wasn't the year 2000 the anticipated date of arrival?"

"Mother, you don't expect Him to go according to human timetables?"

You could hear the H capitalized as she said it.

"No, of course not. All we need is faith. Well, I sell my kind of escape, and you sell yours. What else is new?"

Sandy lowered her eyes for a moment. "Maybe you can see that I'm expecting."

Sam arrived just at that moment with a cryogenic martini decanter and a tray of frosted glasses. He'd left Winnie behind in the kitchen.

"Hey," he said. "Let's drink to that. Too bad you can't join us."

Bob Hunter glared at Sam. His fingers plucked restlessly at his mustache and he turned to look at his wife. "Sandy, I think we ought to bring up that matter before anybody else comes."

Sam looked at Judy over the top of his glass and grinned. *Here it comes*, his eyes told her. "L'chayim," he said, sipping.

Sandy's prim mouth tightened. "As you know, mother," she said, "people in our position are having a difficult time. Between the demographic surtax and the impossible costs of education we are just barely making expenses. And with the new one arriving . . . well, we are just going to need some help from you."

Judy sipped her drink, wishing she could enjoy its cold bitterness. But too much bitterness dwelt in her thoughts. She tried to hold her voice level. "Don't you think you might have considered that before begetting a new child?"

Sandy's eyes glowed darkly. "You know, mother, that artificial birth control is forbidden to us. We must obey the instructions of the Lord."

Judy's lips curled. She discovered once more how good contempt felt. It was such a rare feeling. A pity it had to be directed against her own daughter. "Sandy," she said, "everybody lives with a certain amount of delusion. But I've seen hospital cases with fewer delusions than you carry in your head. You know what the physical results of overpopulation are, and yet you continue to say contraception is a sin. You must practice believing two impossibilities every morning before breakfast."

At this onslaught Sandy simply pursed her lips more tightly. "Mother, you just don't understand. You're so old-fashioned."

"Me, old-fashioned?"

"You simply don't know what's going on. Don't you know that for the past 20 years the number of girls being born has been going down?"

"Of course I know. It's down to one girl for every three boys now. So you're going to add another boy to the four you already have?"

"Of course not. That's what I'm trying to tell you. We had sperm selection performed, and we're going to have a girl."

A sparkle glinted in Judy's eye. "You're sure?"

"Absolutely. It's no sin to make sure the race will be propagated. And it's simply old-fashioned to talk about overpopulation. That's not the issue anymore. The issue is to have enough girl babies to keep humanity going."

For a horrible instant it appeared to Judy that her daughter might be right after all. It was with an electric shock chilling her spine that she realized how obsolete her 1980's type of thinking had become. There was fear for all humanity if the new virus attacking the female chromosome could not be identified and destroyed. You could overpopulate the planet with boys and then boom. Suddenly nobody.

But surely the scientists would win. There was no infectious disease that could defeat the molecular biologists. That was Judy's faith.

"I'm glad you're having a girl," she said. She turned to Sam and touched his hand. "Won't it be lovely to have a granddaughter?"

Sam grinned, somewhat bemused. "I've barely gotten used to having grandsons. Instant family. It's very nice."

He sipped his drink, feeling sentimental. He'd almost given up hope of his own children having children and felt very far away from them, he wondered if they'd visit today. The distance between them had grown to interplanetary dimensions since he'd split from their mother. Literally. Jake was up there building a solar satellite. And Joan was in China being a doctor. Would they know it was Thanksgiving?

"Well, then, Sandy. What is it you want?" Judy was saying. Her lips were practicing to say no, but somehow she knew she was going to say yes.

"It's school. Jerry and Josh already have their own computers, but Amos is just starting, so he needs a new one. Then there's the cost of new bubblecards. The price of software is just killing."

"You couldn't send them to classroom school?" Judy asked, knowing full well why they couldn't.

"Oh mother, you know they can't get an eduction there." That was code for: you know they'd be rubbing elbows with all different kinds of kids. "The only way is the private school with individualized instruction."

"And programs that change every year so you can't hand down bubblecards from one kid to the next," Sam said. "That's how they make their profits." Sam had their number. After all, that was his business.

Judy persisted. "Can't they take turns at the computer? Or . . . ?" What was that term they used to use? "Isn't there a way of sharing a computer?"

Sandy rolled her eyes. Sam laughed softly and put his hand on Judy's shoulder. "Hey baby, if you're thinking of timesharing, that's been dead for 25 years. The whole computer now is no bigger than the terminal used to be. I'm afraid, sweet, Sandy is right. Every kid needs his own computer. Avoid mayhem and conflict."

Still, Judy couldn't say yes without a struggle, even though she knew she was going to say yes. "Let me think about it for a while," she said.

The wall computer pealed a clear, crystalline chime. *"Call coming from Portland, Oregon,"* it said. *"Will you accept?"*

"We'll talk some more after dinner," Judy said hastily to her daughter. To the computer she said, loudly and clearly: "We'll take the call."

The screen split. Sandy and Bob moved over to the left half and two new figures occupied the right. Barry, Judy's son, and Gene, his roommate.

"Hi, mom," Barry greeted. His closely-knit red curls made a fiery cap that blended into a bronze beard. He was tall and thirtyish and his grin was easy. "You remember Gene, don't you." Gene was shorter, a trifle younger, and his beard was a very dark black.

Gene waved a wine glass at everybody and said hi. Their room, seen in the background, was painted dark green and was densely furnished in antique plastic furniture dating from the 1980's. A good stained glass piece was mounted in front of a light, making a spot of rosy brightness in the room.

"Glad to see you boys," Judy said. "And this is Sam." Sam waved his glass, and greetings were exchanged all around.

Sandy and Bob sat more stiffly than ever and gave the two men the same look they would give one of the more repulsive creatures from outer space. Judy thought disgustedly: it's like this at every party. Stuffy Sandy's feelings about her brother always put a damper on the entire proceedings. Actually Barry and Gene were much nicer people than Sandy and that stuffed shirt she called a husband. After all, the boys had been living together for over two years now. That showed some measure of stability. How could a prig like Sandy have sprung from her own loins? She shook her head in wonder. As a professional she understood the mechanism of reaction formation. But as a mother she found the mystery too deep to fathom.

"How are the boys?" Barry asked. "Can we see them?"

"They'll be here as soon as we sit down to dinner," Sandy sniffed. Judy could read her face, transparent as pure crystal. *It's disgusting that I have to expose my children to this kind of filth*, she had to be thinking. *If I didn't have to ask mother for money.*

"If you're worried about corrupting your children," Judy said, "you should take a look at what's going on around you. Yup, right in Austin, Texas. With the boy-girl ratio three to one, either your're going to have some boys going with boys, or some girls going with two boys, or both of the above."

Sandy's eyes glared through the screen. "Take care." Her voice deepened. "You atheistic, liberal humanists are at the bottom of all this."

Judy blinked. "We are?"

"The changing of birth patterns is a curse sent to punish mankind for sinful ways."

July's trained ears heard it and knew that Sandy spoke in all seriousness. A shroud of mourning draped itself over her mind. It had finally happened. To her own daughter. The fanaticism, the delusions had been bad enough. But now there was no longer any doubt. Sandy had come out of the closet as a full-fledged, hard-core paranoiac.

Sam, beside her, fizzed like a warm beer bottle. He sprang up, hissing and sputtering, as his laugh threatened to break out in all directions. He danced to the serving table. "This calls for another martini, my darling. If we must sin, at least let us do so with elegance."

He poured the icy liquid into the two glasses, handed one to Judy, and swallowed a good half of his own. "Let me see how dinner's coming," he said, and disappeared into the kitchen. It was dirty pool, but self preservation was the primary law.

To Judy the party was becoming a busman's holiday. But when the loonies are your own family, then it becomes awkward. She was saved from her black thoughts by a fresh chime from the computer, announcing a call from St. Petersburg, Florida. That had to be Bob Hunter's parents. Jed and Lucy Hunter were the only people she knew from her own generation who were still married, for the first time, to each other. Jed was a retired publisher of religious videotapes; his son had taken over the business. That was how Sandy and Bob had met. Sandy had worked for a store that sold religious materials and had run into him at a convention. Their belief systems had fitted together like a Japanese wood joint and apparently they liked things of the flesh as well, since the children had followed at regular intervals.

When Sam returned from the kitchen with a tray of crackers and cheese, he saw the screen split into three parts. Sandy and Bob occupied the upper left quarter, Barry and Gene filled the upper right, and the newcomers had the whole bottom half to themselves. Bob's parents wore deep suntans and their Florida outfits seemed strangely out of place on the northern screens.

"The heat down here is unbelievable," Jed Hunter was saying. "The only way to survive is to stay out in the bay on the sailboat."

"Look, it's eighty up here, and on Thanksgiving yet." Sam set down his tray. "It's all that carbon dioxide in the atmosphere, they say."

Judy's expression had become glazed. She leaned back in her chair and went into meditation, martini in hand. She had just about tuned all the others out when the chime clanged once more. And then again. And again.

The relatives were beginning to arrive in droves her brother and sister, with their children. Sam's brothers, with assorted roommates of various genders. Finally, Sam's children reported in very briefly, on their way to other parties elsewhere. Personally! On foot.

The video screen divided and subdivided until it became a Mondrian. Conversations and cross-conversations became hard to follow. The level of sound in the room gradually grew to the saturation point, where it was necessary to talk as loud as possible to be heard over the prevailing level of noise.

Suddenly from Judy's kitchen came the clang of a heavy spoon beating against a stainless steel pot. Silence shut down abruptly, like the heavy quiet after the takeoff of a shuttle.

Winnie appeared in the doorway hearing a tray on which sat, dark brown, crispy, and fragrant, The Bird. Winnie had doffed his apron and wore an African tunic that matched the bird's color. His face gleamed in triumph.

"Meet Winnie," Sam said to the newcomers. "Winston C. Mullins—without whom this dinner could not have been accomplished."

Winnie set down his tray and bowed modestly toward the screen. The relatives murmured their greetings. Judy thought: if curiosity could kill, the screen would be filled with dead bodies.

"It's a beautiful turkey, sweetheart," Judy said, quietly. Winnie took her hand elaborately and kissed it. Judy felt embarrassed and exposed, then felt defiance. If Sandy doesn't like it all she has to do is flip the switch. But she wouldn't. She wants the money more.

In silence Sandy Hunter got up to set her own table, her face rock-like. That brazen slut. Her mother. If it were not for the financial discussions that still needed completion, she would never speak to her again.

She touched Bob's hand. "Help me serve dinner," she said. In the kitchen she hissed furiously, "Did you see what I saw? That evil woman is living with two men. And one of them black! Sin upon sin." Her eyes burned with rage.

"Kissing her in public." Bob's cheeks were pink. "Can we take her tainted gold?" he asked, convulsed with morality.

Sandy ground her teeth. "I'd like to take it all."

The four boys trooped in from the TV in the other room and said hello to all the strange faces on the big video screen. Sandy felt frozen. Would the kids see? Would they notice? What would she say if they questioned?

They didn't notice. Another friend was just another friend. Their curiosity was not inflated with spite.

The children gave the other adults a good excuse to ignore grandma Judy and her strange entourage. The old lady was obviously suffering from terminal dottiness and the less attention paid the better. Which was perfectly fine, as far as Judy was concerned.

All over the country dinner tables became loaded. Smoking turkeys, luscious sweet hams, hot baked sweet potatoes, savory mince pie, fragrant mulled cider—their images were converted into electro-magnetic signals that flew from Earth to satellite and back to Earth, splitting and dividing into millions of homes. Everywhere people ate in twos and threes and fours, but were interconnected with other groups by the pictures on their video screens.

Judy and Sam and Winnie ate traditional turkey while watching Barry and Gene setting out a magnificent Columbia River salmon, fresh from the broiler. Jed and Lucy Hunter, needing no big bird, were digging into the swordfish that Jed had just that morning pulled out of the Gulf. In Texas, Josh and Amos Hunter were fighting noisily over who was going to get the remaining drumstick, Jerry, the eldest, having staked out his claim already.

The clamor began to get to Judy Kroll. The trouble with this kind of system was that it was almost impossible to follow a conversation. All the voices came out of the same pair of loudspeakers, and there was not the directional quality that allowed you to filter out one voice from all the others going strong during a party.

The pre-dinner martinis and the wine she was drinking during dinner made Judy feel as though she were encased in a translucent bubble through which all those distant voices and images filtered. Within that bubble she retreated, turning over and over the proposal Sandy had made to her. Logic and feeling battled each other within her mind.

Dawdling over dessert and coffee, she became aware of Sandy's sharp-edged voice penetrating the bubble. She was glaring out of the screen, her face pale and angry. "Barry Kroll, how dare you smoke in our presence? Have you no manners, no shame? If you have no respect for a minister of the Church of the Messiah, you could at least consider the influence you are flaying on these small children present."

Barry leaned back and guffawed. "Well, little sister, you'd think your shit don't stink. First of all, I'm not in your presence. My smoke isn't going to filter through the loudspeakers and contaminate your precious children with essence of cannabis. If you hadn't raised such a fuss about it they wouldn't have known it was such a big deal. And you always have the privilege of cutting me out of your reception."

Barry's eyes shifted to another sector of the screen. "Mom, Gene and I are going to cut out. This scene isn't very amusing. Let's get together some time just by ourselves. Okay? Sorry to eat and run, everybody. Tally ho."

His segment of the screen abruptly darkened, and then the borders shifted so that the other segments filled up the space.

Judy's face was livid with fury. "Sandy," she said, her voice like a sharp sword, "I've had just about enough of your bossiness. Maybe you can tell your congregation how to live, but don't think you can pass judgement on your own family. I wiped your dirty ass when you were a baby, so you don't intimidate me. You've been on your brother's back ever since you discovered he was gay, and the only reason you haven't said anything about my own *menage a trois* is because you're waiting to get some money out of me."

"Mother!" Sandy's voice was a shocked squeal. "There are others listening."

"I don't give a good goddam." Judy waded into battle, reckless and strong, voice throaty, stops all out. She stood up and approached the screen. "All I know is that you, my daughter, have become an intolerable pain in the ass. Now . . ." Her tone suddenly descended an octave. "You talked about money for school, for software. Tell me, Sandy, what kind of school are the children going to?"

Sandy grew frightened. She knew the future depended on her answer. But there was no choice. "They go to the church school, naturally. Academy of the Messiah."

"I thought so." Judy stood there, hands on hips, her body straight, a monument. "And there they'll learn about truth as the church sees it. The real truth, the absolute truth."

"Of course, mother. There's only one truth."

Judy exhaled explosively. Then she smiled, very slowly, very broadly. "Thank you, daughter. You've just hanged yourself. In my book anybody who claims to know absolute truth is a fraud and a charlatan. I'm not spending my money to contribute to the miseducation of my grandchildren. If you want to enroll them in a place like Dartmouth extension, where they'll learn to investigate truth, to examine the world and make their own decisions—then I'll be glad to pay. But I won't pay to have their minds closed up tight. They'd do better in the public schools, even if they didn't learn such good grammar."

Sandy raised a hand like a claw. "Be careful, mother. If you take that attitude you'll never see the children again."

The boys sat in the background, a row of silent, white, puzzled pawns.

Judy looked at them in anguish. A feeling of finality dropped down over her. "Don't threaten me," she said. "It works both ways. Maybe you need me as much as I need them."

Sandy's eyes looked like black marbles, hard, shiny. "Maybe. Maybe not."

Judy shrugged. "Call me whenever you like." Her voice was flat. She noticed the rest of the family still blocked out in their little rectangles on the screen. "It's getting late," she said. "And I'm tired. See you next Thanksgiving. Maybe. Maybe not. Goodnight, all."

She tapped the off tab with one sharp finger and collapsed slowly into the couch as the relatives faded off the screen, waving and saying farewells.

Sam came over to sit beside her. "You were magnificent," he said. Winnie looked at her in awe.

"I feel burnt out. Get me another drink."

Sam emptied the decanter into three glasses. "Well, just think. If they had been here in person you couldn't have switched them off so easily."

"I know." She lifted her glass and stared into it. "But I wanted so much to hold the little one in my lap. It's been so long since I touched the grandchildren. Do you think we'll ever be able to travel again?"

THE DIRECT LINE

THE DING OF the door bell interrupted. Nick Vencel's scrawny head raised up, eyes beady, like a bird startled in the grass. *Damn customers. Always interrupting.* The cloth in his hand kept going over the 27-hour clock from Altair-4. A beautiful piece, lustrous with years of loving polishing. The roar of Westcoast Shuttleport swelled and then cut as the door closed, catching the bell so that it dinged once more. It was a real brass bell, suspended on a spring to catch the swinging door. God knows how far back it went.

Nick carefully placed the clock on the table. He unfolded himself and stood up. Tall, thin, and grey as a cadaver, his tunic spotted and splotched where he had used it to wipe off silverware from Fomalhaut or ceramics from Canopus, he focussed watery blue eyes on the door. ANTIQUES, COLLECTABLES, AND JUNK, it said in reverse on the unwashed glass. BOUGHT, SOLD, TRADED.

Inside the door the customer stood, looking about with steady gaze, waiting for eyes to adjust to the dimness. He was, Nick saw, a survivor. Leathery skin, blackened by radiation from a dozen suns, lay heavily creased along the cheeks. Hair white as bleached sand, hands—hands mismatched. One a prosthesis. Over a black leather jacket he bore a shoulder bag of a design Nick had not seen before. His head turned continually, his eyes peering along the shelves and tables, his thin lips taut with anticipation.

"C'n I help ya?" Nick shuffled to the front of the store. No rush.

"Maybe yes. Maybe no. Depends on what you have." It was a voice that started from deep, deep, down. By the time it emerged it had diminished to a harsh whisper.

"I've lotsa things. It'd save all kinds of time if you told me what you were looking for."

Damn customers think they'll go away with a bargain if they make believe they're not looking for something special.

The stranger's dark eyes shifted past Nick's shoulder and searched along the shelves filled with artifacts from a hundred solar systems. Dusty copper hammerings from Schedar, fearfully ancient *khameti* from El Nath.

The eyes came back to engage Nick's. "It's hard to describe what I want. I'll know it when I see it." His voice held a sibilant accent that Nick could not quite place, but there was nothing unusual about this, for wanderers from all over the galactic sector found their way into his shop from the Shuttleport down the road.

"Well, look around." Damned if Nick was going to argue. "I'll be in back if you see anything you want." He turned and retraced his shuffling steps.

Picking up the clock, he replaced it on the shelf next to his desk, then pulled down from the top shelf a transparent, crystalline object with three octagonal faces in which a set of lights rotated in an asynchronous manner. With a soft cloth he began polishing it, but his eyes followed the stranger as he moved slowly and randomly about the room.

The man's gaze probed along every shelf, into every nook and cranny, missing nothing. Near the front door was the junk—the unpolished rocks from the planets, the surplus cooking utensils from ancient spaceships, the uniforms and assorted gear left over from forgotten expeditions. Bins and boxes, crates and racks, they were piled to the ceiling. Dust swirled lazily in an afternoon sunbeam that managed to squeeze its way through a corner of the front door.

Further in were the collectibles, the badges from old uniforms, archaic weapons, medals from forgotten wars, polished stones, silverware from a dozen Captain's tables. Then at the very rear, the good pieces. The clocks from planets around the galaxy, telling time in units that matched nothing on Earth. The rings and chains carrying stones of unfamiliar hues and shades. The translucent porcelains and breathtaking, blazing jade carved by the diamond-like claws of the Atrians. Glass molded in gravless space lay on the shelves like frozen fire.

These were the pieces Nick hated to sell.

The customer came to the end of it. His eyes finished their sweep and then flashed to fix on Nick Vencel's watery orbs.

"Is this all?" There was disappointment and puzzlement in the whispering voice. A missing expectation.

Nick's mouth twitched in annoyance. *Damn pest. Knows what he wants but won't tell.*

"All that's down here. What is it you're looking for?"

The stranger shook his head slowly, his eyes veiled, as though listening to something far away. Suddenly the eyes lit and he looked at Nick demandingly. "There must be more."

The dealer shrugged. "There's some special things upstairs. But only people I know are allowed up there. Too much valuable stuff."

Too much precious stuff. Stuff to keep for myself, to pleasure my remaining years. To run my hands over the smooth woods and polished metals. My own. All my own.

The man reached into a pocket. "Let me introduce myself. Captain Ephra Kammerer, retired. Formerly chief of the *Andromeda,* line cruiser of the Lyrane navy." His identity card verified the name and rank, but gave no hint as to the location of Lyrane.

Nick's memory nagged. Something about Lyrane lay in back of

his mind. But what? Damn growing old! He could remember better from fifty years ago than from yesterday.

"All right," he whined. "You can go upstairs. Just remember, anything goes out that room, I know about it."

Kammerer glared. "You need not worry." He turned and clomped angrily up the rickety wooden stairs. From the sound, Nick guessed that one of the legs was a prosthesis, also. The Captain must have been in one hell of a fight.

Nick opened his desk drawer and waited for the Captain's image to appear on the video screen hidden inside. He watched patiently as Kammerer strode three paces into the upstairs room and stopped. Catlike, Nick waited while his quarry stood there quietly, turning slowly, as though sniffing the air. When he froze, Nick knew that he had him. The hidden camera did it every time.

Kammerer moved. He moved quickly and decisively toward a shelf where, surrounded by rococo jeweled clocks, mobile sculptures, crystals of iridescent fantasy, was a featureless black sphere, mounted on a base of molded silver. Kammerer's eyes fixed on the sphere with unabashed avidity, his mouth a grin of triumph.

Nick knew that he had him.

But why the sphere? Why that particular sphere?

It had been sold to him a year ago. He had many times seen crystal spheres mounted on similar silver bases, works of gorgeous, perfect art. But never black. Pure black, unreflecting, like a hole in space.

Except that sometimes when he looked at it a certain way there seemed to be something inside, some light, some color, some shadow, leaking out of the featureless dark. But nothing to recognize, nothing to relieve the deep mystery of its origin.

Strange. Out of all the things in the shop, the Captain had gone unhesitatingly to the one item that Nick Vencel did not understand. He did not know where it came from, how old it was, or what its purpose was. Worst of all, he did not know how much it was worth.

It had been brought in by one of the derelicts whose lives oozed away in the slums surrounding Shuttleport. Twenty credits he'd given him. At least the silver was worth that much. And because of its mystery he had put it upstairs among his treasures.

Now, to tantalize him, to tease him, to torment him, this had to be the one item the Captain aimed for like a pointer dog at his quarry, ignoring all the other baubles in the store. Its value instantly leaped and soared within Nick's mind.

And the more it was worth, the less he wanted to sell it. For that was the paradox of Nick Vencel, who bought carefully and sold reluctantly.

*   *   *

A song swelled in the Captain's heart. He had found his *eonos*. After two long, empty years it was there in his eyes, the warm, dark sphere resting on the shelf. And the emptiness of his life was gone.

John, the barkeep at Fritchies, had told him this would be the place to look, but even before entering the door he had felt that song radiating through the walls, the song of a siren drawing him magnetically and unerringly closer to the center of his existence. The fool below could not keep him away.

His teeth bared. Harsh pain of memories cut and burned, pulling him momentarily into the past. The roar of the incandescent atmosphere around his descending lifeboat still echoed in his ears. Its nose glowed red as the ground came up to meet him. The impact had fled his mind. Just that howl of air and then the quiet of the hospital. Of the lifeboat, only a crumpled shell left. Of the crew, a handful of survivors. Of his possessions, nothing. Picked clean by scavengers, he'd been told.

The loss of the *eonos* had been the greatest of all pain—more than the loss of his arm and his leg. Yes, even more than the loss of his family: his wife, his two children. But one thing he had known in every cell of his mind, in every fragment of his mangled body—there was no way the *eonos* could be kept from him forever.

The only thing in the way now was that horse thief downstairs. Give that junk dealer one hint of the *eonos*' true value and he would demand every last credit left to Kammerer's name. Not that Kammerer would mind sharing a million if he had it, but he was a destitute, a wanderer from a planet that no longer existed. Subsisting on handouts, on odd jobs, on charity. . . . His face hardened and his good fist clenched. Then he looked deeply into the center of the *eonos*, saw white radiance extend to infinity, and felt the vanishing of his pain.

Nick Vencel heard the footsteps coming slowly down the stairs. It was about time. The old Captain had spent a long time up there staring at that black ball. Standing there and staring. How much was he going to offer? Not more than five hundred. It was a bet that Nick always won from himself.

The sunbeam had faded and the shop interior was going dark. Nick got up to switch on the meager lights. The Captain emerged from the stairwell as he took his hand from the wall plate.

"Well, Cap'n. See anything that hits your fancy?"

He glanced sideways at the leathery-faced one and thought he perceived a different aspect on the man's countenance. Something brighter about the eyes, the ghost of a thin smile on the lips. Nick laughed to himself. He could tell when a customer had found what he wanted.

But the Captain leaned casually against the door jamb, put his hands in his pocket, and shrugged. "Maybe. Maybe not. Most of your stuff's too rich for my blood. There's a couple of clocks I could go for if they're not too much. I like wood. Old wood. Real wood."

"Tell you what." Nick unfolded himself once more and made his way to the front door. "It's time to close up, anyway. Let me lock the door and I'll go upstairs with you."

"Thank you. That's very considerate of you."

Nick thought, groaning up the stairs, that the Captain put on a lousy act. He had not mastered the art of supreme indifference. He didn't have Nick's decades of experience at buying low and selling high. If he sold at all. Nick wouldn't have bothered with him at all, but he wanted to find out what the Captain knew about the black ball.

The Captain had the grace not to wince when Nick quoted him a price of ten thousand credits for a clock from Hadar-2 with the complex epicycle system for a double star and a case carved from a wood that seemed to conceal a hidden fire in its translucency.

Nick carefully put the clock back on its shelf. "You understand," he said, "this is my personal collection. I sell from it very rarely."

And, what he did not say was: it was because of this personal collection that he dared not die. For once he did, his precious things would fall into the hands of vultures and jackals and tax collectors. His life energy flowed from his possessions.

The Captain tapped his finger lightly and thoughtfully on the black sphere. "Ten thousand." He spoke quietly and his voice was tired and bleak. "That's mighty steep for a retired spacefarer." He tapped the sphere again. "What about this black ball? Looks like a mistake. I've seen 'em crystal, but never black."

"No mistake. The black is rare. Very rare. In fact . . ." Nick made his voice casual. ". . . I have an old customer already interested in it. Of course . . . if I could get a higher bid . . ."

The Captain's mouth widened in a savage grin. "Sure, old goniff. I'll give you a bid. One hundred credits. Tell that to your old customer."

Nick Vencel squawked. He thrashed his arms like a startled chicken. "One hundred . . . I've never heard such . . . You think I would part with that exquisite piece of work for a measly centum? The base alone . . ."

"Cool it, friend. The base is a dime a dozen. A piece of silver worth a few credits. And the globe is just another globe. As a work of art it's not worth a burned out chip."

"The globe's just another globe, eh?" Nick mimicked. "Then go buy yourself one somewhere else. I told you I'm not interested in selling my private collection."

"I hear you don't sell much of anything. You're like a mother hen sitting on her eggs. What d'ya plan to hatch?"

"What do you know about collecting?" Nick grumbled, placing his rear on the corner of his desk. "Collectibles are the only things you can count on in this crazy world."

"The only things? Not people? Not ideas? Not . . ." Captain Kammerer regarded Nick Vencel with contempt. "I've seen a world go up in flames. Your collection would have vanished there just like that." He snapped his fingers under the dealer's nose. "What good will *things* do you in the afterworld?"

"As far as I'm concerned, this is the only world there is, and I'm hanging on to what I've got while I'm here. Afterwards I won't know and I won't care."

"It shouldn't make much difference for you to sell one of your precious pieces. I bet you don't even know how much it's worth. You don't even know what it is."

Nick shrugged and spread his hands in an ancient gesture. "If I don't know how much it's worth, how can I sell it? If you know how much it's worth, you re sure to take advantage of me."

Kammerer leaned forward and forced himself to look directly into Nick's repulsive eyes. "The fact is that it's worth a lot to me, but is worth very little to you. You gain nothing by keeping it, while I gain a lot by getting it."

Nick showed yellowing teeth in a triumphant grin. "The rules of commerce are that the seller charges what the item is worth to the buyer. That's what determines value."

The Captain turned away in disgust. "I've no patience with this kind of dealing. The ball is of absolutely no value to you, yet you hold on to it as though it was your passport to paradise. I've traveled thousands of light-years to get here. I've killed more people than you could count. What's to prevent me from just walking out of here with the thing?"

Nick backed off the desk in alarm. "Don't give me any threats. You wouldn't get a kilometer without being picked up. Every valuable has its built-in beacon. And I have my foot on the big red panic button. How the hell do you think I keep a store here for 30 years without a robbery?"

The Captain suddenly laughed, his head down, ruefully, as though laughing at himself. "It's no threat. I can't stand the sight of blood. Whoever I killed, I killed from a distance of a thousand kilometers. Strictly business. Strictly impersonal." His voice was quiet, thoughtful. "Look," he said. "You don't know where that black ball comes from. And I do. So let's make a deal. I'll tell you what the thing is, and I'll convince you that it is of no value to you, and you'll then let me have it for a hundred credits."

Nick fizzed for a moment. "You're crazy. Once I know what the thing is, then I can find somebody who can use it and will give me more for it. A hundred credits is nothing."

Kammerer shook his head. "I don't think so. I don't think you'll find someone else. But let me buy you a drink, and let me tell you the story. Then I think I can convince you."

He grinned, and he could see fright appear in Nick's eyes as he glimpsed the evil in the grin.

But Nick recovered. "The thing you don't understand," he said, "is that I want the ball precisely because it's not useful, and especially because you want it. But I'll take that drink. And you'll tell me a story."

*　　*　　*

Makumba's Tavern was across the street, an ancient, falling-down brick structure with a rambling warehouse on one side and a shipping office on the other. It was handy for truckers and spacers alike.

The bar was already crowded. Captain Kammerer scanned the dim room, saw the towering bald, black man in back of the bar rake him with glittering, olive eyes. A Captain's cap was not a regular thing in these quarters.

Nick waved at the barkeep. "Hi, Makumba. Meet my friend Cap'n Kammerer. We've got a little business to discuss. Gonna use your back room."

Makumba grinned at Kammerer. "Watch your wallet, Captain. What's your poison?"

They took their drinks to a booth in a dark alcove. Kammerer sipped his klem as he remembered all the spaceport bars he'd haunted during all those years. The klem warmed as it went down, sending fiery tentacles along his nerves, relaxing muscles tired of manipulating an artificial leg. The drink, imported from Canopus, marvelously sharpened the perceptions, so that very soon the faces of the men along the bar were as seen in a microscope, every hair, every twitch, every emotion crisp and clear in his eyes. Colors brightened, edges became hard, time seemed to slow.

He savored it for a time, watching the crowd, getting the feel of the place. The customers were almost all humanoid, descendants of galactic colonists, but there was one group that Kammerer recognized as natives of Sadir-4, tall, willowy, with metallic blue skins and high, tinkling voices. One fine evening somewhere in the past, somewhere in a bar like this . . .

No. Stop it. The past is gone. Nothing remains but the present.

He turned his eyes on to Nick Vencel, saw that the antique dealer had already gulped half his drink. It was in harmony with the rest of his life—rapacious, greedy, knowing nothing of experience, only of obsession.

Vencel returned his stare with a foxy grin. "So tell me where the black ball came from. And what it does."

"What makes you think it does anything?"

Vencel smiled secretively. "I saw you looking at it. I think it doesn't just sit there like a lump. I think that's the story you're gonna tell me."

Kammerer's vision abruptly expanded beyond the dingy room and focussed far off, in space and in time. To tell a story he had to remember, and to remember without pain he had to suppress all feeling.

"Do you know the Lyceae system?" he asked, softly, as though beginning a ballad. "It's far from here, and off the beaten track. Earthmen settled on Lyrane, the third planet, long ago, time enough to build two civilizations. The fourth planet, Lyphore, was already occupied, and was left undisturbed."

Kamtnerer sipped his drink, keeping himself numb, knowing that the more he talked the more difficult it would become.

"We had a good world. Solid people, religious, stable. I had a family—a wife, two children—the most beautiful . . .

He broke off. The feeling was beginning to overpower him. After two years it was still there, a raging despair filling every cell of his body. He put his hand over his eyes. Control was necessary. Retrieval of the *eonos* was absolutely essential.

"We had a good world," he repeated. "It was good because we had a good religion."

"That would sure make it different," Nick commented. Kammerer hated the cynical smirk that twisted the dealer's face.

However, he found himself agreeing. "I can vouch for its uniqueness among the planets I have visited. Our religion was completely personal. Each individual had his own communion with his own God. It was his own strength, his own foundation."

"Sounds like a slippery foundation to me, everybody making up his own beliefs."

What did Nick know about belief? Katnmerer wondered.

"It was not a question of each person making up his own belief," he said. "The belief was there. It existed. And each individual spoke with his own God. You have no idea what that means. The feeling you get from that drink is as quicksand compared with the solid strength obtained from communion."

Nick shifted uncomfortably in his seat. Kammerer saw no comprehension in his eyes.

"Well, what about that black ball?" Nick asked, impatiently.

Kammerer shrugged. "It was like an icon, a symbol. It had belonged to my family, handed down from my father. Handed down from his father."

Nick's eyes gleamed. That he could understand. Then he frowned. "It was your own, you say. How do you know? How do you know it's not another?"

"Very little escaped the destruction of my planet. Very few things and very few humans. But regardless. I know it's mine. Just as I know the sound of my wife's voice. There can be no doubt of it."

"If you can legally prove it's yours you can sue for it. You know that, don't you? Laws of salvage."

"I don't have papers of ownership," Kammerer said, wearily. "I hoped it would be possible to convince you without going through the tedious legal process."

"I hear a lot of stories." Nick Vencel's face was ghostlike in the dim light, and filled with the dissatisfactions of an empty life. "Everybody comes into the store, has a story. Everybody has a scam. What do I know about you?"

"You could find out. You could look over the news from two years ago and find what happened to Lyrane. You could ask Calgeneral Hospital about me. You could find that I tell you only the truth."

"Hell, what a drag. You think I got nothing else to do?" Kamrnerer stared steadily at him, and finally knew what he was going to do.

Hell could be a drag. Indeed.

"Let me tell you," Kammerer said, "what happened to my planet and how I happened to get here and why I am looking for my *eonos*. That's what we called it on Lyrane. An *eonos*."

*   *   *

It rested in its box on the control console of the Andromeda. *The sight of the black sphere caressed his eyes. Its availability was always comforting. Now, before battle, its use was a necessity.*

Throughout the ship each crewmember began communion. What the others experienced, he could not know. Each communion was private, not to be questioned. He knew only that whatever happened, strength flowed from the experience. Strength and stability.

Now it was time. The darkness within the sphere and within his heart dissolved. Radiance prevailed, outside and inside. For a brief time he was in contact with ultimate experience, and when he returned he was ready for whatever might come.

*   *   *

Captain Kammerer stared gloomily into his glass, but it was no substitute for his *eonos*. The operation had been so futile.

"We had the biggest fleet in our history—a hundred and fifty battleships, sailing fifty million kilometers from Lyrane to throw a lethal blow at Lyphore. I commanded the *Andromeda*, second to the flagship."

He lifted his glass and sipped cautiously from it.

Nick had finished his and signalled for another. "Sounds like you didn't like the Lyphoreans much."

"It was not so much that we disliked them. The problem was that they didn't like us. To be more precise, they did not think that we had a right to exist. Therefore we had to get rid of them."

Nick snorted. "Sounds like the pot calling the kettle black." The Captain shrugged. "Ethics becomes very basic when self-preservation is involved. We don't claim to be more virtuous than the others. But we did believe that we were ridding the universe of a deadly menace. I hope we succeeded. If we didn't, you're in for some interesting times. God preserve us from people with strong beliefs."

A wry twist settled on Nick's mouth. "I forget when's the last time I believed something."

"And now look at you. An empty shell. To be solid, filled with life, you must believe in something, whatever it is. Else your life is like try-ing to walk on top of a tank full of gelatin. It gives no support. The Lyranians believed in belief, but to them it was a very individual thing. No person could question the beliefs of another, and no person could force his belief—or the consequences of his belief on another person. It made for heady law, but the result was a lively and healthy civilization."

"Sounds like a mess. Suppose my belief required me to chant naked in the middle of the street at midnight?"

"That would be imposing the consequences of your belief on other people, and they would have the right to object. The nudity wouldn't bother them, but the noise would."

"But then you're imposing your beliefs on me. It ain't fair."

"It isn't always fair, but the rule of privacy always prevails. The Lyphoreans had a much simpler system, allowing for no such contro-versies. On Lyphore everybody had to believe the same thing."

"Oh. One of those places."

"You said it. Lyrane and Lyphore as neighbor planets made a to-tally unstable situation. It had not been intended that way. Descen-dents of Earth settled on Lyrane three thousand years ago. At that time, Lyrane, the third planet of the Lyceae system, was not inhabited by any species close to intelligence. Lyphore, the fourth planet, was a bit farther ahead. Its most advanced species was in an essentially neolithic period. In accordance with accepted policy the Lyranians left them strictly alone. But, surprise—the Lyphoreans were unexpect-edly bright people. Or creatures, or beings. They didn't look much like people. Regardless. It was maybe their communal living style that helped them share intelligence and got them to move ahead so rap-idly. In two thousand years they hit the first industrial revolution, and in another three hundred years they were in space. At that point

Lyrane began to arm itself."

* * *

Kammerer carefully watched the approach to Lyphore on the screen, aware of a feeling of unease circling inside, stalking his mind. The fleet's approach to Lyphore had been open and straightforward, following a smooth arc out from the sun, yet no defense fleet had risen from the planet's surface to meet them. It was not natural. He buzzed Intelligence:"What signs of defensive activity?"

"Nothing. Total quiet. It's weird."

* * *

Kammerer let his eyes rove over the bar, watched Makumba polish glasses, enjoyed the friendly buzz of conversation, droning in the backgound like a bee swarm.

"The Lyphoreans were not like us at all," he said. "Not in appearance, and not in philosophy. The appearance should not have mattered. But the Lyphoreans *believed* that it mattered. And *belief* is always what counts. It was bad enough that they believed all Lyphoreans should believe the same thing. What they believed was that all sentient creatures were made in the image of God, which meant that anybody who didn't look like the Lyphoreans just didn't count. So there was no point in trying to get along with us."

"Not a friendly attitude at all." Nick's eyelids were lowered to half mast as the drinks had their way with him.

"Not friendly at all. Historical evidence proves unanimously that two species so separate in philosophy could not possibly live in harmony within the same planetary system. So our defense fleets grew. My family grew proud in the service."

Kammerer's eyes misted over slightly with the memory of his father and his father's father, and the rest of the line going back for centuries, the records vanished now. And his son, his proud, tall son, half way through the Academy.

"We left the Lyphoreans strictly alone," he repeated. "Until intelligence found that the Lyphoreans were on the verge of developing a new and powerful weapon. At that point we decided on a preemptive strike. Killing an entire civilization is a bitter step to take, but it was strictly a matter of self-preservation.

* * *

The deep, deep voice so familiar to Kammerer issued from the speaker. Fleet Admiral Hargrith flung his ultimatum at the Lyphoreans: Dismantle your armament system immediately. An outrageous demand. Purposely so.

Receivers crackled with scornful reply: "Take heed of your own planet. In three minutes you will see its fate, already consummated."

Kammerer froze in horror. Three minutes was the time for light to race between the two planets in their present position.

Whatever had happened, they were too late to stop it. No time to wonder. The command voice knifed through the loudspeakers. "Attack according to plan."

*   *   *

"We hit them with everything we had. Thermonuclear missiles, laser beams, direct hits on their major cities. By that time their satellite-based defenses had a cloud of missiles coming our way, and our laser defenses were kept red hot. We picked them off nicely, but inevitably a few got through and we started losing ships."

Kammerer's fists tightened. His lips drew back. "Then we heard from Intelligence. 'My God, look at Lyrane,' the observer said. We looked, and each of us began to die at that moment."

*   *   *

On the screen Lyrane bloomed. Blotches of blazing light flashed across the surface of the planet as though it turned under a blowtorch. Furrows of blackness, scorched and smoking, leaped into sudden existence. Gouts of incandescent, molten magma flowed from huge holes fused all the way down to the planet's mantle. Try as he might, he could see no source for the beam of incredible heat that melted Lyrane's surface whereever it touched.

"Admiral! Do you see Lyrane?" Kammerer choked on the words.

Death spoke with the Admiral's voice. "They've completed the wormhole weapon. Lyrane is being burned out by squirting energy directly from the center of the sun."

*   *   *

"From then on," Kammerer sighed, "it was a suicide attack. Our orders were to deplete our weapons and then find shelter someplace. Anyplace. It took about ten minutes, at the end of which time we turned and ran. But turning takes time in space, and while turning we took a missile in the tail. The damage was not major. Except that our propulsion system was gone and we were losing air. I ordered the crew into lifeboats and got into my own spacesuit. After gathering up my own *eonos*, of course."

*   *   *

He would, of course, no more leave without his eonos *than he would step naked out of the airlock.*

Before setting the lifeboat's course for Earth and entering stasis, he stole one final look at Lyrane on the screen. Its entire surface was in livid, violent eruption. gouts of incandescent material spurting from a hundred craters.

Then reality became incorporated and recognized. Reality was his planet, his home, and his family being destroyed in front of his eyes. It made a pain greater than he could bear.

Oh God, they're gone. Sheera, Tomas, Iona. My wife, my children. My civilization. Everything I've worked for. Oh God, oh my very own God. *Eonos,* help me bear the loss. Help ease the pain.

And the sphere heard, and as Kammerer's mind sank into limbo, the peace came that transcended all other peace.

*   *   *

Dark had descended by the time Captain Kammerer and Nick Vencel crossed back across the street to the small building that housed the antique shop. Shuttleport lights made a faint white haze in the sky above. Nick carefully surveyed the dim thorofare before placing his hand on the lock plate and waiting for the click of recognition. A shuttle came in, its nose glowing red. The starships hung high, out of sight.

Inside the shop, as the lights came on and Nick waited for the security system to sniff out his identity, he said, "So you came back to Earth. Not to some other planet that might have been closer to Lyrane."

"I had lost my home. It seemed, at the time, logical to return to the source."

The Captain, head sunk into his collar, eyes hooded, appeared lost in a maze of memories.

Finally he said, "It would have been better to return home. Better to crash there and be dead with my people than to crash here and be alive and alone. But here I am and here I stay."

Nick led Kammerer up the stairs to the room that held his treasures. "Bad landing, eh? That where you lost your arm?"

"An atrocious landing. The computer may have been hit by a solar flare and lost its mind. It took us out of stasis too late to get into proper orbit. We came down burning our hide and pancaked a kilometer from the field."

The Captain shivered, as though struck by a sudden cold wind. Nick turned on the upstairs light. His baubles glittered on their shelves, but he was interested only in the black ball that nestled quietly in its silver stand.

"You were going to prove to me that this thing is your own. Your very own."

Captain Kammerer's eyes turned on to the antique dealer and a thin smile teased the corner of his mouth. "You don't believe the story I told you? That was not enough proof?"

"Anybody can tell me a story." Nick's tone held a lifetime of cynicism. "You said this thing is like a private lifeline to God. That you get a high from tuning in to it. Show me how it works. Let me see it."

Kammerer's smile widened, became wicked. "You're getting religious? You want to hear the word? I can show you how it works, but. . . ." He paused. Then decided. "Yes. I will show you how it works. Then you will give my *eonos* back to me."

Nick's dour face lit with a rapacious grin. "Maybe. You don't con me so fast. First show me. Then we'll see."

Kammerer's smile disappeared. "We will certainly see."

He turned to the *eonos,* picked it off the shelf, and set it down on a small table. "Watch the *eonos* and I will control it to allow you in."

Nick put his hands in his pockets and stood close to the table, staring at the little ball, trying to probe to the center of its opacity. Kammerer stood opposite, watching Nick's face, observing Nick's blatant greed, sensing that behind that greed was a real need to experience the communion, to feel that direct link with God, to purge a lifetime of emptiness.

One thing he understood was that Nick would never openly admit the need that he felt. And because of that he would never be satisfied.

Kammerer began to feel the white surge of power, drawing his consciousness off through an infinitely long tube into the quintessence. The last thing he saw was the perspiration breaking out on Nick's forehead.

*   *   *

The red light blinds! It burns through my eyes and spreads through my body. It burns and I burn in the desert. Out there is a wasteland of red fire where I burn forever. My soul is open and naked—and all the things I've forgotten are pouring out of it, flitting around my head like a swarm of bats, sticking, biting, tearing. After all those years I've kept them locked up and now they're coming out and they hurt. Oh God, they hurt, and I can't bear it.

*   *   *

Kammerer saw the beads of sweat roll down Nick Vencel's face. He saw those pale, wrinkled hands began to shake and those staring eyes grow wider and wider. Finally a rasping sigh burst from Nick's throat, his knees buckled beneath him, and he slid to the floor. His mouth was slack and a trickle of drool issued from one side.

Kammerer calmly continued to make his own communion with the sphere. When he was completed, he sighed in satisfaction and turned to the recumbent Nick beside him. He thumbed the man's pulse and knew he was still alive. Surely the old bastard's heart could stand up under any stress the *eonos* might give him. Cheerfully he slapped Nick's face lightly until he saw signs of revival.

The dealer's eyes popped open with a start of terror. "Jesus Christ! Where the hell was I?"

"That's just where you were, my friend." Kammerer laughed a

short, dry laugh. "You were in Hell. Yes, really. You saw it with your own eyes. The ball leads me to God. It leads you to Hell. Are you convinced?"

Nick creaked to his feet. His face was white, his hands trembling. "I don't know what kind of trick you pulled, but one thing I know is, I don't want that freakin' ball around here. You can just take it and get out of here."

Kammerer laughed. "You know damn well there was no trick. Because there'd be no point in being scared of a trick. What you're scared of is the real thing."

And only Nick knew how real it had been.

His shaking fingers managed to pull the hidden beacon thread from the bottom of the ball's base. Kammerer reached to the back of the shelf, picked up the square box and opened its lid. He watched gratefully as Nick slid the black sphere into its nest.

"Thank you, Nick," he said. "I will not forget this."

"I won't either," Nick growled. "But I'd like to."

The two walked downstairs. Nick wordlessly opened the door for Kammerer. "Well, good luck, Captain," he said, finally. "I don't suppose you know where I could get one of them things. One that works for me, I mean."

Kammerer shook his head. "Lyrane is where they came from, and Lyrane is no more. Except for my little bit of it."

He straightened his shoulders and began to walk down the dim street, feeling a lightness that had been absent for two years. He felt the cubic shape of the box inside his shoulder bag and caressed it with his good hand.

"At last, my beloved," he whispered, "we are together once more."

THE HIDDEN WORLD OF
MILTON ROTHMAN

TONY ROTHMAN

WHEN MILTON ROTHMAN died on October 6, 2001, his career as an active science-fiction fan lay nearly fifty years behind him. His last major function had been to chair the 1953 Worldcon in Philadelphia. This circumstance makes it difficult for me to discuss authoritatively his life in science fiction. I am told I was the youngest fan to attend that Worldcon, but I have no memory of it; I was four months old.

It can hardly be coincidental that 1953, the year in which my father retired from science fiction, was the year after he received his Ph.D. in physics from the University of Pennsylvania. Since his days at Central High in Philadelphia, when he had planned to be a chemist, Milton had set his eyes on a scientific career, and after World War II, careers in physics were for the asking. In mid century, especially after the Bomb, nuclear physics was virgin territory and that is where my father wanted to be. Life, of course, never works out as one expects and from that truth my father had no better luck escaping than anyone else. In 1950 he married Doris Weiss, my mother, and a few years later he did get a first post-doctoral job at the Bartol Research Center in Springfield, Pennsylvania, where he did do nuclear physics. My first memories date from those years. He had hoped to get a position at Oak Ridge National Laboratory in Tennessee, but fate had other plans.

Oak Ridge, where the uranium separation had been carried out for the Manhattan Project, was still a classified installation, and to work there required security clearance. Milton applied. But as it turned out, in his science-fiction days, some twelve years earlier, he had been corresponding with another fan, Chandler Davis (who was to become an author and prominent mathematician in his own right), whose parents—and indeed Davis himself—were members of the Communist Party. The FBI was actually searching Davis's trash and intercepted the letters. Milton was denied clearance. Davis later served jail time for refusing to testify for the House Committee on Un-American Activities. For many years my father wondered whether Davis had set him up, but finally at a recent convention the two old men got together and hit it off quite well. Davis had been duped as much as my father.

At the time, though, Milton was devastated and, I am told,

taught me at the age of one to razz every time I heard the name Mc-
Carthy. (This seems to be true; I still razz when I hear the name.) But
it was the best thing that ever happened to me, and probably to him.
In 1958 the US fusion program, Project Matterhorn, was declassified
and became the Princeton University Plasma Physics Lab. My father
got a job there and the following year the family moved to Lawrence-
ville, New Jersey, not far from Princeton.

For nearly ten years, Milton worked at the lab on the largest fusion device of the times, which was known as the Model-C Stellarator.
It had been the brainchild of Lyman Spitzer, also known as the father
of the Hubble Space Telescope. To a child climbing around on the machines, the lab was a true science-fiction wonderland with colossal
and fabulous devices, which even today would be an extraordinary set
for a Hollywood movie. But the machine was basically a failure; Milton eventually wearied of the grind and the diminishing prospects for
practical fusion, and he left to take up a teaching position at Trenton
State College. There he remained another ten years, in the meantime
moving back to Philadelphia, where he had set up house with an epi-
demiologist at Penn, Anita Bahn. After five years of living together,
they married in the early 1980s, but she unexpectedly died of a stroke
a few months later. Not long afterwards Milton married Miriam
Mednick, a social worker who was heavily involved with the Philadelphia arts scene, and with whom he was to spend the last twenty years
of his life. Once he left Trenton State, Milton lived in semi-retirement,
working for a time at the Franklin Institute and attempting to resus-
citate his writing career.

I should say his science-fiction career. He had never ceased to
write, but in the 1960s he had turned to science fact, publishing his
first book *The Laws of Physics* in 1964. Over the next two decades he
produced seven more books, all science fact. The one he was most
proud of, I think, was *Discovering the Natural Laws* (1972), in which
he actually details the experiments that have established the laws of
physics and with what precision. None of these books was a bestseller,
but he did garner a fair amount of respect in the science-writing field.
Nevertheless, once at Trenton State, and especially once back in Philadelphia, he did turn his hand to science fiction again. The later stories in this collection date from those years.

I need to be honest: he never expressed regret at having left science fiction. To the contrary, as he got older, he became ever more
wedded to science. I can understand this. I also started writing science fiction at an early age, but to those of us with scientific inclina-
tions, the actual science becomes more interesting than the fiction.
What's more, one's deepening sense of what is possible and what is

not actually hinders you from writing SF. I think this is clear from my father's stories. They are extremely conservative for science fiction, rarely venturing beyond the solar system, and the later ones don't venture a millimeter beyond established science.

Certainly one of the reasons Milton gave up science fiction was the number of "kooks" who inhabit the field. John Campbell was a frequent topic of conversation. At one time they must have known each other reasonably well. My father's middle initial was "A." He always denied that it meant anything and so I was surprised to hear from Bob Madle that it stood for Arcot, a character in Campbell's "Arcot, Wade and Morey" series. Campbell also suggested Milton's pseudonym, Lee Gregor. (I believe Bob also says this was because "Rothman" was too obviously Jewish.) Despite the influence, I don't recall many kind words Milton had for the famous editor. Frankly, he thought Campbell was a nut. They had a long running dispute over the infamous Dean Drive—a supposedly reactionless engine that Campbell promoted—that distinctly soured my father both toward the editor and SF in general. The likes of L. Ron Hubbard didn't help either. Milton once told me that at some convention, L. Ron got up and gave a speech in which he said, "If a man wants to get rich, he should start a religion."

None of this means SF had entirely vanished from my father's life. He joined the Science Fiction Writers of America when it was founded, and took me to workshops and the annual Nebula Awards banquets. The attic, already filled with sf books, soon overflowed. To a large extent this explains my own origins as a writer.

The story of the first convention was folklore around our house. It's been told often enough, and I wasn't there, but the world's first officially recognized science-fiction convention did take place in my father's house (more precisely my grandfather's house) on 22 October, 1936, at 2113 N. Franklin St., near 7th and Diamond, Philadelphia. Photos by Herbert Goudket exist to prove it but as the convention is described by Bob Madle in his article, I need not go into details. My father doesn't seem to have attached any great significance to the event; clearly he had no idea of what was being spawned that day.

Another "first" of which he spoke, but not often, was the first Hugo awards, which were presented at the 1953 Philcon. Apparently, the last minute had arrived, the convention had begun and they still lacked a design for the trophies themselves. In a sort of desperation Milton copied one of Chesley Bonestell's rockets from *Conquest of Space* and gave it to Jack McKnight, who spent two solid nights machining the things. It is unlikely a coincidence that Milton's signature in many of his old books is accompanied by a Bonestell-style rocket.

These are just stories. For me, the biggest "remnant" of my father's science-fiction days was his circle of friends. Oldtime fans occasionally dropped by the house, but much more often we saw the pros, his old buddies. Lester del Rey in particular.

Lester Ramon Philippe San Juan Mario Silvo Enrico Alvarez del Rey, to use the short form of his name, had been my father's closest friend since they had first met in 1939, while they were both working in Washington. For many years, I'm told, Lester showed Milton his work for criticism, and vice versa. The friendship endured for decades; certainly there is no time I can remember Lester not being nearby. (Apparently I met him at the 1953 Philcon, when I was four months old.) Our family would regularly go out to his place in Red Bank, or Lester and Evelyn would visit us. After Evelyn's death in a car accident in 1970, Judy-Lynn appeared by his side.

Lester remains eternally vivid in my memory. This little man, with a prophet's beard and coke-bottle eyeglasses seemed to know everything. He had an answer to any question, an opinion on any subject, had rewired his typewriter keyboards to his own system and could quote the Bible from beginning to end. I always regarded him as my godfather and cannot overstate the influence he had on my own life. On many occasions I made the pilgrimage to Red Bank alone, to rummage around in that extraordinary basement (where every square centimeter was covered by a magazine; "my filing system," Lester would say) and to receive his wisdom. With perhaps not even the exception of my father, Lester instilled in me a thirst for knowledge. As I grew older and a little wiser, I saw that he wasn't the all-knowing wizard I had thought. Lester once accused Harlan Ellison of swiping events from his own biography, that in his youth he had run off to a circus and been a boy evangelist. Since then I have heard that Lester had invented these tales himself.

Lester was probably the greatest gift from my father's science-fiction days. The two of them, though, would eventually grow apart. Just as Lester wasn't too charitable toward Isaac Asimov and others, Milton began to feel Lester was an "autodidact," a know-it-all who really knew very little, and one who couldn't see beyond his little world of commercial fantasy and science fiction. When Lester finally died, my father never bothered to inform me. I only discovered his death by accident a year later when reading a "News of the Weird" column that commented on his improbable name.

Lester may have been the closest of Milton's sf friends but he was not the only one. Of Fred Pohl I can only remember him consistently saying, "He is one of the smartest people I've ever known." Unfortunately, although we did sometimes visit Fred in Red Bank, this was when I was very young, and my main memory of him seems to be his knee. Even vaguer recollections are of Fletcher Pratt and Willy Ley at the Jersey shore. Milton always spoke of L. Sprague de Camp as being his other best friend from "the old days" and he remained in contact with Sprague and Catherine until they eventually moved to Texas. I visited the de Camps myself several times in Philadelphia when I was a student at Swarthmore. Sprague of course was tremendously impressive with military bearing and historical knowledge, not to mention his output, which was about 90 books at the time, and I wish I had gotten to know him and Catherine better. Bob Silverberg became an acquaintance somewhat later. As I recall, at my instigation Milton wrote him a fan letter, to which Bob quickly replied. We didn't see the Silverbergs often, but both of us regarded Bob as by far the best sf writer working in the late sixties and early seventies. There are a few tales to be told about Isaac Asimov, but that would take too long.

So the science-fiction world of my father that I saw, I saw through his friendships. For that reason it has come as something of a shock to learn that he had published nearly a dozen stories, including a novella. "Heavy Planet," which he wrote at the age of 19, is of course the most (and perhaps only) famous one of these, having been anthologized forty-three times, if I'm not mistaken, at least dozens, if I am. Lester del Rey once said that he preferred "Shawn's Sword," a remark that piqued my curiosity, though until now I had never seen a copy. The three last tales appeared after I had started writing myself and so I saw them in print. But of the others, he simply never spoke, I don't know whether this was because he was ashamed, uninterested or even perhaps because he had forgotten them, but his silence was absolute, and it is only because of Darrell Schweitzer and Lee Weinstein's research that they have come to light at all. I might mention that Milton did begin an abortive SF novel sometime in the 1970s. He never spoke of this project either, but I saw the manuscript once on his desk. It involved a young girl who was a mathematical genius. I don't think he got very far with it and my guess is that the manuscript no longer exists.

In reading these stories, I cannot truthfully call them "great" in any sense of the word, but I speak as someone who has also grown away from science fiction. Although there is some evolution of Milton's style from first to last, all the stories are written in basically the same way: third person, past tense, from the outside. Most suffer from lack of characterization, too little drama and too abrupt endings; in a few it isn't entirely clear even what has happened.

It has naturally been tempting to try to see my father in these pieces. In some I find him and in others not at all. Many of the defects, I think, are directly attributable to the tension he always felt between science fiction and science. The stories are, as I've said, conservative. The science is fairly conventional; the action is limited almost entirely to the solar system. It is as if Milton could not will himself—or allow himself—to break free of physics. Most of the earlier ones take place on the asteroids and there seems to be a war between the Venusian colonies and Earth in the background. Perhaps he was vaguely outlining a series, or a novel.

In these early tales, including "Heavy Planet," one sees a preoccupation with atomic energy and radiation. The stories were published well before anyone had heard of the atomic bomb. I don't know how prescient they are, but my father was a smart guy; he told me that when around 1942 he read a newspaper clipping about copper wire disappearing into the mountains of Tennessee, he knew immediately that an atomic bomb was in the works.

"Shawn's Sword," stands out as having a protagonist who is none too bright. For that reason, I think it is a little more endearing than some of the others. But here too, the ending is extremely abrupt, leaving one wondering what has been accomplished. It is interesting though, that my father's interest in music is brought to the fore. All his life he was not only an amateur pianist but an ardent Wagnerite. That becomes clear.

When I read "Last Night Out" I frankly didn't believe he had written it until I remembered that during World War II he had been briefly stationed at an army base in Texas, perhaps Ft. Hood. He told a story about a piano competition in which three guys in a row got on stage to play the Bach-Busoni Chaconne. That must have been something. Also Lester once recounted a tale about Milton getting drunk, and analytically noting down the results. "Last Night Out" is probably the weakest tale in the collection—almost nothing happens—but I guess I now believe he wrote it.

"Asteroid" has an interesting premise, that a mining operation is destroying a delicate, ethereal life form that lives there and that the inhabitants can't do anything about it. These beings are clearly the sympathetic characters in the story but, again, one is left wishing for more development.

"Formula for Murder" involves a Soviet agent feigning insanity. Without even glancing at the publication date, I am willing to bet it was written in 1950s under the influence of McCarthyism and Milton's troubles with the FBI. There may also be a few traces of my mother, Doris, who was then working toward a degree in psychotherapy.

A psychologist also makes an appearance in "Formula for Galaxy I," which is the most ambitious story of the lot. A murder mystery set on an asteroid, the protagonist of this novella is a photographer who seems to be based partly on Chesley Bonestell. Some of the subsidiary characters are hardly more than phantoms and so the dialogue about them becomes perplexing and difficult to follow, but on the whole the plot is engaging and one wishes that Milton had fleshed it out into a full novel.

The roots of "Getting Together," which appeared in *Galaxy* in 1972 are clear. The late sixties were a wild time, the touchy-feely age, and my mother, who had become a successful psychotherapist, held weekly encounter groups at her office behind the house. It was not uncommon for fifteen or twenty people—invariably proto-New Agers—to spend the weekend there stone carving or undergoing hypnosis. Occasionally I participated in these groups and, I think my father as well. (We certainly smoked dope together at a few strange parties.) "Getting together" comes right out of those experiences. Milton was quite tickled with it and I remember that Judy-Lynn del Rey, who had bought it, also rated it highly.

Two of the final stories, "Prime Crime" and "Eternal Genesis" take place on space colonies at the Lagrange points (where the gravitational tug of the Earth, Moon and Sun are balanced). In the mid 1970s physicist Gerard O'Neill of Princeton worked out the mechanics of such colonies, showing that they would be technologically and economically feasible. O'Neill became the foremost proponent of space colonization, founding the Lagrange Society, and for several years his ideas were all the rage. At about the same time, Arthur Clarke published *Rendezvous With Rama*, which was based on a similar idea. (Both O'Neill and Clarke claimed priority.) Clearly my father was influenced more by O'Neill than Clarke. He spent a lot of pleasurable hours working out things like coriolis forces on such a satellite and when he was done, wrote the stories.

"Prime Crime" is very predictable, but is of interest to me because for my father's 50th birthday, in 1969, we had surprised him with a genuine pipe organ in the attic, which he began to practice. After moving back to Philadelphia in the late seventies he bought an electronic organ and for a while took it seriously. That history also surfaces. "Eternal Genesis" proved to be something of a sore point between us. It appeared shortly after my own novel *The World is Round*. I had been planning a sequel; many of the ideas in "Eternal Genesis" about the fate of the universe and so on, were implicit in *The World is Round* and explicit in an earlier, unpublished novel, as well as in our conversations. I was quite angry with Milton for confiscating my plans without permission. He didn't deny it, but didn't apologize either, and relations between us actually broke down for some months. At a distance of more than twenty years, it doesn't seem so important, but in rereading the story I must admit I remain convinced that he filched a lot of my ideas.

The genesis of "Fusion" is also crystal clear. This is a story straight out of the Princeton Plasma Physics Lab. Hertzberg, about to retire, is my father. Bill Hawke is Milton's closest colleague at the lab, Bill Hooke. There were also a couple Russian visitors there in the mid 1960s, one of whose name was, I recall, Denis. Matt Brackett is Lyman Spitzer (in hydrogen spectroscopy, one series of lines is known as the "Lyman" series, another as the "Brackett" series). A lot of Hertzberg's feelings expressed in the story about the fusion pro-gram—and his own role in it—were Milton's own. He had always felt himself to be a second-rate physicist, but Bill Hooke has assured me that some of his experiments on the Stellarator, ignored by the top brass, set new records for the day. "Fusion" is a highly realistic tale, basically fact, and for that reason highly technical. I don't know how much the average reader will appreciate the details, but having spent 1995 at the lab as a visitor, I can testify that they are accurate. It may well be that such details hinder the story, but at least one character is more lifelike than the author's other creations, and the writing is more mature. Ironically, my year at the lab was largely to do research for a suspense novel set in a fusion laboratory, an idea suggested to me by Bill Hooke. Perhaps the novel suffers from some of the same problems as the story; at least it has become clear to me that many ed-itors do not appreciate science. As a result the manuscript sits on my shelf.

So there you have it. This small collection does not constitute a career. Milton Rothman was too conflicted between writing and sci-ence to devote all his time to one or the other. As a result, he always felt he had fallen through the cracks. Certainly he was not the world's most successful science-fiction writer or the world's greatest physi-cist, but the fact is, most of us aren't. In terms of the thousands of readers his science books reached, his hundreds of students, the pio-neering research at the Plasma Physics Lab and his early efforts to get science fiction established in Philadelphia and America, he had much to be proud of.

MILTON A. ROTHMAN
SCIENCE FICTION PIONEER

ROBERT A. MADLE

1. *The Early Rothman*

MILT ROTHMAN WAS born in Philadelphia, Pennsylvania, where he has lived for most of his life. Milt was one of the earliest science fiction fans. In 1930, at the age of ten, he discovered *Science Wonder Stories*. This was The Beginning, and he was hooked; stories of space travel, time travel, future science—all of these things made his mind reel. In 1930 there wasn't much science fiction around—practically everything revolved around magazines; *Astounding Stories, Wonder Stories, Amazing Stories,* and *Weird Tales.*

Back then, all the magazines had readers' columns where readers wrote letters of comment, some very lengthy. This became Milt's earliest forte as a fan, or more appropriately, a science fiction addict. Extremely interesting letters commenting on the stories and their scientific accuracy began to appear from Milton S. Rothman—his middle initial then was "S," but he soon changed it to "A," short for "Arcot," who was one of the characters in John W. Campbell, Jr.'s "Arcot, Wade, and Morey" space opera series.

When Hugo Gernsback started *Amazing* in 1926, he was firmly convinced that science fiction would instill in young readers the desire to work in scientific fields, or indeed to actually become scientists. This idea in later years became known as "The Gernsback Ideal" and, in the earliest days of fandom, seemed to be prophetic—two of the earliest clubs, formed by s-f readers who located each other in the various readers' columns were called "The International Scientific Association" and "The Scienceers." Both were organized in that glorious year of 1930. As time went on, however, fans became more interested in the literary rather than scientific aspects of the stories. But not Milt Rothman—because of s-f, even as a pre-teen, he knew that he wanted to be a scientist.

2. *The PSFS*

As a result of his feverish letter-writing to s-f magazines, Milt met Raymond Peel Mariella, another letter-writer. In 1934, Milt and Ray were both fourteen years old with their lives revolving around s-f when they read about the creation of the Science Fiction League in the April issue of Gernsback's *Wonder Stories*:

"The founders of the Science Fiction League believe they have a great mission to fulfill. They believe in the seriousness of s-f. They believe that there is nothing greater than human imagination, and the diverting of such imagination into constructive channels. They believe that s-f is something more than literature. They seriously believe that it can become a world force of *unparalleled magnitude* in time to come."

Milt, greatly inspired because he felt himself part of this "world force of unparalleled magnitude," not only joined the SFL, but also applied for a charter for SFL Chapter #11. One or two meetings were held in early 1935 with a few members present, but soon it was just Milt and Ray, and the club faded into inactivity.

At this time in Philadelphia there were several other fans who had formed another s-f organization, The Boys' SF Club. They were John V. Baltadonis, Jack Agnew, Harvey Greenblatt, and myself. In October 1935, this group, along with another fan, Ossie Train, joined with Rothman and Mariella and the newly-reformed Philadelphia SFL was off to a good start. Milt was unanimously elected president of the Chapter at the first meeting, which featured a discussion of the current issues of the s-f magazines. The big event of the evening, however, was when Milt brought down a cigar box full of rejected s-f stories. One of the rejects (from Charles D. Hornig of *Wonder Stories)* said, "If we were giving prizes for stories, this would receive the prize for the most hackneyed story of the month." Apparently Hornig got a real charge out of rejecting stories by fifteen-year-olds. But we still thought it was incredible that Milt actually communicated with the Gods of s-f. and we all wanted to do the same.

The first great event for the new Philadelphia SFL chapter was the visit of Charles D. Hornig and Julius Schwartz in December 1935. Schwartz was the editor of *Fantasy Magazine,* the greatest fan mag of its day. This was, indeed, the Gods descending from Valhalla. I walked through a snowstorm with John Baltadonis and Jack Agnew to Milt's house for the meeting; the highlight was Hornig telling the group of the great plans he had for *Wonder Stories* and the SFL. But by 1936, things had changed—Wonder Stories was no longer a Gernsback Publication, having been sold to Better Publications and renamed *Thrilling Wonder Stories.* It was about then that Milt decided the club should also change its name, to the Philadelphia Science Fiction Society, the name it continues to use today—the PSFS is the oldest continuing s-f club in the world.

3. *Important Events*

Milt graduated from high school in 1936 and took his initial step toward becoming, as he puts it, a SCIENTIST by enrolling at the Philadelphia College of Pharmacy and Science. The year 1936 was also a landmark year for Milt and the PSFS, for this was the year that the first science fiction convention was held. Don Wollheim advised Milt that members of the New York branch of the International Scientific Association were going to visit the PSFS on Sunday, October 22nd. The New York group consisted of Wollheim, John B. Michel, Frederik Pohl, David A. Kyle, William S. Sykora, and Herbert Goudket, and when they arrived in Philadelphia were met by Rothman, Ossie Train, and myself. Baltadonis and several others showed up later at Milt's home. Milt was elected chairman of the meeting, and it was Wollheim who suggested it be called the "First Science Fiction Convention" (subsequently becoming better known as the "First Eastern Science Fiction Convention"). The following year, the first Philadelphia SF Conference (the "Third Eastern Science Fiction Convention") was held, at which Wollheim presented John Michel's essay, "Mutation or Death," that politicized the science fiction world (but that's another story). It should be mentioned that Philadelphia SF Conventions, or "Philcons" as they are known today, have been held every year since then, except for a break caused by World War Two.

In 1939, Milt became a professional writer, selling two stories, "Heavy Planet" and "Shawn's Sword," to John W. Campbell. Jr., for publication in *Astounding Science Fiction*. Milt had been forced to drop out of college (no money) and had no job. Later that year he was offered a government job in Washington D.C. where he met Lester del Rey, Jack Speer, and Elmer Perdue, who were also working for the government. Milt stayed in Washington through 1941, and following Pearl Harbor returned to Philadelphia and enlisted in the Army. The Army actually sent him to college under the Specialized Training Program and he got his degree from Oregon State University, not in Chemistry but in Electrical Engineering. The Army then shipped him to Europe and, as he says, "put me in front of a typewriter." When the atomic bomb was dropped on Hiroshima in 1945, he was the only one in his company who understood what it was.

In early 1946, Milt was discharged from military service and came home to Philadelphia. Ossie Train, the only active PSFS member not in military service had kept the club alive during the war by publishing a fanzine, *PSFS News,* and sending it to all other members. The post-war 1940s were great years for the PSFS. A clubroom was obtained and meetings rapidly grew in size, with as many as fifty people in attendance at times. There were famous writers who came to meetings—L. Sprague de Camp and George O. Smith actually became members, while David H. Keller and Lester del Rey were guest speakers. But the biggest event of this period was winning the right to host the 1947 Worldcon. Milt took a train to Los Angeles to attend the 1946 Pacificon. When his bid for Philadelphia won, the PSFS became known as "The New Mecca of Fandom."

Milt was the unanimous choice for chairman of Philcon I upon his return from Los Angeles. The 1947 Worldcon was a great convention. With about 200 fans and writers attending, it was as big as the 1939 Nycon, which had been the largest worldcon to that time. Philcon I was the first of the "adult" conventions where alcohol flowed freely; the two major nightly parties were hosted by Lloyd Eshbach of Fantasy Press and Tom Hadley of Hadley Publishing Company. John W. Campbell, Jr., the Guest of Honor, came from New York intending just to give his speech and leave. But he enjoyed himself so much, especially at the parties, that he stayed for the entire convention.

During his Chairmanship of the Philcon, Milt had started graduate work at the University of Pennsylvania. He received his M.S. in Physics, then in 1952, his Ph.D. in Nuclear Physics, and was, indeed, a SCIENTIST. At this point, Milt did what all newly-anointed Ph.D.'s in Nuclear Physics did: he applied for a job at the Oak Ridge National Laboratory. However, that was the time of the Cold War and McCarthyism: unfortunately for Milt, he had been a s-f correspondent of H. Chandler Davis who was an active fan, professional s-f writer, brilliant intellectual . . . and an active member of the Communist Party. Getting a job in atomic energy required security clearances, and neither the FBI nor the Atomic Energy Commission were impressed with Chan Davis. Back in 1940, Davis had asked Milt to join the Party. Milt had refused, but the FBI and AEC felt that Milt's refusal was not indignant enough! And if this wasn't enough, also showing up in his files was his connections with the Futurians fan organization, some of whom had been members of the Young Communist League and Communist Party. This was a difficult time for Milt; his fannish associations had cost him a job opportunity. But as it turned out, that lost opening kept him eligible for a different type of opportunity.

4. *Philcon II and The Great Oblivion*

About this same time the PSFS sent a large contingent of members (about seventeen people) to Chicon II. the 1952 Wordcon. Several PSFS members felt that 1953 would be the year of the BIG Worldcon, and that it should be held in New York City. As the convention wore on, it became evident that the New York fans were mostly in agreement but felt that the PSFS should put on the BIG show. And so, following several "smoke-filled" room meetings, the vote was held and the PSFS won over a competing San Francisco bid.

James A. Williams was elected Philcon II chair by members of the PSFS, but Jim died in April 1953, and a new chairman had to be elected. Milt and I were the two nominees, and we were both reluctant as we were both expecting out-of-town jobs to materialize. Milt finally accepted when I took myself out of contention, knowing that I would almost certainly be moving to North Carolina that summer—too far away to be an effective chairman. With the Philcon II chairmanship, Milt became a true science fiction pioneer with his unprecedented achievements—chairman of not only two Worldcons, but also the first science fiction convention ever held.

Philcon II turned out to be a huge success (including the presentation of the first Hugo Awards) and Milt, despite his job problems, was a great chairman. Following the convention. however, Milt's interest in s-f gradually waned. He'd gotten a job as a SCIENTIST (actually a nuclear physicist) and after 23 years of reading, collecting, writing, and general fanning, he had reached the saturation point. "Gafia" had taken over.

And so Milt was swallowed up by The Great Oblivion—he was gone from s-f fandom for over forty years. But he was not gone from s-f itself; in those years he sold several stories to *Galaxy, Infinity,* and *Amazing.* In 1974, following the publication of "Fusion" in *Stellar I,* he decided he was a much better science fact writer than a fiction writer. In the following decade he had at least fifteen science fact articles published in various magazines.

In 1959, Milt was hired as a Research Physicist at the Princeton University Plasma Physics Laboratory, which was involved in nuclear fusion research. As Milt describes it, the laboratory looked just like a drawing out of old *Amazing* and *Astounding* magazines. He stayed there for nine years, finally leaving when it became evident that commercial thermonuclear fusion was never going to be economically feasible. During this period, Milt wrote his first books on science: *The Laws of Physics* and *Man and Discovery.* In 1968, he became Professor of Physics at Trenton State College, where he stayed until 1980 when he became a Senior Scientist at the Franklin Research Center. He became actively involved in the field of skepticism, becoming a member of the Committee for the Scientific Investigation of Claims of the Paranormal and writing books on the subject, including *A Physicists' Guide to Skepticism.* Milt claims that his interest in this field goes nearly full circle, back to the 1940s, when he argued with "cranks and crackpots" in the pages of his fan magazine, *Milty's Mag.*

* * *

Milton A. Rothman was many things to science fiction and to SF fandom. His early activities—letter-writing, PSFS founder, fan-mag publisher, convention chairman—have helped to make SF fandom what it is today. Also, in addition to being one of the leading fans of his era, he was, as indicated, a prominent writer of science fact and science fiction. I'm delighted that his importance as a SF writer is being recognized by the publication of this volume of his fiction.